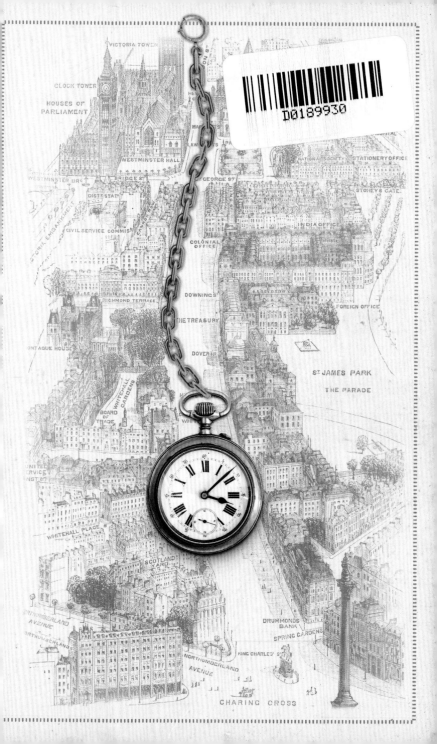

10/12/16
28/01/17
05/09/17

Books should be returned or renewed by the last
date above. Renew by phone **03000 41 31 31** or
online *www.kent.gov.uk/libs*

THE
WATCHMAKER
⚙F FILIGREE
STREET

NATASHA PULLEY

B L O O M S B U R Y
LONDON · OXFORD · NEW YORK · NEW DELHI · SYDNEY

Bloomsbury Paperbacks
An imprint of Bloomsbury Publishing Plc

50 Bedford Square
London
WC1B 3DP
UK

1385 Broadway
New York
NY 10018
USA

www.bloomsbury.com

BLOOMSBURY and the Diana logo are trademarks of Bloomsbury Publishing Plc

First published in Great Britain 2015
This paperback edition first published in 2016

British Library Cataloguing-in-Publication Data
A catalogue record for this book is available from the British Library.

ISBN: HB: 978-1-4088-5428-0
TPB: 978-1-4088-5429-7
PB: 978-1-4088-5431-0
ePub: 978-1-4088-5430-3

2 4 6 8 10 9 7 5 3

Typeset by Integra Software Services Pvt. Ltd.

Printed and bound in Great Britain by CPI Group (UK) Ltd, Croydon CR0 4YY

To find out more about our authors and books visit www.bloomsbury.com. Here you will find extracts, author interviews, details of forthcoming events and the option to sign up for our newsletters.

To Claire

PART ONE

ONE

LONDON, NOVEMBER 1883

THE HOME OFFICE telegraphy department always smelled of tea. The source was one packet of Lipton's at the back of Nathaniel Steepleton's desk drawer. Before the widespread use of the electric telegraph, the office had been a broom cupboard. Thaniel had heard more than once that its failure to expand was a sign of the Home Secretary's continuing mistrust of naval inventions, but even if that wasn't the case, the departmental budget had never stretched to the replacement of the original carpet, which liked to keep the ghosts of old smells. Besides Thaniel's modern tea, there was cleaning salt and hessian, and sometimes varnish, though nobody had varnished anything there for years. Now, instead of brooms and brushes, there were twelve telegraphs lined up on a long desk. Three to an operator during the day, each wired to separate places within and without Whitehall, and labelled accordingly in the thin handwriting of a forgotten clerk.

Tonight all twelve machines were silent. Between six and midnight, one operator stayed in the office to catch urgent messages, but after working at Whitehall for three years, Thaniel had never seen anything come through after eight. Once, there had been a strange, meaningless percussion from the Foreign Office, but that had been an accident: somebody had sat on the machine at the other end of the wire. Sat and bounced. He had taken care not to ask about it.

Thaniel shifted stiffly and turned himself to the left of his chair rather than the right, and slid his book along the desk. The wires from the telegraphs were threaded through holes in the desk and then down into the floor, leaving all twelve trailing just where the knees of the operators should have been. The senior clerk liked to complain that sitting sideways made them look like society girls learning to ride, but he complained more if a wire snapped: they were expensive to replace. From the telegraphy room, they ran down through the building and spidered out all over Westminster. One went across the wall to the Foreign Office, one to the telegraph room at the Houses of Parliament. Two joined the clusters of wires strung along the street until they reached the post office headquarters at St Martin's Le Grand. The others wired direct to the Home Secretary's own house, Scotland Yard, the India Office, the Admiralty, and other sub-departments. Some of them were pointless because it would have been faster to lean out of the main office window and shout, but the senior clerk said that would have been ungentlemanly.

Thaniel's watch ticked around to quarter past ten with its crooked minute hand that always stuck a bit over the twelve. Tea time. He saved tea for the nights. It had been dark since late afternoon and now, the office was so cold that his breath was showing and there was condensation on the brass telegraph keys. Having something hot to look forward to was important. He took out the Lipton's, put the box diagonally in his cup and yesterday's *Illustrated London News* under his elbow, and made his way to the iron staircase.

As he went down, it clanged in a bright yellow D sharp. He couldn't say why D sharp was yellow. Other notes had their own colours. It had been useful when he still played the piano because whenever he went wrong, the sound turned brown. This sound-seeing was something he had always kept to himself. Yellow stairs made him sound mad and, contrary to the opinions of the *Illustrated News*, it was frowned upon for Her Majesty's Government to employ the demonstrably insane.

The big stove in the canteen was never cold, the embers of old fires having no time to die completely between the civil service's late evenings and early mornings. When he stirred over the coals, they came to life with a shimmer. He stood with the small of his

4

back against a table while he waited for the water to boil, watching his own warped reflection in the bronze kettle. It made him look much warmer than his real colours, which were mainly grey.

The newspaper crackled in the deep quiet when he opened it. He had hoped for some kind of interesting military cock-up, but there was only an article about Mr Parnell's latest speech in Parliament. He tilted his nose down into his scarf. With a bit of effort he could stretch out tea-making into fifteen minutes, which was an appreciable chip out of one of the eight hours he had left, but there wasn't much to be done about the other seven. It was easier when his book wasn't boring and when the newspapers had something better to do than look askance at Irish pushings for independence, as though Clan na Gael had not spent the last few years throwing bombs into the windows of government buildings.

He flicked through the rest of the paper. There was an advertisement for *The Sorcerer* at the Savoy. He had seen it, but the idea of going again made him feel brighter.

The kettle whistled. He poured his tea, slowly, and took it back up the yellow steps toward the isolated light of the telegraphy office lamp, cup held close to his breastbone.

One of the telegraphs was clicking.

He leaned in, only curious at first, until he saw it was the machine for Great Scotland Yard and lurched to catch the end of the transcript paper. It almost always scrunched itself up after three inches. It creaked as it threatened to crush the paper, but yielded when he pulled. The newest dots and dashes of code came out shakily, in old man's handwriting.

Fenians— left me a note promising that—

The rest was still ticking through the clockwork, making little skittering stars through the gloomy room. He recognised the style of the operator before long. Superintendent Williamson coded in the same hesitant way in which he spoke. As it came through, the rest of the message was jerky and full of pauses.

—they will detonate bombs in all p—ublic buildings on— May 30, 1884. Six months from today. Williamson.

Thaniel pulled the machine toward him by the key.

This is Steepleton at the HO. Please confirm last message.

He had to wait a long time for the reply.

Just found— note on my desk. Bomb threat. Promises to— blow me off my stool. Signed Clan na Gael.

He stood still, bent over the telegraph. Williamson sent his own telegrams, and when he knew he was speaking to a familiar operator, he signed himself Dolly, as if they were all part of the same gentlemen's club.

Are you all right? Thaniel asked.

Yes. A long silence. *Must admit— a bit shaken. Going home.*

You can't go by yourself.

They won't — do anything. If they say bombs in May – there will be bombs in May. It's— Clan na Gael. They don't bugger about lurking with cricket bats.

But why tell you now? Might be a trick to make you leave the office at a certain time.

No, no. To make us— afraid. They want Whitehall to know the day is coming. If enough politicians fear for their lives, they will listen better to Irish demands. They said 'public buildings'. It won't just be a matter of steering clear of Parliament for a day. They're not interested in me. Honestly, I— know these people. I've locked up enough of them.

Careful then, Thaniel tapped grudgingly.

Thank you.

While the sounder was still clicking out the superintendent's last word, Thaniel tore off the transcript and clipped through the dark corridor to a door at the far end, under which firelight bled. He knocked, then opened it. Inside, the senior clerk looked up and scowled.

'I'm not here. This had better be important.'

'It's a message from the Yard.'

The senior clerk snatched it from him. The room was his office, and he had been reading in the deep armchair by the fire, his collar and tie abandoned on the floor. It was the same every night. The senior clerk claimed that he stayed because his wife snored, but Thaniel was starting to think that she must have forgotten about him by now and changed the locks. Once he had read the note, he nodded.

'All right. You can go home. I'd better tell the Home Secretary.'

Thaniel nodded and left, quickly. He had never been told to leave early before, not even when he was ill. As he collected his coat and hat, he heard raised voices at the end of the corridor.

He lived in a boarding house just north of Millbank Prison, so close to the Thames that the cellar flooded every autumn. It was an eerie walk from Whitehall at night. Under the gas lamps, mist pawed at the windows of the closed shops, which became steadily shabbier nearer home. It was such a smooth ruination that he could have been walking forward through time, watching the same buildings age five years with every step, all still as a museum. But he was glad to be out of the office. The Home Office was the largest public building in London. It would be one of the targets in May. He turned his head aside as if he could avoid the thought, and pushed his hands deeper into his pockets. Last March, some Irishmen had tried to throw a bomb in through a ground-floor window. They had missed and managed only to blow up some bicycles in the street outside, but in the telegraphy office, the bang had made the floor jump. But they hadn't been Clan na Gael, only a few angry boys with a bit of stolen dynamite.

The local beggar was sleeping under the boarding house's wide porch.

'Evening, George.'

'Gngh,' said George.

Inside, Thaniel climbed the wooden stairs as quietly as he could, because the walls were thin. His room was on the third floor, on the river side. Although the boarding house looked bleak from outside – the damp and the fog had streaked the outer walls with mildew – it was much better in. The rooms were plain and neat, each with a bed, a stove, and a plumbed sink. By rule of the landlady, the boarders were all single men, and given a bed and one meal a day for the flat annual cost of fifty pounds. Very much the same, in fact, as the inmates of the prison next door. He felt bitter about that sometimes. He had meant to do better in life than a prisoner. At the top of the steps, he saw that his door was already ajar.

He stopped, listening. He had nothing worth stealing, although at first glance, the locked box under his bed looked valuable. A burglar wasn't to know that it was full of sheet music he hadn't touched for years.

He stopped breathing so that he could hear properly. Everything was silent, but somebody else could have been holding his breath inside. After standing for a long time, he pushed the door open with his fingertips and stood sharply back. No one came out. Leaving the door open for the light, he snatched a match from the dresser and struck it against the wall. While he held the match to the lamp wick, the back of his neck pricked and burned with the certainty that somebody was about to shove past him.

When the lamp caught, the room was empty.

He stood holding the burned-down match, his back against the wall. Nothing was out of place. The match head crumbled off and hit the linoleum with a tap, leaving a smudge of black dust. He looked under the bed. The box of music was undisturbed. So were the savings he kept under the loose floorboard for his sister. It was only after he had set the floorboard back that he noticed the kettle was steaming. He put his fingertips against the side. It was hot, and when he opened the stove door, the coals were dusky red.

The crockery on the worktop was gone. He paused over that. It took a desperate burglar to steal unwashed dishes. He opened the cupboard to see if they had taken the cutlery too, and found the missing plates and bowls stacked inside. They were still warm. He left them and searched everything again. Nothing was missing, or nothing that he remembered to miss. Eventually he went back downstairs, perplexed. The cold outside felt sharper than it had a few minutes ago. As he pushed open the door, it rushed in at him, and he went out with his arms crossed tight. George was still asleep on the porch.

'George! George,' he said, giving him a shake and holding his breath. The old man smelled of unwashed clothes and animal fur. 'My flat's been burgled. Was it you?'

'You haven't got anything anyone would want to steal,' George growled, with an authority that Thaniel decided not to question just for the moment.

'Did you see anyone?'

'I might have.'

'I ...' Thaniel went through his pockets. 'I've got four pence and an elastic band.'

George sighed and sat up in his nest of grimy blankets to take the coins. From somewhere within the folds, his ferret squeaked. 'I didn't properly see, did I? I was asleep. Or I was trying.'

'So you saw ...'

'Pair of boots,' he said.

'I see,' said Thaniel. George had been middle-aged when time began, and however annoying he was, certain allowances had to be made. 'But lots of people live here.'

George shot him an irritable look. 'If you spent all day down here on the ground, you'd know everyone's boots, and none of you have got brown ones.'

Thaniel had not met most of his neighbours, but he was inclined to believe him. As far as he understood, they were all clerks of some kind; like him, they were all members of the crowd of black coats and black hats that swamped London for half an hour every morning and evening. Without meaning to, he looked down at his own black shoes. They were elderly but well polished.

'Anything else?' he said.

'Christ, what'd he take that was so important?'

'Nothing.'

George hissed his breath out between his teeth. 'What do you care, then? It's late. Some of us want to get some sleep before the constable turfs us out at the crack of dawn.'

'Oh, don't whine. You come back forty seconds after he's gone. Mystery person breaks into my flat, does the washing up and takes nothing. I'd like to know why.'

'Sure it wasn't your mother?'

'Yes.'

George sighed. 'Small brown boots. Foreign writing on the heel. Maybe a boy.'

'I want my four pence back.'

'Bugger off,' George yawned, and lay back down again.

Thaniel went out on to the empty street with a half-formed hope of seeing a boy in brown boots somewhere up ahead. The ground shook as a late train passed underneath, sending up a cloud of steam through the grating in the pavement. Less quickly, he turned back inside. Taken twice in a row, the three flights of steps made his thighs ache.

Back in his room, he flicked open the door of the stove again. He sat down on the edge of the bed with his coat still on and held his hands toward the coals. A dark shape just beside him caught his eye. He stiffened because at first he thought it was a mouse, but it wasn't moving. It was a velvet box, tied with a white ribbon. He had never seen it before. He picked it up. It was heavy. On the ribbon was a circular label, etched with leaf patterns. In an angular, calligraphic hand it read: 'To Mr Steepleton'. He pulled off the ribbon and opened the box. The hinge was stiff but did not squeak. Inside was a pocket watch.

Slowly, he lifted it out. It was made of a rosy gold he hadn't seen before. The chain slithered gently after it, the links all smoothed flawless, without the slightest hairline space or ripple of solder to show where they had been joined. He wound it through his fingers until the clasp at the end tapped against his cufflink. The catch would not open when he pressed it. He held it to his ear, but the clockwork was silent and the spindle refused to wind. Somewhere in its workings, though, a few cogs must have been alive, because despite the dank cold, the case was warm.

'It's your birthday,' he said suddenly to the empty room, and sagged, feeling stupid. Annabel must have come. She knew his address from his letters and he had sent her a key for emergencies. He had always assumed, in the absence of money for the train fare, that her promises to come up to London were a sisterly

10

nothing. George's mysterious boy was probably one of her sons. The calligraphy would have given her away sooner if he had been less tired and less distracted. Although it ought to have been the job of the butler, she had always written the place settings if the old duke was having a dinner party. He could remember doing arithmetic problems at their kitchen table when he was too small for his feet to reach the floor, while opposite him, her good pen hissed over the cards and their father made fishing flies in a vice.

He held the watch a moment longer before setting it on the wooden chair by the bed, the one that served as a table for collars and cufflinks. The gold caught the ember-light and shone the colour of a human voice.

TWO

THE FOLLOWING DAY Thaniel could not stop thinking about what the proper name for a fear of big machinery was. He couldn't remember, but he had had it when he first came to London. It had been worst at railway crossings beside overground stations, where the steam engines would stop, fuming, ten feet away from people picking their way over the lines. The lake of tracks outside Victoria station was still not his favourite place. There had been dozens of tiny things like that, things that didn't matter until something went wrong, like getting lost, whereupon, catching at thoughts as they did, they made thinking much more difficult than it would have been anywhere else.

He was sure that Annabel was all right. She had been pragmatic even before she had her boys. But she had never been to London before, and she had left no messages with the landlady or the Home Office porters.

More to soothe his own unease than out of any real fear for her, he sent a telegram to her post office in Edinburgh from the desk at work, in case she had had to go home already. He bought some biscuits and some sugar for proper tea on his way home, though, in case she hadn't. The grocer at the end of Whitehall Street had started opening in the early mornings to catch the home-going night-workers.

Annabel wasn't there when he got back but he was cooking when there came a small tap at the door. He opened it with his shirtsleeves still rolled up, beginning to apologise that the flat smelled of dinner at nine in the morning, then stopped when he saw that it wasn't Annabel but a boy with a post office badge and an envelope. There was a clipboard for him to sign. He signed it. The telegram was from Edinburgh.

What do you mean? Am in Edinburgh as usual. Never left. HO driven you mad at last. Will send whisky. Told can be beneficial. Happy returns. Sorry to have forgotten again. Love A.

He put the paper face down next to him. The watch was where he had left it on the chair. Because of the steam from the pan, it was dull from condensation, but the gold still hummed its voice colour.

He went to the police station on his way to work the next morning, incoherent from the switch of time that always made midweek difficult. He was snorted at by the desk officer and asked not completely unreasonably whether the culprit might be Robin Hood. He nodded and laughed but as he left a creeping worry seeped back. At the office he mentioned it during a tea break. The other telegraphists looked at him oddly and made only vaguely interested noises. He stayed quiet after that. For the next few weeks, he expected someone to own up, but nobody did.

The sound of the ships creaking outside his window was not something he usually noticed. It was there always, louder when the tide was in. It stopped on a cold morning in February. The river had frozen the hulls into place overnight. The quiet woke him. He lay still in bed, listening and watching his breath whiten. Wind hissed in the window frame, which was loose where the pane had shrunk. The glass had mostly steamed over, but he could make out part of a furled sail. The canvas didn't move even when the hiss became a whistle. When the wind dropped, there was nothing. He blinked twice, because everything looked suddenly too pale.

Today the silence had a silver hem. He turned his head against the pillow, toward the chair of collars and cufflinks, and a faint sound became clearer. The outer side of the blankets felt clammy when he moved his arm to lift up the watch. It was much warmer than it should have been, as usual. As he moved it, the chain slipped almost off the edge of the chair, but it was long enough not to fall and made a gold slack rope.

Holding it close to his ear, he could hear mechanisms going. They were so quiet he couldn't tell if they had started just then, or had been turning all along and masked by other things. He pressed it against his shirt until he couldn't hear it at all, then lifted it again, trying to compare it to his memory of yesterday's version of silence and its shadow colours. Eventually he sat up and pressed the catch. It still wouldn't open.

He got up and dressed, but stopped with his shirt half buttoned. He didn't know whether it was even possible for clockwork to start itself after two months dead. He was still thinking about it when his eyes caught on the door latch. It was up. He pushed the handle. The door was unlocked. He opened it. Although the corridor was empty, it wasn't quiet; water mumbled in the pipes and there were steps and sudden bright thumps as his neighbours got themselves ready for work. He hadn't left the door unlocked once since the burglary in November, or not that he knew; he did forget things spectacularly every now and then. He closed the door again.

On his way out, he stopped, thumped his knuckles slowly against the door frame, and went back for the watch. If somebody were tampering with it, leaving it out in his room all day only made the task easier. The thought made his stomach turn nastily, though God knew what kind of burglar came back to adjust previously deposited presents. Not the cricket-bat-and-mask kind, but then, he didn't know all of the kinds. He wished the policeman hadn't laughed so much.

The open latch was still on his mind as he climbed up the yellow stairs, unwinding his scarf. From a combination of the cold and tapping at telegraph keys, his fingertips had roughened and kept catching on the wool. He was halfway up when the senior clerk came down and pushed a sheaf of papers into his chest.

'For your will,' was the explanation. 'No later than the end of next month, understand? Or we'll drown in paperwork. And sort out Park, will you?'

Puzzled, he went on to the telegraphy department, where the youngest clerk had burst into tears. He paused in the doorway, then dredged up something that at least looked like sympathy. He believed firmly in a soldier's right to cry in public upon surviving the attentions of the surgeon, and a miner's after being lifted from a shaft collapse. He wasn't convinced in the least that anyone in an office at the HO had anything to cry about. He was also aware, though, that this was probably a very unfair thing to think. Park looked up when he asked what the matter was.

'Why do we have to make out wills? Are we going to be bombed?'

Thaniel took him downstairs for a cup of tea. When he shepherded him back upstairs, they found the others in a similar state.

'What's all this?' he said.

'Have you seen these will papers?'

'It's only a formality. I shouldn't worry about it.'

'Have they issued them before?'

He laughed, had to, but forced himself to keep it slight and quiet. 'No, but we're up to our eyes in unnecessary forms. Remember that one about not taking money from the Prussian intelligence services for secret naval information? For what, when we run into a Prussian spy in one of their many haunts near the Trafalgar Square tea-and-horrible-coffee stall? I expect we've all been very vigilant there. Just sign it and lob it at Mr Croft when he comes past.'

'What are you going to write?'

'Nothing, I haven't got anything anyone would want,' he said, but then realised that it was a lie. He took the watch out of his pocket. It was real gold.

'Thank you for looking after me,' Park said. He was folding and refolding a handkerchief. 'You're awfully good. It's like having my dad here.'

'You're no trouble,' he murmured, before he felt a little sting. He almost said that he wasn't so much older than all the rest of them, then saw that it wouldn't have been fair. It didn't matter how much older. He was older; even if they had all been the same age, he would still have been older.

They both jumped when all twelve telegraphs burst into clattering. Transcript paper crumpled under the speed of the messages, and there was a scrabble as everybody reached for pencils to take the code down by hand. Because they were all concentrating on individual letters, he was the first to hear that the machines were all saying the same thing.

Urgent, bomb detonated in—
Victoria Station destroyed—
—station severely damaged—
—hidden in cloakroom—
—sophisticated clockwork in the cloakroom—
Victoria Station—
—officers dispatched, possible casualties—
—Clan na Gael.

Thaniel shouted for the senior clerk, who ran in, looking like thunder with tea spilled down his waistcoat. Once he understood, the rest of the day was spent speeding messages between departments and the Yard, and refusing comments to the newspapers. Thaniel had no idea how they managed to get hold of direct Whitehall lines, but they always did. From down the corridor, there came a bellow. It was the Home Secretary shouting at the editor of *The Times* to stop his journalists blocking the wires. By the time the shift ended, the tendons in the backs of Thaniel's hands hurt and the copper keys had made his skin smell of money.

None of them discussed it, but instead of parting ways at the end of the shift, they walked together to Victoria. They found crowds, because the trains had been stopped for the day, and then, closer to the building, bricks everywhere. Since everybody else was more interested in finding out when the services would resume, it wasn't difficult to get to the edge of the wrecked cloakroom. The wooden rafters were blasted as though something monstrous had broken out. A top hat still sat in the rubble, and a red scarf had turned greyish where frost stuck it to the bricks. Policemen were clearing the wreckage from the outside in, breath steaming. After a while they started to look warily at the four telegraphists. Thaniel could see it must have looked strange, four thin clerks lined up neatly in black and staying to look for much longer than anyone else. They broke apart. Rather than go straight home, he walked around St James's Park first, soaking in the nearly green grass and the empty, raked-over flowerbeds. It was so open, though, that the great fronts of the Admiralty and the Home Office still looked close. He wished for some proper woods. On the wish's tail came an urge to go up to Lincoln for a visit, but there was another man living in the gamekeeper's cottage now, and a new duke at the big house.

He went home circuitously, avoiding Parliament.

'See this?' George the beggar said, holding up a newspaper at him when he went by. The front page was mostly taken up with an etching of the blasted station.

'Just now.'

'What times, eh? Wouldn't have had this when I was a lad.'

'But they burned all the Catholics in those days, didn't they,' said Thaniel. He looked down at the picture. Seeing it in a newspaper made it more real than seeing it in person, and suddenly he felt annoyed with himself. They were supposed to have their affairs in order. In order meant a state which relatives could make sense of if it all went badly in May. Annabel would never sell something like a watch, even if she was scraping to keep the boys in clothes that fitted. It was no use willing it to her.

'Oh, har har,' snarled George. 'Wait, where are you going?'

'Pawn shop. Changed my mind about something.'

Just beyond the prison was a pawnbroker who called himself a jeweller despite the three gold balls outside the shop.

The front window was hung about with shabby-looking gold and pasted with advertisements for other shops or by people with second-hand things too big to bring in person. The newest was one of the police notices to keep watch. It was clerkishly pedantic of him, but he was starting to feel tetchy about those. Bombers did not go about trailing wires and fuses.

'Silly, isn't it?' the pawnbroker said, seeing him frown. 'Been coming round pasting those up all over the place for months. I keep saying, all our bombers are safe locked up.' He nodded to the prison. 'But up they go.' He had one stuck to the top of the counter too, and peeled it off to show another underneath. The paste had made it translucent and there was another under that, so that 'keep watch' had a diagonal, fading shadow.

'They're everywhere at Whitehall,' Thaniel said, and then took out the watch. 'What's this worth?'

The pawnbroker glanced at it, and then looked again, and then shook his head. 'No. I'm not taking one of his.'

'What? Whose?'

The pawnbroker looked annoyed. 'Look, I'm not falling for this again. Two was enough, thanks. The marvellous disappearing watches, brilliant trick, I'm sure, but you'll need to try it on someone who hasn't seen it before.'

'It's not a trick. What are you talking about?'

'What am I talking about? I mean they don't stay pawned, do they? Someone sells one on, I pay good money, the sodding things disappear a day later. I heard it all round town, it's not just me. You get on before I call the constable.'

'You've got a cabinet full of watches there that look like they've managed to stay pawned,' Thaniel protested.

'You don't see one of *these*, though, do you? Just get out.' He showed the handle of a cricket bat he had under the counter.

Thaniel held his hands up and left. There were some little boys playing Indians outside, and he had to weave around them. He looked back at the pawn shop, wanting to go back and ask for the names of the people who had tried to sell on the watches before, but he doubted he would get much but a swing from the cricket bat for his trouble. Frustrated, he went home and put the watch back on to its dressing-table chair.

If what the pawnbroker had said was true, he wouldn't find anyone who would take it. A prickling terseness started about halfway down his spine, as though somebody had rested their fingertips gun-shaped between the vertebrae there. He bent his arm back and pressed his thumb into it hard. People did run scams around·expensive watches, and he did sometimes forget to latch the door. In the balance of probability, it was unlikely that somebody had broken into his flat twice, wound the watch, then made it impossible for him to get rid of it. The money it would take to upset all the pawnbrokers in London, for a start. He couldn't convince himself.

The next day Thaniel retrieved the will papers from the back of his drawer, under the Lipton's packet. They came out gritty with tea powder. He swept it off and filled out the blank spaces in carefully clear handwriting. As he described the watch and where to find it, a ball of ink tipped down the nib of his pen and burst above Annabel's name. He shook his head once and went through the rest of the unnecessary pages before signing the last.

The weather took a sudden turn for the brighter soon after that. Spring was coming, and he began to catch himself looking at butter and cheese in shops and adding up in his head to see if they might outlive him. He took some old clothes and pillowcases to the workhouse over the river, and cleaned the outsides of the window frames when he came back.

THREE

OXFORD, MAY 1884

THE ACADEMIC YEAR was nearly over. In the almost-summer light, the sandstone had turned gold and wisteria ran down the high walls. Under the blue sky, where the air smelled of hot cobbles, Grace rubbed her hair and felt like a Philistine for wanting rain.

Throughout winter, she always believed that she was a summery sort of person. Unfortunately, this was not true, and after a week of good weather, she was sick of being too hot. The sky showed no sign of greying, so she had resolved to spend the day in the cool of the library with a book she had ordered the previous week. She had an experiment in mind and wanted to check how it had been done before. It had seemed like a fine idea when she set off; now that she was nearly there, she was sweating and wishing that lemonade was allowed inside.

As she passed through the main square of the Bodleian, posters advertising college balls and plays fluttered on the walls in the hot breeze. She had been permanently put off the latter by a horrific performance of *Edward II* at Keble last year. Edward had been an ancient classics professor and Gaveston an undergraduate. Grace did not mind what classics professors and undergraduates got up to in their own time, but she objected to being charged a shilling to watch. Adjusting her false moustache as subtly as possible, she tapped up the steps of the Radcliffe Camera. Its basement floor was the darkest reading room in the library. She touched her hat to the porter at the door. He ignored her, already moving to intercept a young woman not prudent enough to have stolen a gentleman-friend's clothes.

"Scuse me, miss. Where d'you think you're going?' he said amicably.

The woman blinked, puzzled, and then remembered that she had no escort. 'Oh, of course! I am sorry.' She turned around at once.

Grace felt her eyebrow twitch and went on down the spiral steps. She had never understood why anyone listened to the rule about unaccompanied women and libraries. Everybody, professors and students and Proctors the same, knew that if the sign said 'do not walk on the grass', one hopped. Anybody who didn't had failed to understand what Oxford was.

The arrangement of the reading room was circular. All the bookcases were identical, and even though she was now at the end of her fourth and final year, she was disorientated while she looked for the main desk. Until recently, she had navigated by the signs on the pillars that showed which subject the nearby shelves represented, but they had switched around the theology section last month. Having found the desk, she crossed the tiled floor and asked in a whisper for her book. She had ordered them under the name of Gregory Carrow, an ancient cousin who had left the university decades ago, but the librarians never checked names, requiring only that the identity offered belonged to a student or an alumnus.

'*The American Journal of Science* – whatever do you want that for?' the librarian asked as he handed it over, a little irritably. Like museum curators, the librarians were loath to allow anyone to touch anything. It was pretty clear that they felt the whole university would be better off it weren't full of students.

Grace smiled. 'I'm putting up shelves. It's quite solid.'

He blinked. 'You can't take books out of the library.'

'Yes,' she said. 'I know. I've built a secret cellar. Thank you,' she added, and took the books away to a desk.

Food was forbidden in the library, but she had secreted a couple of biscuits in her pocket. Risky, since this was an offence punishable by banishment from the whole library for the day, though necessary. In relation to the centre of Oxford, Lady Margaret Hall might as well have been in Brighton, and she didn't have enough time left before the end of term to waste library days going back and forth for meals.

She had, in any case, waited more than a week for the journal. The Bodleian kept a copy of every book ever published since its establishment, but that meant that only the most often-used could be out on the shelves. Unusual books lived deep in the stacks, which covered a space underground much bigger than the library above, and obscure things had to go to old tin mines in Cornwall and be put on a train when a request came through. The only books more difficult to get hold of than little American journals were first copies of the *Principia*, which were chained to the desks in the manuscript library and inaccessible without written permission from a tutor.

'I've been looking for that *new* jacket everywhere, Carrow.'

Grace swung around in her chair and then squeaked when Akira Matsumoto ripped off the false moustache.

'You are quite a convincing man without that,' he said as he sat down opposite her. He flicked it across the room.

Grace kicked him under the table. Her lip hurt. She was about to tell him to be quiet when she realised that she was the only other person here except the librarian. Everyone else was outside, taking advantage of the sun. 'What are you doing here?' she said instead. 'I thought you were nurturing Japanese poetry in the Upper Reading Room? Or did you have to come and borrow my moustache before they'd let you in?'

Matsumoto smiled. He was the elegant son of a Japanese nobleman, not so much a student as a very, very rich tourist. Enrolled at New College, he had the run of the university, but as far as Grace knew, he had done no work; only perfected his already impeccable English and translated some Japanese poems. He insisted that it was hard work and important. The more he insisted, the more Grace was convinced the project was mythical.

'I was at the coffee house,' he said, 'and I saw my jacket walking past. I followed. May I have it back?'

'No.'

He levered down her book with one white-gloved finger. Outside, Grace had been uncomfortably warm in the borrowed jacket and starched collar, but Matsumoto seemed not to sweat. '*The Relative Motion of the Earth and the Luminiferous Ether*. What in God's name is a luminiferous ether when it's at home?'

'It's the substance through which light moves. Like sound in air, or ripples in water. It's incredibly interesting, actually. It's one of those things like the missing elements in the periodic table: we know mathematically that it must exist, but no one has yet proved it by experiment.'

'Dear me,' he sighed. 'How frightfully dry.'

'The man who wrote this essay almost managed it,' Grace pressed on. She had decided some time ago that it was her duty to make Matsumoto learn some science. It was embarrassing to be associated with a man who thought Newton was a town. 'His experiment was unsuccessful, but that's because his parameters were too lax and he conducted it among too many extraneous vibrations. But his design is excellent. This thing here, this machine, it's called an interferometer. It should work. If I could build one, with some improvements, somewhere absolutely vibration proof – a college's stone cellars, say – then it could be very exciting—'

'I'll tell you what's exciting,' he interrupted. 'My *finished* translation of the *Hyakunin Isshu*.'

'Bless you.'

'Quiet, Carrow, and pretend to be thrilled.'

She wrinkled her nose. 'Show me, then.'

He lifted the book from his canvas bag. It was a pretty quarto, and when he opened it, it was printed in Japanese on one side, English on the other. 'All polished and done with, at last. I'm quite proud of it. I only printed the one, for vanity; well, my father's vanity. I fetched it from the printer this morning.'

Grace flicked through it. The poems were only a few lines long.

'I direct you to number nine,' he said. 'Don't pull that face. These are the finest poems in all of Japan and medicine for your numerical soul.'

Grace turned to the ninth poem.

The flower's colour
Has faded away,
While in idle thoughts
My life passes vainly by,
And I watch the long rains fall.

'Not a very great example of manly frankness, is it,' she said.

Matsumoto laughed. 'And if I tell you that our word for colour is the same as our word for love?'

Grace read the poem again. 'Still trite,' she said. It was one of his faults to bombard all his acquaintances with persistent, suggestive charm until they adored him. He couldn't stand anything less than adoration. Grace had met his other friends, and disapproved. They followed him around like dogs after the huntsman.

'Hopeless,' he sighed, taking the little volume back. 'Now do put that awful science book away, Carrow, or we'll be late.'

Grace was lost. 'Late?'

'The National Society for Women's Suffrage. At your college. In quarter of an hour.'

'What? No,' Grace protested. 'I never said I would go. They're all tea-drinking idiots—'

'Don't speak of your fellow women in such an abominable way,' Matsumoto said, tugging her upright. 'Leave the book and come along. These things are terribly important and besides, the movement is becoming a little frightening. Certainly that Bertha girl looks fit to go at you with a knitting needle if she discovers you've shunned her meeting.'

Grace tried to pull against him, but he was a head taller than her and unexpectedly strong beneath his immaculate clothes. She only just managed to lean far enough away from him to drop the journal back on the re-shelving trolley. 'You don't give two figs about women's suffrage, what are you playing at?'

'Of course I do, of course you ought to have your rights.'

'You have to say that, you're afraid of the knitting needles too—'

'Ssh,' Matsumoto said, and they walked silently past the librarian. When they reached the steps, he took her arm and steered her up. 'If you must know, I have organised the most exquisite poker match in the anteroom where the various put-upon husbands and brothers will be waiting, but dear Bertha won't let in a member of the unfair sex if he is unaccompanied by an example of the fairer.'

'I see. I'm your ticket to the game.'

'Yes.'

Grace thought about it. She wanted to be indignant, but even an octopus would have had difficulty finding a leg to stand on after spending the last four years towing him around every library in Oxford. 'Well ... yes, all right, fair enough.'

'Excellent. I will buy you some wine tonight.'

'Thank you. But once the game has finished, if you could announce loudly that you intend to go to your club ...'

'Yes, yes, of course.' He kissed the top of her head and she caught the scent of his expensive cologne. She felt herself redden.

'Will you get off me!'

They had just reached the top of the steps. The porter gave her a suspicious look.

'You rather gave yourself away just then,' Matsumoto laughed once they were out of earshot again. 'Women haven't cultivated the art of proper friendship.'

'Women don't climb all over each other—'

'Oh, that's a cab – can you catch it? They never stop for me, they all seem to think I'm a harbinger for the invasion of the Yellow Man.'

Grace ran to catch the cab. The Oxford sort were always in a better condition than their London equivalents, and despite the hot weather, the seats inside smelled only of leather polish and cleaning salt. Matsumoto ducked in beside her.

'Lady Margaret Hall, please,' Grace called. They ground off over the cobbles.

Lady Margaret was at the far end of a long, wide avenue. The cab took them past other libraries and townhouses, then the redbrick walls of Keble College with their zigzag patterns, which looked ridiculous and spoke, Grace suspected, of the general unavailability of proper Cotswolds sandstone. Matsumoto's college had bought it all for their new buildings.

There was talk of new buildings at Lady Margaret, too. Grace hoped the plans would go through. As the cab stopped outside, the hall looked impoverished even after Keble. Because she almost never took a cab and so never made the transition between the great spires of the town and here in so little time, she rarely noticed how tiny it was. Nobody could have called it a college in the sense that the others were. From the outside, it looked like nothing more exciting than a white stone manor house, nicely planted about with Virginia creeper and lavender, but hardly impressive. There were only nine students in residence.

Today, though, there was much more activity than usual. Other cabs were arriving, and women with parasols were gravitating towards the doors two by two, or slightly ahead of husbands. Some of the men saw Matsumoto and made a beeline across, looking hopeful.

'Ah, Grace, joining us at last?'

'Good afternoon, Bertha,' Grace smiled, though she could feel that the smile had a certain rictus-like quality. Bertha lived in the room next to hers, but she studied classics, the most pointless subject in the university. It was hard to communicate with somebody who spent every waking hour poring over the linguistic cleverness of men who had been dead for two thousand years. Matsumoto was bad enough, but classicists were honorary Catholics. Now, Bertha was manning the main door like a bishop.

'Perhaps you'd like to change into something more suitable before attending?' she said, lifting her eyebrows at Grace's borrowed clothes.

'Yes. This is far too hot.' Grace pulled off the jacket and gave it to Matsumoto. 'I'll be in in a minute. There's no need to wait for me.'

'Who's this?' Bertha demanded. 'You can't bring in your servants, there isn't room.'

'This is Akira Matsumoto. He isn't my servant, he's the Emperor's second cousin.'

'Do you speak English?' Bertha asked him, too loudly.

'I do,' Matsumoto said, unruffled, 'though I'm afraid my sense of direction is somewhat hazy in all languages. Can you remind me where I ought to wait? Somebody did tell me last time, but I've quite forgotten now.'

Bertha was wrong-footed. 'Through there on the left. There are refreshments and … yes.'

Matsumoto smiled and slipped past her towards the anteroom and the smell of pipe smoke. Grace watched him go. She couldn't tell whether he was charming because he had a deep-seated love of humanity, or because charm always got him what he wanted. It was tempting to think that the former notion was naïve and the latter far more likely, but he kept it up all the time. Her own reserves of bonhomie ran low after twenty minutes. She shook her head once and went slowly upstairs to change.

Her brother had bought her a fob watch for her birthday. It opened in two ways. On one side was the clock face, on the other, a filigree latticework. When the back lid opened, the filigree rearranged itself into the shape of a tiny swallow. Clever tracks of clockwork let it fly and swoop along the inside of the lid, silver wings clinking. She took it down with her in order to have something to fiddle with. The meeting had started by the time she arrived and she had to slip in to sit at the back. She ran her fingernail over the maker's mark on the back of the watch. *K. Mori.* An Italian, probably; Englishmen were rained on too often to come up with anything that imaginative.

Bertha stood on the stage where the high table usually was, her hands clasped in front of her and blushing prettily while she gave her speech. Every now and then, there was a smattering of applause. She was saying the usual things. Grace clicked open her watch and clicked it closed again three times, watching the swallow flit. The clicking was sharp and probably irritating to the women further along the bench, but two of them were knitting.

'And so,' Bertha was saying, 'I propose that this society offer its support to Mr Gladstone's establishment in any way possible, whether through our influence over male relations, or through party donations. Would anyone like to say anything?'

Someone in a white bonnet lifted her hand. 'I'm not sure about Mr Gladstone,' she said. 'He doesn't seem entirely trustworthy. My uncle is a phrenologist and says that the shape of his skull is typical of a liar.'

'That's utter nonsense,' someone else said. 'My husband works at the Home Office and has found him to be an absolute gentleman. He provided wine for all his staff at Christmas.'

Grace turned over the watch and wished that the ingenious Mr Mori could have devised a way to make time speed up. It had only been fifteen minutes. The meeting would last at least an hour. It took Bertha nearly that long to carry her motion. Almost as soon as there was a general agreement, the porter leaned in and cleared his throat.

'Ah, ladies? The gentlemen are declaring their intention to repair to their clubs.'

There was a flurry of movement as the women hurried to intercept their relatives before they could be left behind. Grace slipped out first and found Matsumoto waiting for her just outside, leaning against a door frame.

'There,' he said. 'Duty done. That wasn't so difficult, was it?'

'You weren't there. Outside, outside. If women ever get the vote, I'm moving to Germany.'

His lip quirked. 'How very unfeminine of you.'

'Have you listened to them? Oh, we can't support Gladstone, he's got terribly odd hair, but wait, he's a lovely man really, even if he does have a queer nose ...'

As they passed back outside, where the air had cooled now, he lifted his eyebrows at her. 'I hate to state the obvious, Carrow, but you are one of them.'

'I am an atypical example,' she snapped. 'I've had a proper education. I don't spend my time mumbling about crockery. Anyone who does shouldn't be allowed anywhere near the damn vote, never mind Parliament. Christ, if women members were allowed now, foreign policy would be decided according to the state of the Kaiser's sideburns. I'll kick anyone who asks me to sign a petition, I swear.' She paused. 'Did you promise me some wine, earlier?'

'I did,' Matsumoto smiled. 'If you'll come back to New College.'

'Yes please.'

'You are ludicrous, I hope you understand.'

'I understand.' She sighed. 'Is it white wine? Red tastes like vinegar.'

'Of course it's white wine, I'm Japanese. I'd like to walk if you don't mind, now it's cooler,' he added, nodding at the clouded sky.

'Yes, me too.'

As they walked, he took her arm. 'I must say, I don't approve of this dress. It's ghastly. My tailoring is infinitely better.'

'It is. May I have that jacket back?'

'You may.' He put it around her shoulders.

It smelled of him rather than her. 'This is the one you were wearing earlier.'

'I wanted to keep my new one new. I enjoyed the biscuits, by the way.'

The wind rose and Grace pulled the sleeves over her hands, then paused. Each sleeve had only one button, and each button had been made in the shape of a silver swallow. She looked up. 'These are good.'

'Oh, do you think? I bought them specially, actually. I've always had rather a weakness for swallows. When I was a boy, we used to watch swarms and swarms of them from the castle walls. They fly in enormous numbers sometimes in Japan, and they make the strangest shapes. One can see why people in medieval times thought they were seeing spirits and suchlike. Reminds me of home.'

Grace took out her watch and showed him the filigree swallow inside. Matsumoto almost never talked about Japan. Or, he would mention it in passing as a way to illustrate the deficiencies of the English, but he had never told her what it was like there. She had assumed, wrongly, that he didn't think of it.

He smiled. 'May I?'

She passed the watch to him. He turned it around and around. The weighted swallow stood upright whichever way the watch was held.

'There's something familiar about this,' he murmured. His black eyes sharpened. 'Who's the maker?'

'Some Italian.'

He looked relieved.

FOUR

LONDON, 30 MAY 1884

THANIEL LAY IN bed and watched the sun brighten his ceiling. He hadn't slept until an hour ago because he had been doing the last of the cleaning – the grate and the hearth, and the insides of the cupboards, completely empty except for the crockery. Now he felt as though he were trying to get up at midnight. Usually he took a night shift on Fridays, but the senior clerk had reshuffled the timetable to bring in the fastest coders for eight o'clock, and leave the slowest for the night. Today, the night shift wouldn't matter; if Clan na Gael kept to their promise, the Home Office would be safe or gone by midnight. The tall ship outside was creaking again, rigging squeaky from the damp and loud because he had left the window open overnight. Somebody was repairing the hull. He could smell the tar.

He waited for the clock to reach seven. The mist outside made the air close and stuffy, and he had to peel himself off the sheets.

In the morning quiet, the click of the watch's clasp was sharp as it unlocked itself. He turned his head without moving the rest of himself. Pressed down by an invisible finger, the button on the catch lowered, and the case eased open, no quicker than an oyster shell. Once it had opened wholly, it sat inanimate again. He waited, but it did not move again. At last, he lifted it up by its chain.

The face was glass, to show off the clockwork underneath. It was working. The time was right. Under the hands, the silver balance swung on a hairline wire, and the cogs that wheeled round the seconds ticked under jewel bearings. Behind those was more clockwork, very dense, much more elaborate than an ordinary watch. He couldn't tell what it was measuring. From the open cover, a round watchpaper feathered out and settled on his knee, face down. He turned it over. A border of fine leaves encircled the maker's mark:

K. Mori
27 Filigree Street
Knightsbridge

Mori. He didn't know what kind of name that was. It sounded Italian. He fitted the watchpaper back into the lid and kept staring at it in snatches while he got up – shave at the mirror, tie, collar. He had gone through the same motions in the mornings and in the nights for long enough to know, without looking at a clock, that it took twenty-one minutes to dress. It was so well established that if he tried to do anything unusual, or go any more slowly, he felt a pressure on the base of his skull. It made his study of the watch difficult, and the question of whether or not to bring it with him more feverish than it needed to be. At last he picked it up. He wanted to show it to Williamson. As he closed the door behind him, he took one last look around the room. Everything was clean, cleaner than he had found it, and there was no clutter. If Annabel had to come down to see to it, she would only have to spend half an hour packing up what he had left.

He set off in the thready mist. It was still dense over the river, where it made skeleton ghosts of the ships' masts and trapped the stale smell of the water. The way took him past Parliament and Westminster Abbey, whose high walls threw the path into a shadow that still held the night-time cold, then up to Whitehall Street and its rank of new, bright buildings. The knot that had been forming deep in his intestines tightened. The bomb at Victoria had been a little clockwork device that might have fitted into a shoebox. The springs of even an ordinary watch could go strong for more than a day. There was every chance that the new bomb was in place already.

The yellow of the stairs sounded far away, and the telegraphy office on the second floor seemed further up too. He had to stare at the nearest telegraph machine for a few minutes before he could lift his hands and wind in a new reel of transcript paper, and when he did, he gripped it too hard and bent the upper edge in five places where his fingers had been. He had no time to put in a straighter one before the machine thrummed and began scratching out a message. Being forced to concentrate, and do something, made him pull himself together. It was stupid to think there would definitely be a bomb in Whitehall. If everybody went about paralysed, Clan na Gael wouldn't need to bother with dynamite to bring the civil service to a grinding halt. He had never even met an Irishman, but he felt suddenly determined that he'd be damned if he was going to worry and shudder his way through the day.

The clicks and pauses came in the hiccuping rhythm of Williamson's code.

Clockwork bomb found and— disabled at base of Nelson's Column. Field officer reports it looks— complex. Decent springs used and sixteen packets of dynamite. Timer set to go in— thirteen hours i.e. 9 p.m. Sending uniforms to search HO again today please confirm receipt…

While the code ran, Thaniel held the end of the transcript paper with one hand and rested the other on the bronze knob of the key. As soon as Williamson stopped, he replied, *GM Dolly message received.*

A pause. GM was good morning, but Thaniel realised then that Williamson, with his meticulous typing, probably did not know it. His own English had devolved rapidly since he had become a telegraphist. There was a shorthand for everything. GM, good morning, GA, go ahead, 1, wait a moment, BO, bugger off, generally to the Foreign Office.

How do you— always know it's me?

The way you type.

You HO boys are— disturbing sometimes. Going— for a drink after? Everyone seems— to be planning to descend on the— Rising Sun.

It was a bar opposite the Yard, just down from Trafalgar Square.

Hope so, Thaniel sent back. *Plan not to die in service of British Government. Pay insufficient. Remember that watch that was left at my house?*

Y—es?

It was locked before. It opened this morning. I think you should have a look at it.

How big?

Watch-sized.

Not explosive then. It's— bloody odd, but no time today for anything without— dynamite in it. Sorry. Must go.

Wait. You said the timer on the column bomb was set for nine tonight. If there are other bombs, should we expect those at the same time?

A long pause. Then, *Yes.*

Thaniel delivered the first message to the senior clerk and threw away the rest of the transcripts. By the time he came back, they were uncrumpling slowly in the wastepaper basket like the tendons of a dead thing relaxing. He watched them and felt crumpled too. His neck had been aching lately because there was never time to stretch or walk.

'Williamson says to expect it all at nine o'clock tonight,' he said to the room.

There was a small silence as the other three paused in their coding. As they did, a boom of gunfire cracked the air. It made the four of them jump, before they all dissolved into nervous laughter. It was only Horse Guards. They fired shots in the parade ground at eight o'clock every morning. Thaniel lifted out the watch anyway to be certain. Sure enough, the filigree hands showed eight. The rose gold sheened its familiar voice-colour.

'Phew!' Park said, with a brittle enthusiasm. 'Where did you get that?'

'It was a present.'

Park's transcript paper creaked and then crackled as it buckled in on itself. When he had written down the message, he peered down at the watchpaper in the lid. 'Mori,' he read. 'He's quite well known, isn't he?'

'I don't know,' said Thaniel honestly. The other central exchange machine started up too, and they had to turn away from each other.

The senior clerk passed a folder full of notes over his shoulder while he wrote. The notes were messages to be telegraphed today. Still listening to the central exchange and transcribing with his right hand, Thaniel opened the file and began to tap out the top messages with his left, to the rhythm of the opening chorus of *Iolanthe*. He had seen it last year. Arthur Sullivan's music tended to be disguised behind silly lyrics in comic opera, but underneath, its real colours were as good as anything by more respected composers. He still had the programme and a lithograph print at home, locked in the music box.

'How do you do that?' Park said, talkative now that they had broken their usual silence. The two operators on his far side glanced toward Thaniel too, eavesdropping.

'What?'

'Write with one hand and code with the other.'

'Oh. It's like playing the piano.'

'Where did *you* learn to play the piano?' said Park.

'My ... father was gamekeeper at a big house, and the gentleman there was a concert pianist with no children. He was bursting to teach. If I'd said no, he would have tried the dog.'

They laughed. 'Are you any good?'

'Not any more.'

Williamson's officers arrived soon after. Thaniel wanted to make them look at the watch, but Williamson had said it was nothing, and insisting would have frightened the other operators. Once they had searched under the telegraphs, Thaniel faded back into the scratching of the code, and worked his way through the file of notes. They were mostly meaningless to him, being snippets of conversations whose totality he had not heard. A few did make sense. The Foreign Office was throwing a ball next month and there was a message confirming an order of six casks of champagne for the Foreign Minister.

'Steepleton, is that from Gilbert and Sullivan?'

He looked round at the senior clerk. 'Yes?'

'Pay attention to the messages! The fate of the nation might well be in your hands!'

'It isn't. They're full of Lord Leveson's champagne.'

'Get on with it,' the senior clerk sighed.

The policemen returned three hours later and declared an all clear. In that time they couldn't have done anything but stroll the halls and glance in a few cupboards. The senior clerk announced suddenly that all those who had begun on the early shift should pause for tea and some food. They would work on until nine. They would be free after that, one way or the other.

Glad for the chance to stretch, Thaniel drifted to the small canteen, where he waited in line for a cup of soup that was, just for today, being provided free of charge. The usual canteen chatter had dulled almost to silence. The sound of soup being ladled into cups was too loud. He tried to think how he had ended up here.

He had taken the job four years ago and had considered himself lucky to get it. Before that, he had been a ledgers clerk at a loco-motive factory in Lincoln. That had been cold and horrible. The Home Office paid more and did not expect its employees to buy their own coal. But telegraphy never varied. It was as easy as writ-ing, once you knew Morse Code, and he wasn't educated enough to advance much further. There were vague prospects of becom-ing an assistant senior clerk at some point this year. He had been pleased about that when he heard, then horrified to be pleased, because being pleased with something so boring meant that without noticing, at no particular point that he could see, he had shrunk to fit the job. He had never meant to be a telegraphist for four years.

But the fact was that you could not support a widow and two boys with orchestral work. After Annabel's husband had died he had sold the piano. He hadn't been able to go to concerts or opera for a good while, but gradually that wore off. Now, he bought a cheap ticket once every season or so. The part of himself he had amputated still twinged sometimes, but letting her go to a work-house would have been worse than a twinge.

Now, when the Irish were not threatening to blow up Whitehall, he worked between eight and eleven hours a day for six days or nights a week except at Christmas. He was not poor – he could afford ten candles and two baths a week. He wasn't going to throw himself in the Thames for the misery of it all, and God knew most of London was worse off. All the same, he had a feeling that life should not have been about ten candles and two baths a week.

'D'you reckon we'll blow up today, then?' the cook asked him as he handed over the soup. He had a South Riding accent that sounded like home.

'Not up here. Last time they threw a bomb at the ground-floor window, didn't they?' He caught the cook's disconcerted expression. 'Still, blowing up would be a change from paperwork.'

The cook laughed, too high.

As nine o'clock edged around, the office began to slow. The clip of Morse was more spaced as the telegraphists listened for an explosion. In the larger office across the corridor, the typists lost their rhythm and lowered their voices. Thaniel saw Park's knuckles whiten over his telegraph key. He leaned across and took it from him gently, and got up to cross the corridor. The telegraph room was windowless, but the typists' office had huge windows overlooking Whitehall Street. The others followed him. They found the typists standing too, going to the same window. It was open now and letting in the smell of ozone. Thunder growled around the city steeples, quietly, as though it knew that hundreds of men were trying to listen.

Nine chimes tolled out from Parliament and the city remained its ordinary self, unlit by flashes or smoke. Rain tapped on the window panes. The clerks exchanged glances, but nobody moved. Thaniel took out the watch. A minute past, two minutes, and still nothing. Ten. Then a gust of laughter came from the street. The clerks from the Foreign Office were already on their way home. They were sharing umbrellas.

The senior clerk rang his bell.

'Well done, everyone! Early shift is over, late begins in two minutes. Clear out, and if you see an Irishman on your way home, give him a good kick from the Home Office.'

There was a cheer, and he took his first deep breath for months. He hadn't been aware of breathing shallowly. It had happened gradually; someone had put a penny on his chest every hour since November, and now the weight of thousands of pennies had lifted at once.

Everyone was going to the Rising Sun and to other bars and clubs near Trafalgar Square. He walked along Whitehall Street among the exodus of clerks, past the long rank where the night cabs waited in the rain. He always kept an umbrella at the office, and once he had put it up, he half closed his eyes as he listened to the thrum of the rain on the canvas. It made a wash of rippling half colours. While somebody behind him told an Englishman, Irishman and Scotsman joke, he bent his neck and lifted his shoulders to let his spine stretch. The wet cobbles were orange with the reflections of the lamps. He couldn't remember seeing that before.

A man standing in the doorway of the Rising Sun would see a man standing in the doorway of Scotland Yard, and as such, it was the most orderly pub in London. He pushed open the doors and walked into the smell of beer, furniture polish, and damp clothes. It was filling fast with clerks and policemen, and though nobody was drunk yet, they were calling across heads and laughing. Dolly Williamson was at the bar, chatting to the girl behind it. He was a big man with a beard that he had cropped since Thaniel had seen him last. He saw Thaniel in the mirror and turned around, beaming.

'You're here! Drink? What d'you like?'

'Brandy, thanks,' Thaniel said. He shook his hand, and Williamson thumped his arm.

The girl, whose name was Miss Collins, was pouring out their brandy when he felt the watch in his pocket clicking. When he opened it, the dense clockwork behind the timekeeping set was going fast, and getting faster. He just had time to wonder what it was doing before it screamed. Not an alarm, but a horrible, keening siren noise. He spun it over to search it for a catch, painfully conscious of the startled looks coming from all around, and half expecting to be tackled and shot. There was no catch.

'Sorry,' he shouted to Williamson over the noise, and ducked outside with it to the deserted alley on the right of the building. Some waiting cabbies looked across curiously from where they stood with their horses. He was able to keep just out of sight, as long as he kept his back pressed against the Rising Sun's angled wall.

The watch stopped. He sighed, and half came out.

A titanic bang made the ground leap. Smoke and fire roared out from the Yard. A wave of heat shoved him, and he saw a cabby fly across the road, then smash into the front windows of the pub. There were a series of crashes from inside that were the heavy tables dominoing. The noise made white bursts across everything. A spray of typewriter keys floated by. When he turned his head away, his skin was stiff from a coating of soot. Standing in the alley, he was shielded almost completely, except from the few shards of glass and brick from the far edge of the blast. They pattered down around his shoes. Then all the noise was gone and there was a long silence, filled with smoke plumes and rags of floating paper, and isolated fires. The aftershocks of the flashes stayed in his eyes and sank slowly, then rose again whenever he blinked.

He stood still. He couldn't hear anything, although he could see that other people were shouting. In his palm, the tick of the watch felt much too slow. A young policeman caught his arms and looked into his eyes. Thaniel could read his lips just well enough to see that the man was asking if he was hurt. He shook his head. The policeman pointed him back towards the Home Office, to avoid the rubble. It was everywhere, completely blocking the road that should have led to Trafalgar Square.

Beside him, smoke billowed from inside the Rising Sun. The kegs had exploded and the bar was burning. A few men staggered out, smacking at their sleeves to extinguish the orange ashes there. Dolly was not among them. Ignoring the constable, he bent under what was left of the doorway.

'Dolly!' He couldn't hear his own voice, and couldn't tell if he had shouted loudly enough for anyone to hear over the fire.

It was a small place, and he soon found Williamson half-trapped under one of the big tables. They had been made to seat twelve people, Viking style, but the blast had hurled them all against the bar. The corner of one had smashed the floorboards where he had been standing before he left. Ruined splinters flanked a hole that looked right down into the cellar. Lit by the flames racing along the spilled brandy over the bar, they were a bloody red. He did not stop and stare but the sight of them branded itself into his mind, and imaginary pain flashed across his ribs where the table would have crushed them if he had stayed.

He pulled Williamson out. Williamson staggered on the way up, his pupils different sizes, but he seemed to catch his balance after Thaniel held him still for a second. Between them they lifted down the barmaid, who had to climb over the taps. They couldn't find the door in the smoke, and climbed out instead through the shattered windows.

'I've got to go,' Williamson said, gripping Thaniel's arm. 'I must deal with all this, understand? Get yourself—'

He was cut off by a distant boom.

'Christ, another one.' Williamson stared that way. 'Get yourself home. Away from the city centre, for God's sake. Stay by the river, do *not* go too closely by Parliament. And you, Miss Collins, go on.' Without pausing, he ran after the policemen already streaming toward the ruined buildings of the Yard.

The girl stared blankly at Thaniel and began to pick her way over the rubble. He stood still for a second, then turned back the way he had come. Williamson was right; there was nothing for him to do but go home and hope that the Irish had no interest in Pimlico.

The smoke from the explosion drifted with him all the way along Whitehall Street. As he walked he became one of a company of ghosts. The watch's tick thrummed through his palm. He would have to give it to Williamson, he should have, just now. Only the bombmaker knew exactly when a bomb would go off. That alarm had been set as a warning. The lights of Westminster underground station filtered up its steps and through the smoke. He was further toward the middle of the road than he had thought.

'Out the way, out the way!'

He stepped to the left for the two men with a stretcher. They were running toward a hospital; the doctors were already outside, rolling up their sleeves as they waited for the injured, white coats already grey along the creases from the grit in the air. The man on the stretcher was dead. Thaniel stared at him. His eyes were still open and he had died with an expression of complete passivity. He had a pair of spectacles hooked over his breast pocket and ink on his fingers. Just a clerk. He looked as if he had seen the flames and let them come.

It would have been him. Thaniel saw white flashes again, though there was no noise to provoke them. He could see it as clearly as memory, as if he had missed it so closely that his mind had strayed down the wrong arm of time and had yet to come back. He would have heard the bang and turned around; the glass windows would have shattered inward, and then the force of the blast would have knocked him back against the bar as the tables fell. The corner of that nearest table would have crushed his ribcage, and within a minute or so, he would have died of the puncture to his lung, with his fingertips stained silver by the pencil lead from telegraph transcripts.

He opened the watch lid, which was alternately smoke-smudged and not where his fingers had been closed over it. The round watchpaper was still inside. *K. Mori, 27 Filigree Street, Knightsbridge.* Fifteen minutes away on the underground. The watchmaker would know who it had been sold to. The familiar well-scheduled pressure on the back of his skull wanted him to go home, like Williamson had told him to, but if he did, Williamson would only have to send someone else to do it tomorrow, and by then, this Mori might have heard enough of what had happened not to want to talk to policemen.

He turned down the station steps. There were still ticket officers in the forecourt, newly alert after hearing the explosion.

Some of them were dusty – they must have been up the road to see. He bought a ticket to South Kensington, aware that the officer was staring at him as he fished four pence from his pocket.

'We heard a bang,' the man said tentatively. 'Someone said that half of Whitehall was blown up.'

'Only Scotland Yard,' Thaniel said. 'Is it this platform or the other—'

'This side. Are ... you all right?'

'Yes. Thank you,' he added, holding up the ticket as he turned away.

Grainy steam churned around the westbound platform. It tasted of soot and the walls were black with it. He leaned against a pillar while he waited. He was starting to feel light-headed, and couldn't tell whether it was the noise from the explosion or the thick air. He almost never used the underground. Pimlico was close enough to Whitehall for the walk to be comfortable, and in any case, he didn't much want the respiratory failure that would ensue from frequent trips. It wasn't just a neurosis. Opposite him, on the other side of the tracks, there were posters pasted on to the walls. The two nearest advertised a new kind of restorative elixir for bronchial problems. He became aware of a rattling, and realised that he was still holding the watch in his pocket. Because his hand was shaking, the case kept clipping the chain.

Two women were looking at him half over their shoulders. He looked back, then around when they averted their eyes again. There was an odd movement in the small crowd of waiting people. Men were seeing him and leaving their women on the platform to go back towards the exits to see what was happening above ground. They must have felt the bang of the bomb, but it could have been anything down here – a train hitting the bumpers too hard or workmen in one of the new tunnels further down – but he was covered in dust, and now the dust was following him down the steps. He heard voices calling down that it was like fog outside, and that there were fires. A policeman came on to the platform and stopped by the conductor near Thaniel.

'How deep are these lines?' he asked. 'Do any of them run under Scotland Yard?'

'No? Why? Not too deep—'

'South Kensington!' shouted a guard. It made Thaniel jump, which sent a shooting pain across the back of his head. He pressed his hand against the nape of his neck. The two women were watching him again.

The train arrived in a thundercloud of steam, through which its front lights glowed red. Almost as soon as he was inside, the engine fired and the train was leaving again. Once the lights of the station had been left behind, everything beyond the windows was dark. He let his temple rest against the glass and thought how good a place a train would be to plant another bomb. People were on and off trains all day, and there were too few guards to keep combing every carriage. He started when the train jerked to the side and the gaslight above him flickered, but it was only bumps in the track.

He had the carriage to himself. All greyed, his reflection looked like his father, who had already been an old man by the time his children were born. He had lasted until Thaniel was fifteen and Annabel eighteen, and then, duty done, died suddenly. There was no will, so they had gone to a séance in Lincoln, where the old man asked via a girl medium if they minded helping the duke hire a replacement gamekeeper, and said his savings were in his tackle box, behind the bronze fishing hooks.

It was only twenty feet or so up to street level at South Kensington. The guards, distracted by his coating of ash and dust, didn't check his ticket. It was too far from Westminster for them to have heard anything. Outside, he lost his bearings before his internal map realigned and placed the station just at the top of Knightsbridge. The rain was coming so hard that there was a mist above the ground where each drop ricocheted back up into the air. The noise sprayed spectra across everything and he put his hand to the wall. The prism colours ought to have been lovely, but his eyes ached and for a long few seconds, until he got himself used to the sound, they might as well have been strobe flashes. Putting up his umbrella, which had left a damp patch across his knees where he had held it on the train, he started down the long road.

Filigree Street was a medieval row of houses whose upper stories leaned toward each other. At its far end, the gap between the gables became so small that people standing in opposite bedroom windows could have shaken hands. It was too dark to see house numbers, but number twenty-seven was obvious because it was the only shop still alight. In the window, a single lamp illuminated a clockwork model of a city that grew new towers and bridges until it became London. When he pushed the door, it was unlocked. There was no bell.

'Hello?' he called into the empty workshop. His voice was spiderwebbed with cracks. Electric lights hummed on as he came in and he stopped still, not sure what he had done to turn them on and waiting, his spine stiff, for something else. The lights were set into the ceiling in looping rows. He had only ever seen them at the illuminations, never in anyone's house. The filaments glowed orange first and then a yellowy white, much brighter than a gas lamp. The fizz of the electricity made him set his teeth. It sounded wrong, in the same way that the great river of tracks at Victoria felt wrong. But nothing else happened except, at last, a fractional brightening. In the new light, everything around him shone. Across the wall beside him was a tall pendulum clock, its movement regulated by the jointed wings and knees of a golden locust. A mechanical model of the solar system spun in mid-air, floating on magnets, and up two steps in the tiered floor, little bronze birds sat perched on the edge of the desk. One of them hopped on to the microscope and tapped its beak hopefully on the brass fittings. Things glimmered and clicked everywhere.

There was a sign by the door.

Room to let. Ask within.

He was about to call out again when, behind the desk, another door opened. A small man with blond hair came through it, backwards, because he was carrying two cups of tea. When he turned around, he nodded good evening. He had slanted eyes. Oriental. Thaniel floundered.

'Oh, er – do you speak English?'

'Of course I do, I live in England,' said the man. He held out one of the cups. His hands were thin, his skin the colour that Thaniel would have turned after a week in the sun. 'Tea? It's horrible outside.'

Thaniel set down his soaking umbrella and took the cup. It was green tea. He breathed in the woody steam, which cleared the soot from the back of his throat. He had meant to start asking questions straightaway, but the little foreigner had blindsided him. Although his clothes were English, they looked worn, and with his bad posture and his black eyes, they made him less like a breathing human than an expensive, neglected marionette. Thaniel couldn't think of a country that was known for turning out broken-toy men. Then he shook his head at himself. There didn't need to be a country for that. A man could have a character independent of his nation. His thoughts were starting to take on a strange ring: they had shrunk from their usual size and now the ordinary attic that was his ordinary mind looked like a cathedral at night, with endless galleries and rafters lost in the dark and nothing but the echoes to show where they were. He forced himself to sip the tea. The echoes eased.

The man was frowning at Thaniel's greyed clothes. 'You're bleeding.'

'I'm what?' Sticky blood had seeped through his shirtsleeve just above his elbow. He couldn't feel it. 'I'm all right. Are you Mr Mori?'

'Yes. I think you ought to come through and—'

Thaniel closed his hand in the air to stop him. 'One of your watches – it saved me from an explosion in Whitehall.'

'An—'

'There was an alarm,' he ploughed on. His bones ached, and he was grimy, and cold, because he had come out without his coat in the warm morning a hundred years ago, but he could see that if he sat down, he wouldn't be able to hold on to his thoughts. 'I didn't buy it; I don't know where it came from. Someone gave it to me six months ago. Left it in my flat with a gift tag. It wouldn't open until today. A watchpaper with your name and address was inside. Do you remember who you sold it to?'

He had been holding out the watch all the while, and now, carefully, the foreigner took it from him. He turned it over twice. 'I didn't sell it. I thought it had been stolen.'

'I didn't steal it!'

'No, you said, it was left for you. Come and sit down, please, your arm—'

'Damn my arm! It was a bomb! The alarm – it wasn't an ordinary alarm, it was a siren, you must have made that to order. It made a horrible noise, it made me move and I would have been killed if I hadn't. What was it for?'

'It really doesn't—'

'Half of Scotland Yard is going to think I knew when the bomb was going to go off, what was it *for*?'

'I set several watches to do that.' The watchmaker held his hands up in the way people do when they speak to hysterical children or wild animals. His fingertips were trembling, but from fear or cold it was hard to tell. The unfamiliar structure of the bones in his face made him hard to read. A draught had come in when he opened the door. On the desk, one of the clockwork birds fluffed up its metal feathers and shivered like wind chimes. 'I keep the shop open until late on Fridays. A horrible noise is a good way to force customers to leave on time, without having to herd them out myself – it's next door's children, they come in and break things. I hate children.' He looked at Thaniel helplessly, as if he were afraid that it wouldn't be a satisfactory explanation.

It wasn't. 'But then it should have gone off every Friday.'

'I – was explaining the alarm, not the timing. Anyone could reset it.'

'The damn thing had a gift tag on it!'

'That's . . . interesting and strange,' he said, glancing at the door as if he were gauging whether he was fast enough to slip by and out before Thaniel lost his temper.

Thaniel let his breath out. 'You don't know a thing about it, do you?'

'I don't think I do.' There was a little space of quiet. Thaniel felt exhausted. His eyes burned and everything became a fraction clearer as the tears lensed the light, like spectacles would have.

'Right. I see. Well, I'd better go.'

'No – no. Come and sit down, for God's sake, before you bleed to death on my floor.' As he said it, his voice sank low into a red gold that didn't suit his size. He must have seen Thaniel's shoulders ease, because he held out his arm to show him through the workshop's back door where he had just come with the tea. 'The kitchen's warm.'

He held open the door and waited for Thaniel to go through first. It led down two dented stone steps, very old, like the kind in churches, and straight into a neat kitchen that smelled sweet from baking. Thaniel dropped into one of the chairs and trapped his hands between his knees. There were lamps but no electric lights. Those must have been in the workshop for show. He was glad – the dimmer light hurt his eyes less.

He gazed around, expecting opium pipes and silk drapes, but everything was English. On the table in front of him was a plate full of scones, and a pot of tea that still steamed. The cups, he thought, were Chinese.

'Were you expecting someone?' he said, but didn't hear the reply. Now that he had nothing else to think about, his arm throbbed and the back of his neck felt as though the bones were fusing together. He clothes were stiff with damp and blood. 'Is there some water I could … ?'

The watchmaker filled a brass basin and set it down in front of him, followed by a new bar of lemon-scented soap. 'I'll go next door and see if Dr Haverly has a spare shirt that might fit you. I think I should bring him too.'

'No, no, I'll go home—'

'You wouldn't get past the front door,' the watchmaker said. There was a touch of the north in his accent. It was bizarre, but then, there was no reason to think so; Orientals had just as much right as anybody else to visit York or Gainsborough, although it was difficult to imagine why any of them would want to. 'I'll be back soon.'

'I'm all right,' Thaniel said. He would have liked a doctor, but he couldn't bring himself to push the watchmaker's good will so far as to ask him to pay for the consultation.

'Well, you need the shirt, at least.'

'I ... thanks, then. But only if he has one he doesn't want.'

The watchmaker nodded once, then slipped out through the back door and clicked it shut again before the rain could blow in.

Thaniel pressed his clean sleeve to his eyes until they were dry again, then peeled off his waistcoat. It was more horrible to feel the fabric move than to sit still in it. His left sleeve was brown. He rolled it back past his elbow to see the cut. It was long and deep, with a shard of glass still stuck in it. It hurt much more now that he could see it. He closed his fingernails over the protruding edge of the glass and pulled it out. It wasn't painful as much as it was shocking, like almost falling down the stairs. He dropped the shard into the water, where it plumed little ribbons of red.

The watchmaker came back then, rain-starred and holding a fresh shirt. He set it down on the chair next to Thaniel, along with a roll of bandages, and paused when he saw the glass in the bowl. 'Christ.'

'It's better than it looks,' Thaniel lied. It was difficult to believe that he had come from Westminster to Knightsbridge without feeling it. The pain was sharpening now that he was calmer. His neck sent spasms down his spine whenever he moved.

'You had better eat something. Sugar is good for shock.'

'Thank you,' said Thaniel, who was too tired now to argue. He rinsed out the cut as best he could and wound the bandage over it one-handed, trapping one end against his hip with his elbow when it came to tying it. Once he had tucked the ends back into the knot, he unbuttoned his shirt one-handed but stopped halfway, unable to go further. It was too much to be half naked at a stranger's kitchen table. He looked up at the watchmaker, meaning to excuse himself after all, but the man had turned around. He was fetching down crockery and cutlery. When he stretched to reach some plates from the cupboard above him, the hem of his waistcoat lifted and showed the dull brass buttons on his braces.

Thaniel ducked into the new shirt as quickly as he could, and felt better. The watchmaker must have been waiting to hear the clatter of fabric, because he turned back then and gave him some more tea and a scone, then crumpled down opposite him. He saw Thaniel watching him and smiled. It traced small lines around his eyes. Thaniel thought of cracks beneath the varnish on old porcelain.

'Do you know if there's somewhere nearby I could stay?' he asked. 'I think I've missed the last train.'

'You can stay here, I've a spare room.'

'I can't cause you any more trouble.'

The watchmaker lifted his shoulder. 'There are hotels along Sloane Street, if you brought money.'

He had a grand total of tuppence left. 'I ... didn't.'

'Or you can try the Haverlys next door. They keep the attic for lodgers.' Almost before he had stopped speaking, some banging and shouting reached them through the wall. 'There are the children, mind you.'

'I can walk home, actually.'

'I wouldn't have asked you if it were inconvenient, I'm not that much of a Samaritan. The room has been ready to rent for months. Nobody wants it. And you can't walk home,' he added, letting his ink eyes draw a line down Thaniel's head to the floor.

Thaniel saw the truth of it when he looked toward the door and felt reluctant about going even that far. Helplessness spread through him like damp. When he was small, Annabel had had a horror even of eating too much at somebody else's house. He had never dumped himself on anyone for a whole night, never mind a stranger, nor even thought of it. It felt presumptuous, and selfish, because he couldn't return the favour.

'You must let me pay you for the trouble later, then,' he said at last, and heard how stiff he sounded. He shut his eyes for a second. 'I'm sorry. I'm not trying to be rude, I mean it's – mortifying to stumble in here and—'

'Please don't be mortified,' the watchmaker said quietly. 'It isn't your fault.'

Thaniel thanked him unhappily and concentrated on achieving an even spread of jam across his scone. The high-pitched whine came back, greenish. The longer he was quiet, the louder it became, until it was the roar of collapsing brickwork.

'How do clockwork bombs work?' he said, to drown it out.

The watchmaker set down his teacup. If he thought that the question came abruptly, he didn't show it. 'They are explosives wired to a trigger switch, wired to a timer, which could be a clock or a watch, or something more in the region of a marine chronometer, if they must stand unattended for days rather than hours. The purpose of them is to remove the necessity of lighting a fuse in person. The only reason they have not been widely used before now is that until recently the technology did not exist to keep timers accurate in very cold or very hot weather. It's the springs. The metal expands and contracts. You can lose half an hour a day in winter.'

While he spoke, he stood up and took Thaniel's plate to the sink, where he turned the tap.

Thaniel half rose. 'I meant to do that—'

'Sit down.'

There was a bump under the sink. He jumped, but the watchmaker was unflustered and leaned down to open the cupboard. An octopus fell out. It was made of clockwork and it gleamed in the lamplight, but it was so like the real thing that Thaniel recoiled. The octopus seemed to consider things for a moment, then waved two of its arms. The watchmaker lifted it up and put it in a small water tank on the windowsill, where it drifted around with every sign of contentment.

'Er . . . ' said Thaniel.

'He's called Katsu.'

'I see?'

The watchmaker looked around. 'It's only clockwork. It's not some strange fetish.'

'No, no. It was, you know, unexpected. It's good.'

'Thank you,' he said, placated. He inclined his head at the octopus, which mirrored him. 'That said, I suppose it's not much of a mystery why I can't rent out the room.'

Thaniel watched the octopus too. It was hypnotic. The mechanical joints moved as fluidly as the water, glinting with the warped colours of the kitchen. It took him a little while to realise that it was watching him back, or it looked as if it was. He straightened up, feeling caught out. 'Have I told you my name yet?'

'I don't think so.'

'It's Steepleton. Nathaniel, but Thaniel if you like. I know it's a bit … but my father was Nat.'

'I'll stick to Mr Steepleton, if you don't mind.'

'Why?'

'In Japan, first names are only for who you're married to, or if you're being rude,' the watchmaker explained. 'It sounds wrong to me.'

Japan. Thaniel couldn't remember where it was. 'Can we negotiate down to Steepleton? Mr Steepleton makes me sound like a bank manager.'

'No,' said the watchmaker.

Thaniel laughed, then touched the back of his neck awkwardly when it occurred to him the man might not have meant to be funny. 'So I shouldn't ask your first name?'

But the watchmaker was smiling again. 'It's Keita.'

'Sorry, what … ?' It was a simple sound, but knowing that it was Japanese and therefore difficult, his brain had refused to hear it properly.

The watchmaker spelled it for him. 'Rhymes with later,' he added, and, unoffended, poured them both some more tea.

The spare room was crooked, as though it had planned to be L-shaped but changed its mind at the last minute. In one wall was a diamond-paned window, warped into a wave; under it was a bed with fresh sheets, and under that, floorboards bleached into a diamond cross-hatch pattern by the sun. Once the watchmaker had lit the lamp, he left the door open on his way out. His bedroom was only a few feet away across the landing. Thaniel sat down on the edge of the bed to check the bandage on his arm, and faced that way. The two doors made a double frame around the other room, where the watchmaker sat on his own bed in a pool of lamplight and wrote in a diary. His hand moved up and down the page, right to left. As he shifted the book over his knee to start the next page, the previous one fell down into view. The writing was all tiny calligraphy pictures. The watchmaker lifted his eyes and, realising that he was in fact spying on a man writing a diary, even if it happened not to be a language he knew, Thaniel eased the door closed, and turned off the lamp. Although he moved slowly, his joints were stiff and grinding. He had to undress without bending much. When he got into bed, he stayed kneeling, working up the courage to move his spine and knowing it would hurt that nerve in the back of his neck again when he did.

Despite the thunderheads, the night was light now, and silver light cross-hatched itself across the floor. He leaned on the windowsill, resting his cheek against the wall. Below him was a garden, quite long, where he could make out the rough shapes of bushes and trees through the rain. Off to the left were the city lights, but beyond the garden there must have been some kind of heath, maybe even Hyde Park – he had lost his sense of direction – because everything that way was black.

A swarm of lights sparked into life in the garden. Frowning, he found the latch, old but well oiled, and pushed the window open. He couldn't see what the lights were, only that they were floating above the grass. He flicked a farthing at them, but they didn't scatter. Suddenly they all went out. Nothing moved but the rain.

FIVE

KATSU WAS AN octopus. Still half asleep, Thaniel tried to remember how he knew that and why he had thought of it. After some false starts, his mind coughed up a memory of a foreigner and a medieval house full of clockwork. He curled on to his side and heard the scratch of stubble against the cotton pillow-case, then of his lashes as he opened his eyes. The room was gold in the morning. He had thought that he had dreamed it all, but the crooked floor was still crooked, and his skin still smelled of lemon soap. The watchmaker's footsteps went back down the uncreak-ing stairs. He had been on the landing, and talking, because as he went, so did the gold in the air, and gave way to ordinary sunlight. Thaniel watched it fade. It was the wrong shade for English.

Somewhere, a clock struck eight. Eight already. He sat up in a heap and shrugged into yesterday's borrowed shirt, then swore when the dry blood on his arm caught on the bandage. He turned the sleeve back, carefully, and unwrapped the bandage to see. It was no worse than the things that had befallen his knees when he was a boy. He got himself used to the idea, ignored the ringing inside his ears, and looked around for his socks.

He was putting them on when the first strains of piano music sang up the stairs. It was a morning song. The key was cut glass with prism colours around the edges. Distracted, he almost didn't notice when the top drawer of the dresser opened by itself.

The clockwork octopus came out. It extended a tentacle with a clicking of metal joints. Around it was looped the chain of his watch. He hesitated, but took it. The chain skittered over the metal tentacle with a high, thin pitch like incoming sea. It was quite a coincidence for a mechanical sea creature and he was speculating whether it could possibly have been done on purpose when Katsu stole his other sock and flopped on to the floor with an unbiological bang, whereupon it octopused out of the open door and slid down the banister.

He exclaimed at it, was ignored, and then went after it just in time to see it disappear into the parlour. It was climbing up the leg of the piano stool when he caught up. The watchmaker confiscated the sock and threw it over his shoulder to Thaniel, who caught it with the tips of his fingers. The octopus settled in his lap.

'Thank you for finding him,' he said. Against the piano keys, his hands were too warmly coloured for the watery morning. 'I was looking for him earlier. He plays hide and seek.'

'Don't you suppose that it would be easier to find a permanent tenant if you could persuade it not to do that?' said Thaniel, narrowing his eyes at the thing as it looked at him over the watchmaker's hip.

'I've tried. No, you can keep that,' he said when Thaniel tried to give him the watch.

Thaniel stopped. 'What? No, I can't. I'll only break it—'

'You won't break it, it's elephant-proof. I've tested it at the zoo. How is your arm?'

'Much better, thank you. Sorry, at the zoo?'

'Yes,' said the watchmaker.

Thaniel stood for a second, but no elaboration was forthcoming. There was no furniture in the room, except for the piano and a low table by the hearth. He sat down on the floor so that he could put on his second sock. In front of him, the watchmaker was bothering with only one pedal; whenever he leaned on it, the piano bumped gently and notes came up through the floor. The heels of his brown boots were imprinted with the mark of a Japanese manufacturer in their dense pictographic writing.

Thaniel frowned. Chinamen were not rare in London and God knew what George had seen. If he wasn't very careful, he was going to start jumping at imaginary ghosts. He didn't want to spend the rest of his life staring at everyone's shoes. The ringing noise from yesterday started up again. He closed his eyes but still saw white spots.

'Mr ... Mori, am I saying that correctly?' he said, probably more loudly than he should have.

'Morey.'

Thaniel nodded. 'Thank you for letting me stay. You've been very kind, but I ought to get to work now.'

The watchmaker turned his head to the side as a token backward look, though he didn't twist to see over his shoulder. 'It's Saturday.'

'It won't matter. I work at Whitehall. Everyone will be expected to go.'

'Rubbish, you were almost killed. They don't know you haven't a terrible concussion.'

'I haven't.'

'But you're not fighting fit either, are you.' He took his hands from the keys and the last cadence hung for a while, foggily. 'I'm going out for breakfast. Why don't you come with me?'

Thaniel's mind stopped working for a second, tumbled by the friendliness. 'I'll have a day taken from my pay.'

'Is it governmentally necessary that you go?' the watchmaker asked, without any trace of irony. It was a real question, and he was waiting for a real answer.

'No, I'm just a clerk. But I need the money,' he said, feebly.

The watchmaker stood up. 'In that case, the most efficient use of your time would be to go later and then faint over your desk. That would be considered a heroic effort, they wouldn't dock your pay, and you would only have been for five minutes. But not if you can't act,' he added, just as serious as before.

'Er ... all right,' Thaniel said. He smiled. He was beginning to think that losing a day's pay would be worth it. 'I'll give it a go.'

When the watchmaker gave him his hand, he was unexpectedly strong.

Yesterday's storm had left long puddles in the road, and they made islands of the taller cobblestones. Some of the water had condensed overnight into a mist thick enough to obscure the leaning houses. The washing lines strung between the nearer windows were empty and dripped into the puddles. Because it was still early, the shop-fronts were dark, all except the watchmaker's own. Small lights hidden in the displays glowed on as they passed and sparked over the tiny model of London: among the church spires and the familiar government buildings were strange glass towers. He only saw them for a second before they took themselves apart again and became ruins. The watchmaker made a disapproving sound at the cold. Now that they were walking side by side, he was taller than he had seemed last night, but still small.

'Mr Mori, are you half English?' Thaniel asked as they turned from Filigree Street on to Knightsbridge. The mist furled in the wakes of the cabs and rang with disembodied whistles as cyclists rounded corners. There was a halo of bright light coming from the other direction. When he looked at it hard, he saw that it had 'Harrods' written down the middle. An electric sign. Pimlico it was not. He felt perversely glad to have been forced to stay out for the night. He had been running on tracks between home and the office for months, unvaried. If he had parachuted into his thoughts now not knowing the context, he would have assumed he was seeing a day when he was just coming out of a long, long fever. He could think again.

'No?'

'Your hair is light.'

'It's dyed. I like being a foreigner, but not one who's identifiable at a hundred yards. No one in England has black hair.'

'They do,' Thaniel protested.

'That's brown,' he said firmly.

Thaniel smiled. 'What's Japan like?'

The watchmaker gave it some thought. 'Very similar to England,' he said at last. 'People have their factories and their politics and their preoccupation with tea. But you'll see.'

Thaniel was about to ask how when they passed under a gaunt red gate and came out in the middle of Tokyo.

Paper lamps lit the way through the fog. They hung from wooden frames above little shops where sliding doors were already open for business. Kneeling on the floor beside coal braziers, artisans worked on the porches. One nodded to them, then turned his attention back to a spidery wooden framework of indefinite purpose. Thaniel slowed down to watch him. His hands were so swarthy that it was hard to see if he was dirty or tanned, and he held his tools in an awkward way, but he worked unfalteringly and the wooden framework soon resolved itself into the skeleton of a parasol.

'Three shillings,' the man said, having seen him watching. His English was slurred but decipherable. Thaniel shook his head, wishing he did have three shillings. Annabel would have loved a real oriental parasol, although she would have been hard pressed to use one in Edinburgh.

Beyond the parasol shop was a potter finishing the enamel on a tall vase. He had laid out his colours in rough bowls, but the painting was glossy and perfect. A tailor nearby spoke in broken English to a white woman dressed in the plain style of a governess. There were no other occidentals there. Thaniel jumped when he heard a bump, and the ringing in his ears came back, but it was only a woman sliding open the door of a tearoom. She saw him looking and bowed. As she turned away, the hem of her green dress brushed the ground. She had stuck a closed fan in the back of her belt.

'But this is—' he began.

'All imported from Japan,' the watchmaker explained. 'It's part of an exhibition. It opened last week. They serve an English breakfast in the tearoom there.'

'Does it really look like Japan?' Thaniel asked as they went by a shrine housing a painted figure that might have been a god, or something that ate gods. A little boy put a coin in its bowl and rang the bell inside.

The watchmaker nodded. 'Near enough. The weather is better in Japan, and it would be difficult to find English food. But I think they do draw the line here at brown tea.'

Thaniel could smell the bitterness of green tea now. 'What's wrong with brown?'

'Don't be stupid.'

He snorted and let the watchmaker lead the way.

A group of men sat beneath the tearoom's bamboo portico. They were passing round some sort of magazine, which was making them smirk. Some of them glanced up, and when they saw Thaniel, they stared at him. He slowed. They looked rough. All of them wore their sleeves tucked up despite the morning cold, showing brown, muscular arms and powerful hands. Cross-legged and angled forward, they seemed to take up far more space than they really occupied.

'Morning,' the watchmaker said to the men. It was the same tone that he would have directed at somebody dressed up as Shakespeare. The ones blocking the way in moved aside more readily than Thaniel had thought they would.

The step up into the teahouse was steep. It had sliding doors like the other shops, and the paper had been inked with a picture of two cranes wading through a river, waxed waterproof. China cups clinked inside. The woman in the pale green dress glided up to them and bowed a little, her hands flat to her thighs and her fingers pressed together. Past her shoulder, he could see that the teashop had its own piano, a rickety thing with silver candleholders built into the music stand. The case was up.

'Good morning, Mori-sama. Would you like the table by the window?'

'Please,' said the watchmaker.

She smiled and led them across to the table. The windows were more like the sliding doors than the usual sort, but their panels were glass rather than paper. Just beyond the small steps down to the grass outside, there was a flooded patch, and six small herons lined up in a shabby row. Living so close to the river Thaniel was used to the gloomy fishing birds and the black coots, but the watchmaker shifted to see a seventh land, less close. The girl did too, and the strength of their interest made Thaniel look again. For a fraction of a second, he saw how strange seven herons were. The two of them were stranger. With her black hair and her spring-coloured clothes, it should have been difficult to see that the girl was from the same country as the watchmaker, but in the bright light, their eyes were the same, and their fragile bones made them look like children.

'Mrs Nakamura is cooking breakfast,' the girl continued, seeing that he was watching her and mistaking it for impatience, 'but she is not very good. Would you still like to try?'

'Please,' he said.

'And tea? She is better at tea.'

He nodded and watched her go, and noticed that the watchmaker didn't. 'Is there a Mrs Mori in Japan?' he asked.

'No,' the watchmaker said. 'Women think that making clockwork leads to an attic full of model trains.'

'It mainly does,' Thaniel pointed out.

'Actually mine is full of clockwork pears. Although I suppose that sticks to the broad principle,' he admitted.

'Pears, why?'

His shoulders went back. 'My old tutor was a botanist, so I started making them for one of his birthdays a while ago and then couldn't stop. It's like those origami swans.'

Thaniel narrowed his eyes at the salt cellar, worried that origami was word he ought to know. 'What swans?' he said eventually.

'You haven't...?' He made one out of the paper napkin and scooted it gently across the table to Thaniel, who had to take it apart to see how he had done it. The tea arrived while he was trying one of his own. It came out more like a duck. The watchmaker laughed when he slid open the window a fraction and sailed them both along the puddle, toward the wary herons.

'Oh,' the watchmaker said, and leaned forward and caught the balled-up newspaper that would have hit Thaniel's shoulder. He did it slowly, as if he were taking a money-spider from the air, and Thaniel didn't understand where it had come from until he saw the boy in the doorway.

He was staring straight at them. He wore the same clothes as the men on the porch – traditional robes in bleak colours, the sleeves pushed up – but he was different. While the men had made a show of being surly, the boy's eyes were flat and expressionless. A prickle crawled down the back of Thaniel's neck. The eyes of pike had that dead shine when they were hung outside the fishmonger's. The boy was shredding the edge of another newspaper page between his fingertips, slow, perfectly spaced tears of uniform length.

'Missed,' the watchmaker said to him.

The boy snapped something back in Japanese. Thaniel didn't understand, but it came with a sharp nod in his own direction.

'This is England. You'll find there are a lot of foreigners here. I think your father was looking for you, Yuki-kun, you'd better find him.'

'Yuki-san.'

'You're only fifteen. It's no use growing up too fast; you can't get away with half as much,' the watchmaker told him. He had the schoolmaster trick of sounding benign over a warning. It made Thaniel look at him again, because he had assumed he was young, and now he didn't think so.

The boy threw the rest of his shredded newspaper at them, but the shot fell short and bounced off the keyboard lid of the old piano, which was on a fragile hinge and bumped shut, just hard enough to disturb the strings and bring out a red hum. In tune, despite the draught. Then the sliding door slammed and bounced off the wall, and slid back open again, but then the boy had disappeared. A silence settled over the other customers that lasted for an uncomfortably long time. They were all white, Thaniel noticed; the village was not like the Chinese districts of Limehouse. People had come to it like they would to a fair and the silence was not the awkward kind but more irritable, as though actors had abandoned their lines for a row midway through a play. At last, a woman two tables along wished loudly that the locals would keep their feuds out of the public eye.

'As opposed to ours, which are always quiet and never involve exploding buildings,' Thaniel murmured, but loudly enough for her to hear. He was pleased when the watchmaker looked down at his tea with the porcelain lines around his eyes again. 'Why was he upset, the boy?' he asked, more quietly.

'He was aiming at me,' the watchmaker explained. As he spoke, he went to the piano to retrieve the ball of newspaper. He put the keyboard cover up again. 'The men dressed up outside are nationalists; they want Japanese people to be Japanese, and he's taken it more to heart than the rest. I'm sorry.'

'I was blown up yesterday, I can cope with newspaper.'

Some of the ivory had chipped off the middle keys, but it was still polished enough to reflect Mori's watch chain. He must have seen something else while he was there, because he tilted up the lid to see inside. There was a small squeak as he twisted one of the wing-bolts that held taut the strings. The hum turned to a weird, acid sharp. Thaniel folded his hands around his tea, not sure what the purpose of that had been, but he had a feeling that if he were to ask anything about a piano, his entire musical history would come spilling out. The watchmaker came back to his seat.

'Are you all right?' he said. 'Your colour's gone.'

'I was thinking about what it would have been like to do something else for a living,' Thaniel said. He pushed his fingertips hard against the hot cup.

'Why don't you?'

'No money.'

'I'm sorry. That seems to be quite common.'

'Seems?' said Thaniel, looking back at him again.

The watchmaker moved his head awkwardly. 'My cousin was Lord Mori. I grew up in a castle. Then I was an aide for a government minister, so ... yes.' A little pause. 'I'll be buying the tea.'

Thaniel put his cup down. 'Why in God's name do you need to share the rent of the house, then?'

'I don't. I'm lonely.' As soon as he said it, he pursed his lips at his tea.

Thaniel almost said that he was lonely too. He swallowed it. 'What happened to your government minister?'

The watchmaker blinked once, slowly, as if two people had spoken to him at once and he was having trouble hearing which was which, though the conversations around them were still all at a low mutter in the strange boy's wake. 'Nothing, he's negotiating in China now. I prefer clockwork to the civil service though.' He hesitated. 'What is it that you do now? Did you say?'

'I'm a telegraphist at the Home Office.'

'Well, I'll bet you a guinea that you will have a better position soon.'

'What makes you think that?'

'How old are you, twenty-five? People don't usually stick where they are at twenty-five for the rest of their lives.'

Thaniel shrugged. 'All right. I could do with a guinea.'

SIX

HAGI, APRIL 1871

ALTHOUGH IT WAS not so much further south than Tokyo, measuring by latitude, Hagi was distinctly warmer than the capital; it bred plants not found in the north, and as the carriage rounded the final bend of the mountain road, Ito saw the yellow flowers nodding in the castle gardens, where workmen laboured on a portion of the wall. Then the garden was lost behind the old masonry and the driver went along the street for a few hundred yards, respectfully overshooting the castle gate. Ito had told him to stop outside, but he was unsurprised to be disobeyed. They stopped instead at the side of the wide road, just before a market. None of it had changed since he had left as a boy.

Stiff, he stepped out into air that smelled of pollen and summer, and felt grateful for the chance to walk and stretch. Five hundred miles in four days nettled him far more than the piousness of the driver. The employees of the British Legation always arrived at their posts with the same question: where are the damn trains? He assured them that the government was doing its best, but the fact was that they would have to wait until next year even for a line between Tokyo and Yokohama, a distance representing a short afternoon walk. Connecting lines all the way to the far south belonged to an altogether more distant future. He pushed his arms out in front of him, wishing that he could hurry the future along, if only in the interest of not developing arthritis at thirty-one.

He caught sight of his hands. They were wan and tired. So were his three aides. The countryside sun had a frank habit of showing all the lines and wrinkles that the mist in Tokyo politely obscured.

'Mr Ito?'

A man was standing five feet from them. Unlike Ito and the aides, he was nearly luminous. His skin was gold, his hair glossy in its long tail, and his clothes, strictly traditional except for the pocket watch clipped to his belt, looked cool and comfortable in the heat.

'I've been sent from the castle to fetch you,' he explained. 'My name is Keita Mori.'

Ito bowed for the Mori name. The man bowed back, unnecessarily. Ito's father had been a bookseller; the Mori were knights. Well-informed knights.

'I didn't send any word ahead,' Ito said, puzzled. 'We were going to stay at the inn on Kamigoken Street.'

'You can't stay at an inn when we have eighty rooms sitting idle,' the man smiled.

'That's very kind, sir,' Ito said, wondering which of his staff was the spy. Almost any of them. It was not only carriage drivers who retained their respect for the great houses.

'Not at all. It's this way.'

Ito fell into step beside him. Behind them, one of his aides murmured in English,

'Someone has warned them. Lord Takahiro would never usually be so generous to civil service people.'

Mori looked back. 'He took the precaution of assuming that if the Minister of the Interior arrives on short notice, the purpose is probably both important and urgent.' He spoke English with a British accent.

They all stared at him.

'I am sorry, sir,' the aide mumbled in Japanese. 'I meant no offence.'

'I'm not offended,' Mori assured him.

Ito considered him more closely. He had thought Mori was much younger, but in fact they were more or less of an age. Ito would be thirty in October and had spent some time lately feeling distressed about the grey in his hair. There was none in Mori's.

'So … is English now required at the castle?' he asked. 'When I lived here, it was unheard of.'

'It's still banned. But I like it.'

The road to the castle gate was crowded, and Ito worried about crushing his already dusty suit, but the carters and sweepers and market women melted apart before them. An apple seller didn't see them until they were only a few feet away and, mortified, dropped straight down on to his knees and pressed his forehead to the dusty cobblestones. The genuflection was aimed at Mori, not Ito's party.

'Up you get,' Mori said gently, and the man apologised again before hurrying away, shoulders hunched in an effort to make himself smaller.

Hagi castle was on the far side of a short bridge. Ito had grown up seeing it, but his memory had hazed around the edges. Under the blue sky, the castle was stark white and black. It rose from the river on foundations twenty feet high, and above them, the walls towered over the city. Built over decades, it was really a conglomeration of lesser castles spliced together. Mori led the way in through the black gates. Ito slowed. He had never been inside before – commoners unrelated to or unemployed by the Mori clan were forbidden entry.

A huge cherry tree snowed petals in a wind that brushed them eddying over the flagstones. They were well past their best now, brown at the edges. Fresh, apple-cheeked servant girls not in the least past their best went by with their hands clasped before them, eyes down even when a group of young men clattered by with bows and quivers. If Keita Mori had told him now that there was some ingenious lens built into the gateway that allowed a visitor to see into the past, Ito would have believed him. There was no aspect of the people or the buildings that would have been out of place a hundred years before.

'Lord Takahiro is engaged for now,' Mori said. He had gone on ahead to wait by the door of the main hall. 'But if you would like to come in, I can show you where to wait.'

'Thank you,' said Ito. He doubted that Lord Takahiro was busy. Feigning occupation was a standard tactic among noblemen faced with civil servants. He had spent half his life waiting in foyers and outer halls, but patience was always the key. Time waiting was time to plan.

Mori led them inside. As soon as Ito followed, the wooden floor squeaked slowly. He winced. He hated nightingale floors. The name made them sound as though they ought to chirp and sing, but in fact the noise was horrible. Mori's own steps were silent, and Ito followed them as exactly as he could, though in vain. Above them were two tiers of galleries where long silk banners rippled in the draught. The rest of the hall was empty and echoing.

Through a set of sliding doors lay a long corridor. It was lined with suits of armour. Ito counted ten sets before the next doors. Bullet holes riddled the tenth.

'Is this from the war?' he asked.

Mori didn't look. 'Yes, most of our knights fought for the Emperor. Their armour was retrieved afterwards.'

There was tea ready in the room within, and the window had a splendid view down over the gardens. The old wall looked very tumbledown indeed from here. The repairs they had seen on the way into the city were overdue. Mori waited with them and served the tea himself.

'I'm sure one of the maids can do that,' Ito said, unsettled.

Mori lifted his head fractionally at the tea. 'Most of the maids are more important than I am.'

Ito watched him. As he spun hot water around each of the cups to keep the porcelain from cracking, the motion of his hands was fluid. Ito hadn't been to a real tea ceremony for a while – they always took such a tremendous amount of time – but he remembered it well enough to know that Mori folded the red cloth in the correct way before using it to lift the iron handle of the kettle. When his sleeve fell back, it exposed four finger-shaped bruises around his wrist. Ito pretended not to notice and asked him about castle life instead. As was usual for his class, Mori replied briefly and pleasantly. While he spoke, he twisted the red cloth between his hands. Ito had a fair idea of what he really wanted to say.

Mutsuhito had summoned Ito to his study early in the morning, last Tuesday. He was a new emperor, only nineteen, and four years ago there had been a war to put him on the throne – the same war that had so thinned the ranks of the Mori knights. Nervous that the titans of the court remained unconvinced that he was worth all the trouble, Mutsuhito was in the habit of rising before dawn and of reading everything any minister gave to him. He frowned in photographs; in person, he had an open face, and young, so young that it was possible to see what he would have looked like as a small boy. Ito wanted to tell him to leave governing to the government and enjoy his youth while it lasted, but such personal advice was not the prerogative of a civil service minister, or anyone.

'Minister,' the Emperor said. He was standing by a window with his hands behind his back, a posture he had adopted in order to seem older than he was. He was dressed in an exquisite morning suit. 'Lord Takahiro Mori has still not attended court. We invited him particularly.'

Ito nodded once. 'I have noticed his absence, your majesty.'

Mutsuhito turned to him, though only from the waist. 'Takahiro behaves like a king and always has. I will not be Emperor of all Japan except Hagi city. He has his own army and a fortress the size of Mount Fuji, and now he is being deliberately rude. If he does not bow, the other noblemen will think ...' he trailed off. 'Go to Hagi today and do something about it.'

Ito lifted his eyes. He was the Minister of the Interior, but Mutsuhito was not a constitutional monarch; it was impossible to divide government into interior and exterior, one department or another, when the young Emperor sat at the centre of all of them, tinkering. 'Something, your majesty?'

'Anything,' Mutsuhito said. He looked very alone. 'He agreed to be a prefectural governor just like the others. He agreed that policy would come from Tokyo now, not from him. Does he not understand what that means?'

'I think he understands, your majesty, but I think he is choosing to ignore it.'

Mutsuhito's frustration leaked past his careful manners. 'Well, I don't understand. You wouldn't catch England or America allowing feudal lords to run everything, it's medieval!'

'They no longer do here, your majesty.'

'Takahiro does not appear to have noticed.' He looked away and swallowed. 'What can you do? Can you take his castle? Will you need soldiers?'

'No,' Ito said gently, 'we will not be needing soldiers. Accountants will do nicely.'

Mutsuhito frowned. 'How does one storm a castle with accountants?'

'One buys it, sir.'

'But ... Lord Takahiro does not want to sell his castle.'

'He will,' Ito promised.

Ito straightened when he heard a banging of footsteps in the corridor. The sliding doors opened and Lord Takahiro Mori strode through. Everyone around the table stood up, except Keita Mori and the girl who had brought in the tea; they bowed so quickly that Ito thought they had collapsed. The nape of his neck prickled. Most people at court responded with less alacrity to the Emperor.

'So you're Ito.' Lord Takahiro studied him frankly. He had a weathered face. Behind him, four retainers stood against the wall, arms folded. They were all southern men, dark-skinned. 'Sit down. Familiar name. What's your father do, is he on my staff?'

'No, sir, he was a lower-class samurai from the town,' said Ito as they all knelt down again.

'Samurai, really. Didn't see him take up arms in the Satsuma rebellion.'

Ito, who had just returned from a long stint in America, thought of escaping oranges. 'No, indeed, sir, he sold books.'

Takahiro snorted. 'They're sending me peasants now. What d'you want?'

Ito folded his hands around his teacup. He had never been cruel, or he hoped that he had not, but he couldn't help noticing that Takahiro was setting himself up beautifully.

'The government would like to buy this castle.'

Silence fell like a brick. The only sounds left were the calls of the workmen outside as they moved along the outer wall, and the tick of Keita Mori's pocket watch.

Suddenly Takahiro laughed. 'With what? It would be cheaper to buy Korea.'

'Government bonds,' Ito said.

'To be honoured when, in a hundred years?'

'Quite possibly.'

On the periphery of his vision, Ito saw Mori shrink. Takahiro set his teacup down with something between a clink and a bang. 'I'd like to see you try,' he said flatly.

'I don't think you would like it at all,' Ito said quietly. 'The Emperor is anxious about your loyalty. If you decline, tomorrow will see an army of accountants and lawyers from the ministry descend on every record here. I suspect they will discover a great many interesting things.'

'You have no right—'

'The government has every right to investigate the financial state of one of its own prefectural offices.' Ito lifted his hand a little to encompass the castle.

Takahiro's eyes flared. Ito doubted he had been interrupted before in his life. 'I am still a prefectural governor, and I submitted without a murmur to the indignity of allowing the civil service to saddle me with a deputy—'

'Yes, he was a lucky man. I believe you gave him ten thousand yen and a fine residence in Kyushu, where he now keeps bees. It must be a long commute.'

'How dare you speak to me in this way!'

'I'm here to negotiate terms, of course.'

Takahiro stared at him but said nothing for a while. When he did speak, his tone was hard. 'I don't see what there is to negotiate. I have done nothing but live in my family's holdings, all within your new laws. My authority to rule my own land is subject to Tokyo's every whim. My retainers, loyal to my family for generations, are now civil servants, paid by the government. Our records are sound. Bring your accountants.'

Ito nodded once, though he was disappointed. The clerks would come and Takahiro would cause a riot, and by next week, all the other governors would have burned their ledgers. Hagi would be a one-off trick.

Keita Mori squeezed Ito's wrist under the table. 'You need only give him something he already has,' he said in English, lifting the teapot as if he were asking whether Ito would like some more.

'Pardon me?'

'The retainers,' he said. 'They're paid through the prefectural office as Tokyo requires, yes, but Lord Takahiro is the governor. This *is* the prefectural office. He's paying them far more than the government salary. None of them are really government men. They're his own private army. Look at them.'

Ito looked. The four men behind Takahiro stared at him unblinkingly.

'You lose nothing if you offer him control of his own men again. He can't admit he already has it.'

Everyone looked at him.

'Yes, please, more tea,' Ito said quickly in Japanese.

Takahiro wasn't fooled. 'My cousin should be careful of tying his shoelaces in a melon field,' he said, almost mildly. 'Anyone might think he was stealing.'

'I was asking whether Westerners put milk in brown tea,' Mori said.

'I doubt it. You won't talk again until I speak to you.'

Mori bowed his head.

'Lord Takahiro, nobody wishes to see you make an ignominious exit,' Ito said. 'If you agree to the sale now, the Emperor would be very happy to allow you financial control of your own retainers, should you accept.'

Takahiro remained expressionless. 'Why?'

'He knows what he is asking you to give up. He hoped for a gesture of good will; he does not want to force you out.'

'Or perhaps Keita here suggested it to you.'

Ito felt another flicker of unease. The singing tick of Mori's pocket watch was the room's only sound once again. He was holding it between both hands to muffle it, but he was a poor insulator.

'Is it necessary to have something with you that always makes a noise?' Takahiro asked him.

'It might be mine, in fact,' Ito said, touching his own watch chain. It was a shabby excuse for an intervention, but he couldn't think of anything better.

'Tokyo fashions. Watches and golden spectacles and silk cravats; what are you going to try next, corsets and petticoats?'

His retainers smirked.

'And the matter at hand?' Ito asked. He had heard it all before. The conservative newspapers liked to list things that modernist politicians did; an inability to speak without peppering one's arguments with English phrases, the wearing of Western high collars, complimenting one's own wife in public, forgetting how to speak Japanese. They weren't wrong. Ito himself did all of those things except the last, and he had no intention of donning a kimono and bullying his wife. Mrs Ito would have hit him with her shoe.

Takahiro folded his arms. 'I accept, of course. Anything in the service of the Emperor.'

Ito bowed a little from where he sat. 'You have the Emperor's gratitude, sir.'

'Yes.' Takahiro stood up and went to the window. The workmen on the wall stopped talking and put their heads down. Without any warning, he caught his cousin's collar and slapped him so hard that Ito heard his teeth knock together.

'If you ever interfere in clan business again, I'll cut your hands off like the commoner you are. Give me that,' he added, wrenching the pocket watch from Mori's hands. 'Effeminate piece of rubbish.'

He threw it hard out of the wide window. It smashed on the crumbling wall between two startled workmen, spraying cogs and broken glass. The other builders saw it too and melted away, leaving tools and half-eaten food behind them. Some white fish rolls caught the sunlight sadly.

Ito's aides stared into their teacups; Takahiro's retainers looked satisfied.

'Out,' Takahiro said.

Mori bowed and left quickly. As he disappeared into the corridor, Ito saw him spit something into his hand.

Takahiro smiled. 'So. Better have some wine.'

After the wine, one of the omnipresent maids showed Ito and the three aides to separate rooms. Ito stepped in front of her as she was leaving. She shied, as if she expected him to grab her, so he held up his hands quickly. Where to find Keita Mori was a simple question, but he found himself dressing it up so politely he might have decently been asking the Empress. The alarm in the girl's face turned to a shade of puzzlement that implied she worried for his cognitive health before she caught her neutrality again and directed him down the corridor to the left. When he arrived, he tapped his knuckle against the door frame.

'Mr Mori?'

No answer. He slid the door open by an inch or so, and almost walked into a small boy. The boy had an old book and a guilty expression. He put the book behind his back as soon as he saw Ito.

'Hello,' Ito said.

'I didn't steal it.'

'Perhaps I ought to take it?'

The boy twisted his nose and handed the book over. Ito ruffled his hair.

'Off you go.'

The boy departed with the self-conscious walk of the knowing wrongdoer. Ito knocked again and went inside. The room turned a right-angle, and there was another sliding door through which he could hear a faint clicking, like clockwork being wound up. He put the stolen book down on the nearest table as he went through. As he did, the book fell open; it wouldn't close because so many extra things had been pasted in. On the open page was a photograph of

Mori and five other men, one of whom had him in a crushing bear hug from behind. They were all very similar to each other, and nothing like Mori himself.

Ito knocked on the second door. Inside, Mori was sitting at a Western desk with his back to the door, putting together cogs and springs with a pair of tweezers. The desk was otherwise bare, with only a calligraphy scroll and a pen lying rather ostentatiously on the corner in clearest view of the door. Mori looked back and slid the clockwork mechanism into the desk drawer with his left hand. There was a tiny click as he locked it. The key disappeared into his sleeve. There was a teacup next to him. It held a tooth with bloody roots.

'I'm sorry,' Ito said quickly. 'I didn't mean to intrude. I, er … intercepted a small boy with one of your books.'

Mori nodded. 'Akira. Lord Matsumoto's little boy. He stays here in the summer and steals anything interesting.'

Ito smiled. 'Are you all right?'

'Of course.' Mori's hand went to his belt, where the pocket watch should have been, and then he stopped and folded his hands in his lap instead. 'I don't suppose you know the time.'

Ito consulted his watch. 'Ten past eight.'

'Takahiro always goes for a walk around the gardens at eight.' He looked at the door as if he hadn't quite convinced himself that Takahiro was not about to knock it down and shout at him for his secret clockwork-making.

'Does he often beat you?' Ito asked.

'He was showing off for you.' He was quiet, and, from the way he shifted his jaw, he must have been probing the empty space left by the tooth. 'And he's much kinder when he isn't flustered.' He sounded, if not sad, then at least heavy. 'Shame he's always flustered now. We used to get on before he had a title.'

Ito glanced toward the window in the pooling silence. In fact, it was less a window than another door. It was open, and led out on to a balcony. The sky was a brilliant red and low on the horizon hung the Golden Star. Ito had never seen a view like it in Hagi. The city sparkled below; the city he had lived in, and yet, how unfamiliar it looked from here. He felt as though he had found a secret room in his own house after walking past it for years.

'I wouldn't mind some air,' Mori suggested, lifting one hand to let Ito go out first. Ito went gratefully, and tried to keep his pace slow. He had always wanted to see inside the castle, and now that he was here, he suspected that his schoolboy curiosity was showing. Mori was chivalrous enough not to mention it.

The air was still warm, and in the light wind, the pale pink cherry blossoms had blown up on to the balcony. The petals sat on the mossy wood like the bubbles of silver air on coral.

'Thank you, for your advice,' Ito said.

Mori shook his head.

'You won't be sad to see the castle taken away from your family?'

'It's falling down anyway.'

'No, really.'

Mori studied the banister. When he spoke again, it was in English. 'Honour is leaving your family behind because your own conscience is more important. This place breeds it. Everywhere like this place does.'

'I'm sorry.'

Mori shrugged.

'The armour, in the corridor ...'

'It was my brother's. I had four others too, but their armour is a bit burned, so it's not much to look at.'

'Were you too young to go with them?'

'No, I'm a bastard on the wrong side.' He lifted his arms a little to show that he wasn't allowed to carry a sword.

So his legitimate brothers had gone to the wars and left him to the tender mercies of Takahiro. Ito tried to think how long ago that must have been. Three years or four. A long time, however impervious Mori seemed to his cousin's temper.

'You know,' Ito said at last, 'I need someone like you on my staff. We're going to America again in the winter. Your English is astonishingly good. It's almost impossible to find fluent aides, but I can't do without them.'

'No need to be polite,' Mori said.

'I know.'

Below them, a grey cat bounced on to the new wall from an overhanging tree. It had seen the abandoned fish rolls. As the cat landed on the stonework, Lord Takahiro passed beneath one of the wide archways, returning from his evening walk. He paused, just in sight still, to look at the lilies that had grown through the stone.

The wall collapsed. Not slowly, or in pieces, but all at once, as though it had been dropped from a height. One moment it was there in the quiet evening; the next it was gone, and the crash was resounding and clacking around the castle, the echoes warped by the sharp angles of the roofs. Dust rose in uneven plumes down the ruined length of the brickwork. Ito stared. The cat shot away and stopped twenty feet from the wreckage, hissing. Takahiro did not emerge.

'The weight of the cat . . . ' Ito said, stunned. His fingernails felt odd, and he realised that he had closed his hand hard over the banister when the wall came down. Now they were full of moss.

Mori had folded his arms. Neither of them spoke for a while. They both leaned forward against the banister to watch while servants poured toward the fallen masonry, calling out for Takahiro.

'I had better arrange for the coroner to come,' he said.

'That was—' Ito said. He had never seen anyone killed before.

'Not a tragedy,' said Mori, who must have seen it often.

'My offer was serious, you know. About America.'

'I know.' He hesitated. 'I do want to go. But I can't swear life-time service. I'll have to leave in ten years.'

Ito laughed. 'How specific. What will happen in ten years?'

'I'm going to London. There's someone . . . well, I must go to London.'

'I see,' Ito said, mystified.

SEVEN

LONDON, 31 MAY 1884

DESPITE THE FOREBODINGS of the waitress, whose name was Osei, breakfast was good. Thaniel would have stayed much longer, but at nine o'clock Mori said that he had an appointment at St Mary Abbot's workhouse to buy some clockwork parts. Since the train station was close to the village entrance, they left together. They had almost reached the red gates when Mori handed him a little golden ball, about the size of a curled dormouse. As soon as Thaniel touched it, it whirred to life and slid between his fingers, cleverly weighted to cling on at almost any angle, and warm, like something alive. It gave a little hoot and puffed steam at him.

'What is this?' he laughed. 'And why have I got it?'

'A steam engine toy,' Mori said. 'It's an old design. The Ancient Greeks had them.'

'The Ancient Greeks? If they had steam engines, why didn't they have trains?'

Mori twitched his shoulder. 'They were philosophers; they put two and two together and got a goldfish. As to why you've got it, silly things help with nerves.' He inclined his head fractionally to the east and Whitehall. 'Or I think so.'

Thaniel began to say that he wasn't nervous, but it would have been a lie and he didn't want to lie to him. 'Thank you. But is this real gold?'

'It is. But you can send it back later. Or bring it,' he added without looking at him.

'I will. Bring it, I mean,' said Thaniel. 'I've got to give your neighbour back his shirt, anyway.'

He looked down at the steam toy, which skimmed around his hands unerringly no matter how slowly or quickly he moved. Its weight felt solid; the surface was polished to a sheen that showed convex reflections of his fingertips and the buttons on his waistcoat. Above them, the sky was clearing, and there was a patch of bright blue that the gold turned to green. A black reflection appeared. A tall gentleman had stopped just in front of them.

'I say,' the gentleman said, looking at the toy, 'wherever did you get that?'

'He made it,' Thaniel said, gesturing to Mori with his elbow.

'Made it? My dear fellow, might I have your card?'

Mori gave it to him. It was nearly as beautiful as the toy. A clockwork pattern had been cut around one side and edged with silver, but the gentleman seemed not to think that it was anything extraordinary.

'Mr Mori,' he said, without stumbling over the pronunciation, 'I think I've heard of you, actually. I shall call on you later; I've been looking for a good clockwork maker for weeks.' He gave Mori his own card. 'Will four o'clock be convenient?'

'Of course. I'll expect you then.'

Thaniel gazed after the gentleman and began walking again. 'That was lucky.'

'Hm?' said Mori. He smiled suddenly. 'Oh, yes. Very.' He inspected the gentleman's card before saying, 'What does this say?'

'Fanshaw,' said Thaniel.

'How does Featheringstonehough spell Fanshaw?'

'The upper classes accumulate unnecessary letters. There are other names like that. Risley is spelt Wriothsley. Villers is Villiers. It makes them look old and important.' He put his hands back in his pockets, his left around the steam toy. The right clipped the watch. 'Oh. I was going to – I didn't say. The watch was locked when it was left for me. It didn't open until yesterday. How did it do that?'

'There's a timer inside. For gifts, you know, anniversaries and things, so that it won't open until the day.'

'How do you set it?'

Mori held his hand out, and when Thaniel gave him the watch, he twisted the clasp anticlockwise, and the back opened. On that side were small dials that showed the months and days and then the hours. 'Here. Why?'

'I was worried I was going mad.' He paused uncomfortably. 'Are you sure I can keep this? It must be worth a fortune.'

'I'm sure. I thought it had been stolen. I won't miss it.'

When they had reached the gate, Mori lifted his hand to show that he was going right. The station was on the left.

'I'll see you tomorrow,' Thaniel said, holding up the steam toy. As they parted, he looked back. Since Mori had already faded into the mist, there was nothing to say that any of it had been real but the weight of the toy in his pocket.

Whitehall swarmed with workmen. They were clearing the ruins of the Yard; salvaged bricks stood in stacks, while the broken ones were being taken away on big carts. Even though it was the weekend, the Home Office was alive, and because the bomb had snapped half the telegraph wires, the yellow spiral steps had become a byway for a stream of clerks. Thaniel stood at the foot for a while, waiting for the whining sound to stop throwing its greenish tinge over everything, his hand closed around the steam toy. When it did not stop, he took the toy out and watched it roll about its happy way. Mori was right: it was silly enough to banish any serious thoughts or fears or the need for a pretend fainting fit.

He had barely reached the top of the stairs before the senior clerk dumped a pile of paper into his arms. He winced.

The senior clerk didn't notice. 'Take those down to the basement.'

'What? Why?'

'The basement,' the senior clerk insisted.

He sighed and did as he was told. The small weight of the papers made his arm throb, and when he reached the basement, his sleeve was blooming red. He swore quietly, wishing he could have managed to not bleed over a borrowed shirt. Because of the starch, the red stopped when it reached his cuff. He tucked the papers under his other elbow so they wouldn't stain, though he didn't know why he bothered. The basement was for storage. It was a forest of cabinets, all filled with outdated files on matters that had been resolved years ago. He reconsidered fainting.

Pushing the swing doors open with his shoulder, he was enveloped in the smell of old paper. And lamps. There was light everywhere. After the gloom of the stairwell, it let him see very sharply for a few seconds before his eyes adjusted. A policeman with gleaming buttons smiled at him and nodded to the papers.

'Those for us?'

'Er...'

The policeman angled down the top of the first file. 'Oh. Over there. Stick them in the in-tray.'

Not wholly sure what was going on, Thaniel made his way around the desks that now filled the wide aisles between the filing cabinets. They were all old desks, abandoned down here for faulty legs or chipped tops, but the policemen had propped them level again with paper and broken mousetraps. Most of them were unoccupied, but between the archives for A–P 1829 was Dolly Williamson. He was using somebody's hat as a wastepaper basket. There were scratches on his cheek that Thaniel hadn't seen through the smoke yesterday, raw-looking still.

'Thaniel,' he said, with a careful neutrality. 'Where have you been? I sent a man to see you yesterday but—you're bleeding,' he added, to Thaniel's arm.

Thaniel dropped the papers into his in-tray. In fact it wasn't a tray, but a space of desk labelled 'in-tray' in chalk. 'It's nothing. What's all this?'

'Temporary lodgings. The Yard is completely gone. That other explosion was the Carlton Club, so I shouldn't wonder if they— open a smoking room down here somewhere too.' He paused. 'So. Where were you?'

'I'm not Clan na Gael, or I wouldn't have told you about—'

'I know. I had some checks run this morning.' He propped up a piece of paper and held it long-sightedly away from himself. 'You're from Lincolnshire. So is your family. Mother died in

79

childbirth; father was a gamekeeper at a manor until his death in seventy-five. You haven't got any friends. No wife. You write to a widowed sister in Scotland, who receives half your salary by postal order, monthly, but who rarely writes back. Have I missed anything? Any Irish relatives?'

'Not that I know. I don't know much about my mother's family though. Shall I tell you about the watch or are there papers you need?'

Williamson shook his head. 'No, go on.'

He held it out. Williamson took it from him and turned it over twice before opening it. 'I told you before how I found it. I went to see the maker yesterday night. His name is Keita Mori, he's Japanese. He says the watch went missing from his workshop six months ago. He doesn't know who took it, but look at this.' He opened the front and the back, and showed him the dials, and explained the alarm. 'I don't think that somebody stole any random watch. This is perfect for warning someone about a bomb, but you wouldn't know how it works to just look at it. I had months with it and didn't. I think Mori has either met the man or one of his customers has. Someone would have had to explain how to use it.'

Williamson rubbed his beard and was quiet for a while. He looked much less happy than he ought to have.

'I'm in trouble, aren't I?' Thaniel said quietly.

Williamson glanced up at him, then waved his hand once. 'No. You put the wind up us, that's all, disappearing like that. Your flat was almost empty. Looked like you'd bolted.'

'I cleared everything out, in case my sister had to ...'

'Christ. Yes.' He sighed. 'Do you know anything about clock-work?' He was speaking more quietly than before, and lower. The change of shade was the same as when the shadow of a cloud crossed a field. Things dulled and sharpened.

'No.'

'I do. I've brushed up, since February. The main thing is— it seems to be bloody difficult to keep accurate time. It's why people never made bombs out of the stuff before, it's too unreliable—'

'The springs—'

'Shift depending on the temperature, yes. The point is— there isn't much that can keep time down to the second. There are naval prizes for that kind of thing. This watch was superlatively accurate. But if that's what it was for, a warning, then it was also relying on the bomb being just as accurate. I ... would find it hard it believe, if they were not made by the same person.'

Thaniel fell still. 'Dolly ...'

'I'd like to send this for analysis. We have a man who has been consulting in the bomb cases since Victoria station. We must compare the clockwork. And in the meantime – we should keep an eye on this Mori. You've met him already. How good are you at making friends?'

He thought about the Japanese marks on Mori's brown boots. And last night, when there had been two cups of tea. Mori had been expecting someone. He had been surprised, but no doubt that was because through some administrative error or other, the wrong person had arrived. Any idiot would have seen it, or any idiot not so very busy feeling sorry for himself that the promise of tea and a few kind words brought on selective blindness.

'Thaniel?'

'The beggar outside my flat said he thought he saw a boy with some kind of foreign writing on the heels of his boots. Mori's about ...' He touched his knuckle against his collarbone. He let his hand drop and it bumped his pocket, where the steam toy still sat. 'I'm seeing him again tomorrow.'

'Good. I know I'm landing you in it,' Williamson said, as though he expected to argue for a while. But there was a subtle edge in his voice, and Thaniel realised that if he were to argue, he would be quietly reminded that he had been under suspicion five minutes ago.

'No.' His voice sounded wrong. He tried again. 'No, it's sensible. What should I look for?'

'For now, just let me know if he suddenly disappears. May I have that watch back?'

'No,' Thaniel said. He had to grip the edge of his chair to keep his resolve when Williamson's grey eyes narrowed. 'If he is involved and I go without it tomorrow, he'll know something's the matter, he's sharp. Who's your consultant?'

'I'd rather not—'

'Please; I'll do this, I'm happy to, but don't make me do it hobbled. He will notice if I don't have the watch.' He swallowed. 'And I know I'm not in uniform, but I'm certain I've signed more secrecy oaths than you have.'

'Right.' Williamson sighed down at his desk and it was plain he was still unhappy. Thaniel waited. 'I haven't got a card, I don't leave things lying around. Can you remember a name and an address?'

'Yes.'

'Frederick Spindle. Throckmorton Street, near Belgravia.'

Thaniel rubbed the back of his neck, which ached again. He felt frayed, whether from relief or worry he couldn't tell. 'No Chinamen from Limehouse for you, then.'

'Wealthy men are hard to bribe,' Williamson said drily. 'And he's the best.'

'If he's the best, then I want to know why my ironing isn't being done by a mechanical man singing *Die Fledermaus*, because Mori has got a clockwork octopus.'

'You're angry,' Williamson said, sounding too surprised to snap back at him. 'I know this is difficult, but if he knows you already then—'

'Sorry. God, I didn't mean to snap.'

'Everyone's nerves are shot to bits. It's all right.'

Thaniel gave up. 'He was kind, Dolly. He sat me down at his kitchen table and made tea for me. With scones, for Christ's sake. I don't remember the last time—' He stopped himself and looked down at the desk, with its chalk-marked inbox. 'I'm going to order you some proper stationery, you look like you're playing hopscotch.'

'Look, it could have happened to anyone. Especially anyone in your position—'

'And a bin. You can't use that bloody hat.'

'Thank you,' he sighed.

Thaniel nodded once and went back upstairs to fill out the order forms. He was forging a signature when the senior clerk stopped by him.

'Good God, Steepleton, go *home*. Before you bleed all over the telegraphs.'

'Thank you, sir.'

'Is that my signature?'

'Yes.'

He considered. 'Good. Carry on.'

EIGHT

THE STEAM TOY woke him. It rolled out of his pocket and over the blanket, where it pushed itself about in zigzags.

He had gone home thinking he was more or less well, and had continued to do so until he collapsed into bed. He had no time to undress or to check the cut on his arm before his mind switched itself off. He did not dream. When he opened his eyes, he couldn't tell how much time had passed, though he could see that it had. The room was bright and warm, and the sun had burned away the mist.

He felt around for the watch, his sleeve stiff with dried blood. Apart from its ticking, the only sound was the cotton quilt cover creaking against his fingernails. It was past one. He pressed his face against the pillow. He could feel the watch chain digging into his hip, but couldn't summon the will to move. When he did sit up, the room didn't look the same as it had before yesterday. It was tiny and bare, and clean, as though nobody had lived there at all. In the overhead of his thoughts, he hadn't much expected to return. He sat looking at the dust in the sunbeam. It was exactly the same now as it had been four years ago when he had first taken the tenancy. Everything since then had been nothing but laps.

When he stood up at last, the sleeve of his borrowed shirt was brown and stiff. He had to ease it off little by little because it had stuck to the cut and the fine hairs on his arm. Once he had cleaned the blood from his skin, he boiled the kettle and put the shirt in the sink to soak, but it did no good. He would have to apologise to Mori's neighbour. The idea of going back brought on a fresh wash of lethargy. What Williamson wanted was straightforward, but doing it wouldn't be. He was by far the worst man for a job that involved spying objectively on somebody built of paternal kindnesses.

He pushed a handful of cold water through his hair. It woke him up. He cut part of the hem from the ruined shirt and used it as a bandage in the absence of anything else, put on a new shirt of his own and then found his map of London. Throckmorton Street was, as Williamson had said, just off Belgravia. His eyes strayed to Knightsbridge, where the inward curl of Filigree Street was so small that it wasn't named. He folded the map with a snap.

Spindle's watchmaking shop was in fact not far from Mori's, nor from three or four other watchmakers in neighbouring streets. When Thaniel opened the door, which clanged a loud bell, Spindle himself was dissecting a tangle of clockwork with two pairs of tweezers. Flat on the desk lay a green velvet cloth marked into numbered squares, and in each square lay a tiny clockwork part. Spindle looked up from his work. Behind the several lenses of his glasses, his left eye, pale green, was more magnified than his right. He took them off and pulled a cloth over whatever the subject of the dissection was, hiding all but the outline of it.

'You took me by surprise,' Spindle said, smiling. 'I was rather absorbed in this. Government work, you know. These are the remains of the Scotland Yard bomb. Is something the matter?'

Thaniel had stopped five feet shy of the desk. Williamson had told him the man was consulting, so he should have known the bomb would be here, but he hadn't expected to see it. 'No,' he said, and came the rest of the way. 'Superintendent Williamson sent me, actually.'

'My report isn't ready yet—'

'No, he wanted you to look at this.'

Spindle glowed until Thaniel took out the watch, when his face changed. He took it with his delicate fingers and clicked it open. 'This was made by Keita Mori.'

Thaniel nodded. 'What can you tell me about it?'

'In what sense?'

'Anything.'

'Well, the mechanisms it uses to tell the time are in perfect working order. As usual,' he added bitterly. He prised apart something in the case and lifted out the glass face to expose the cogs below, and was silent. After a moment, he put his spectacles back on and clicked two extra lenses into place. He examined the watch for long enough for Thaniel to lose interest in him and glance around the workshop instead. The display cabinets contained only watches; there was no evidence of anything like Mori's flights of whimsy. Behind the desk was a bank of square drawers, each labelled in even handwriting. It was seventeen drawers wide and seventeen down. He studied them for any sign that some were used more than others, but all of them had worn patches on their handles. Nothing like the chaos of loose parts over Mori's desk.

Spindle made an interested noise. Thaniel willed him to hurry along. Despite its wide front window, the shop was dark, and the light that did come in only glittered on the dust motes. The dead bomb under its shroud kept catching his eye.

'This clockwork behind the main mechanism was made to work for only fourteen and a half hours,' Spindle said at last. 'Powered by self-winding springs.' He slid it under the microscope beside him. 'God knows what it was supposed to do. Typical Mori. Has he paid you to come and annoy me with this?'

Thaniel blinked. 'No.'

'No, no, forget I said that, pardon me. Do you know, I used to make clockwork for the royal family? Not since Mori arrived in London.' He smiled what he probably hoped was a self-deprecating and sportsmanlike smile, but it was more of a grimace.

'So you can't tell me what the extra clockwork is for?'

Spindle adjusted the microscope so that the lens almost touched the workings of the watch. 'I cannot tell you what it was for, but I can tell you what it did,' he said. 'It has a microscopic compass and spirit gauge, to which everything else is connected. This watch would know if you twitched. The weighting is such that one cog here turns by...' He picked it up and swung it experimentally by the chain, 'yes, turns by one tooth with every step you take. It compares that to a pre-set distance, represented by a fine-toothed and slow-turning cog in the centre here, and to that is connected an alarm bell, which was set to go off across a range of three or four seconds, or not at all, depending on where you were at – when did it go off? It would have been a big noise.'

'About half past nine at night.'

Spindle became very still. His hands stopped flicking over the settings of the microscope. 'I see. So just before the bomb.'

Thaniel said nothing. Spindle took off his glasses again and looked toward the bomb with his lips pressed together hard. He had seemed nearly happy before, taking it apart, but he was frightened now.

'Mori,' he said, as if he were having to look at the idea from different angles. Thaniel thought he would say something else, but he took a deeper breath then and shook his head slightly. 'You know you're carrying this around awfully casually for something made with about two hundred pounds' worth of diamonds.'

'Two *hundred* pounds?'

The watchmaker nodded. 'There are about ten times more jewel bearings in here than even the best chronometers need. Something like this is ... well, it would be only a method of hiding jewels, not using them.'

'Hiding them.'

'Yes.' He pulled his fingers down his long nose and touched his already-perfect cravat. Having peered into the watch again, he twitched aside the cover he had placed over the remains of the bomb, and lifted out a blackened metal coil with a pair of tweezers. 'Bimetallic mainsprings,' he murmured.

'Pardon?' said Thaniel.

'One of the problems of clockwork is lost time. A solution is to use a mainspring made of two different metals. They expand and contract at different rates in heat and cold, which evens out the time loss caused by using just one. It is a signature of Mr Mori's to use steel and gold, so that you can see the colour difference. Like you can here.'

He held up the watch. Thaniel leaned close. The mainspring gleamed silver on the outside and gold inside. Without speaking again, Spindle lifted the tweezers to present the bomb's mainspring. Although it was charred, the colour difference was still clear.

'Don't springs come from factories?'

'Raw parts, yes, but the man who mentioned bimetallism to factories would be lynched. We do that ourselves. Every watchmaker makes his clockwork differently. This is not a business of patents. If factories got hold of our secrets, we would be finished.'

Thaniel took a breath to say he understood, but Spindle went on over him.

'There is no such thing even as a standard cog; they arrive rough-cut and we all file them down ourselves. Each watch has unique cogs, each maker has his own methods, and his own inventions. This is one of Mori's, for certain. But, of course, anyone could have taken it from one of his watches knowing it was the best, and put it in here. Which is why I would not go so far as to suggest the provenance of this quite yet.' He touched the bomb and Thaniel clenched his hands. 'However, this *is* his watch, and it is full of diamonds, and whatever the purpose of these extra mechanisms, they were measuring where the bearer was at half past nine yesterday. May I ask who was carrying it?'

'I was.'

There was a pause. 'Do you know Mori, then?'

'No. That watch was left in my flat months ago. I think it must have been meant for a different Steepleton.'

'Indeed.' He looked worried.

'You know, Williamson is going to some pains to keep you a secret and you're here telling everyone you've got the Yard bomb. Are you sure you should be?'

Worry turned to indignation. 'How I do business is rather my own affair, don't you think?'

'All right,' said Thaniel.

Having been charged a punishing fee for the inspection – probably revenge for owning something of Mori's – he left the shop slowly and stopped in the sun. If he had been an organiser for Clan na Gael charged with the execution of a bombing, he knew what he would have done. He would have found a very good clockwork maker to put together the bomb, a long while before the fact so that there would be no demonstrable contact between the maker and the group in the months running up to the explosion. He would have had it planted, though, only a few minutes before it went off, or certainly after nine o'clock, because the chances of the police finding it in their own headquarters during their extensive searches was otherwise too great. He would have given the man who planted the bomb a watch made with identical clockwork and an alarm set to go off just before the explosion, so that he would know exactly when to get undercover as he left the Yard. And he would have put the bombmaker's payment in that watch, so that he would only receive it if the alarm worked and the bearer was not blown up before he could return it.

Of course it all went wrong if the watch was delivered to the wrong man. He watched a pair of white horses sail by and could not think how it had been delivered to the wrong man. It had been his name and his room. Williamson was probably checking census records now to see if there were other Steepletons in Pimlico.

There was a post office a short way from Spindle's shop, so he ducked in and wrote out a short telegram for Williamson, outlining what Spindle had said about the clockwork and the diamonds. When he took it to the desk, the woman glanced at the message, which he had written ready in code, and smiled at him.

'Telegraphist?'

He nodded and touched the call code he had pencilled in automatically in place of an address. 'I know half the wires are down in Whitehall. Is it still possible to get this to the police headquarters?'

'Everything for Whitehall is going through the Foreign Office, actually. Theirs are the only working lines. I'd think there's quite a delay by now,' she said, looking at the service box he had ticked. 'There's probably no use sending it expedited. You may as well send it as a day letter.'

'No, I'll try this all the same. The clerk at the other end might take it downstairs before lunch rather than after.'

'I shan't charge you,' she said. 'You've done all the work for me.'

'Oh, thank you.'

'Which office are you?'

She meant which post office, and a second later he saw he should have lied, but his attention was not wholly there and so the truth came by default. 'The Home Office.'

'Oh,' she said, and her expression closed into something tangled around pity and wariness. 'Well, good meeting you.'

When he left, he walked toward the train station, but slowed before he reached it. It was a watch full of diamonds. Williamson would scream if he found out he had gone home and left Mori unobserved. He crossed the road and started for Knightsbridge.

In the warm day, Filigree Street had come alive. He passed a stationery shop selling glass pens tied on ribbons to a great pair of antlers, and a bakery where a model Ferris wheel spun tiny fancy cakes slowly around and around in the window. When he found Mori's workshop door open and Katsu sunbathing on the step, the clockwork octopus did not seem out of place, and certainly nobody else seemed to think so. The people looking into the shop windows were nicely dressed, and some of the women were carrying packages tied with Harrods blue ribbons. Feeling shabby, he stepped over the octopus.

'Afternoon,' said Mori from his desk. 'Did the fainting go down well at work?'

'I didn't try, I bled all over the place instead.' He had to take another breath, although there ought to have been plenty left over after such a short sentence. 'I'd like to take the rent on that room, if it's still free.'

'Really?'

'Yes, mine's depressive.'

Mori opened his shoulders. He was only straightening out of his more usual bad posture, but it made him seem smaller, like a boy told to recite a poem. 'Why is it?'

'It ... Well, I had cleared most of it out, before yesterday.'

Mori did not ask why again. Instead, with his left hand, he took a kettle from where it had been resting on its stand and poured out the water into two waiting cups. It turned green with the powdered tea. He leaned over the desk to give one to Thaniel, who took it and was surprised to find the cup almost too hot to touch, the water having only just boiled.

'You've got a knack for this. Oh, here.' He held out the steam toy. 'It helped. Thank you.'

'I think it's that I drink too much tea,' Mori said as he took the gold ball. The heat from the kettle was making some of the moons in the floating solar system above him turn a fraction quicker on their axes. Saturn's rings had shifted upward. Now that he looked, there were too many planets; on the outer edge were two extra, spinning around each other as well as the sun. He wasn't surprised. Only reading the newspaper on the night shift was a good way to miss major astronomical discoveries.

'Can Six try?' said somebody else, and Thaniel jumped. There was a tiny girl beside Mori. She had been leaning forward and sitting still, and though she was in plain view, he hadn't seen her before. She was a mouse of a thing. Her hair was cropped short and her dress made of lumpy black stuff hardly finer than hessian. Mori gave her his own cup and she tried the tea solemnly before making a face and giving it back.

'Is she yours?' he said, confused.

'No. This is Six; she's making some fusee chain for Mr Fanshaw. The workhouse is the only place that produces it these days, but they throw it away; apparently the children make it only to stave off idleness.' He let his voice drop lower as he quoted the workhouse slogan. 'So I had to rent her for the day. Six, Mr Steepleton.'

'Six?' echoed Thaniel.

'They're numbered at the workhouse. Give them back,' he aimed at her.

The girl aimed owl eyes at him. 'Six hasn't got anything.'

'Left pocket. And I think you're old enough to speak in the first person.'

Looking annoyed, she pulled out a pair of multi-lensed glasses of the kind he had just seen Spindle use. Thaniel stared hard at them. He knew the name, but he couldn't think. His tired brain gave him wolves. No; loupes.

'Thank you.' Mori took them back. 'There are still scones in the kitchen if you like,' he added to Thaniel. 'Make yourself at home.'

'Can I have another one?' Six said.

'Yes.'

Six slid down from her high chair and bobbed through the workshop's back door. She clunked – her boots were too big for her. Thaniel followed her slowly, and carefully, because like Mori she was more fragile than the usual model of human.

She couldn't reach the table, and so he had to pass her the scone. 'It's a fine day out, isn't it?' he said, for something to say.

Mori must have made her scrub her hands, because they were brilliantly clean against the rest of her grubby and rumpled self. Under it all, she couldn't have been older than four or five, and if Mori had been allowed to take her away from the workhouse, she was an orphan. He could excuse her stealing.

'Six saw a caterpillar.'

'What kind?'

'Green, with purple and white zigzags.'

'I see,' Thaniel said slowly. Liking children did not keep him from being perplexed by them. He was recently too old to remember his own childhood with any clarity. 'I imagine that was exciting?'

She glanced up at him warily. 'No. It was just a caterpillar.'

'Do you know what caterpillars turn into?' he tried again.

'Yes. Babies know that.' She bit into her scone, quickly, as if she thought he might take it from her. 'How does it decide if it's going to be a butterfly or a moth?'

'I ... don't know.'

'They're different species,' Mori said from the workshop. 'It's the way you decided not to be a monkey before you were born.'

Six considered. 'Matron says I'm a monkey,' she countered.

'Matron will find she is anatomically incorrect.'

Nodding to herself, Six clunked back into the workshop with the remaining half of her scone. Thaniel followed, wanting to see what she was doing and why Mori wasn't doing it himself. Once she had stopped eating, she picked up a pair of pliers in one hand, and lifted something invisible in the other. The light glinted on it and he thought he saw a strand, only a fraction thicker than hair.

'Give back Mr Steepleton's watch,' he said.

'You've got a stupid girl's name,' she mumbled, but she held out the watch to Thaniel. He took it, embarrassed. He was no good at making himself at home and he could see he was drifting pointlessly. Something about the way Six was holding herself was proprietorial: she had taken the watch to offend him and make him go away. She wanted Mori to herself.

'No. That would be Keiko. I'm Keita. Your idea of gender markers is nationally subjective.'

'What does that mean?' she snapped.

'Stupid,' he said. 'Do your work.'

She snorted at him but did as she was told. 'What is this *for*?' she asked.

Mori had put on his glasses, and now he moved them down again. 'You know when you wind up a spring and let it uncoil, it moves fast at first but then slowly?' he said.

She nodded. Thaniel looked too.

'Springs regulate the movement of clocks. You can't have a clock starting too fast and becoming too slow. So, if you wind that chain around the spring, and wind the other end around a cone shape – the mainspring barrel – the clock will keep even time. Modern clocks work differently, so almost nobody makes the chain any more. Hardly anyone could make it, even if they wanted to. The links are too tiny. I managed four in an hour.'

She smiled, pleased with that. 'Six can do a hundred and fifty.'

He adjusted his glasses again. 'Keita is impressed.' He lifted his eyes at Thaniel and widened them to ask why he was still standing up and wearing his hat.

'Sorry, I was watching.'

'How are you with machinery?'

'I – fix telegraphs sometimes.'

'Sit down,' he said, and when Thaniel sat, he set in front of him a framework mechanism, a spring, and six or seven cogs. He separated them gently and showed him how to fit them on to their spindles, and how they linked, and how to file them down. Because he had to lean close, Thaniel could smell the lemon soap from his skin and his clothes. The colour of his voice and the warm air from the open door made the workshop feel far from London. When Thaniel looked up next, it was counterintuitive to see the medieval street beyond the window and the black cab pulling up outside.

'Oh, that's Fanshaw,' he said.

Six looked interested and Mori prodded her. 'No,' he said.

'I haven't done anything!'

'Go and play in the garden, if you don't want to be arrested and sent to Australia.'

'There's nothing in the garden,' she grumbled.

'Well, there's a cat, and some fairies, and a watering can. You're five, you'll make do.'

She looked up. 'Fairies?'

'Hm?'

She was gone before Fanshaw reached the door.

'Won't she be disappointed when there aren't fairies?' Thaniel said.

'There are, I made some.'

'What? Why?'

Mori nodded toward the Haverlys' house. 'Those little bastards from next door have stopped coming in here and breaking everything since there have been magic things to chase in the stream.'

'Afternoon!' Fanshaw called from outside. He paused to take off his hat and coat. 'It's turned rather hot, hasn't it? Good God.

Right, now I come without much hope, I have to say, because this seems to be a sticky job.' He folded his coat over his arm and then stopped dead just before the doorstep. 'What – is that?'

'An octopus,' said Mori, making no move to rescue him.

Thaniel ducked in front of him and picked the thing up. The clockwork was so well-jointed that it was upsettingly like the real thing. He put it down quickly on the worktop, from where it flopped into Mori's lap and wrapped itself around his arm. He stroked it absently.

'You were saying about the clock,' he said.

Fanshaw seemed to go to some effort to force his eyes upward again. He cleared his throat. 'Yes. Yes, the ... it's quite old, you see, and it has some sort of chain that apparently nobody makes nowadays. Something to do with fuses. Ah, it's quite heavy, you might need that other hand ...'

Mori took the old clock with only one and let Katsu keep the other. He tilted open the back panel. 'No,' he said. 'It's all right. I had some fusee chain made this morning, I can mend it while you wait.'

'Really? Thank God.'

'Tea?'

'Oh, is it green? Thank you very much. Wonderful,' he said, and looked over the display cases while he drank the tea. By the time he had chosen two watches for his nephews, Mori had finished too, and Fanshaw went on his brisk way promising to mention the shop to everybody at work.

'He's going to say not to come unless you want a disturbing experience with an octopus,' Thaniel said, watching Katsu slide squeakingly down the table leg. 'How did you know he wanted that chain? He didn't tell you before.'

'No, but he said he had been looking for someone for a while, and most watchmakers can mend most things. It's only antiques that are difficult, so I thought it was probably ... oh, bugger,' he said, as the octopus fell off and on to a heavy switch in the wall, near the floor. It turned on the electric lights, one of which blew, as if it had been caught unready. Mori pursed his lips at it. 'Do you mind electricity?' he said. The others, the undamaged lights, were already fading.

'No?'

'Would you change that bulb, then?' He held out a fresh bulb from the drawer beside him. It was a perfect glass bubble with a tangle of fine wire inside.

Thaniel took it and felt unqualified to be doing anything with it. 'Why can't you?'

'I'd have to stand on the desk.' He shifted. 'I'm afraid of heights.'

'And you can't even stand on a desk?'

'Shall we not dwell on it?' Mori said, at a slightly higher pitch than usual.

'Sorry. Is there anything important I ought not to stand on … ?'

'No, no, just these … ' He chivvied two of the clockwork birds off the edge of the desk. Thaniel climbed up. The dead bulb screwed loose easily, and when it came away from its fixture, he studied the insides. Its tangle of wire had snapped. The ends touched the glass with a skittering noise as he turned it around in his hands.

'Who usually changes them?'

'I pay beggars,' Mori mumbled.

He screwed in the new bulb. Nothing happened. He frowned, thinking he had made a mistake, but then Mori leaned across to wave his arm at a patch of air by the door. The lights crackled on, and Thaniel felt the heat through the glass almost at once. He climbed down feeling disproportionately pleased with himself. It was a very modern thing to do; for a moment, at least, he could see why people became so excited about motorised engines and automatic mills.

Mori was still watching him with anxious eyes.

'I can't tease you when I'm afraid of that thing,' Thaniel said, nodding to where Katsu had stretched out in a new sunbeam.

'Why are you afraid of him?'

'I don't know, I feel like it's going to run up my shirt.'

'Oh. Nothing like that. I reset him every morning so that he does a certain set of things throughout the day. He has random gears, so whether he turns left or right out of the workshop is not predetermined, but that's all. He isn't thinking, or deciding. Look, I can show you.' He caught the octopus and clicked open a panel.

Thaniel went to stand beside him, and Mori gave him a pair of his several-lensed glasses. He didn't need them to see that the clockwork inside, dense as honeycomb, sparkled with hundreds of tiny jewels. They threw colours on to the walls.

'Those are diamonds.'

'Yes,' said Mori, as if it were the most usual thing in the world. 'All good bearings are jewels. The harder the substance, the less they twist, the more accurate they are. Diamond is hardest, so I use industrial grades for inner clockwork. If you have something on show then rubies look better, but no one except me sees this, so it doesn't matter.'

'Isn't that expensive?'

'Not overly. There's about a thousand pounds' worth in here.'

'A thousand ... pounds.' It was a year's salary for a man like Fanshaw. 'Are you rich, then?'

'Yes.'

Thaniel watched the diamonds turn and wave. He had a murky feeling that he was seeing the payment for the Victoria bomb. 'Which reminds me, about rent?'

'Housekeeping. Just your own food and so forth.'

'But in Knightsbridge—'

'So, these are the random gears, here,' Mori said, pointing with the end of a brush pen to a miniature series of magnets that spun among the clockwork. 'He won't attack you, but he may well chance to live permanently in your top drawer, and over that I'm afraid I've no control whatever. At least, not without gutting him and starting again, which I'm not going to do.'

Thaniel nodded once, slowly. 'Housekeeping sounds fair enough.'

'I think so.' He clipped Katsu's back panel closed again. The octopus stole his pen and made off with it. Mori looked down at his microscope. 'I was about to do something, just now,' he said blankly.

'Take back Six?'

'Not yet.'

'A watch? More octo ... pi?' Thaniel said, knowing that it sounded wrong, though so did puses and podes. He tried to think where he had heard it last, but he did not often have business with more than one octopus at a time.

'No, I saw you and I thought ... oh, yes.' Mori caught one of the clockwork birds and opened it up. From inside came the faint but distinct smell of gunpowder. 'Would you like some more tea?'

Thaniel sat down again. 'Please.'

NINE

OXFORD, JUNE 1884

IT HAD BEEN a fine morning. Misty rain cooled off the scorched feeling in the streets and saved the crisping grass. With her window propped open, the grumbling humming of the bumble-bees came up from the broad flowerbeds with the smell of damp lavender. Grace was trying to read, but at some point in the last week, she had lost her watch, and her mind kept chafing about where it could have gone. She had looked through all her pockets, drawers, boxes, asked the porter, who hadn't seen it, and at the Bodleian, where three watches had been handed in, none hers.

She worked in her nightdress and a shawl until her eyes got tired, then, not wanting to find anybody to tie corset strings, dressed in some of Matsumoto's old things. It was good to get up and she wanted suddenly to go out and have a walk in the garden, or take the work out with her, but then the unharmonious bells rang out noon round the city. Going anywhere, even the garden, felt like too unconscionable a waste of time. She had turned her calendar over at midnight last night. The end of term was circled in red next week. She sat down in the uncomfortable chair again and propped her chin on her knee while she scanned down the essay to find her place.

She jumped when someone tapped on the door.

Bertha opened it. 'There's a lady here who says she's your mother.'

'My mother's a chronic invalid.'

Bertha nodded and mimed being wrapped in shawls. 'I thought I'd better not send her up, lest she dies of shame.' She let her eyes go around the room. It wasn't that bad, even if she had been stacking used cups into a pyramid rather than taking them back downstairs.

'Thanks. Always magnanimous. I'll come down,' Grace said. She wondered if it might be Matsumoto playing a joke.

'Put some proper clothes on, won't you?'

'Oh, are we all for corsets and bows now there's no podium? No, sorry, that wasn't very good. All my clothes are in the laundry. I didn't expect anyone today.'

'Well, perhaps you'd like to borrow something?' Bertha said, with a particular, clear politeness.

'Better not. I'll get it burnt or spill something on it.'

Bertha only looked impatient and left. Grace followed, slowly, listening for Matsumoto laughing, but in the airy sitting room at the back of the house, with its fine view over the lavender borders and the long roll of grass down to the river, was her mother. Her mother, who hadn't left London for years. Her mother who hadn't left the house for years.

'Mama, what's happened? Is it William? Or James? I thought they were both coming home on leave, what—'

'No, no, nothing like that,' her mother said quickly. She tugged her shawl closer around the shoulders, though she was in a broad sunbeam. 'Goodness, what are you wearing?'

'My clothes are in the laundry – what is it, then? Papa?'

'No.' She took a deeper breath. 'Francis Fanshaw is going to be at the Foreign Office ball on the fourteenth.'

Grace felt the lines draw themselves across her forehead. 'What?' she said helplessly.

'Francis. You were children together, don't you recall? You used to fish for tadpoles in the lake at his father's estate in Hampshire. He's a few years older than you.'

'I – yes, I recall. Is … he ill?'

Her mother looked blank. 'No? He's going to the Foreign Office ball, I told you. You know his first wife died some years ago?'

'I read about it I think,' Grace said, still floundering. She sat down opposite on the horsehair couch, which creaked and brought her into a familiar haze of violet perfume.

'Well, the old earl is very sick now,' her mother said quietly. Her eyes were watering in the bright light and with a small noise she took out her shaded lenses and put them on. The case had been made with antique blackwork. 'And your father of course has been invited to the ball too. It really couldn't be better timing, could it?' She smiled, a real, joyful smile. Because sugar and coffee both made her feel ill, she still had pristine white teeth that looked strange in her lined face. She had put earrings on to come out, Grace noticed suddenly. At some point recently, though, her earlobes had lost their elasticity and the gold studs pulled them downward. She was an old woman. She wasn't yet fifty.

She misinterpreted Grace's expression. 'Don't you see? It will be so romantic. You can meet up again after all these years and dance, and if you're lucky he will have proposed by the end of next month. It's a very good match, very straightforward.'

'Yes, I see. Mama, I'm not … this is very sudden.'

Her mother nodded sympathetically. 'These things always are. You know, I didn't want to marry your father, I had a horror of him at the time, I thought he looked ferocious in his army clothes. I should have much preferred to marry a parson, and lived somewhere pretty in the countryside. But of course I came to get used to it, and I should never have it any other way now.'

Grace chewed her tongue and didn't say anything about imagination or lack of it. 'No, no. I know. Of course. But—'

'Oh, Gracie!' her mother burst out, and there was a soft thump from behind the door. Grace didn't look that way. It seemed unkind to let Bertha know she was spying less secretly than she thought, especially having been rude once today already. 'You're far too old to live with us! You need your own house, your own husband. You'll stop fighting so with your father the moment the two of you don't share a roof, don't you see? And you'll be able to continue … whatever it is you do here, once you have your aunt's house.'

'It'd be simpler if I could have my aunt's house without having to marry somebody to carry the keys for me.'

Her mother took off the dark glasses again, her eyes full of reproach. 'That can't be helped. Of course if it were up to me you should have it in an instant, but I don't know a thing about it. It's very complicated, the law. I'm certain your father knows best, I really am.'

'Yes, I know. I'm sorry. I was only being waspish. What I meant to say was, I'd much rather support myself. I'm about to do an experiment and it might be important. If it goes well, I won't need to marry anyone. I'll have a fellowship here, and rooms.'

'Yes, but what if it doesn't?'

'Well, I … I think it will.' She swallowed and tried to think of a way to explain that wouldn't sound as though she were speaking downward. 'It's been done before, but not done well. I'm correcting bits of it now. It should be fairly simple.'

'But what if it isn't?' her mother insisted. 'Just say you'll come to the ball. Then I shall be happy. I hate to think of your having to come home and moulder.'

'If I do have to come home, I'll find some teaching work at a school,' she said, and tried to sound enthusiastic about the idea.

'And that would be better than marrying Francis Fanshaw, would it?'

Grace's carefulness cracked. 'Look, if I get married, I'll be someone's wife. Wives have duties. If I have children I'll go insane for a year and a half – don't look like that, you did, with James and with William, it was terrifying – and that will be a year and half of weeping over nothing and a brain made of soup in which I can't work. And then it will happen again with the next child, and then slowly I won't want to work at all, and I'll always be soup, and I'll just be …'

'What?' her mother said, her voice rising. 'You'll be what? Just like me? Is that so very awful? You have such scorn for me, but I got myself here, didn't I, to tell you about it all? There are plenty of women who wouldn't want to venture out fifty miles from home quite alone!'

Grace didn't argue, because like always, it felt like slapping a kitten, and now she could feel how frail its bones were under her hand. She apologised and apologised instead, and then, slowly, because her mother could not walk fast, took her into the empty dining room to order a pot of tea. While it brewed and steamed between them, Grace reflected aloud, trying to sound offhand, that perhaps it would be fun to go to the ball.

All seemed to be mended then. Since Lady Carrow had not booked herself into any hotel but was too tired to go back immediately on the train, Grace put her in the guest house opposite the college. Knowing that the new place would unsettle her, she stayed with her the rest of the day. By the time she came back to the college, the night was gathering. A grasshopper had come in through her open window to sit on the ether essay. She nudged it out again. Still bent awkwardly over the desk, she stood staring down at the pages for a long time. Her back began to hurt. The bed had been freshly made while she was out, and it had developed a magnetic pull, but she had lost too much time already. She dropped into the uncomfortable chair again and lit the lamp, and pinched herself awake to finish reading.

It was only when she stopped, after midnight, that she found her watch sitting on top of the stack of books she had already finished. She picked it up, annoyed with herself, and flicked it open to wind it up. It was already wound as much as it could be. The time was correct. Somebody had polished it, and inside the lid, cut tiny and circular to fit, was a new copy of the original guarantee from the maker. She looked over at her own closed door, perplexed, and meant to ask the porter in the morning. Because she had to take her mother to the train station, she forgot.

TEN

LONDON, JUNE 1884

THE SENIOR CLERK glided by on roller-skates. Thaniel didn't ask why. He had got up that morning to find Katsu nesting in his suitcase, which had altered his gauge of strangeness for the day. The suitcase was already missing some socks and collars. He couldn't bring himself to mind. It was like being by the sea, sitting in the clean kitchen with the workshop door open and the clicks and sighs of the clockwork coming through. After Spindle had made his report and Williamson's men came, it would all be gone.

He pushed his fingertips against his eyelids and watched the colours of the incoming code while he drew in the will to visit Williamson again. He wanted to be sure he had received the telegram, and to mention Katsu's diamond workings. He had not gone yet because he had a clear sight of his future self, who would have to go back to the shadow of the prison and the damp riverside after making a hanged ghost of a man who used his diamonds, however ill-gotten, to make clockwork. He jumped when a hand landed on his shoulder.

'By George, it is you! What are you doing hiding away here?'

It was the gentleman from yesterday, Mr Fanshaw.

'Oh – morning,' Thaniel said. 'If I'd known you worked here, I would have said something yesterday.'

'I'm not really here,' Fanshaw stage-whispered. 'I'm a Foreign Office minion, I'm scrounging people.' He gave Thaniel an intrigued look. 'I'm surprised we haven't recruited you already, with your oriental experience.'

'My what?'

'Croft! Croft, I'm stealing this one. Last one, I promise.'

'I don't know why the Home Office must fall prey to the Foreign Office's parties,' the senior clerk said waspishly.

'Any particular reason for the skates?'

'Conservation of motion.'

Fanshaw grinned. 'You'll have him back by next Friday, don't worry. This way, Mr...'

'Steepleton.' He had to hurry to keep up. Fanshaw walked quickly. Soon they were on the ground floor again, in the long, ornate gallery that connected the Home and Foreign Offices. A full-length portrait of the Queen hung on the wall above the staircase, which creaked with stately echoes. Mahogany. 'I'm sorry, sir, I don't know what's going on—'

'What's going on is that the Foreign Office is having a ball,' Fanshaw said, 'and Foreign Office balls come with a Himalayan range of administration. It's vital that various ambassadors come, but that they each speak to so-and-so or such-and-such at a particular time, and no, they can't sit with the Indians, and what, we haven't got green tea, and is Italy coming, because if so, Hungary isn't – you understand the gist.' He shot an arch look at the Queen. 'And that of course takes priority over whatever coup might be developing in China, or whether Kiyotaka Kuroda wants to invade Korea again. The diplomatic negotiations surrounding the ball inevitably leech staff away from areas considered less key. If we don't have British citizens in the country, no one cares. That of course is a stupid view, so I'm drafting people in from other departments. No one here speaks Japanese, and we need someone other than me on the desk.'

'But I don't speak—'

'Yes, but you'll know what it sounds like, which is a start, and you're in a position at home to learn quickly,' Fanshaw said, turning sharply left into what could have been a war-room. The walls were covered entirely with maps, and six or seven men worked at desks lined up as they would have been at school. Stacks of books stood everywhere, and somebody had even made a serviceable ottoman from one, on which now stood a tray of tea-making equipment. One of the men was on the telephone to what sounded like a journalist. Fanshaw motioned Thaniel to the spare desk in the corner. 'Japan there. I'll be around, of course, and when you aren't busy, you'll be doing the usual. Telegraphy, accounts, and so forth.'

'Hold on, learn quickly? You said I'd be back at the HO by Friday.'

'I lied, obviously.'

'What? I don't know what you *do* here.'

Fanshaw waved his hand. 'Sit down. Mostly you'll be talking to the chaps who own the Knightsbridge village, but there are other Japanese scattered about London, and since there aren't enough of them to open an embassy, they come straight to us if they get stuck. The ambassador – that's Arinori, he isn't here today but mind out for him or he'll have you signed up for foreign service by Tuesday – keeps office hours here three days a week. You'll help with lost papers, advice about housing, language – anything, really, that people might have difficulty with. That stack of paper there is requests filed in the last week. Work through those you can, and hand on to me those you can't. Johnson here will explain how to fill out any forms and suchlike.'

The man he had motioned to, Johnson, looked up and noticed Thaniel for the first time. He smiled the brief smile of a busy person. 'Morning.'

'Johnson, this is Mr Steepleton, I've stolen him from the HO telegraphy boys.'

'Oh, thank God,' he said, throwing down his codebook and motioning to Thaniel to come over. 'Here, send this for me. I'm talking to Shanghai, but it's taking an age, and Fanshaw's stolen our telegraphy chap for the fellows dealing with America. See you, Francis,' he added.

Fanshaw had gone. Thaniel sighed and sat down at the telegraph, automatically sideways, and drew out the transcript paper gently. This telegraph was a far superior machine to the battered ones in the Home Office; it was running faster and more smoothly, and he could hear from the precise clicking of the mechanisms that the paper was not going to screw itself up after three and a half inches. He held it from habit anyway. The message was a request for a form that confirmed Britain knew about a Mr Feversham's lost passport, and would let him through the gate at Dover.

Once he had sent a message back via the operator at the main exchange, he wound the transcript spindle tighter to keep it from rattling as it had done before. He was clicking the machine closed again when he became aware that Johnson was watching him.

'I don't suppose you could do this one for me too?' the man asked meekly. 'I'd soldier on myself, but our last chap wasn't half as quick as that and it won't take a minute at the rate you go. Can you hear the code?'

'Yes. You start to after a while.'

'Is that so? That's remarkable.'

'It's not difficult.'

'Oh, yes, and I'm sure pure mathematics isn't so difficult once one gets the hang of it,' Johnson laughed. 'Anyway, glad to have you with us. Nice break from the norm to have a working chap who knows what he's doing, rather than some duffer fresh out of Eton and killing time till Pater gets him an embassy post.'

'I'm sure,' Thaniel said, shaking his head once. He quite liked boarding-school men; there were plenty of them around Whitehall, and though they were a different species to everybody else they spent a good deal of time good-naturedly pretending not to be. He glanced up when Johnson did not dictate anything and saw that the other clerks were all exchanging significant smiles over his head, although he didn't understand exactly what the signification was. 'Ready?'

'Um – yes. Yes. So: hello Henry, stop. I have a new fellow on the telegraph now, stop—'

'You can just talk,' Thaniel said to the key.

'Really? I thought it had to be specially phrased ... you know?'

'I'll do it for you, we'll go quicker.'

'Oh. Splendid. Gosh, you know your work, don't you?'

'There are monkeys that know it. Telegraph, stop ...'

After that, Johnson was off. Not infrequently, he stopped his dictation so that he could explain what he was talking about, and the others chipped in. They seemed pleased to have somebody to show off to, and Thaniel listened and remembered everything, because he had never heard of any of it. The message to Shanghai was a reply to diplomatic dispatches, and therefore long; there were Chinese customs scams to address, and a strange cult in the east, and the problem of British botanists sneaking into forbidden regions in order to collect tea samples. After the Shanghai message, the dispatches from Tokyo ticked through, only half intelligible because the minister there spoke in a mad English-Japanese pidgin full of gozaimases and shimases that Thaniel had half-heard at the show village the day before, but whose meaning he couldn't tell. After a while, Johnson wrote out a list of them.

Despite their enthusiasm, the others seemed oddly wary of him, and he was not invited to wherever they went for lunch. He didn't mind. The quiet was a chance to catch up with himself. He sat alone at the Japan desk and learned the list of words. The more he looked at them, the more remarkable it seemed that Mori managed to speak with no accent. He was still reading when his eye caught on the filing cabinet opposite him. It was marked 'Japanese Aliens'.

He stood slowly and opened the drawer for N–R, which was dominated by Nakanos and Nakamuras. There were only two people whose name was Mori. Keita was the second. Inside the thin file were copies of immigration forms. The forms were a sort of printed certificate divided into columns, where the information was written by hand and signed by the Customs Officer of, in this case, Portsmouth. He read through the details.

Name: Baron Mori, Keita b. June 14, 1845
Country of citizenship: Japan
Country of embarkation: Japan
Occupation: Governmental aide to Mr H. Ito, Minister of the Interior
Certificate date: January 12, 1883.

There was nothing else except a letter of reference from Mr Ito that acted as proof of identity. It was sealed with something official-looking in Japanese, and the paper had the crest of the Emperor at the top. Thaniel let the file tilt down on to the top edge of the cabinet. Mori had mentioned his cousin was lord of somewhere. It should not have been a surprise to learn his name began with 'baron', but the thought had never occurred. With his heart tightening, he read the letter and certificates again and realised he had to let Williamson know, before the police tried to arrest a nobleman for having diamonds.

The telegraph clicked.

Scotland Yard c/o Foreign Office…

The Home Office machines printed code only in pencil lead, but this one produced text in a pretty, flowing script like handwriting. Soon the first message was followed by a second, and a third. The main exchange must have collected everything for the Yard and sent it on all at once, like ordinary post.

To A Williamson I had the watch examined by Spindle as you asked and—

He tore out the transcript paper and sat with the reel clamped between his hands while the rest of the message played out. The telegraph carried on printing letters straight on to the paper roller, which, being small, soon developed three or four layers of illegible palimpsest before the ink ran together and turned it black. As if the message were completely unremarkable, the next message followed it, and the next. He took them down by hand. Once they had stopped, he unclipped the roller and rolled it over a spare sheet of paper to clean off the ink. He clipped it back on. Having put the transcript reel back in too, he sat still with his hands pressed together between his knees, looking at the ink smudges on the piece of paper in front of him.

'Everything all right?' Fanshaw had arrived silently. 'Your face is rather dark.'

He straightened. 'No, it's my ordinary face.'

'The others are huddling outside over their sandwiches, you know. They seem frightened. Did you say something stern about cotton mills?'

'No? I don't know anything about cotton mills.'

Fanshaw laughed. 'I see. How are you getting on?'

'I looked up Mori in that cabinet. Apparently he's baron of somewhere.'

Fanshaw's eyes widened with interest. '*That* kind of Mori. Really.'

'Are they famous?'

'They're a huge samurai clan in Japan. Lots of money, very conservative, usually. Their current head is the Duke of Choushu, which is very like being Duke of Northumberland. O-oh ... I know. I know; there was a Mori on Minister Ito's staff. Left a while ago. I remember someone said in dispatches he'd upped sticks to make clockwork in England. Never thought I'd meet him. Bizarre.'

'Maybe government work was boring.'

Fanshaw laughed. 'Doubt it. Ito's going to be prime minister as soon as he can wangle a cabinet system, not a shadow of a doubt. Anyway, a present for you,' he added, and dropped a Japanese dictionary on Thaniel's desk. It landed with a bang that made the papers jump. 'Learn that.'

'All of it?'

'All of it.'

Thaniel angled the cover open with his fingernail and winced – he had used his left hand. The tiny exertion made the scab on his arm crack. On the tissue-thin pages, the text was minuscule. 'But don't you speak—'

'I'll be here for only a third of the time; I have a dozen other things to do.'

'What things?'

'Everything,' Fanshaw sighed. He dropped into his chair. From his desk drawer he took out a tweed pincushion, full of glass-headed pins, and a piece of fabric with a needle pushed through it. Thaniel could only see the underside of the stitching, but he thought it was half an ivy pattern. 'Though I swear I spend at least half my time directing Lord bloody Carrow to Lord Leveson's office. It isn't as though he's moved in twenty years. These people seem to think it unnecessary to memorise the layout of a building when fellows like me are around to do it for them.' He cast around aimlessly.

'I've forgotten something. I've always forgotten something. You know how one ends up with a constant nagging sense that one has walked out of one's house without some vital item of clothing and so one lays out a second pair of trousers for the express purpose of forgetting them? Tickets!' he said suddenly. 'FO employees get tickets to the ball, you can pick one up in Chivers' office round there. Wouldn't want you to miss it. Not after all the effort I've put into the damn thing. Oh, and you'll need to sign some more secrecy oaths, I shouldn't wonder. If you thought HO material was sensitive, wait until you see what comes through the wires here. The salary is proportionately enlarged, I should add.'

'I ... my God, you were serious?'

'Quite.'

'Thank you.'

Fanshaw waved it away. 'Can't waste a Japanese speaker on Home Office telegraphy.' He sighed again, falling back into his previous lethargy. He looped the needle through a new stitch and the green thread hissed quietly.

'What are you doing?' said Thaniel, who had held it in for as long as he could, which wasn't long.

'What? Oh, the embroidery. Symptom of overwork, I'm afraid. If I don't work at it a bit every now and then I go gently mad.'

'Why does embroidery help?'

'You are such a genuine fellow, aren't you. I think it's to do with doing something with one's hands that doesn't much involve one's brain. I suspect it might be a developing neurosis, I have been meaning to see someone. Runs in the family. I'm not a patch on my brother, you know. He has to go around the estate counting the railings. There are quite a lot of railings. I suppose numbers, being immutable, are comforting when one feels isn't quite in control of things. Three will always be three.'

Thaniel nodded, slowly. He had never understood proper mathematics. There was always a gaping hole in the middle of the idea – namely, that he had never been able to see what *three* was. From what he could tell, it was a thing of its own, but he had only been able to envisage it as its sign, which was like trying to conceive of a piano by looking hard enough at the letters in the word.

'I was about to make some tea,' he said eventually. 'Would that help?'

Fanshaw put his hands together and leaned back in his chair as though he had arrived in the Promised Land after forty years wandering a tealess desert. 'Rather, thank you. Oh, by the way, all telegrams for the Yard are coming here, so when they come in, do take them down to the basement, won't you?'

For the last week, cracks had been baking into the mudbanks of the Thames, but the Home Office cellar was cold. Some of its clutter, and therefore its insulation, was gone now, and when he went down, the young officer at the front desk was holding his hands around his lamp. Among the old filing cabinets and the brassy noises of the men moving about in heavy boots, Williamson looked criminal in a pair of fingerless gloves.

'I think I saw the Franklin expedition in a cupboard back there,' Thaniel said.

'We're just missing dog teams and— ice picks,' Williamson said gloomily. 'Are those our telegrams from the FO? What are you doing with them?'

'Francis Fanshaw recruited me this morning.'

'Oh, that's good.' He took the transcripts, and Thaniel's handwritten notes. He put them aside. 'So,' he said, and his voice dropped as it did when his stammer was about to disappear for a while. 'Frederick Spindle was in here this morning talking about hidden diamonds and extra mechanisms.'

Thaniel moved a chair across and sat, arms folded in the cold. He was in his shirtsleeves. 'I've come about that too. I've just looked up Mori in the oriental desk records. He's a baron in Japan. His family is rich. Fanshaw says very rich. I don't think the diamonds signify.'

'What's he doing making watches in Knightsbridge?'

He shook his head. It was not impossible to explain Mori's oddnesses, but he was wary of trying to do it now. He would rosetint them too much.

Williamson leant his elbows against the table and pushed his fingertips under his scarf. 'But it's not quite right, all the same.'

'It's not quite wrong either.'

Williamson's sharp eyes caught on him for too long and read his bones. 'Nevertheless,' he said, more slowly, 'the watch arrived at your flat on the night of the threat. It opened on the day of the bomb. The alarm went off just before. And special mechanisms that measure where the bearer is at a certain time? I don't know what that was intended for, but Spindle says it's one of the most complicated pieces of machinery he's ever seen. You don't make the most complicated piece of machinery ever seen by one of London's best watchmakers if you only want to set an alarm, do you?'

'I took the room he was letting,' Thaniel said quietly. 'To keep an eye on him. I don't say I think he's innocent. I'm saying you can't assume the diamonds are payment when the man's from money. Old money, from the way Fanshaw talked.'

Williamson sat back a little. 'Well, that's good. That's very good.' He looked sorry but did not say it. 'You know, you should be in Special Branch, not typing for Fanshaw. You're steady enough.'

He smiled. 'Out of interest, how often do Special Branch officers die when they let slip to the Irish?'

'If they do let slip? Always.'

'It's good to work with efficient people, though, isn't it, so it's all swings and roundabouts.'

Williamson coughed as he laughed. 'Tell me about Mori.'

'What kind of thing?'

'What's your impression of him, forgetting the clockwork mysteries?'

'He's kind,' said Thaniel. He looked down at the floor, which was scuffed in semicircle shapes where the desk had been pivoted. 'He's afraid of heights, he doesn't like next door's children. He has a pet octopus made of clockwork. It collects socks. They seem to know him well at the oriental show village in Hyde Park, so I don't think he is the completely solitary sort.'

'How are you getting on?'

'Well enough.'

'To the extent that you could have a good look around the house without raising suspicion?'

'I couldn't take up the floorboards,' Thaniel said slowly.

'No need to take up floorboards. I'd like you to search for correspondence. If he is involved with the Irish, he might have burned everything pertinent, but he might not have. People feel safe at home; he might have kept letters, pamphlets … they're not above blackmail, either.'

His teeth stung. 'All right.'

'If you find anything, tell me straightaway. Spindle's final report should come in soon, but I can't arrest anybody for suggestive clockwork and there's … well. Pressure from on high.'

'You look like it,' he said.

'No, no, say what you really think,' Williamson tried to huff, but then put his hand to his head. 'Do I really?'

'Dolly, it will be all right. I thought you'd already arrested most of the men involved in all this?'

'Yes. We knew who they were months beforehand, but couldn't take them until after we found the bombs. No evidence otherwise. But no bloody bombmaker. If we don't have him, it will be the devil's work trying to connect the rest of the bastards direct to the explosion, and none of them know; no man knows more than he needs to lest he's arrested. Just – be careful. If you spook this man, the case might … '

Thaniel sat back. Williamson must have seen his expression close, because he lifted a placatory hand and then pulled it over his jaw.

'Don't imagine for a moment that I don't know this is a vast administrative cock-up, resting so much on a civilian.'

'What happens if I don't find anything?'

'Then I'll have to arrest him anyway and shake a confession out of him, and quickly, before the Foreign Minister hears I've arrested an oriental nobleman.'

Thaniel's lungs stiffened hard, and then hurt because they wouldn't move. 'Dolly, it might not be him. You've got the clockwork in the bomb, but any watchmaker could have taken apart some of his watches, and you've got a suggestive watch, but any other watchmaker could have set it to do what it did.'

'And the beggar outside your house, who saw a boy with foreign marks on his shoes?'

'Half the watchmakers in London are Chinese.'

'Is that what you really think, or do you only want it not to be him?'

Thaniel stood up. 'What I want is for you not to be personally thrown out by the Foreign Minister on the not very unlikely chance that a samurai manages to hold fast against a few coppers long enough for someone to hear of it.'

Williamson stood up too. 'Sorry.' He held his hand out.

Thaniel shook it and turned away before the policeman could see his face clearly.

With a gilt invitation to the Foreign Office ball in his satchel, Thaniel let himself into the house through the front door rather than the workshop. Mori had looked busy through the window, or at least, occupied. He set Fanshaw's dictionary down on the kitchen table and put the kettle on, and read through the first few pages while he waited. It was a dictionary not of words but of single characters, some of which happened to be words, arranged by stroke number. It began with numbers, and the signs for person and sun and big. He moved the block of the pages left to see the entries toward the back. They were rambling and mazy, and ancient-looking. The meanings were all philosophical terms.

'There's tea in here,' Mori called when he heard the steam.

Thaniel shut his eyes. 'I thought you might not want disturbing.'

'Disturb away.'

He tilted the door between them open. It had never been quite shut, resting on its stiff iron latch. It was heavy oak, pointed at the top, but the weight was familiar; he had spent years putting his shoulder to a similar door in the duke's chapel organ loft. This one didn't creak. On the other side, Mori had his back to him, his neck bent over a microscope. Whatever he was doing must have been difficult, because he didn't look back to see why there was still quiet. He passed a pencil from his right hand to his left and made a note on a blueprint. It was plain he wouldn't have thought it was rude if no conversation was forthcoming after all.

Thaniel went up behind him to catch his elbows and set a guinea down by his hand. His shirt was real linen and, because he had been sitting side on to the draught, cool down the left arm. He twisted in his chair.

'What's this for?'

'Your winnings,' Thaniel said. 'I work for the Foreign Office, as of this morning.'

Mori inclined his head. 'Well done.'

'Thank you. Baron Mori.'

'Oh, who told you that?' he said crossly.

'Nobody. I looked at your immigration papers at the office. Why didn't you say?'

'I'd like to be a watchmaker before I'm a samurai, somewhere in the world.'

'Must be terrible for you, being a samurai.'

'Shut up, peasant.'

Thaniel laughed and knew what Williamson would say if he could see him, and then pushed the thought into the bicycle shed at the back of his mind. Williamson wouldn't have to live in Pimlico after it was all over.

Dinner was not much later: fresh bread, real grapes, and a bitter oriental wine that, after two cups, he decided he liked. He also liked watching Mori eat rice with chopsticks, which he could use far more accurately than Thaniel could use cutlery. Mori seemed to disapprove of cutlery as a sort of unnecessary decadence and by way of reinforcing the point, he did all the washing up except Thaniel's fork, which he left in a jar like a chemical specimen. Thaniel prodded him and Mori smiled at him in the reflection in the dark window.

Outside, among the birch trees in the garden, soft balls of light rose from the grass. They were what he had seen on his first night, but here he was nearer to them than before, and he could see that they were differently coloured, in shades of amber and yellow. Every now and then, one flickered, as if something were moving between them. The Haverly baby, left outside the back door again, noticed too, and whooped.

He set down the plate he had been drying. 'What are they?'

'Fireflies.'

'There are no fireflies like that in England.'

Mori took a key from his pocket. As soon as he opened the door, the floating lights disappeared. They both went outside to look around anyway, but they found nothing but Katsu, who bubbled at them from a watering can.

PART TWO

ELEVEN

OXFORD, JUNE 1884

G RACE HAD WORKED all week on the interferometer. Term
would end on the fourteenth of June – tomorrow – and then
it would be too late. Accurate measurements would be impossible in London, where there were trains above and below ground
and building work everywhere. That was why the American's
experiment had gone wrong. He had been in the cellar of a naval
academy with five hundred men running drills above his head. But
she was hopeful now. She had done everything properly: re-run
the original calculations, found the errors, corrected them. As she
had taken the last of her notes from the last of her stack of reading, she started to feel a bubble of lightness coming up through
her ribs. It had been very fragile at first, but she thought now
it was made of something stronger than suds. The new experiment would work. She would still have to go back to London for
a little while, but not for ever. Once the paper was published, the
college would have her back.

She had set up in Lady Margaret Hall's deep, silent cellar, where
everyone left her alone. Mostly alone. Matsumoto called every day
at three o'clock to make sure that she hadn't blown herself up. She
had tried to explain that she hadn't got any explosives and therefore couldn't explode, but he only said it was dangerous to imagine
she wouldn't find a way.

It was nearly three o'clock now. Having balanced the last
mirror on the interferometer, she straightened up. In the way
things do after a long period of concentration, the room looked
inexplicably different. It was bigger, and fuller. Along the back

wall was the college's infant wine collection. Everything else was hers. She had set up a trestle bench, scattered with bits of mirror and several hacksaws. Next to that was the font she had borrowed from New College chapel. Sitting within it was a flat plane of wood, on which sat the four arms of the interferometer in a cross shape. Although one could still do proper science with a magnet and some iron filings, it felt professional to have made something that looked like a mutated windmill. Science had to have some mystery, otherwise everyone would find out how simple it was.

The can cut into her forearm as she poured the first of the mercury into the font. It glimmered and swam. When she poured in the second can, the mercury already in the font jumped and splashed, but nothing like as much as water. It was too heavy. She moved the can around, making shapes in the surface, which dented under the new weight pouring in.

A cane tapped on the door.

'Coming in, Carrow,' Matsumoto called. 'Anything nasty I should know about?'

'Yes, stay back a bit. You shouldn't breathe in these fumes.'

He pushed the door open with the handle of his cane. 'What in God's name are you doing?'

'It's mercury.'

'I can see it's mercury, Carrow, the question is why is there mercury in this otherwise delightful cellar?'

'Wait, last one,' Grace said. She was breathless now. The mercury cans weren't big, but they were so heavy that they might have been steel all the way through. 'It deadens vibrations. It's heavier than water.'

'I've brought some friends. I thought it might do you good to see other humans.'

'What?' Grace put down the empty can and straightened up to find that six of Matsumoto's minions were already halfway down the steps. They were all dressed in close-cut jackets and silk ties that rippled with magnificent petroleum colours. When they came into the lamplight, they made polite, appreciative noises at the cluttered room. One came across to her and bowed too formally.

'Albert Grey. I think we might have met once, but I may have been preoccupied at the time.'

He meant he had been unable to tear himself away from his Ancient Greek. Grace shook his hand carefully, her fingers stiff from lifting the heavy cans. 'Sorry about the fumes.'

He glanced at his palm and rubbed it against his trousers. 'What's all this machinery, then? Some kind of wonderful alchemy?'

'N—o, it measures light.' She heard a clink and had to jerk past Grey to take one of the mirrors from somebody else. 'Don't touch anything, please.'

'Physics a rather analytical pursuit for a woman, don't you think?' Grey said, dipping his finger into the mercury pool.

'Oh, don't be such an ass,' Matsumoto snapped, just as Grace opened her mouth to defend herself. 'We all know you fancy yourself a bit of an enlightenment man, but face facts, for God's sake. You've got the analytical capacity of a dead rabbit. No need to bad-mouth real scientists to cover it up.'

There was a small, shocked silence. Matsumoto never lost his temper with anyone. Grey looked across at him with the startled eyes of a suddenly rebuked child.

'You should all leave,' Grace said at last. 'These fumes are poisonous if you breathe them for too long.'

But Grey, anxious now, tried a false little laugh. 'Only poison? Matsumoto here was telling us about explosives. Apparently you nearly blew up the college once. Are you certain you aren't behind the Whitehall bombing?'

'The what?'

Matsumoto's eyes widened. 'Carrow. I've been bringing you a newspaper every day.'

'I've been … meaning to read them later.'

'The bomb at Whitehall? Destroyed Scotland Yard? Fenians?'

'Oh, Christ – were they all killed? The police I mean?'

'No, they were all out.'

'Then why is it important?'

'Can you hear yourself, I wonder?'

Grace heard a small splash and spun around. 'Get your fingers out of my bloody mercury, Grey! Matsumoto, if I wanted to speak to humans, I would go upstairs and eat in hall. Everyone get out. I said not to touch it,' she said, and smacked Grey's hand with a steel ruler, hard. He gasped and snatched it back.

'All right, I'll see you all at dinner,' Matsumoto said. He herded them back toward the steps. They went in a quiet cluster, Grey last. He caught the arms of two others when he reached the top. Men in Oxford seemed to occur in chains, like conspiratorial atoms. She wished it would stop. A gale of laughter came down the stairs, and she knew that the joke had been about her.

'You didn't really think I'd be overjoyed about having them climb all over my experiment?' she said to Matsumoto. 'My very important experiment, which has taken a week to build?'

'No, but medicine never tastes good.' He sighed and came to look at the mercury. Compared to the others, he had a quiet, unpretentious way of standing, but just at that moment, Grace resented it. He enjoyed his own ease.

'Being solitary isn't a disease that needs a cure—'

'Invariably a claim made by the imminently hysterical. The man who looked after me when I was small spent all his time alone and became quite psychotic before long. Anyway, this mercury no doubt has some kind of purpose veiled to the unscientific. Is it dangerous? This isn't going to be like the magnesium thing again, is it?'

'It isn't explosive,' she said, for the fourth time that week. 'And the crater wasn't that bad, and your eyebrows were perfectly all right.'

'I think you'll find the crater is still perceptible in the lawn, despite the valiant efforts of the gardener.' He looked up. 'You know I hope you haven't gone around involving the other girls in all this chemistry stuff.'

'Why, because they'd burn off people's eyebrows?'

'No, because then they would know how to make bombs, and what would happen if you gave someone like Bertha a bomb?'

Grace paused. 'She does classics. And the others are biologists, which means they spend all day with yeast and ... ooze.'

'All right, what is all this, if not lethal?'

'It is an interferometer.' She even liked saying the word. She gave it a gentle push and it spun slowly on the mercury, mirrors winking. 'It measures the speed of light as it passes through ether.'

'Ether is like air to sound. Light has to ... move through something.'

'You remembered,' she said, surprised.

'I do sometimes remember science by accident,' he sighed. 'What's the point?'

'The point,' said Grace, 'is to prove the existence of the ether. Usually, ether just sits – it permeates everything. It's very fine: imagine something that makes grains of icing sugar look like boulders. But the earth is moving through it, which drags it, so you get what's called ether wind, or ether drag. That's very useful, because we can measure it. If you can show ether has a flow, you show it exists in the first place.'

'How, I ask dutifully?'

'With light. It's the only substance affected purely by ether and not by air. The device has four arms, as you see, and mirrors at the end of each arm in order to reflect light back and forth. The light that moves in the direction of the ether flow will go quicker than the light that moves horizontally across it. Just like a boat following the current of a river will go faster than one crossing it. This mirror here puts the two light beams together again and feeds them into this telescope, which is casting what are called light fringes on this piece of paper. They look like coloured lines as the waves overlap. If the light is moving through ether, the lines won't match up properly. If it isn't, they'll be very clear.'

'I see. And why is that useful to know?'

'Any of number of reasons,' Grace said, ignoring his expression. 'If we can prove ether, it could explain a great deal. Ether penetrates everything, including vacuums, including the human brain, so the impulses there assuredly affect it.'

'Impulses.'

'Thinking is a physical process, Matsumoto, it's electricity flashing and chemicals moving, it's not magic. Moving things push ether about.'

He looked put out. 'Electricity.'

'Yes. Anyway?'

'Yes, yes.'

'Anyway,' she repeated, 'ether could explain how real mediums work, and how ghosts could exist, generally how thought has physical effects beyond the cranium. If you could study ether, you would be halfway to understanding what happens to your consciousness after you die.'

'Oh,' said Matsumoto, sounding more interested. 'What happens now, then?'

'Now, I have to turn off all the lights, and turn on the sodium lamps here to tune it, and make some observations.'

'It's already boring,' he said, but he helped her turn off the lamps on the desk until only one was left. She used it to find the switches for the interferometer's powerful sodium lamps, then blew it out too.

'I'm going to make sure the arms are exactly the same length. Look at that piece of paper by the telescope.'

'Look for what?'

Grace tweaked one of the arms. 'Can you see dark stripes on it now?'

Matsumoto looked startled. 'Yes.'

'Those are the light fringes I was telling you about. Tell me when they sharpen.'

'How sharp?'

'As if you'd drawn them with a pen.'

'Now,' he said after a moment.

Grace checked. 'Good. Right, now we'll use white light.' She relit her lamp and turned off the sodium lamp.

'What? What the devil difference does it make?'

'White light splits into colours. It's easier to count the lines because the colours will change as they radiate outward. You get lost if you try counting only in grey.'

'Oh, yes,' he said, sounding unsettled.

'Something wrong?'

'No. This is all very bizarre. I feel rather as though God has put some malicious booby traps into everyday objects.'

Grace laughed. 'They're not malicious, they're rainbows. Right, we'll start. We're hoping for little lines to start appearing between these strong ones. It should make them look fuzzy.'

She put the sodium lamp on to the edge of the turnstile so that it glowed towards the central mirror. On the piece of paper, the dark stripes turned coloured, except for one black line in the middle.

'They still look pretty sharp to me,' Matsumoto said. He jumped when a small camera attached to the telescope took a picture of the lines. Grace had rigged the shutter to snap every five seconds after the light was turned on.

'Hm.' She turned the interferometer in the mercury. The lines winked out until the light aligned through the telescope again. They were exactly the same as before. They remained exactly the same through three hundred and sixty degrees, and then again when she tried in the opposite direction. She had expected only faint interference lines, hence photographs that could be accurately examined and measured, but they should have been visible to the naked eye. A nasty weight settled in her stomach.

'I've done something wrong,' she said.

Matsumoto took the lamp off the turnstile. 'Enough for now, the mercury is making me dizzy. Would it be stupid to say that perhaps there is no such thing as ether?'

'It's there, we know it is. All modern mathematical models of the universe predict it.'

'Enough for now,' he repeated, and tugged her away. Once they were at the top of the cellar steps, he patted her arm.

'No, no, I need to try it again, I'll have just misaligned something, or—'

'Fresh eyes. You'll have them in ten minutes. Come along.'

After the gloom of the cellar, the daylight looked too yellow. It was lancing in through the open door in perfectly straight lines.

Light travels in straight lines, but is a wave. Not for the first time, her brain bumped against the question of what, exactly, was doing the waving. It was a tired, stale question.

'I don't want to be out for long,' she said. 'I won't have access to a laboratory after tomorrow.'

'Why?'

'Term ends. I'm going home.'

'I thought that horrible aunt of yours left you her house in Kensington? Set up there.'

'It was left as part of my dowry.'

'So marry some poor bastard and then boot him out. Didn't somebody pass a law recently saying that what's yours is yours, regardless of passing menfolk? The Bertha crew were rather jubilant for a while, I recall.'

'Y—es, but it's not mine. My aunt didn't settle it on me, she settled it on my father, for me. He thinks anyone related to my mother must be just like her and therefore wouldn't trust me to efficiently manage pencil shavings. It will never be in my name. When I marry it will be my husband's, in the good old-fashioned way. Which would mean I'd have to find a husband who didn't mind ether experiments in the cellar. Which I think is unlikely. Unless you're willing. There's a house in Kensington in it for you.'

He laughed. 'I'd be delighted to, but unfortunately an English bride would cause a horrible scandal. The English are too ugly.'

Grace cleared her throat. 'Charming.'

'Have you seen Japanese women? Such delicate creatures. Anyone meeting an Englishwoman in Kyoto could be forgiven for thinking he had run into some sort of troll. Oh, speaking of trolls. Are you going to the Foreign Office ball tomorrow? Your father's friends with the minister, isn't he?'

'Yes. That's why I can't stay here a few days longer. Are you?'

'The ambassador invited me. You'll like him. He's just like me.'

'Well, if you hear I've shot myself beforehand, you'll know why.'

He laughed again.

Grace pushed her hands into her pockets as they began their usual walk around the edge of the lawn. She had to duck an overhanging rose. Everything was left semi-wild here. Even the college looked as though it might have grown. She glanced back – the Virginia creeper across the wall had finally turned red, nearly purple at the bottom, where it blended into lavender bushes. It would all be glorious for a fortnight, then become a mess of bare stalks for the autumn.

She had once met a scientist who worked in more or less the same area she did, one Oliver Lodge of the University of Liverpool. He lectured on ether, and on electricity. She had gone up to Liverpool last year to hear him. He had explained how the electrification of particles, including water particles, would make them coalesce; he had even manufactured a fine rain in the lecture theatre. It was fascinating stuff, and if it was developed properly it would have applications in weather control and in the search for ether, which was only extremely rarefied particles. But she had a feeling that Lodge was one of a kind, and he was already married. What was left, down that road, was to find someone willing to make a bargain, house for laboratory, but since she was neither charming nor personable, she couldn't imagine how she would go about anything like that.

What she could imagine were two paths. Down one, she found some stupid mistake in the experiment and mended it, and wrote a decent paper, and secured a teaching position; down the other, there was no mistake, and it was all wrong, and perhaps, if she was lucky, she would be able to teach schoolgirls how to make little magnesium fireworks between their literature lessons and sketching. She didn't much like moments when things split so clearly. It was much better to be able to think that anything could happen, even if it couldn't. Seeing it made her feel claustrophobic, though dark cellars didn't.

'Where will you go once term ends?' she asked.

'Japan. I shall take a leisurely route through Europe, though. No rush.'

Grace frowned. 'So is that it, after London? You're going home from there? You didn't say.'

'You didn't ask.'

'Withholding basic information until someone asks is a bit vain, don't you think?'

He lifted his eyebrow. 'And making a point of not asking is ... ?'

'Whatever I do, you'll construe it as an infatuation,' she said irritably, though it was just his usual teasing. But her temper was ragged from the heat and the experiment, and sometimes, there was an edge to his playfulness.

'You were the one who asked me to marry you a moment ago.'

'For God's sake, Matsumoto, what is this, Camelot? Marriage and love are not the same thing. In fact, they tend quickly to become mutually exclusive.'

'You used to take my arm,' he said.

She stiffened. 'What?'

'And then you stopped,' he said, without bothering to repeat himself. 'I am flattered, but I hope it won't make things difficult. It has been splendid knowing you, but I'm afraid my family simply would not approve.'

She had stopped six months ago, when she caught herself thinking how charming he was. It was bizarrely difficult to keep resisting somebody who, although not naturally striking in any way, behaved as if he were Adonis. 'Nor would mine. I stopped taking your arm when you started wearing that god-awful cologne.'

'I see,' he said. He didn't sound convinced. 'In that case, I do apologise.'

'Good. Listen, I'm going inside, I've got to see if those mirrors were misaligned, I've still got nearly an entire day before I must be in London.'

'I'll see you in London, then?'

'Perhaps, but if you call at the house, do use the back door; the servants will laugh if you try the front.'

As she turned away, she saw him frown. She didn't stop. She had always known that he strove for regard so that he could laugh at it, but she didn't think she had known him to be spiteful before. It clanged around inside her head and made her wonder if he had been laughing at her all along.

TWELVE

LONDON, JUNE 1884

THE DRESSER RATTLED urgently.

'Yes, well,' said Thaniel, spinning the key over his knuckle. 'Give back my socks. And my good tie. I need it for tonight.'

Katsu subsided. His springs must have been winding down by now, so perhaps it wasn't deliberate, but the silence sounded sulky.

Having plotted the kidnap the night before, Thaniel had the day's clothes out already and so dressed uninterrupted, but the victory soon felt guilt-tinged. Very big to have outwitted a little mechanical octopus whose only ambition was the acquisition of socks. He turned back to let him out. Katsu stayed curled at the bottom of the drawer. Thaniel lifted him out, but he stayed stiff. He put him back. After looking down at him for a little while, he tucked some of the last remaining socks around him by way of an apology.

It was Saturday again, the third that he had spent at Filigree Street, and the morning of the Foreign Office ball. There had been no word from Williamson, and Thaniel hadn't searched the house yet. Mori rarely left it except to buy groceries, and since the grocer's was at the top of the street, he was only ever gone for less than half the time it would have taken to sift through the workshop and his bedroom. Thaniel was beginning to think Mori was a little agoraphobic, although that was hardly shocking. Boisterous socialites didn't often become watchmakers. But he was feeling the old weight against his chest again. He was nearly sure that Williamson wouldn't storm in without telling him, but not positive, and the more time went by, the more often he looked toward the street outside, expecting men in uniform.

He was still not used to full weekends, and as he made his way downstairs, the time stretched out incredibly. He couldn't get himself out of his old habits of saving time, though, and while he waited for the kettle to boil on the stove, he cleaned the table and put some fresh water in Katsu's tank on the windowsill. Once he had made the tea, he took two cups through the workshop's back door. Mori had provided breakfast at seven on every weekday morning, along with Japanese conversation tailored to Thaniel's vocabulary. He had a knack for speaking clearly and grammatically without sounding as though he were talking to an idiot, and Thaniel was learning at the speed of sound because of it. Bombmaker or not, he was owed tea.

'Morning.'

'Oh, morning.' Mori said it mostly into his microscope. He was building up some miniature clockwork beneath the lens, with very fine, thin tools that looked like something that belonged to a surgeon. 'Sorry, I'm counting.'

Thaniel stayed quiet and sat down in the high chair. One of the Haverly children was just outside, his nose pressed piggily against the window while he watched the display. He jumped when Mori threw a mint humbug at the glass. It bounced off and landed in the doorway. The boy grinned and took it, and went on his way. Mori was already looking into his microscope again. Thaniel couldn't see his fingertips moving, only the tiny shift of the tendons in the back of his hand. Beside him was an empty jar. He had tipped the parts out over the desk in a little heap of cogs and things whose names Thaniel didn't know. Mori put his left hand out without looking up and lifted a tiny metal framework from halfway down the nearer slope.

'I've stopped counting,' he said once he had set it in place.

'I think I might have broken Katsu,' Thaniel confessed. 'He was ...' He tried to decide whether Katsu's having stolen most of his socks and his good tie was a morally sufficient reason for locking him in the dresser. 'He was moving, but then he stopped,' he said instead.

'If you can't find it, you can take one of mine for tonight,' Mori said.

'Pardon?'

Mori straightened and put his hands against the base of his spine. 'Your tie.'

'I said that Katsu might be broken.'

'I misheard, sorry.'

'No, he has stolen my good tie,' Thaniel said. He paused. 'At least if watchmaking falls through, you can make your living as a mind-reader.'

'I – yes,' said Mori. 'Morning,' he added as a postman came in with a big, flat parcel. 'Yes, down there. Thank you.'

'What's that?' Thaniel said, curious. The postmarks and stamps weren't English or Japanese.

'A painting. There's a depressed Dutchman who does countryside scenes and flowers and things. It's ugly, but I have to maintain the estates in Japan and modern art is a good investment.'

'Can I look?'

'I wouldn't bother,' he said, but Thaniel untied the string and folded down the top half of the paper packaging anyway. It was a strange painting. The paint was laid on so thickly that it stood up in bumps from the canvas, all in muddy colours and lumpy strokes. Mori was right, it was ugly, but it was swirlingly distorted as if the wind were a visible force in the air, and in the greens was the sound of the hay moving.

'You should keep this here. It's good.'

Mori made an unwilling sound. 'I don't like Western art.'

'No, look at this.' He lifted it from its package. It wasn't heavy. 'It's clever, it looks like busy Mozart.'

'What?'

'I ...' Thaniel sighed. 'I see sound. Mozart looks like this. You know. Fast strings.'

'See? In front of you?'

'Yes. I'm not mad.'

'I didn't think so. All sounds?'

'Yes.'

Mori waited, and then prompted him, 'For example?'

'For example, when you speak, everything tints this colour.' He held up the watch. 'Ticking watches are ... what. Lighthouse flashes. The stairs at my old office clang yellow. It's nothing.'

'Do you ever draw them?'

'No, because it looks like I belong in an asylum.'

'It would be much more interesting than a picture of a field and some mud,' Mori said seriously.

Thaniel dipped his head down, knowing he had turned red. He hadn't meant to tell him any of it and now felt exposed. 'No, it wouldn't. I'm going to hang this up.'

There was a crash from upstairs that sounded a lot like an octopus breaking through the back of a dresser. 'Katsu seems all right,' Mori observed.

'Do you know where he's put my things?'

'No, sorry. As I say, he works partially on random gears, so I don't always pre-set where he goes. I'll look later, but I can't leave this for now or it will fall apart. You can take one of my ties. Top drawer,' he said, pointing to the ceiling. His bedroom was directly above.

Thaniel didn't move. It was the chance he had been waiting for, but it was a harsh thing.

'Go,' Mori said. 'I haven't cursed the threshold. Christ, Englishmen and privacy.'

The room was without character. There were no pictures, no souvenirs, no paper lamps, not even any books. Only a chest of drawers and the bed. He looked through the drawers. Clothes, no papers. The top left was all ties and collars. He checked the windowsill and under the bed, and when he found nothing, he shook his head at himself and went back to the ties. A green and a blue one were buried under greys in a way that suggested they didn't come out often. When he moved the dark ones aside to reach them, he uncovered a book. He stopped. Ancient and cracked, the cover was otherwise blank, but the spine had been broken and restitched to allow for the insertion of extra pages. It was in Japanese. Although he didn't know nearly enough yet to read well, he opened it.

It was not a diary. There was text, but most of it was in bullet points, and they surrounded other things: cut-outs from newspapers, precise ink sketches of clockwork, people, annotated maps. After a while, he recognised dates too, though they were written Japanese-fashion, with the year noted according to the length of the present Emperor's reign. He tried to remember what Fanshaw had told him. There had been a civil war in Japan in sixty-seven, and then the Emperor had taken power in sixty-eight. Now was eighty-four; this year would be the sixteenth. The dates in the diary were only vaguely clustered. Early on were dates from before Mutsuhito's reign, though he couldn't read the name of the previous ruler, and they hopped around a few years and months in either direction. Later were nearer dates. Once or twice, this year cropped up. Towards the back were entries for this year and for next year, and the year after. He frowned and recalculated the difference, but he was sure he was right. He flicked back. In the middle, next to an entry about the twelfth of April in 1871, was today's date, the fourteenth of June, 1884. The ink was old and faded, just like the entry from the earlier date. The first word of the entry was his own name.

He looked round, pointlessly. He would hear Mori coming up the stairs. He closed the book over his finger and took it into his own room, where Fanshaw's dictionary still lay open on his bed. He learned forty new words every day. It was less difficult than it had seemed at first. Seeing sounds was useful for quick remembering, and the pictograph writing system was sensible; the word for mountain looked like a mountain, and the word for forest was three trees together. Things like 'beautiful' threw a spanner in the works – that was a combination of 'big' and 'sheep' – but as Mori pointed out, context helped. Monks in remote parts of ancient China had probably developed some unorthodox opinions about sheep before long, and their doctrine explained too why three women together were evil and why every second word had a temple or a shrine in it somewhere. He could read a little now, at least, and he only wanted to translate a tiny portion. The grammar was assuredly beyond him but the character system allowed semi-coherent parsing.

There was a hole in the back of the dresser where Katsu had escaped. He brushed up the splinters and tilted the door closed. With the diary open on his knees, he began turning the pages of the dictionary. Each character was listed in order of the number of pen-strokes required to construct it, and this being logical but laborious, it took him a little while to find them all. But Mori had neat writing, and he didn't mistake any. After half an hour, he had something like a translation.

JUNE 14, 1884
Thaniel bought some music. I can't say the composer's name, but I like the song; it makes me feel young. There is blue cake, with an icing duck on it. He says it's a swan, but I think it's a duck. Red wine, too. I don't like it but according to him I must learn to like it if I'm to be accepted in civilised society. We both have too much, although it's hardly a celebration unless somebody embarrasses himself.

And: might need new dresser in his bedroom.

He shut the diary and put it back in Mori's drawer. He re-read his translation. None of it had happened but the broken dresser, and there was no way Mori could have known that until this morning. He didn't understand the rest at all. He knew he would have made horrible mistakes throughout. Whatever it really was, however, it was nothing to do with Clan na Gael or bombs.

Having torn up his translation and scattered it into the grate, he made his way back downstairs in order to gauge Mori's opinion of the ties. He had been gone for too long and he wanted to imply he had been deliberating. Vanity was better than spying for Special Branch.

'Blue,' he said as soon as Thaniel came in.

'Green it is.'

Mori lobbed a tolerant look in his direction as he took the blue tie back. 'I stole your invitation to see what they're doing tonight.

It said there's a pianist playing halfway through, Endymion Griszt; if I gave you the money, could you buy the sheet music for me?'

'Griszt, are you sure? He's the lunatic with the pink ribbon round his hat.'

'I know, but still.' He held out the invitation.

'I'm not sure about this ball,' Thaniel said. 'There will be no one there I know and there's this … special section in the invitation listing all the ambassadors, look. Arinori Mori, is he a relation of yours?'

'I don't think so. His Mori means woods. Three trees.' He sketched the character on a scrap of paper. 'I'm Mo-*u*-ri, which is the same in English spelling but different for us. Like this.'

'Featherworth.' Thaniel looked up. 'You're the Japanese equivalent of Fanshaw.'

'It probably used to be woods, with a pretentious drawl. Must you go?'

'Yes. But I'm going to try and come back early. I'll steal some food and run, I think.'

Mori laughed low in his throat, mostly to the clockwork in front of him. He looked tired; he was holding himself brittly, with his neck still and straight. 'Mr Steepleton, at the ball. If you meet …'

'Who?'

'No. Never mind.'

'Someone you know?'

'Yes, but I realised that I'm not interested.'

Thaniel snorted and clapped his back, gently, in case he broke him. Mori bent forward over the microscope again, away from his hand. Thaniel watched him. He didn't seem right. The creeping sense that he might have seen him reading the book came up from the ground, but that was more anxiety than evidence.

'Are you feeling well?' Thaniel said at last.

'I'm getting a cold.'

'It's summer, go outside. You'll feel better for the sun.'

'It is not summer, England doesn't have summer, it has continuous autumn with a fortnight's variation here and there. And the Haverly children are outside. Stop laughing at me.'

Thaniel did stop laughing then, because he had just seen a constable through the window. The man only told the Haverly boys to quieten down. Mori gave Thaniel a puzzled look and he realised he had been staring. He shook his head and mumbled something about going to the post office. When he got there he sent a wire to Williamson, asking for more time.

THIRTEEN

T HE CARROW HOUSE in Belgravia was big enough to lose the
cavalry in, but it was not big enough for Grace to lose her
maid, Alice, or for her brothers to pass beyond the range of her
hearing. Both of them were in the army, and both were on leave
for the ball tonight. Their father had insisted. Lord Carrow had
organised a good part of the proceedings, and he wanted, he said,
to show off his children. It was code for padding out the numbers.

While Alice was sighing over Grace's evening dress, he knocked
and came inside. He had the awkward way of a man who sees his
colleagues more often than he sees his children.

'Gracie. Get everything down from Oxford?'

'Mm. There wasn't much, I brought most of it home at Easter.'

He looked around the room. So did Grace. It was smaller every
time she came home. An ancient rocking horse still stood in the
corner, just beside the desk. The desk was scattered with squared
paper and pencils, and the pieces of a calculating engine she had
been building during the last holidays. A glass prism in the window
shone rainbows over the chests and Persian carpets and assorted
astronomical equipment, all put patiently in order in her absence.
Provoked by the shifting of the old floorboards, the rocking horse
squeaked. The blackboard was bolted to the wall in an asymmet-
ric position. She had had to nail it in herself; the maids had kept
putting it in the cellar.

'Dress up properly,' he said. 'Francis Fanshaw will be there,
remember.'

'Yes. I remember.'

'You'll upset your mother if you don't make an effort.'

Grace looked at the ceiling. Her mother occupied most of the top floor, curtains drawn and fires burning. She was ill now, had been, said the servants, since she had come back from Oxford, so Grace hadn't seen her yet. But when Grace opened her own door that morning, she had walked into a faint cloud of lilac perfume. She was almost certain that her mother must have been standing there just before, watching her through the hinges.

'How I spend the rest of my life can't depend on what might or might not upset her,' she said quietly.

His eyebrows lifted. 'I beg your pardon. I seem to recall I sent you to Oxford, despite the wishes of your mother, and that she ailed all the faster after that. You've had four years doing quite as you please without anything to show for it. Unless this fabled fellowship is just around the corner?'

'No,' she said.

'Well then. I'm doing for you what I can and I shall be damned if you turn your nose up. One of the great evils of our time for men and women is to be educated beyond one's purpose in life.'

'Not malaria, then,' she said, without laughing, because ten years ago it had been funny that he was a stupid person. It was not funny now. 'Or those insufficiently educated for their purpose.'

'Your mother will be wearing yellow,' he said. He had a great capacity to ignore what he believed made no sense. 'She hopes you will wear something complementary.'

'I've only got one dress that will do and it's green, I'm afraid.'

He went stiffly to the door, where he stopped suddenly. 'In ten years' time, you will be glad to have been given a push.'

'You're doing all this on the strength of your certainty that you are qualified to say what I will think in ten years? You idiot.'

'Miss!' Alice exclaimed.

'We shall all meet downstairs at eight,' he said. He was straining to keep his voice quiet. Grace tilted her head at him by way of asking why he had not left yet.

The door clicked behind him, and Alice burst into the scolding that had been brewing all along.

'That will do,' Grace said, once she had let her run for a while.

Alice sat down with a bump to return to her stitching. She was sewing beads back on to the green evening dress. It had been years since Grace had worn it, and it had shed them gradually over the base of the wardrobe. She sat in front of the mirror and watched her reflection push pins into its hair, though what she saw was her room at college, being cleaned now and made ready for whoever was to have it next term.

When the concierge announced her name, heads turned briefly. She hadn't been out in London society since going to Oxford. She was glad when she saw some familiar faces, Francis Fanshaw for one. She started to lift her hand, but his smile was glassy and he turned away quickly. She let her hand drop again and felt ugly. While her brothers shot toward cavalry friends, she looked around for black hair, but if Matsumoto had already arrived, he wasn't dancing. She could only see diplomats and their elegant wives, and the pristine clerks of the more important Foreign Office sections, all Englishmen with similar hair and similar posture, though there were a dozen languages fluttering under the chandeliers. She didn't think that any of them were Japanese. She swallowed and started to look instead for somewhere to sit down.

A snatch of expensive cologne drifted past her just before a pair of white-gloved hands settled over her arms.

'Come along, Carrow, stop frowning at those poor women and come and play a proper game.'

She turned. Matsumoto nodded toward the far corner of the ballroom, where the stewards had set up a miniature gentlemen's club. It had card tables and roulette, and deep velvet armchairs arranged by the fire.

'Alice chose the dress?' he offered after a moment.

She nodded and smoothed down the front, though it wasn't creased. It was still fashionable, but she felt gaudy in it, and aware that it looked strange with her short hair. 'What do you think?'

'Oh, it's ... it's ... well, it's a catastrophe with sequins.'

She laughed, then took his arm and let him lead her across to the roulette table. His entourage was already there, turned out beautifully in white ties. A couple of his aides were speaking animatedly to one of the interchangeable clerks in Japanese. Grace watched the man, curious to know where he could have learned. The banker nodded to Matsumoto and handed him a black dice case, with the roulette ball inside. He held it under her nose.

'Blow. Not that it will affect a random process, of course. See? Science.'

'Probability theory is mathematics.'

'Shut up.'

Grace blew, and Matsumoto tipped the ball gently on to the wheel. Everyone placed their bets while the silver wheel spun, black or red, or for those who did not understand probability, a number.

'Zero?' Matsumoto said to her.

'One in thirty-seven chance,' Grace said.

'Gambling is about fun, Carrow, not mathematics. Zero,' he added to the banker. 'Think of horse races. People like to bet on the one with three legs and a wheeze. They don't bet on that one because they think it will win, but because they can see how very glorious it would be if it *were* to win.'

Grace looked up. 'Sounds like religion to me.'

He laughed. 'You poor pedantic thing. Your science can save a man's life, but imagination makes it worth living. Take that fellow there, look at him. Clerk written all over him,' he said, looking past her to the man still speaking to the three aides. 'The highlight of his day is probably an excursion to the canteen to buy lukewarm vegetable soup, before it's back to dishing out passport forms for Chinese immigrants. How do you think he carries on? Knowing that the world is statistics and probability, or imagining what it would be like to see impossible things?'

'Statistics and probability are only methods of describing things, they don't make them less interesting.'

'Think you'll find most people disagree. Oh, here we are,' he said suddenly.

On the roulette wheel, the ball was clicking to a halt.

One of Grace's brothers arrived. 'What are we playing?' he said. He was already flushed from the wine. Matsumoto gave him the amused look of an experienced dandy meeting his younger self, and flicked a few counters to him.

'Oh, thank you ... oh!' James added, having caught sight of Matsumoto's black hair and slanted eyes for the first time. He beamed. 'You must be Gracie's Japanese beau!'

'I don't think she has any beaux of any sort. She frightens them off with numbers and sulphur,' Matsumoto said. She thought there was coldness in his voice, but Matsumoto was bulletproof: anything that was not a compliment pinged off him and hit an innocent bystander.

The ball crept over one last number.

'Zero!' announced the banker.

'Oh!' laughed Grace. She threw up her hands without meaning to, just like Matsumoto and her brother. When she stepped back from the wheel to let Matsumoto collect his winnings, she bumped into someone just behind her. Twisting around, she found the clerk who had been speaking to Matsumoto's aides.

'Oh – sorry,' he said, smiling a little. His eyes were an unusual bright grey, like storm light. 'I didn't see you.'

Grace smiled too. He had a completely incongruous northern accent, not strong, but hardly Foreign Office Eton either. 'No, no. My fault. May I ask where you learned Japanese?'

'Oh ... out of a dictionary. And at home. My landlord's teaching me. I'm not very good.' He looked her over and didn't bother to pretend that he hadn't noticed her hair. 'Anyway, I'm sorry, ma'am ...'

'Actually, would you stay a minute?' Grace said, and then felt stupid. 'It's ... I'm sorry. It's just that I think my friend might be annoyed with me and I haven't got anyone else to talk to.'

His grey eyes went over Matsumoto, and then to her again. He had the quiet unflustered manner that usually came of army service, but she didn't think he was otherwise military. There was no oil in his hair, and he did not hold his hands behind his back.

'Why don't we see about the next dance, then?' he said. 'I won't be very good, but it might be better than roulette.'

'Please. I'm Grace, by the way, Carrow.'

'Thaniel. Steepleton.'

'Like Nathaniel?'

'Yes, but my dad was Nat, so . . . ' He tipped his head as he trailed off, in a way that suggested he had explained it often already tonight, mainly to people who couldn't pronounce a 'th' anyway.

'No, no, I see.'

Pleased, she tapped Matsumoto to tell him where she was going. He looked Steepleton up and down once, then turned away without saying anything.

FOURTEEN

SHE WAS AN odd-looking woman. The fashion was for whites and pale blue, but her dress was hummingbird green and her hair was very short. She moved like a faulty bicycle, by turns too fast, and then too slowly. It reminded him of Mori, or, Mori as he would have been if he weren't so closely tangled with the fires at Scotland Yard. When she spoke, it was with his serious truthfulness.

'So, you've got an unusual voice for someone who works at the Foreign Office.'

'You've got unusual hair,' he said. It was a gamble to say anything; he had only just learned to dance and talk at the same time. Fanshaw had been giving lessons at the office all week on the principle that if even the oafs from the Russia desk were competent, he wouldn't be having any of his fellows embarrass the section.

She nodded, two short nods, as though her springs were too tightly wound. 'It used to be long, but I set fire to it once and it seemed better to cut it after that.'

'How?'

She looked away from him and he heard her teeth click together as she set them, just, over the well-rehearsed strings orchestra at the edge of the room. The colours from there were blurring with the shapes people made dancing, and sometimes he couldn't tell whether he was seeing the flash from diamond pins in a woman's hair or from a high violin. The hems of skirts moving over the floor made their own shades and men's voices were lost sometimes under the red cello. It was the brightest place he had been since Gilbert and Sullivan's last operetta.

Then, 'I read physics at university. There were a few experimental mishaps.' Without giving him chance to ask anything about it, she said, 'I take it you're at the Orient desk?'

'That's right.'

'You know Francis Fanshaw, then?'

'I work for him. You?'

'We used to go fishing when we were small. It... how is it, interesting?'

'Less interesting than reading physics at university,' he said, wanting to get back to that before they strayed too far from it.

'Well, that's all done now,' she said, and asked him instead about the work, and what sort of a language Japanese was, and whether it was difficult. When the music ended, she ducked an abrupt curtsey. She pushed her fingertips against her thumbnails. 'Well. Lovely meeting you.'

From the far end of the hall, a steward announced that Endymion Griszt's performance would begin in a few moments. Thaniel glanced that way and then down at her. She was watching an older man, her father from his jaw, speaking to Francis Fanshaw. 'Come and listen to this with me, will you? I don't want to sit in there by myself.'

'Why would you be?'

'Because the composer's pretentious and his music is bloody hard to listen to.'

She laughed. 'Are you hiding from someone too?'

'No, but I promised to buy the music for my landlord. I want to hear it first, so I know what I'm letting myself in for.'

'All right,' she said, and looked relieved.

They skirted the hall toward the grand piano and the rows of tapestry-upholstered seats. In fact there were plenty of other people sitting down already. Probably they weren't overly familiar with Griszt. The man himself was arranging his music on the stand, pink ribbon around his hat as always. He adjusted it in the reflection of the piano's black body, where the lacquer had been polished so well that when he dropped his silk gloves on to the top, they slipped straight onto the keys. Grace slouched down in her chair, not much, but enough for the shoulders of her dress to have lifted above her own.

'Do you know about music, then?'

He shook his head. 'No. I sit at the back of the Royal Albert sometimes.'

'Only you sound rather as if you know,' she said, letting her voice fall low.

'Really?' he said, making an effort to be confusedly flattered. 'He's starting.'

She met the shoulders of her dress again.

As he had expected, the introduction was a flush of unpleasant colours and clever theory. He knew it was unfair to think Griszt pretentious for that; a good number of people listened to, and wrote, music because they liked to hear the sound of mathematics. But he always wanted to say, if he ever fell into the trap of reading critics' good reviews of Griszt concerts, that if the method and the mathematics were championed over the real shape of the thing, there would never be another Mozart. Mozarts would come along, but they would all be banished to comic operetta and never allowed a symphony orchestra. He listened and felt disproportionately sad, and hoped he could persuade Mori not to play it often. Not that he would have to put up with it for long. He wondered if Williamson was here.

The music drifted into a familiar, rushing melody that was almost like the rest, but not. He looked up when he realised he could have hummed it. He looked at the ceiling in order to have a blank space on which to see the colours, thinking it was an absent-minded mistake of his own, but the shades and the shapes were the same. It was the piece Mori played in the mornings. In the programme, it had said that the sonata was new for the occasion.

'That's better,' Grace offered.

He nodded, gradually.

At the end, he excused himself and caught Griszt just as he was about to make his way to the next room, where they were selling sheet music. There was already a queue of girls waiting to see it.

Some of them were arguing about the second movement, singing snatches of it to each other as they tried to remember it.

'Excuse me?'

'Hm?' said Griszt. He was powerfully German, which came through even over a small sound. Vienna Conservatoire.

'The second movement. Have you played it somewhere before?'

'No,' said Griszt, looking wary, 'never. The sheet music was printed only this morning.'

'Steepleton!' Fanshaw's voice.

'Steepleton?' Griszt said. 'Didn't you used to ...'

'Sorry,' said Thaniel. Fanshaw smiled briefly at Griszt before claiming his arm and steering him away.

'You seem to have made friends with Miss Carrow.'

'Oh. It wasn't anything improper—'

'I didn't think it was. But you didn't go to Eton and you're fortunate enough not to be the second son of an earl, so you can get away with bad manners, no, wait for the end of the sentence; would you mind continuing to make friends with her in a socially clunky but determined way for which I will be eternally grateful while I in my gentlemanly meekness fail to get a word in edgeways?'

Thaniel moved his hand gently, but Fanshaw held his fingertips instead and squeezed them by way of showing his urgency. 'Why?'

'Lord Carrow wants to marry her off, and I, alas, *am* the second son of an earl. You've met her. Would you want to marry her? We've known each other since we were children, and don't get me wrong, she's very interesting, but she has always been the madwoman in the attic full of explosives. For God's sake, Steepleton, before I have to go and start an embroidery pattern at the buffet table.'

'I like her,' he said, beginning to laugh.

'Splendid! Good man.'

He took a deep breath as Fanshaw disappeared among cavalry officers, and went to insist on another dance. Grace looked confused.

'Did Fanshaw ask you to keep me occupied?'

'Yes. I'm not just an inept idiot.'

She laughed. But he saw her look toward Fanshaw where he was chatting with the officers. There was strain around her eyes and in her back.

'Do you want to marry Fanshaw?' he said.

'I have to marry someone, if I want somewhere I can work properly. My aunt left a house,' she said, shaking her head, and didn't go into it. Then, without preamble, 'Anyway, I shall be at the Westminster Hotel restaurant tomorrow and I should like to buy you some tea, if you don't work on Sundays. Half past ten?'

'Yes, please. What for?'

'Because you've been awfully kind, and there's no reason for you to be. Have you got a scientific sister?'

'No, but I've got a friend who's ... in the same chemical group, I think.'

She laughed and so did he, until he realised that he had called Mori a friend, despite having spent two weeks taking care not to.

Grace inclined her head to catch his eye. 'Everything all right? Your eyes went rather dark just then.'

He told a vague lie he couldn't remember later.

The ball did not finish until after midnight, and it was nearer one o'clock by the time he turned on to Filigree Street. It was ghostly in the empty lamplight, but not in the way it had been when he had first come after the bombing. Without the rain, he could hear the houses settling as the old timbers cooled, and see which had bachelor tenants from which windows were still lit. The water in the drains below the cobbles muttered. When he passed the bakery, the model Ferris wheel was still turning and glinting, and casting a moving reflection in the glossy surfaces of the cakes, colours all lost with the display lamps turned out. A sugar swan sailed over one of them.

The lights were still on downstairs at number twenty-seven. Odd strains of piano music stopped and started in the parlour. He banged his forehead against the wall. Yes. Music. He had forgotten it. He pushed the door open with his knuckle.

Mori was sitting with one leg curled under him, playing the same section again and again, but he was slipping – he never made it past a difficult octave leap. There was no light except a candle on the empty music stand.

'I'm sorry, I forgot it,' Thaniel said, annoyed with himself.

'Never mind.' He let his hands drop, flexing his fingers until they cracked. 'How was—'

'But it was what you were playing just now,' said Thaniel. 'I asked Griszt about it and he said that it was new for today, but he must have been lying. Play it again. I'm sure it's the same.'

'I can't, I've forgotten it.'

'You don't forget something overnight.'

Mori tacked his shoulders back like a bird deciding whether or not to fly away. 'You might not, but you've got middle age to look forward to. Was Miss Carrow on form?'

His smile was paralysed halfway to fading. 'How did you know that?'

Mori frowned. 'You just ... told me.'

'Oh. I'm more drunk than I think. Or middle age is closer than I think. She was interesting, anyway. I'm about to make some tea, do you want some?'

'No, I think I'd better take my cold to bed. I didn't mean to stay up so late. Night,' he said on his way up the stairs.

While he waited for the kettle to boil, Thaniel looked through the cupboards for some honey. Lemons they had: Mori kept a bowl of them on the kitchen windowsill because the juice was acidic enough to clean oil from mechanical parts. Some searching yielded a small jar with a piece of honeycomb suspended inside. He spooned some into a cup and squeezed out half a lemon too, then stirred in the hot water. He thought, as he was making it, that he should not have been making it. He ought not to have cared whether or not Mori had a cold. Dolly Williamson would have murmured something, if he could have seen. The old warning bells were sounding tired now, though. He took it up with his own tea and tapped on Mori's door with his elbow.

'Let me in, I've got something for you.'

Silence, then the click of the lock. 'What sort of something?' said Mori. He sounded hoarse now. 'Oh. Thank you.'

Thaniel stopped.

Mori pushed his hand over his red eyes. 'Is this lemon?'

'And honey. Try it, it helps with …' Thaniel hesitated. 'Is there something else?'

'No. Go to bed and stop fussing. You're going to need to sleep if you're to make it to the hotel for ten tomorrow.'

He stopped with his own cup almost against his lip. He managed only to turn it into a pause and forced himself to continue and drink, but it was hard to swallow. So Mori, or somebody, had been following him. His hand stiffened slowly around the cup as he tried to gauge how long for. If it had been since the start, they knew he was working for Williamson. He had never made any effort to hide his long visits to the Home Office cellar. But if they knew that, he would have been dragged into a warehouse already and asked what he knew by somebody with a pair of sturdy pliers. It was more recent. Down the back of his neck, like the breath of a man standing just behind him, came the prickling awareness that his life might depend on chatting a little, finishing his tea, and leaving before dawn.

'I don't need that much sleep, if you want some looking after.'

But he had paused for too long. Mori's shoulders lifted as he realised what he had said, and the two small lines between his brows, where he always frowned anyway, deepened. Thaniel lurched toward the stairs but Mori was fast and in front of him before he reached the top. He looked down at Mori's hand on his chest, and then made an X of their arms as he did the same.

'I will push you down these stairs if you don't get out of my way now,' he said softly.

'Don't. I wasn't following you, it's not what you think – please.' His voice had cracks in it and Thaniel could feel his heart through his waistcoat. 'I wasn't following you. I thought that you had told me. You were about to tell me. I'm tired, I get things confused when – you've heard me do it before. I answer the wrong question, I answer the one that you were going to ask, and not the one that you did.'

'What are you saying?'

'I'm – I remember what's possible, and then forget what becomes impossible,' he said without moving. 'You've just watched me do it. You forgot to buy the music, so I've forgotten how to play it. You were about to tell me about the hotel,' he repeated. 'You must have been.'

Thaniel didn't let his hand drop. 'What do you mean, *remember*?'

'I mean not seeing or knowing or deducing.'

'What's possible.'

Mori's shoulder twitched and though he didn't look back, it was plain that he could not forget the steep stairs behind him. Thaniel didn't let him move. 'Past,' Mori said, tracing a line in the air with his fingertip, 'what has been and is. Future.' He opened his hand to show many lines. 'What's possible.'

'Keep going.'

'Likely things are very clear, like recent past, which is … why I get them confused so often. Unlikely things are patchy, like things that happened a long time ago, because there are hours or years of more likely ones stacked up before them.'

Thaniel was quiet for four long ticks of the workshop's locust clock. Mori couldn't look at him for so long. 'In your book – the diary. You wrote about today, but it was wrong.'

'It isn't a diary. It's for …' He struggled. 'Of everything that might happen, only one thing does, but I start out knowing all of them. Sometimes what's unlikely is much better or more interesting than what's likely. So I write it down so that there's a record of it, when I forget. The book is for dead memories. Today was a nearer miss than usual. I wrote it ten years ago when I never thought I would leave Japan.'

Thaniel let his teeth close. He wanted to say that it was nonsense, but what had been written had almost been right. If the dice at the roulette table had rolled differently, Grace wouldn't have walked into him, and Fanshaw wouldn't have come for him just as he was about to buy the music. He would have had time to buy it, and then to remember reading in the Foreign Office file that today, the fourteenth, was Mori's birthday; he would have come back in time to bring the sugar-swan cake and some cheap red wine. They would have gone out into the garden in the warm night. It was so clear that it was a shadow memory, as clear as dying in the Rising Sun.

'I know there's no test for what might have happened. But tomorrow,' Mori said, and nodded slightly when Thaniel's attention sharpened more. 'At the hotel your waiter will drop the tea tray. He's developing palsy in his left hand but thinks it will go away if he ignores it. Miss Carrow will wear green, and there will be tulips on the table. You don't like tulips. It will probably rain at half past ten. There will be a man there with a wolfhound that likes jam, unless there is a traffic accident involving two carriages by Charing Cross.'

Thaniel took his hand back and stepped sideways to let him by. 'I suppose we'll know tomorrow afternoon, then.'

Once Mori had his back to his bedroom door, he was very still. 'You can lock me in if you like,' he said quietly.

Thaniel blinked. He had been gearing himself to make the long walk back to Pimlico, late though it was. 'Yes.'

Mori gave him the key obediently. It had been in his pocket all the while. 'Just ... I know I'd leave a house if I thought the landlord had followed me for whatever reason, but – why did you want to run away just then? What did you think would happen? I'm not really of a size to do anything to you.'

Thaniel watched him for a heartbeat or so. It was either a real question, or it had all been a mad story by a sleepy bombmaker caught off his guard, and who now wanted to know if he had been wholly or partially found out. 'People who follow civil servants aren't usually alone,' he said at last. 'All kinds of things have crossed the wires recently. I've signed nearly as many secrecy oaths as I've coded documents. You know that; you were civil service too.'

'Yes.' He drew his teeth over his lower lip. 'Anyway, I'm sorry.'

'It's all right.'

Mori nodded fractionally and then stepped back. 'You have to push it a bit,' he said as he closed the door.

Thaniel turned the key. The lock ground quietly into place, and from the other side of the door, there was a soft thunk at about shoulder height that he thought was Mori bumping his head against the panel.

Taking the key, he went back to his own room, where he sat down on the bed to take off his cufflinks and borrowed tie. He couldn't think any more. His mind would go no further than to report that his collar was hurting his neck.

FIFTEEN

IT WAS ONLY when the daylight arrived that he saw he had a new dresser frame into which the original drawers had been transposed, with everything in them, including Katsu. The octopus must have approved, because he had brought back the stolen socks, along with a collection of brightly coloured beads and spare watch parts. Thaniel eased out a collar and was putting it on when the drawer closed by itself. Katsu whirred grumblingly from inside.

Once he had dressed, he went to Mori's door to unlock it, but then stopped on the landing. Through the slim balusters, which were made of varying shades of oak in varying stages of newness and oldness, he could see that the workshop door was ajar. He put the key back into his pocket and went down.

The electric lights hummed on as soon as he crossed the threshold. The sound made him pause, because it was easy to hear through the floor upstairs. Some long seconds of quiet went by before he stepped inside.

Beginning furthest from the front door, he made a search of the cabinets and the desk drawers. In the cabinets were watches in boxes, some labelled with the names of the customers who had ordered them. He checked everything, but there was nothing more interesting than a set of marine chronometers already paid for by the navy. The drawers were mainly full of clockwork parts – raw cogs and springs, tiny diamond bearings, different sizes of chain and wire – and when he did find one of papers, it was only receipts and an accounts ledger, kept in neat Japanese numbers. On top was a bill from a goldsmith for watch cases.

Behind the papers was a plain box, with a square cut from the lid as if it were planning an inlay. He opened it briefly and closed it when he saw nothing inside but clockwork, but opened it again when it pinged musically. With the lid open wholly, a quiet song played. The turning music tumbler was still exposed because the base of the box hadn't been put in yet. A tiny silver girl began to spin, and her parasol opened little by little. He watched it for longer than he meant to. Annabel had had a music box when they were children, but since they quickly became boring for anyone over the age of four, he hadn't seen one for a long time. The silver girl slowed under her parasol as the springs ran down. He could see them loosening. Before she stopped, he closed the box and put it back.

The last drawer clinked as he opened it. He had disturbed a wide rack of glass test tubes. He glanced toward the empty doorway and then back at them. They were all stopped with identical corks and unlabelled. At first he thought that there was nothing in them, but when he held one to the light, its shadow showed that gas had settled in the base. If he held it very close, he could make out the tiny particles swimming inside. One of them snapped blue and a hairline spark flickered out to the glass.

A clockwork bird fluttered down on to the desk then with a rush of the same chemical smell he had noticed before. He had to set the vial down to catch it. As soon as he closed his hand around it, it fell still. He found the catch that opened it and exposed its workings, then slowly sat down on the high chair by the microscope to look.

There was a square space in the centre of the clockwork. It was filled with a tightly bound paper block that smelled sharply of salt and chemicals, and in a neat, red Japanese stamp, it was marked inflammable.

He jerked his hands away from it, too quickly. His elbow nicked the vial he had put down, and he couldn't catch it before it spun off the edge of the desk and cracked on the floor. It was only small, so the smash of the glass was hardly more than a sad plink, but it crashed in the silence. He snapped the bird's casing closed and threw it into the air, where it flew off again to the window, fluffing its silver feathers.

On the floor, grey not-quite-dust rose from the glass shards. Almost straightaway his eyes felt dry and a strange sigh came from an old cup of yesterday's tea. The liquid level was retreating, leaving a green stain behind it where the tealeaves were stranded around the sides. He stood up and stepped back, but the dust had already formed a patch of dark mist just above the desk. The air tasted of tin. He retreated to the door and was about fetch Mori when there was a snap and the fog patch began to rain. The water pattered down on the floor, just catching the edge of the desk and the half-emptied teacup.

It stopped only when the little cloud was exhausted, and left everything nearby looking as though he had spectacularly dropped a cup of water. He stood for what felt like a long time, waiting to see if it would do anything else. Eventually he touched his finger-tip to the nearest wet patch. Once he was sure it was only water, he cleaned it up as well as he could and hung the wet tea towels to dry on the back of the kitchen chairs. Gunpowder and nameless chemicals to make emergency rain. He went back upstairs to be sure that Mori was still there. The key was stiff in the lock and left a dent in his middle finger when he pushed it. He eased the door open, almost expecting an empty room, but Mori was still asleep, his head on his arm and the sun on the back of his neck. Someone might have dropped him there.

On Sundays, only a skeleton staff worked at the temporary police headquarters in the Home Office cellars, and Dolly Williamson was not among them. Thaniel left a note on his desk, with thick underlinings, before going to find the hotel where he had arranged to meet Grace. It began to rain.

The hotel was closer than he had imagined. He had walked past the wedge-shaped building a dozen times thinking that it was owned by the government; it was opposite Westminster Abbey and nearly as big. Coming in from the rain, the guests left their umbrellas in a mahogany rack by the door, where a steward took them away one by one to dry. The vaulted ceiling glittered with broad chandeliers. He watched their rainbows instead of the other diners, who wore clothes from Savile Row and laughed over tortes piled with marzipan fruit, and into crystal glasses. Beside him, the clatter of the rain on the window pane sharpened. He shifted. He felt as though somebody were about to tell him to get out, although nobody had shown any sign of it.

Grace appeared from behind a waiter, her hair wet. He only had time to half stand up before she bumped into her chair. 'Miss Carrow.'

'Miss Carrow? I thought we'd settled on Grace,' she said, re-arranging the tulips between them so that she could see him past them. They shed a few of their over-fragile petals, and as her fingernails brushed the rim, the little crystal vase sang. She was wearing green again.

'How are you? Have you ordered?' she said.

'Not yet. The waiter thinks I'm a tramp.'

'Pish.' She lifted her hand and a waiter glided over at once. After ordering tea and scones, she leaned back in her chair and studied him. 'You didn't say how you were,' she said.

'I know, sorry. I'm still thinking.'

She laughed. 'Interesting.'

'Any progress with Fanshaw after I left?'

'No. I think I might be doomed to live in the room under my mother's until I stab myself with a pair of compasses. Or her.'

He smiled. 'That bad?'

She opened her eyes wide at him. 'Do you not have a mother?'

'No, I never knew her.'

'Oh, God, sorry.'

'No; as I say, I never knew her. She might have been dreadful. Dad was ... mainly he didn't talk, he only twitched his fishing flies in a telling way.'

Her ease came back again. She slouched forward to put her fore-arms on the table. 'Just you?'

'No, I've a sister.' That made him pause, because he had thought of Annabel less than he should have lately. He was a week late with the money he usually sent. 'She lives in Edinburgh with two boys.'

'Oh, right? What's the husband do? I'm trying to find a relative you don't like so you understand my mother.'

'Hah. No, he was a soldier. Afghanistan. I only met him twice. He seemed like a bastard actually, but I might have misunderstood. He was from Glasgow. Everything past "good morning" was a bit of a blur.'

'I see. Everyone you know seems to be dead. You'll have to take my word for it that mothers become unbearable after you're about nineteen.'

'I believe you, I believe you. Is it not quite a big house, though?'

She ducked her head once. 'It is. The Sahara wouldn't be big enough.'

'Oh. Suddenly I feel lucky.'

'You damn well should. The luck of orphans is greatly understated by the press.' She paused. 'But then you must be supporting the sister?'

'It's no trouble.'

'That is almost certainly a lie.'

'It … is,' he admitted, and had to laugh with her. When they stopped laughing, there was a strange pause in which she only watched him, her lips pressed together as though she were keeping herself from saying something else. He cast around for something to say himself, but was saved by the waiter arriving with the tea and scones. Across from them, a wolfhound puppy looked up and cocked its ears hopefully. It was tethered to the chair of a big man in tweed. While the waiter fussed over the arrangement of the tea and the cream, the dog clambered into the man's lap and put its nose in his bowl of jam. Thaniel bit the tip of his tongue. Because he was watching for it, he was quick enough to hear the clinking of shaking crockery and to catch the edge of the tray when it dropped.

'Oh – I'm sorry,' the waiter mumbled.

Thaniel gave back the tray and looked him in the eye, but it was impossible to see if he was only embarrassed, or frightened to be asked if an oriental man had paid him to do it. 'You should go to a doctor about your hand.'

'I ... yes. Yes, I've been meaning to.' Pink to his ears, the waiter left again.

Grace lifted her eyebrows. 'You're quick,' she said admiringly. 'You know, paperwork and telegraphy are usually what Special Branch men say to put one off the scent. No?'

He had to look at the swirl of the cream rather than at her. 'No. My landlord told me about it yesterday.'

'Oh, he comes here often?'

He teetered before coming down on the far side. She would be able to tell him if it was possible, at least, or she would know of another scientist who could. 'No. I can't decide whether it's real or not, but he just knows things. He knew about you, he knew your name, he knew you'd invited me here. He knew about that dog over there, and the waiter's hand. The rain. What you would wear.'

She had begun to sit further forward halfway through the list. 'Why, in what context? General showing off?'

'No. I thought he'd been following me and I was an inch off pushing him down the stairs.'

'And it's all correct?'

'Yes. But I've heard of channelling ghosts. I haven't heard of predicting jam-loving wolfhounds. Is that possible, even?'

She pushed the tip of her tongue into her teeth. 'Of course it's largely fraud, but the reason there are so many successful frauds is that it is extremely possible. It's easily tested, mind.'

'Is it?'

'Of course. You just need a blind test of some kind. Like, laying out seven cards face down. If you're not a fraud, you can predict all of them.'

'Might need to be a bit cleverer than that,' he said, watching the rain against the window in the surface of his tea. He was so used to green now that brown tasted odd. 'I think it must be fraud. But he had thought about it carefully. He'll know some card tricks.'

'You look as though this has been upsetting you.'

He lifted his eyes. 'If he's lying, he's been following me. Often. Which would be less unsettling if I didn't work where I work.'

'Well – why don't you let me test him, then?'

'How?'

'Oh, good evening, I'm Thaniel's friend, I've brought cards. Play poker? Excellent.' She inclined her head. 'I know what to look for, it's no trouble. It's actually to do with what I was working on before I left university.'

'Are you sure?'

'Tomorrow evening at seven, will that be too early?'

'No, that's good; I'll be at home by six,' he said, and then caught his tongue between his back teeth. He couldn't remember when he had started to think of Filigree Street as home.

She nodded once. 'Good. Tomorrow at seven it is. Address?'

He had to borrow a pen and a piece of paper from a waiter. 'Thank you,' he said quietly.

'No, no. Glad to be of service; it will make up for my useless damselling last night.' She poured him some more tea, the tendons standing in her wrist under the weight of the pot, and talked about the weather and Newton. She left after an hour, after paying for both of them. He watched her go past the window, fast in the rain and peculiar in her green dress. Her short hair made her look like a workhouse girl.

Mori was not in the workshop when he arrived back at Filigree Street. Katsu waved three or four tentacles at him from the desk, where he was prowling after the clockwork birds. They flew away to the window display in a cross fluster as Thaniel passed by, and the little octopus dived down the table leg to follow them, his metal joints sighing sea-coloured as he crossed the floor. Hoping that Mori was out, Thaniel went upstairs to take off his cufflinks, and to think of how to explain tomorrow's visit. When he reached the landing, however, he heard a rush of water. Turning a very sharp corner past his own bedroom was another, tiny stairway. He had thought when he first arrived that it led to the attic, but the room at the top was a plumbed-in bathroom.

Although the top of the house seemed like an odd place for it, he had realised as he got to grips with the geography of the old building that it was directly above the boiler. The water came out of the silver taps scalding, with the fearsomely clean smell of hotel steam presses.

'The kettle's just boiled downstairs,' Mori said through the door, which was open on its latch.

'Can I come in?'

'Yes?'

Thaniel opened the door, then shut it again. 'You're in the bath.'

'What did you think I was doing?'

'Cleaning.'

'I'm not talking to you through the door. Come on. I'm not a girl.'

He sat down on the floor with his back to the door, where he could see Mori only from his shoulders upward. With his hair wet, he was sharper than usual, and the water shone along the bones in his spine. Although he often went about with his sleeves folded back, his skin was the same colour across his arms and his chest. He wasn't dark, but not pale either; where a white man's veins would have shown through blue, there was nothing. It made him look more finished.

'So, I've invited Grace Carrow here tomorrow night,' Thaniel said. Turning in the air between them was the morning's timely rain and everything that had been correct at the hotel, but he talked past it.

'I'd rather not have unmarried women in the house,' Mori said carefully.

'She's a Belgravia lady, she's not coming in the capacity of an unmarried woman. And I'm sure she will have a chaperone.'

'I can stay out of the way for an evening, then.'

'I'd like you to meet her.'

'I wouldn't.'

Thaniel pushed his hand over his mouth. 'But you'll like her. She's clever. She's a physicist. I think she might be a suffragist.'

'No. I haven't got time for women's suffrage.'

'But she – what?' he said.

Mori did not quite move, but the bone in his wrist shifted. His arm was resting on the edge of the bath. 'Women won't have a vote until it's in the fiscal interest of the state to give it to them. They'll have it when all able-bodied men die and not before. Protesting now is pointless.'

'Good. Reasonable as usual.'

'Do you still want to expose her to me?'

'Yes,' Thaniel insisted, and then tried to swallow the lump in his throat. 'Look, you were right about everything at the hotel. You can do what you say, so you know I don't mean for anything improper. I like her, that's all, she's interesting, but she's from the sort of family who will have me horsewhipped if I don't see her in the company of someone respectable. Barons are respectable. Please?'

Mori looked across and was, briefly, a languageless, inhuman thing rescued from the sea and asked for an impious favour. He was not his ordinary self until he moved again. 'For the sake of your not being horsewhipped, then.'

'Thank you.'

Mori let his hand slide from the edge of the bath and back underwater. 'You will, of course, be buying the good cocoa from Harrods, since you forgot the music, and you locked me in all night, and I don't like Miss Carrow.'

Thaniel hitched. He had meant to squeeze his wrist. 'Yes. Of course. Then – tomorrow at seven?'

'Mm. And not that Brazilian rubbish. The green packet from Peru.'

'Yes.'

When he reached the bottom of the stairs, he stopped with his hand flat on the polished orb on the banister. The rail was squeaking because Katsu was swinging from it by two tentacles. Watching the octopus play, he held his thoughts very still, and eased open an imagining of what it would be if Mori were telling the truth. He stopped himself and banged it shut before he could see too much. He went back out in the rain to buy the cocoa.

*

He left for work the next morning much earlier than usual, when the air was still cool and his wisdom teeth felt sharp from not having eaten. While he waited in the Home Office cellar, opening and closing the lid of his watch, a young constable gave him a cup of tea that tasted of dust. The dust was everywhere; the policemen were settling in, and everything had been moved. The filing cabinets stood like jumbled building blocks at the edges of the room now, surrounded by stacks of mouldering papers and an assortment of horrible, expensively framed paintings. Unwanted gifts from foreign emissaries. He opened his watch again. Williamson came around a bank of cabinets and stopped when he saw Thaniel at his desk.

'Thaniel. Found your note. Come— with me,' he said quietly.

Thaniel followed him along the rows of desks and cabinets. They passed through a small door and along a corridor, unlit and pitch black, so that he had to follow the silver resoundings of Williamson's boots, and then into the light again and a small room with brooms stacked by one wall. A table had been set up in the centre. Mr Spindle waited on the other side, his hands resting on either side of a blackened mess of clockwork.

'If you could repeat your findings to Mr Steepleton here,' Williamson said. His stammer was gone again.

'Why?' said Spindle, sounding irked. Without his tri-lensed loupes, his green eyes were of an ordinary size. He looked like any other shopkeeper. 'I thought you were fetching the Home Secretary?'

'The Home Secretary doesn't live with our man. Go on.'

Spindle pursed his lips, but he lifted a pair of long tweezers, and handed Thaniel a magnifying glass. 'As you wish. You'll need to be closer than that,' he said.

'I can see.'

'Very well. You see the mainspring here? I showed it to you before. Gold and steel, as per Mr Mori's style. The main mechanism uses jewel bearings of course, as all good clockwork does, but these are industrial-grade diamonds. Rubies are far more standard. I have here a comparison watch I bought from Mori's workshop last week; as you see, there are diamonds inside. Nothing like as many as in yours,' he added to Thaniel, and glanced at Williamson. 'I still think it's foolish to believe he has that sort of money to—'

'I've seen his records at the Foreign Office.' Thaniel interrupted. 'He entered the country as Baron Mori, with a letter of confirmation from the Minister of the Interior in Japan.'

'And how would one check the veracity of a letter from the Minister of the Interior in Japan?' Spindle laughed.

'By wire,' Thaniel said. 'From my office. It's Japan, not Mars.' He had done it last week, when he was sending through a reply to diplomatic dispatches. It had been only an overhead note, aimed at the operator rather than the official channels. The reply had come through quickly only a few hours later; the clerk had not even needed to check. He had met Mori, who used to come to the Legation often as a translator on behalf of Minister Ito. Same man: remarkable northern accent, knack for dressing sensibly despite belonging to a nation of civil servants who favoured morning coats with buttonhole flowers. Not to be faced over the bridge table.

'Well, I suppose I'll have to defer to the spy on matters of espionage. Shall we return to this? You see these small cogs here? They are unusually small. It takes small hands to achieve work this fine.'

'Workhouse children make clockwork parts.'

'So do oriental watchmakers. Finally, this large cog.' He lifted it out. It was blackened and bent from the immense heat of the exploding bomb, but still carried a glint of silver in places. 'You can just see the engraving pattern on it. Vines and leaves, yes? I believe his name means woods.' Spindle set the cog down and opened the sample watch. Inside the lid was one of Mori's hand-drawn watchpapers. 'Same pattern. Short of his having signed the thing, I rather think all this is conclusive.'

Thaniel turned to Williamson. 'All this means is that whoever made the bomb did it with reliable clockwork, and Mori's is the most reliable in London. If Mr Spindle here were as good, it would be his work in the bomb.'

Spindle flinched at that.

'I know,' Williamson said, 'which is why I haven't sent anyone round to arrest him straightaway.' He sighed and took Thaniel's arm. 'Come back out here. Thank you, Mr Spindle. If you could wait here a moment longer.'

Thaniel let himself be guided out into the main cellar, but then he shook Williamson's hand from his arm. 'You can't go to the Home Secretary with that, Dolly, you know you can't.'

'Of course I won't, I was going to make him wait for an hour and then tell him the Home Secretary can't see him. He's a pompous little tick; I like to waste his time when I can. Sick of the sight of him. He's been with us since the Victoria bomb.'

Thaniel eased, but not much. They made their way to Williamson's desk in silence. Thaniel's supplies had reached it; there was a real wastepaper basket now, and a packet of tea serving as a paperweight.

Williamson took a breath and then paused. 'But I am going to investigate those explosives you found.'

'Now?' Thaniel said heavily.

'Tomorrow. There's another raid today. We're still chasing down some of the other men involved. The ones who put the damn thing in place, in fact.'

'Then what happens to him?'

'How do you mean?'

'You go to the house, and then . . .'

'We hold him there while we search. When we find something, he'll be arrested.'

'What if I'm wrong, what if it's nothing? You'll just shake it out of him?'

Williamson tucked his head down as if he were talking to a child. 'I'd suggest you stay in an hotel— tomorrow night,' he said. The debate was over: his stutter had returned. He sighed through his nose. 'I know you like this fellow, but even without everything else, an inch square of dynamite in a watchmaker's shop worries me. There's no telling how many *other* inch-long packets he might have, and . . . small amounts are becoming popular. Easier to bury in clockwork, harder to disarm. A bomb is not a cluster of dynamite sticks any more.'

Thaniel had nothing to say to that. They shook hands across the desk.

'Stay with him until tomorrow,' Williamson said. 'Last leg now.'

SIXTEEN

A CRASH CAME FROM downstairs. Both of her brothers were at home. Since it was six o'clock, the servants' dinner hour, neither the butler nor Alice was about the house to scold them. Grace sighed and checked the deck of playing cards again.

That morning, she had gone into town with Alice and bought two identical packs of cards. After removing the ace of spades from one and inserting it into the other, she had replaced the tampered version in its package and resealed it. It was a simple test, but having thought about it all Sunday afternoon, it seemed like the best way. Anything more complicated and Thaniel's friend would know that something was going on. The results would be clear. If he took out the extra ace before they played, it would go a long way to proving Thaniel's hypothesis. If he did not, it was safe to assume he was a fraud. He was a watchmaker, and Grace had never met a mechanically minded person who could leave a mistake in place. He would take the extra card out if he knew it was there. He had no reason not to.

Beside the mirror, the barometer clicked around to 'rain' as the mercury column shrank. She watched it for a few seconds, then looked back through the open door. The corridor was empty; Alice had only just gone down to the kitchen. They had agreed to leave in twenty minutes. Grace slid the tampered cards into the pocket of her summer coat and draped it over her arm. It would be interesting to see how the watchmaker reacted to an early and unchaperoned arrival.

She was at the bottom of the stairs when her brothers charged past. They were not much younger than she was, nineteen and

169

twenty-one, but whenever they were on leave, they regressed to childhood.

'Out of the way, out of the way!' shouted James. He was carrying a rugby ball.

Grace flattened herself against the wall. 'You are not playing rugby in the house.'

'No, we haven't got enough men. Do you want to play?' William asked, beaming. He was the youngest, and Grace suspected that it was he who had acquired the rugby ball. The game had been unheard of when Grace was small, but William had played it at Eton when it first became popular, and now he spoke of it in a reverent tone he normally saved only for women and rifles. Since she had once been with him to see the Harlequins play at Hampstead, she had tried to convince them both to take up cricket instead. Cricket had rules: one was not allowed to stamp on the head of another player and pass it off as enthusiasm.

'No,' she said. She peered past them into the drawing room. 'Did you break that vase?'

'Oh, probably. James! Here!'

It was, she decided, nothing to do with her. She was busy.

Outside, the heat was as viscous and sticky as honey. It rippled along the marble fronts of the townhouses. As she walked, summer coat still over her arm, the deck of cards was a sharp shape in one pocket. Her skin prickled, and she rubbed her wrists to brush away the thunder flies. They were everywhere today – she could see them in the air, like grain on a photograph.

The storm clouds were ahead as she turned out of Belgravia. Good.

By the time she reached Filigree Street, the rain was sheeting and she looked as though she had fallen in the Thames. She had expected to shiver on the porch and squeak to be let in, but in fact the door of number twenty-seven opened just as she was coming up the steps. Inside, Thaniel smiled.

'I'm so sorry, the rain…' She watched as the water skittered into a row of empty bottles on the bottom step. She had seen the servants at home put them out too, but no one had mentioned what they might be for. The bottle necks were too narrow to be an efficient way of catching rain water.

'I know, we saw the clouds coming from the workshop. Mori's making tea. Come in, it's warm, we've got the fire going now ...' He trailed off and his gaze eased over her shoulder. 'Is there no one with you?'

'No,' she said. Mori. The name sounded familiar, but she could not remember why. 'I'm sorry. I was supposed to have, but my brothers were playing rugby in the house and I decided I'd had enough, so I left without my chaperone.'

'Rugby? Why?'

'God knows,' she said. He stepped aside to let her in. Taking the pack of cards from the pocket, she hung her wet coat up on the hooks in the hallway. 'They're soldiers; when they're not charging at Africans they want to charge at each other.'

He showed her into a neat parlour. It was small but warm, with a piano in one corner and a low Chinese table by the fire. An armchair had been relegated to the window. He saw her note the odd arrangement.

'I hope you don't mind sitting on the floor ...'

'No, that's quite all right, it's Bohemian. Anyway, I'm freezing.' She dropped down on the rug with her back to the fire and he knelt opposite, straight, like a pianist. She had thought he might be, despite his protestations at the ball.

'Shall I fetch you a blanket?' he asked.

Grace coughed. 'No, no need.'

'You've gone blue.'

'I'll warm up in a minute.' Her eye caught on a grey jumper folded over the arm of the chair. It was the kind that sailors and workmen wore. 'Actually, would you mind if I borrowed that?'

'Oh ... it's not mine, but I'm sure Mori wouldn't mind.' He fetched it for her. When she took it, she found that it was exactly the right size for her. She pulled it on. It smelled of lemons, and the wool was expensive and soft.

They both twisted around when a clink of china came from the door.

He had not told her what Mori looked like, and she had imagined a grave, traditionally dressed man of an age with Matsumoto's father. He was not. His clothes were Western and his hair was short and dyed, and he looked very young. When he leaned down to set the tea things on the table, he gave her a polite smile. The smile drew lines around his eyes that gave away his real age, but they disappeared when the smile faded. She smiled back, feeling shabby.

'Mr Mori, I'm delighted to make your acquaintance,' she said. She held out her hand across the table. 'Grace Carrow. I'm sorry to have stolen your jumper. And I'm sorry I'm so early.' She watched him carefully.

'Never mind.' He shook her hand with a grip too strong for his thin fingers, and knelt down beside Thaniel. He seemed not to mind her being early, but that was as much an oriental trait as a clairvoyant one. 'Where's your chaperone?' He had exactly Thaniel's accent. He must have learned his English from him.

'I had to go without her, I'm afraid.'

He looked at her as though he could read her motives listed on the back of her skull. 'Are you certain you should be here alone?'

'She's already inside now,' Thaniel pointed out. Mori hadn't taken his eyes from her. She shifted and straightened up.

'Yes, of course,' he said at last, then held out a plate of beautiful, multi-coloured cakes to her. She didn't recognise them, but she took one anyway, curious. It was sponge and cream inside, and easily the most wonderful thing she had eaten for months.

'My God – where did you find these? They're delicious.'

'He bakes,' Thaniel said.

Grace expressed her admiration and took one more, then stopped. She could have eaten half a dozen, but she was bulky next to Mori, and it was making her increasingly uncomfortable. 'So, why London, if you don't mind my asking?' she said.

'The best clockwork in the world is here.' The more he spoke, the stranger his voice was. It was too low for his frame, and although even Matsumoto had a trace of his native sibilance sometimes through all the Oxford elocution lessons, Mori didn't.

'Oh, of course.' She stopped, then pulled out her swallow watch. 'Hold on. Clockwork. This is one of yours, isn't it?'

He angled it down with one fingertip. 'Yes. I sold this one to a William Carrow. Your brother?'

'It was a present. It's excellent,' she added, opening the back to show Thaniel the interior bird. 'I knew your name was familiar. For some reason I imagined that you were Italian. Oh, I've brought some cards,' she added, itchily aware that he could have nothing to say against an accusation of being Italian. She hadn't imagined that speaking to him would be difficult, but it was. For all he was more fluent, he was far more foreign than Matsumoto. The way he sat had a schooled look to it, and so did the care he was taking over the tea. He had turned her cup so that the blue Chinese design on it faced her, and Thaniel's. He had done it while they talked and she didn't think he meant either of them to notice it was ritual. But it was. The china deserved it, too. She recognised the designs. The Belgravia house was full of examples of her mother's old auction house habits. It was Jingdezhen china, more than three hundred years old and still uncracked. Matsumoto had said once or twice that there was something of a generation gap at home, but she hadn't known it was so wide.

'What are we playing?' said Thaniel.

'Poker?' said Grace. 'Do you know that?'

'I'll lose, but yes.' He looked at Mori. 'Heard from the British Legation in Tokyo that you've got a bit of a reputation at cards.'

'What are you doing talking about me in dispatches?'

'Finding out whether or not we should be playing with real money. Have you got any matches?'

'It wasn't that bad,' Mori said, but he took a box of matches from his waistcoat pocket and flicked them to him.

'Really. I heard it was a house in Osaka.'

'Nobody wants a house in Osaka,' he said, and it was strange to hear him switch suddenly to foreign pronunciation in the middle of his English. 'It would mean you had to live in Osaka.'

'What's wrong with it?'

'It's like … Birmingham.'

'We're still playing with matches,' Thaniel said. Grace smiled. Mori saw her and smiled too, apologetically. He had the natural quiet of a man who did not entertain often. She slid the deck across the table to him. She had taken care to put the jokers at the top and the extra ace a few cards up from the bottom. He wouldn't find it by accident.

'Will you do the honours?' she said.

'Mm.' He picked it up and untied the string on the paper packet. He unwrapped the paper fold by fold and then folded it up again once it was off the box. That, at least, she had seen Matsumoto do, though she had no idea why either of them bothered. The pedantry was faintly grating, but it made her more certain he would take out the ace if he knew it was there.

'Ten each to start with?' Thaniel said, counting matchsticks.

Mori set the first joker on to the table, then set the second precisely over it.

'Stingy,' said Grace, trying to disguise how she was watching Mori.

'I haven't played in years,' Thaniel grumbled in his good-natured way. 'Last time I lost to my sister.'

'Oh, yes, what was her name again?'

'Annabel. She lives in Scotland.'

Mori picked up three-quarters of the pack, exposing an ace of spades, took it out and set it down on top of the jokers. He put all three on the floor, out of the way, and dealt the cards.

If it was a trick, she could not see how it was done. She spent the first game thinking about it, to no avail. In the meantime, he played like a professional, without looking at his cards. When he won, he turned them over to show a handful of middle numbers. He made a matchstick house out of the winnings, with too much concentration. He was bored, more than bored, although he had been politely careful enough not to let it show in his face. She saw Thaniel watching him too and their eyes met past his shoulder. She nodded slightly and Thaniel looked as though he might break soon. She couldn't tell what it was, because he was sitting and chatting naturally, but something about him was being held together with willpower and drawing pins, and it made her suspect that there was more to it than being followed and generally worried.

'You're good,' she said to Mori.

'I had too much spare time and too many brothers when I was young.' The matchstick house had a chimney. He had very steady hands.

'I'll make some more tea,' Thaniel said.

Mori surfaced. 'Would it be all right if we were to play something else? With dice?'

'I've got backgammon upstairs.'

'Why? You've done well,' said Grace.

'It's not fair on the two of you.'

'Oh, bold words.'

He sighed. 'Factual ones, really. Sorry.'

As Thaniel went out, he turned sideways as if he was avoiding something. The something soon appeared, in the shape of a life-sized but very clearly clockwork octopus. It shuffled into Mori's lap, seemed to survey the table, and then set about dismantling his matchstick house.

'Oh, what is *that*?' she said, impressed.

'This is Katsu.' He held it up a little and it coiled around his hands.

'Ka...'

'Katsu. It means Victor. For the Queen actually.'

'Christ, that's amazing. May I see?'

'Yes. Careful, he's heavy. You can see inside if you like.' He picked the octopus up and passed it over the table to her. When she took it, it was weighted in the way a living thing would have been, toward the centre, but as he had said, much heavier. 'The clip at the back there.'

Katsu sat still while she opened the panel at the back of its head. The interior gleamed with strata of clockwork, bolted together with miniature diamond bearings. She knew enough about mechanics to follow the cogs until she found the gears. They were tiny, and there were hundreds. It made her feel like a giant looking down into a mine. 'Good God. Are these random gears? How did you make them?'

'Spinning magnets,' he said. He didn't seem surprised to be asked. 'Hence that insulation, otherwise he goes wrong whenever he goes near the workshop generator.'

'That's ... I've never seen machinery like this. This is years ahead of ordinary calculating engines.' She looked up. 'Decades.'

'No, no. Clockwork is much further along than most people think. Nobody patents anything. Factories would put watch-makers out of business.'

'I suppose.' She clipped Katsu back together and the octopus waved three arms at her as she lifted it by its middle to see how it moved. Perfectly. She tickled it and it curled up. Whatever the unseen advances of clockwork, they were not this advanced. A calculating engine could just about do its twelve times table: there was nothing in the world that could mimic life. She watched Mori closely and decided that at some point in the next minute or so, she would drop the octopus. He gave her an odd look.

'Careful,' he said.

She set it gently back on to the floor, where it edged under the table again, back to Mori and the matchsticks. His expression cleared. 'Fantastic,' she said.

'Thank you. Have another cake, they don't last.'

The sun had come out again at last, and in the warm, late light, the hard icing gleamed different shades of blue and green and red, bright enough to be a pile of sea anemones. She took one and was halfway through it before she saw that he hadn't joined her.

'Aren't you having any?' Grace said. She felt freshly clumsy. If they had stood together, she was reasonably sure they would be about the same size, but he had a knack of taking up less space.

'I don't much like them, actually. I made them for Mr Steepleton. He sees colours in music. He says that if you play these colours in this order on the piano, you come out with "Greensleeves",' he said, nodding to the careful arrangement.

Grace studied the cakes, and doubted that it was a real thing so much as a common metaphor used by the musically minded for those who were not. She had heard one of Matsumoto's choir friends talk the same way. He had been an odd person. 'Whatever the tune, you should make these more often. They're very appealing.'

He lifted his head and there was fathoms-deep dislike in his eyes, but then they were only mirrors again and Thaniel was coming back with the tea. He pushed the door gently shut with his elbow, his hands occupied with the tray and the backgammon case under his arm. She watched him and liked his quietness, then stopped when she realised that Mori was watching her.

Whatever knack he had for cards didn't carry over to dice. They were all more or less equally lucky and unlucky, and though there was much less skill in it and much more chance, he seemed to like it better.

Sunset had come and gone by the time Thaniel took her to find a cab. In the dark, the crooked street was warm, even though she had returned Mori's jumper, and the drying pavements smelled of rain. Lines of washing hung between the leaning gables. There was almost no noise except the hissing gas lamps and the singing of unseen crickets. They walked in silence for a while.

'He is certainly a genius,' she said at last. 'That octopus is far beyond anything the rest of the world can produce. I put in that extra ace, and he took it out, which means that either somebody from my household told him about it, or you're right about him.' She looked up at him. 'That said, why would he bother? I know that mad geniuses have their pastimes, but fooling a Foreign Office clerk for the sake of it is ... odd.'

He was quiet for too long. She saw his chest rise before he spoke. 'Six months ago, a watch was left in my flat in Pimlico. It let off an alarm a few seconds before the Yard bomb exploded. Saved my life. I had it analysed. The alarm was set for that time and on that day, and no other day. I'm living here because the police told me to. It's possible that he's the bombmaker. He could have told me all this to explain away the watch, which otherwise must have been meant for someone else. A big lie for a big mistake.'

'A bombmaker. That adds a certain urgency.' She thought about it. 'All right. Well, if it's a fraud, then he has someone in my house. It's the only way he could have known about that extra card. And what I would wear yesterday. I think I'd better speak to my maid before I come to any conclusions. I'll send a telegram as soon as I know.'

'Send it fast, if you can. The police are coming tomorrow.'

'Of course.' She took his arm. At first he almost pulled away, but then he leaned against her fractionally and she squeezed his hand. 'You seem to trust me an awful lot,' she said quietly.

'You're a scientist.'

'Not any more.'

'You never explained about that.'

'Well, I've left university.'

'But you were talking about a house of your aunt's, or—'

'Oh. It's … yes,' she said, surprised that he remembered. 'She left me a house, but as part of a dowry, held in trust to be handed to my future husband because the women of the family are traditionally stupid and my father won't put it in my name. If I want it, and its very spacious and laboratory-sized cellar, I need to marry. There's money too, which is also not in my name. Very simple really.' She thought of stopping there, but his was an open, inviting quiet. 'But not likely. The main candidate was Francis Fanshaw, which you know, but he's a widower. His boy is five. Sensibly enough he doesn't want the child running about after a stepmother whose cellar is full of noxious chemicals.'

'So go and rob a bank and do your work in secret in an attic somewhere,' he said, with unusual force.

Grace had the impression of having come to some thin ice. 'You sound as if you know what you're talking about.'

'I don't know any science.'

'You know something.'

He looked as if he wouldn't say, but then, 'I used to play the piano. But then my sister's husband died and so I had to start sending her money, and music isn't lucrative. But I mean it,' he continued, without giving her space to be sorry for him. 'However you do it,

178

doing it is better than giving it up. You can publish under my name if you like. I can send your post on and no one would know.'

She looked up. 'Would you really?'

'You didn't have to come here today. If I could set you up in a laboratory, I would.'

They were both quiet for a few paces.

'Well, you could, actually,' Grace said at last. 'All that's needed is a warm body. I want my laboratory. Do you want a house in Kensington?'

He laughed, not much. She felt it through his ribs. 'Your family would have a thing or two to say about that.'

'No, no. Unsuitable matches are very easy to make if one just walks around Hyde Park until midnight. Immediate disgrace and a certain urgency ensues. One of the Satterthwaite girls did it a few years ago so that she could marry a Catholic Frenchman. When a sign says don't walk on the grass, one hops.'

He was looking ahead, up the long road and its dots of street lamps to the dark gates of Hyde Park. 'No, I can't do that.'

'It was only a thought,' she mumbled. 'I didn't mean to sound serious.'

'No, I mean the park isn't safe. There's a pub here.'

She looked up. 'What?'

He let his breath out. 'My sister has two boys. She gets by on an army pension and what I send, which isn't much, even now. They go to school at church on Sundays and that's all, I think. If I could ...'

'They could go to Harrow,' she said, and he looked away as if it were a dangerous imagining that he didn't want to touch or examine too well. She watched it make him wary, but couldn't think what to say to reassure him. Money didn't matter when there would always be more of it, but she didn't want to put it like that. It was such a commonly spoken thing that it was hard to see the real meaning. 'Why don't I explain exactly what it would entail, and then you can decide?' she said eventually.

He nodded and held the pub door open for her. Pipe smoke and men's laughter washed out to meet them.

SEVENTEEN

SHE KNEW WHEN she came through the front door that the house was not sleeping yet. The air didn't have that undisturbed taste, and the lamps were burning well on fresh-cut wicks. Before she could take off her coat, Alice rushed down the stairs, her eyes blotchy, and ushered her into her father's study. He was sitting behind the desk, where the density of the smoke around him showed that he had not moved for some time.

'What's this about a telegraphist from the Foreign Office?' he said. 'I was about to fetch out the police.'

'He has a friend who might be a clairvoyant, which has a bearing on what I was working on at Oxford, so I went along. I did tell everyone where I was going.'

'Is this clairvoyant friend of the male or female persuasion?'

'Male.'

He breathed out another furl of smoke. 'I suspect it is an unfortunate consequence of your mother's condition that you have had nobody to reprimand you for unmaidenly behaviour in the past,' he said quietly. 'I wish I had thought of that earlier, before letting you run so wild. Do you know what time it is?'

'Yes.'

'Did it not occur to you that to be seen, or known to be out until after midnight in the company of men would very much damage any chances of a decent match?'

'It was an accident.'

'That matters very little,' he said. 'And I believe you have made your mother freshly ill.'

'Moths and dust make my mother ill. I think it would be in vain to arrest all of my movements in the hope of maintaining her in good health.'

'For God's sake!' he burst out, suddenly much louder, and although it was what she had been angling for, it made her lean back jerkily. 'Give me the man's name.'

'You're not going to bully him—'

'I said give it to me! Write down the address. Now.' He pushed a pen across to her, and the inkwell.

She wrote. As she did, she felt sorry. She had half thought he would see what was going on, but he hadn't; he wasn't even close to it. She had always known she disliked him mainly because he had charge of her and tended to botch the job, but now that he soon wouldn't, he was only a worried, not very bright man trying to do what he was thought was best. It was cruel to execute this piece of strategy above his head. When she had finished the address and drawn a small map, she picked up the paper and gave it to him rather than pushing it across the desk.

'Well, I see you might be coming to regret your actions after all,' he said stiffly. 'It wouldn't hurt to apologise to your mother in the morning. She has been sedated for now.'

'Yes, of course.'

'I shall see about this in the morning. Go to bed.'

She let herself out into the hall, and shook the worst of the cigar smoke smell from her clothes. She put her nose to her sleeve, but the last of the lemon soap from Mori's jumper was lost. Thinking she was alone, she sighed and closed both hands through her hair, then shied to one side when she saw a human form shift on her left. It was Alice, who had been waiting for her at the foot of the stairs. She was still crying a little.

Grace bent her knees to speak to her under the banister. 'Buck up. Everything's all right.'

Alice sniffed. 'Is it really?'

She went around to sit down beside her. The stair creaked. 'Alice, whatever you reply doesn't matter in the least, so I'd like you to tell the truth. Has anyone been asking you questions about me recently? What I'm going to wear, what I'm doing? That card trick I was arranging, the one I told you about? I don't mind if they have.'

Alice looked blank. 'Questions? No. I would never tell anybody anything of the sort.'

'Nothing at all?'

'Nothing. I don't speak to anybody about you, ma'am, I'm your lady's maid, not a gossip.' She swallowed. 'Were you really out all night with a pair of men, ma'am?'

'Yes. I played cards.'

'But if anyone finds out—'

'Yes, yes, I'm a fallen woman, pariah, et cetera, et cetera. I'm going to do some work upstairs.'

'Work? But it's the middle of the night—'

'A cup of tea would be lovely, thank you.'

She set down her chalk. The trail of dust still hung in the air between her and the blackboard, dry-tasting. Previous mists of it had settled over the folds in her sleeves, lending to the cotton the illusion of the bright lights in silk. When she stood back, seeing the entire board for the first time rather than only a part of it, it looked crowded. Crowded and nonsensical. No matter what speed she assigned to the ether, it would not match the other side of the equation, which was the assumption of Mori's veracity. If a clairvoyant could sense movement in the ether, if the effects of an event were to hum and knock through it as her breath made shapes in the chalk dust, they would not get far before the movement of the earth destroyed those shapes with its tailwind. It was possible, that much was obvious, but only at a very short distance. If he were genuine, he should have been able to predict things that were only just about to happen, very close to him. Inches.

'He's a fraud,' she said to the chalk. 'Thaniel is living with a bombmaker who can do card tricks. Magnificent.'

The dust in the air puffed gently, and then swirled when Alice came in with another cup of tea, having taken away the first when Grace failed to notice it until after it had gone cold. She watched the white particles float off to the side.

'What was that, ma'am?' Alice said.

'Shut up,' Grace said, staring at the dust. 'Shut up, shut up.'

Alice straightened her neck, more curious than offended.

'That chalk is still moving because you opened the door.'

'Chalk?'

Grace ground some more against the blackboard and, when the powder fell and drifted beside the white patch she had made, she traced her finger through it and watched the disturbed particles. 'I mean to say it holds the shape.'

'Are you feeling well?' Alice said. She preferred Grace not to write out equations and talk about them in the house. She seemed to acknowledge that while numbers were a necessary part of life, they were, like French postcards, not suitable for a lady.

'No, I'm an idiot. We're all idiots. I don't understand how anything is ever discovered in physics if we keep on like this. Motion is relative. You can stand still on earth without feeling that you're spinning at a hundred and fifty thousand miles per hour and hurtling round the sun, which in turn moves … and chalk dust can hang almost still, despite all that.'

'What does chalk have to do with—'

'Alice,' Grace said, still looking at the board, 'I asked you before whether you had spoken to anyone about me, and I said it didn't matter. I was lying: it does matter extremely. Your employment now depends on the answer. Were you telling the truth?'

'My employment does not depend on the answer, I've been here since you were four.'

Grace turned around. 'I'm afraid loyalty is a continuous phenomenon. You don't score points for past action.'

Alice faltered. Rather than set it down, she stood holding the new tea, which took on a thin white film as the chalk in the air began to fall and settle. 'No, ma'am. But – I am telling the truth, I swear—'

'Can you tell me where you were today, when you weren't with me?'

'Eating, in the kitchen!' Her eyes had filled with tears again.

'So if I ask Mrs Sloam, she will tell me what she cooked for you?'

'Yes, it was ham and egg!'

'Unusual for you, you never seem too keen on ham.'

'She ran out of beef, so we . . . I haven't spoken to anyone!'

'Have you seen anyone around the house? Oriental?'

'I wouldn't speak to a Chinaman, they're dirty!' She began to cry again. 'You can't turn me away now. I shall talk to Lady Carrow about it, she always—'

'Alice, of course I shan't turn you away. I just wanted you to answer properly.'

Alice stared at her with a mixture of relief and resentment.

Grace turned side on to the blackboard. 'The fact is that there are two possible scenarios. One, my friend lives with a bombmaker who has very convincingly pretended to be a clairvoyant—'

'Bombmaker!'

'—to the point that he must have been spending hundreds of pounds on it. Or he . . . well, he's living proof of a static ether. So you see, it does rather matter if you're telling the truth.' Grace rubbed her face. Her skin felt too dry after an evening spent in front of a fire and a night dusted in chalk. 'He found a spare card I had planted in a deck on the first try. I didn't tell him there was one. If he didn't have that from you, he didn't have it from anyone.'

Alice was frowning. 'I never told anybody that, ma'am. Certainly not a horrid little Chinaman.' She hesitated, then regained her nerve. 'What exactly does ether have to do with clairvoyants? I hear everyone say it, at séances and so forth, but nobody says what it is.'

Grace nodded once. 'Ether is to light as air is to sound, but far more efficient. You will have noticed that when fireworks ignite, you hear the bang after the flash? That is because sound travels more slowly, much more slowly. So we can say that the medium of air conducts sound at a certain speed. As does ether. It conducts light at a speed of about two hundred thousand miles per second. Yes?'

Alice dipped her head.

'Light can go anywhere, so ether must be everywhere. Everything moves through it. I always thought that the movement of the world would be measurable, but movement is relative within a closed system, like a planet, as any monkey with a basic understanding of thermodynamics would have guessed if we hadn't all been so busy trying to measure the wretched stuff. That means that it doesn't move at all at ground level, except for the other things that move at ground level. People, light, insects, bacteria. The synapses of human brains. Which is where clairvoyance becomes possible, and why the Institute of Psychical Research funds quite a few physicists now. Ether particles knock together like dominoes as soon as they're disturbed, at the speed of light. If a human being could sense those disturbances, he would know about possibilities as they formed, not as they unfolded. He would know you were going to do something when you decided to do it, not when you did it. And he would know if you were considering it, because that would make a wave too. Oh, for God's sake,' she said suddenly.

It made Alice jump. 'Ma'am?'

'Not you, I'm sorry. I've just understood why he lost a dice game. Ether conducts possible effects. But a die has—'

'Exactly even chances?' Alice said in a small voice.

'Yes. The only thing the ether drag of a regular-sided falling object can tell you is that it is falling. One could be the most sensitive clairvoyant in the world and still lose a game of backgammon.' She touched the back of her head, which was aching. 'I had better send a telegram to Thaniel. I should think he would like to know that his friend has been telling him the truth.'

'It's three in the morning, ma'am, the post office is closed.'

'Of course it is. First thing then.' She leaned back against the blackboard.

'Oh, ma'am, your dress—'

'Chalk washes out.' She picked up her tea. It tasted good after working for so long, though chalk-dusty.

Alice sighed. 'Did it have to be a clerk from the Foreign Office?' she said.

'He's much better than anyone else it could have been.'

'And does he know that he's going to get an angry visit from Lord Carrow tomorrow?'

'Yes. I asked him. I stayed out late on purpose. Alice, stop looking that way.'

'Well! Oh, and of course his nasty little Chinaman friend didn't have a word to say about you doing such a foolish—'

'Actually he wasn't there when we spoke.' She paused. 'In fact, I think he would have had something to say about it, if I'd given him the chance.'

'Oh, yes?'

'Yes. I think he…well. He didn't like me. They seemed quite close.'

Alice's expression turned inward. 'Ma'am,' she said at last. 'It can't be safe to upset a man who knows the future. What's to stop him making sure that you stray into a carriage crash or under a falling pile of bricks?'

'Human decency, same as everyone else,' Grace said, but she looked into her tea and felt something twist in her insides.

EIGHTEEN

Grace had promised to send a telegram once she was sure of what was going on. Although Thaniel could see that it was unreasonable to expect anything before half past seven in the morning, he kept listening for the door bell while he watched rice boil on the stove. Usually he liked seeing the steam rise, because rice steamed differently to anything else, but he couldn't concentrate on it. When he opened the workshop door, wanting to see the street through the big window, he found Mori there already. He was transposing some of the most delicate clockwork from the cabinets and into deep, velvet boxes. Thaniel dug his fingernails into the door frame.

'What's going on?' he said. Since it was before half past seven, prior agreement obliged him to do it in Japanese, which was fortunate. It was difficult to sound unusually strained in a new second language: it was strained all the time.

'Oh, it's ...' Mori clicked one of the boxes shut. Thaniel saw him try to arrange the sentence into vocabulary that was easy to understand, then give up. He broke his normal rule and went into English. 'The police are coming. I suppose I've got an Irish-sounding name. People are more careful with things in boxes.'

'Are they?' Thaniel said.

'Sometimes. Look ... they're angry, and want to fit up the first likely-looking foreigner, so I'm going to be arrested. But it will get to your office quickly. The British treaties in Japan are fragile at the moment and the Ministry of the Interior will implode when they hear. I'd rather do that and be cleared today than go off to the

Lake District and drag it out for weeks. Stop looking at me like that and go to work.'

'They'll hurt you.'

'Not imaginatively.'

Thaniel looked to the window again. The street was still empty except for one of the middle Haverly boys. He was weaving through things in the mist no one else could see. Katsu was on his shoulder.

'Are you waiting for post?' Mori said. 'It won't come until tonight. The Knightsbridge office doesn't open in the morning today.'

Thaniel let his breath out. 'I forgot.'

'Go to work,' Mori said. 'You'll be arrested too if you stay.'

'Why?'

'If somebody hits you, you will hit him back. Which is ... impeding police business, I think. Go on. Watch for a telegram around five o'clock and hand it over to Francis Fanshaw quickly, if you don't mind.'

'Mori—'

'Steepleton.'

He did as he was told.

When he arrived at the office, he stopped at the corner of his desk and looked down at the sleek telegraph machine for a long time. The gears were still shiny and there was no grime yet in the grooves of the transcript wheel. For all things seemed to have changed over the last few weeks, it was hard not to think that, when he boiled it all down, all he had really done was exchange a rickety telegraph for a new model that did just the same thing, more smoothly.

Fanshaw came in and tipped a folder into the crook of his arm. It was full of lumpy papers pasted with raw telegraph transcripts. 'Tokyo and Peking dispatches. Go and brief the Minister.'

'Me?'

'You're the only one who's read them all. Off you go. Quick march, he's waiting.'

Lord Leveson did not wait for any introductions before he began to ask questions. He was a big, white-haired man who barked more than he spoke. The questions were staccato bursts. All he required was the relevant parts of the dispatches, but since the raw transcripts were peppered with overhead and snatches of shorthand code between operators, he couldn't read it himself. It dragged on for an hour, and then two, and having decided that Thaniel was better than usual at reading from the transcripts, Leveson handed him the Moscow set too and it all began again. He was only a few lines in when Fanshaw tapped on the door and leaned in.

'Sorry to interrupt. Steepleton, there's a telegram for you. There's a courier here who won't go away until he gives it to you in person.'

The young post office runner came in and waited while Thaniel signed for the wire. It had been marked double urgent. When he opened it, there was only one line of text inside.

Mori is genuine. Grace.

'Emergency at home,' he said. He gave the dispatches to Fanshaw and left.

He took the train back to Knightsbridge, counting off the stations as the lights came and went through the dark. When he came out, the sun was too bright, and too hot. He had hoped he might arrive before the police, but before he was even in sight of number twenty-seven, he knew they were there already. The street was always busy, because the sort of people who could afford Filigree Street did not work in offices, but the crowd was much denser at the far end than it should have been. The passers-by who were coming toward the shop were looking ahead and slowing, and the ones who had passed it were looking back. He walked quickly and a way opened up for his official-looking clothes.

Mori was sitting on the pavement. Beside him, close enough to touch him, stood a tall policeman in a uniform too heavy for the heat. He hadn't chosen to sit there. There were dust-marks on his knees where someone had forced him to kneel down.

'Stop there,' the policeman said. 'He's not open for business.'

'I live here. Mori, are you all right?'

'What are you doing here?' he said, but he didn't sound surprised.

'Have you been out here all day?'

The policeman aimed a brief kick at Mori's hip. 'Not a word.'

'Jameson,' someone called from the door. 'Bring him in for minute. We'd like to see what he has to say about this.'

The man pulled Mori up by his arm and pushed him to the door. Thaniel followed. A serious-looking officer met them there. He was holding one of the clockwork birds. It had been smashed to get it open, and the gunpowder packet inside was exposed.

'So then. What do you call this, hey? Jameson, call the four-wheeler down, we're just about – bloody hell!'

Mori had snatched the bird and the powder from him. He pulled the string out of the packet. There was a snap.

'Get down!' the sergeant bellowed.

Thaniel didn't. Mori was looking at him, holding the packet in his open hand for him to see, as if there were nobody else in the room. It burst into flame, and a spray of sparks lifted and spun gold and purple through the air, glittering and crackling. Just a firework. It made the workshop seem gloomy by comparison, and the sparks and the smoke smell of the gunpowder made it all, for only a second or so, blend into bright memories of fairs and carnivals. The sparks thinned. The paper packaging had burned to ashes on the instant. Mori brushed his hands and the soft grey rags floated down to the ground.

There was a fractional silence in which everything was still. It was long enough for Thaniel to see what had happened to the workshop. Every drawer from the desk was out and emptied, and all the cupboards under and over the cabinets stood open. Everything from inside was over the floor. If it had been put down carefully at first, there was nothing careful about the way the policemen had kicked things aside to make pathways.

One of the policemen knocked Mori on to his knees again, and there was shouting, and someone pulled out a truncheon.

'Williamson!'

He hadn't seen him, but a Clan na Gael bombmaker was an important arrest, and like he hoped, Williamson appeared behind his men. He had been sitting at the back of the room, only watching.

'Either,' Thaniel said to him, 'I am going to wire the Foreign Office and tell them that you're about to beat a false confession from a Japanese nobleman with no motive and no evidence except a firework, and in view of your having not found the Yard bomb in time in the first place, you'll probably be sacked. Or, you can take your men away. And if you don't take your hand off that thing now, you'll have to fight someone your own size,' he added to the man with the truncheon.

Williamson was staring at him. 'You will keep your mouth shut or I shall arrest you too.'

'Then Francis Fanshaw will be asking after me tomorrow when I don't come to work, won't he, and it will all be the same but twelve hours delayed.'

'You ... idiot.'

Thaniel shook his head once and waited.

'Everyone! Clear out,' Williamson shouted, without looking away from him. 'Yes; now, come on, out.' To Thaniel, very quietly, 'And when we do prove him guilty, you'll damn well go to Broadmoor as an accomplice, you stupid, *stupid* bastard. Get out of my way.'

Thaniel moved, and stood by Mori to see them go. Once the last uniformed man was out of the workshop, he took Mori's hands and pulled him up. The people who had been watching were drifting off now. The Haverly boys on the wall looked disappointed that there had not been a real fight. Thaniel waited for a little while, watching, because he could not imagine that police were a common sight on Filigree Street, and he did not think well enough of London to be sure that everyone would put it down to a mistake. Some women were talking behind their fans as they walked, heads close together, looking back sometimes.

'Did you know that Gilbert and Sullivan are at the show village today?' Mori said, bringing him back.

'What? Why?'

'Research, for an operetta set in Japan. The signs have been up all week.'

'Are you hurt?'

'No.'

Thaniel held his neck to move his head and see if any of the shadows on his face were bruises. One was. 'Liar. I should have stayed this morning. I'm sorry.'

Mori smiled, only with his eyes. 'I know you mean that well, but I have to say, I'm a bit offended that you think I couldn't live through some bruises and some shouting without a man who was born well after I was first on the wrong end of naval guns.'

'When were you?'

'When the British fired on Canton. I mean ... they weren't aiming at me personally, but I think it should still count.'

'Yes, it counts.' Thaniel coughed, because his throat had closed.

'Thank you,' Mori said, quietly. Thaniel let him lead him through everything across the floor, back to the front door.

At Osei's teashop, the air smelled of rice wine and orange blossom, from the incense frames that the women draped their kimono over after washing them. There was so much pipe smoke in the air that it held the lamplight and turned amber. Whenever anyone moved through it, it was tugged after them, whorling where people went to and fro with drinks and money. Arthur Sullivan, in the flesh and looking younger than he did from the back of an operetta, was playing a jaunty piece on the old piano. He winced whenever he hit the middle C, which had become a horrible chlorine sharp. It was the note Mori had changed two weeks ago. Thaniel looked at him to ask why, but Mori ignored him and ordered some sake.

The space around the piano had been cleared of tables and chairs, and some of the girls and the children danced while another man with a magnificent grey moustache struggled to explain a story to a group of young men. William Gilbert, he supposed, though he had never seen the man in person. Mori pulled him into the nearest seats as Osei glided by again, this time to set cups between them. Her hair was twisted up with flowers that matched the new sash on her dress, and made her look like summer. She smiled at Mori, who was reading the Japanese newspaper on the table and didn't notice, or chose not to. Thaniel crinkled the paper down with his fingertip once she had gone.

'What does that say?' he asked. He could read each character of the headline, but couldn't tell what they said put together.

'Government plans to destroy Crow Castle,' said Mori. He followed the characters with his knuckle. To order them in English, he had to skip about.

'Are you sure?'

Mori smiled. 'It's a modernist policy in Japan. The castles represent the old shogunate, so they've been force-auctioned by the new government. Some were knocked down, most are re-garrisoned with imperial troops or sold. Crow Castle is Matsumoto Castle. It's black. They tried to take it down about ten years ago, but the locals protested.'

'Matsumoto. Did I meet someone called Matsumoto recently?'

Mori tipped his head and Thaniel saw him sift through memories. 'Akira?'

'No idea. Tall man, immaculate suit. Very dandy. He was with Grace. I mean Miss Carrow.'

'Yes. Same family, it's his father who owns the castle now.'

'Where do the knights who lived in the castles go?'

'Townhouses in Tokyo.'

'For God's sake, the closest I can get to medieval England is a Walter Scott novel. People shouldn't be throwing away their history when it's still doing archery practice forty miles up the road.'

Mori looked doubtful. 'I lived in a castle. It was cold.'

'Philistine.'

'Call me Delilah,' he said, unmoved.

Thaniel touched their cups together.

Sitting down had taken them below the haze of pipe smoke. He was glad of it. It made an illusion of distance. Now that he was here, he wanted not to be. He had seen every Gilbert and Sullivan operetta, but it was different to see the composers close, unseparated from everyone else by the fourth wall of a stage or the slope of tiered seats. It was pulling at something that still stung.

'I say!' bellowed Gilbert, looking in their direction. It made him jump. 'You in the proper clothes, do you speak English?' He was aiming at Mori.

Mori nodded.

'Get over here and help.'

Mori looked at him, but Thaniel shook his head. 'No, I'd rather—'

'But he thinks that Japanese sounds like baby talk and he has a ridiculous moustache, and he's talking to those men of twenty and twenty-five thinking they're twelve. You're *missing* it.'

Thaniel laughed, a little and helplessly. 'You're ridiculous.'

They skirted around the girls, who were teaching each other to waltz, badly, because they didn't seem able to hear the rhythm well. Gilbert motioned them into seats close to him. He was smoking a pipe while he talked and there was already a volcanic cloud around him. As soon as they were sitting, he thrust at Mori a sheet of paper with the story written on it and told him to get on with it by himself. Thaniel frowned, but before he could tell him not to be rude, Mori touched his arm.

'Enough crusading for the one day,' he said. 'Pace yourself, before you're ransomed by irate Muslims.'

Thaniel kicked his ankle, but Mori paid no attention.

'Another Englishman, thank God,' Gilbert said, oblivious. 'You forget you're in London with this rabble, don't you? It's like Peking in here. What brings you here? Interested in music?'

'We saw the posters for the new show. The *Mikado*, is it?'

'That's right. Satire set in Japan. Supposed to be for October, some foreign notable coming then. We want some real Japs to come in and coach the actors, though none of them seem to speak English.'

'Most of them do,' Thaniel said. He had been to the village often enough now to know that almost all the smallest children had English nannies, and that not everyone was fresh from Japan. Osei and her father had been in England for years. 'They've been told they should be as Japanese as possible around tourists.'

'Hah. Contracts.' Mr Gilbert blew out a lungful of smoke and then banged the bowl of his pipe against the edge of the table. 'I see. You're pretty knowledgeable. Speak Japanese, do you?'

'Only a bit. What's the story, of the operetta?'

'It's about a wandering minstrel, Nanky-Pu, who falls in love with an unsuitable girl called Yum-Yum and afoul of the tyrannical emperor. How's that?'

Thaniel was careful not to move his face much. 'Good. Not quite like real Japanese?'

Gilbert shrugged. 'No point. The safest way to success is to write according to the capacity of the stupidest member of the audience. If the actors say "ping" often enough, everyone will get the gist.'

Another twang came from the piano.

'Can't someone sort that bloody thing out?' Gilbert shouted across the room.

'I can, I can,' Thaniel murmured, having decided to go himself anyway the next time the bad note sounded. It was making his fingernails feel stretched.

He wound his way back across the room and tapped his knuckles against the top of the piano. 'Give me a second and I'll tune it properly.'

'Oh, would you?' Sullivan said. He had a very clipped voice, and his relief had to squeeze itself through the cracks without showing much. 'There never is a blind piano tuner about the place when one has need of such a person, is there? I take it you work with pianos?'

'I used to,' Thaniel said. He tilted open the piano top and leaned down to loosen the small key that held taut the faulty string. 'Try that.'

Sullivan smiled. 'You've got perfect pitch?'

Thaniel nodded.

'I'd be much obliged if you'd have a listen to this middle part, then. Come and sit down.' He moved up on the piano stool. He was plump, so there wasn't much space, but Thaniel was slim enough to fit. 'So, it's for an operetta set in Japan, and there's a little oriental part in semitones here, which melds into a jauntier theme here, but the bridge is rather clunky, like this, you see …'

'I'm not qualified to tell you anything.'

'Yes, yes, but what do you think?'

'I … think it's clunky.'

'Exactly. You look like you know this place, I don't suppose you know much about oriental music?'

Thaniel pinned his hands under his thighs, not wanting to touch the piano keys, but he described what he meant and Sullivan played it slowly once or twice before he understood and lit up.

'Not qualified my foot! Which theatre do you belong to, I didn't ask?'

Thaniel shook his head. 'I don't. I'm a clerk at the Foreign Office.'

'A clerk at the – what a waste. Pianist, though?'

'Mm.'

'I don't suppose you'd feel like turning up at the Savoy for the Sunday rehearsals? I've been looking for a pianist for a while, I've been on the edge of writing out the part altogether. Can't play and conduct at once. There wouldn't be much money, but it would certainly be good to try you out. Will you come along?'

'I don't know if I'd have the time,' he said slowly, feeling heavy.

Sullivan swept the air with his hand as if he could erase the words. 'It's not like a symphony orchestra; I don't rule the pit with an iron fist or shout at anyone who can't play the Bolero with his eyes shut. Short rehearsals. The show will be in October sometime. What do you say?'

Thaniel didn't know what he wanted to say. The idea of it made him afraid. He hadn't touched a piano in years; he couldn't tell if he would still be able to play well, or, come to that, if it would still have any of its old shine now. He was on the edge of refusing when he saw Mori watching him and understood suddenly what it all was. Mori had changed the note, weeks ago. It was Mori's version of a present. A strange warm feeling prickled down his arms.

'Yes, why not?'

'Excellent!' Sullivan wrung his hand. 'And thank you for your help today. It really would be a tragedy if you were never to do orchestral work. By God, I've contracted you to work for me without even asking your name, Mr ...'

'Steepleton.'

'Well then, Mr Steepleton, I must buy you a drink.'

The drink became five drinks and the hours melted, and it was evening when things began to break up at last. When he looked for Mori, he couldn't find him at first. In fact he was in plain view, in a far corner with some of the more austere-looking village men. He was listening much more than he was talking. From the way they were moving their hands, they were describing disputes and troubles. He excused himself as Thaniel started to make his way across and the men stood too and tipped deep bows.

'What was that?' Thaniel said as they met at the door. He opened it for him and they both went carefully down the steep step and into the cool evening. It wasn't dark yet, but the twilight was doing its trick of flattening everything, so that the way to the gates was harder to see than it would have been in full night and bright lamps. The air tasted clear after the smoke inside.

'Some of the boys have been going to nationalist meetings and bringing back Western friends lately. No one speaks enough English to explain to the owner.'

'Yes, probably best to stop that. Nationalist meetings are usually run by Clan na Gael.'

'People can be nationalists if they want,' Mori said. His eyes lifted upward as they passed the shrine and its two pale trees. He wasn't devout, but for the sake of sightseeing he had shown Thaniel how to write a prayer card a few days ago, and it was still hanging up. There was only one priest, who could only go through so many each morning. 'Especially if it's the kind of nationalism where Japanese boys go to hear Irishmen speak in London and make friends to bring home.'

'Have you gone ... oh, I see what you mean. I still don't think—' He choked when Mori put his arm out across his chest to stop him walking on. Yuki, the angry boy from his first morning, was pointing a sword at them. Its tip was just in front of his face. Yuki inclined his head at them and moved it toward Mori instead. For what felt like a long time, nothing moved around them except the leaves and the prayer rope strung between the trees. The paper lamps outside Osei's shop swayed on their cord and moved the candlelight about in waves.

'You've seen the newspaper, then,' Mori said in Japanese.

Thaniel started forward in the hope of drawing Yuki's attention, but Mori's arm across him tightened.

'You could stop it,' Yuki said. Though his hand didn't flicker, there was a catch in his voice. 'You are a Mori. You are a knight. You could stop it. Japan is falling down and you make watches!'

'I want to go home, it's getting cold. Let us by.'

When Yuki feinted, Mori only batted the sword away with the back of his hand. It looked easy, but there was a bang that was steel hitting bones. The impact went visibly up Yuki's arm. Mori caught him by his elbow and twisted until he dropped the sword. Because the lower part of the blade had no edge, he held it there and gave it to Thaniel hilt-first. It was very light, and too short for a white man.

'Come on. I'm taking you home.'

'Get off me, you—'

'Shut up,' Mori said.

Yuki walked with them unforced, but resentment steamed from him. Once, he tried to push Thaniel away, but Mori smacked him over the back of his head. He was calmer after that and Thaniel didn't understand, until he realised that it was something the boy understood, from an older world. He wanted samurai, not modern manners. It was what he had been saying all along.

The village occupied the south-west corner of Hyde Park, but one side of it was blocked off by a long building that Thaniel had vaguely in mind as having once been a hotel, five or six storeys tall. There were shop canopies outside now. Past it was the pagoda and the small lake, water black and orange by the paper lamps. They made fragile silhouettes of the bridges that looped between the two islands, and the prayer gate in the shallows. It would be a fine view during the day, but it was eerie in twilight. Stiffly, Yuki led the way into one of the middle shops.

The light was almost too dim to see by. Pegged high near the ceiling were miners' lamps, closed around low flames that only showed through slits. Despite the fresh air from the open door, the smell of saltpetre was strong. Crowding the banks of shelves were paper packets in bright colours, all different; some were ordinary squares and rectangles, but others were paper dragon heads or red cylinders painted with tiny, perfect pictures of knights or women with long hair. All of them had labels pasted on their sides somewhere, in big Japanese characters.

'Nakamura's Flower Fires,' Thaniel read. He looked at Mori. 'What does that mean?'

'Fireworks.'

Toward the back of the shop was an open space with tatami mats and a low workbench, where an old man knelt cutting straight, thin sticks from bamboo canes. He looked mortified when he saw them, and fell straight on to the floor in front of them. Thaniel thought he had fainted, but it was a bow. When he sat up again, there was a smudge of dust on his forehead. Although he wiped it away, the deep lines in his skin remained lighter. Mori helped him up. He was younger than Thaniel had thought, but ailing with something difficult. Behind him, a curtain rustled and a woman eased the edge of it aside, but she dropped it when she saw them all.

'You can't do that whenever you see me,' Mori was saying.

'Mori-sama is very kind, but I know my place.' Nakamura looked helpless. 'What has he done now?'

'It was nothing,' Mori said. 'But perhaps he shouldn't have a sword.'

'Where did you find a sword?' Nakamura demanded of his son. Thaniel propped it against a bench, out of Yuki's reach 'Mori-sama, I am so sorry—'

Mori interrupted him quietly in Japanese. Nakamura started to reply, and then hung his head. Yuki snorted, but there was an awkwardness to his impatience.

'He needs to be apprenticed,' Nakamura said miserably. 'He has nothing to do but label boxes here and go to his meetings in town.' Thaniel glanced at Yuki. He was probably popular among the more insane Irish. 'I was wondering, Mori-sama, if perhaps ...'

'I'm not sure clockwork would suit him,' Mori said quietly.

'I don't understand?'

Yuki did. His expression hardened again and his black eyes strayed to the shelves of fireworks. Thaniel was inclined to agree with him. Forbidding the boy clockwork seemed like a vain effort when he already worked in a firework shop. The longest rockets stood in ricks tied with string, or baled tightly on the shelves. There were hundreds. The workbench was scattered with planed sticks and coloured paper, and labels, and bowls and packets of powders whose shades varied from silvery grey to white. One set of jars were opaque black to keep out the sun. Their tags were built of old, complicated characters, the sort that had first been drawn in the sand of sulphur-seamed caves to describe what there wasn't a word for yet.

'Never mind,' Mori said. 'I think Mr Yamashita is looking for someone to help him.'

'But that's bow-making.'

'It's a good solid trade and it's difficult enough to be interesting, and it's traditional. And Yamashita is strict.'

'Yes,' Nakamura said. 'Yes, sir.' He pushed his son's shoulder. 'Apologise to Mori-sama. Now!'

Yuki looked away like a cat. There were frustrated tears in his lashes.

'If you're polite,' Mori said quietly to him, 'Yamashita might teach you how to use that sword, too. You could be good.'

Yuki blinked, startled by the praise, and his father seemed unable to decide between pleasure and shame.

'Good night,' Mori said, bowing slightly. Nakamura hauled his son on to the ground, where they both stayed.

Thaniel led the way out. After a short while he said, 'Nationalist meetings and a shop full of fireworks sound like two things that would be better not lined up.'

'True.'

'Couldn't you have arranged for him to be without one or the other?'

Mori was quiet. Then, 'You said to that policeman that he should fight someone his own size.'

'Y—es?'

'Yuki isn't my size. I'll take a bomb from him if he makes one, but I don't want to stop him making one. It's shaking a baby or kicking a kitten.' He sighed. 'I mean—'

'No, I'll take your word for it.'

'Bet your life on it?' Mori said ruefully.

'Yes.' The truth of it had a helium lightness. As they started back to the village gate, he took Mori's hand to see what damage Yuki had done. There was a long cut across his knuckles where the sharp edge had just caught him, and a red stripe from the flat that would bruise later. Mori watched him look, not for long, then pulled his hand back and folded his arms. It was a lonely thing to do, Thaniel thought. He wanted to ask what the matter was, but he saw Mori's shoulders stiffen at the approach of that future, then ease again when he stopped intending it.

'Lord Carrow is outside our house,' he said. Thaniel sighed, because he had forgotten about Grace and he was tired now, and not keen to argue with a man he didn't know. Mori didn't look at him, but his nearer shoulder eased back, like an opening door so that they could speak from adjoining rooms. 'You needn't do it.'

Thaniel shook his head. 'I think it's a bit late for that.'

NINETEEN

The carrow carriage had stopped opposite number twenty-seven. It must have been there for a while, because the horses were restless and shaking their heads. Its lamps illuminated the family crest painted in blue and white, and once Mori had slipped inside the house by himself, the carriage door opened and a tall man with a silk-lined cape stepped out. He stood with his cane in front of him, looking at Thaniel hard.

'Do you intend to marry my daughter?'

'Yes.' Lord Carrow's expression tightened. 'She was very straight. She said she had to marry somebody and means didn't matter.'

'This is utterly ridiculous—'

'It is, but that's not her fault, is it.'

Carrow looked as if he would have liked to hit him with the cane. 'You will sign a contract agreeing to keep the Kensington house, which I'm certain she's mentioned to you, in perfect repair, which will require you to live there. You will not sell it. The dowry will be given in instalments, not all at once. Control of it will remain in my hands. By God, if you think you're marrying money, you've another thing coming.'

'I don't want her money.'

They stood in silence. Thaniel looked across at the workshop window, where the lights were now on. Mori was starting to put the wrecked workshop back into order. There were lights in the other shops too, and their windows were doll's house tableaux of men working or talking, or eating.

'I rather think,' Carrow said, 'that this is a stunt of hers to prove a point, and that she will refuse you in order to be unmarriageable. However, I believe in calling bluffs. So I do hope, Mr Steepleton, that you are happy to live the rest of your life with a woman you don't know.' He looked Thaniel up and down once again. 'I find you insolent.'

'You must have known that she would hop if you put up a sign that said don't walk.'

'How dare you!'

Thaniel sighed. 'Would you like to come in for some tea?'

'Of course I wouldn't.'

'Good night, then.'

Carrow gripped his cane hard again but didn't raise it. Instead he turned away suddenly and stepped up into the carriage, which moved off with a jolt. Thaniel let himself into the workshop. Mori had been setting things back into the glass cabinets, but he turned at the sound of the door and there was a silent catch in which Thaniel didn't know what to say to him.

He took a plain steel ring from his waistcoat pocket and held it out. 'This is the right size for her. You'll need to show it to the jeweller tomorrow.'

Thaniel took it carefully. In Mori's hand it had looked larger. After sliding it into his pocket, he stood for a moment with his fingertips resting on the workbench.

'Come and have a drink,' he said at last. 'I ... seem to be getting married.'

Mori brought some sherry from the cupboard and curled himself into the armchair while Thaniel sat on the hearth to light the fire. Feeding curls of sawdust into the kindling, he heard the mellow noise of the wine flowing through the bottle neck, and caught the smell of it over the burning twigs. When he turned back, the fire snapping behind him, Mori held out a glass.

'Do you want to be married?' he said.

'She says that we can send Annabel's boys to a proper school. In London, so I could see them.' It would have made more sense of the thing to say that it was because of Grace's work, not real trust in Mori, that he had come back from Whitehall, but he couldn't. Having seen what the police had done and how they had done it, he wanted to take that particular story to his grave. 'People say marriage first and love later. Is it true?'

'In this case yes.'

'That would be …' He didn't finish, because he couldn't find a word. He had always thought he would never marry, so he had never strayed into imagining it.

Mori clipped their glasses together softly. 'Congratulations.'

Thaniel took a breath, and a sort of indignant, surprised happiness spilled out. He worried about dealing with Lord Carrow and what would be the state of the ominous-sounding Kensington house, and ran on until he realised that he was waiting for Mori to say something without having given him space to, or any indication that he ought to interrupt.

'I sound like an idiot,' he said, not sure how else he could apologise without sounding dishonest.

The sharp line of Mori's collarbone traced a brief angle before falling back to the horizontal. The firelight pooled in the hollow between the bones. He had taken off his tie and collar. 'You do. But that's a very good sign.' He smiled, but only half. If he had not been speaking, he could have been Yuki's age.

Thaniel set down his glass, and took out the watch. Mori's black eyes followed his hand.

'You left this for me, didn't you? Why?'

'You're my friend and you would have died. You wouldn't have listened to a stranger in a coffee house. It had to be something you were wondering about for a long time.'

'I did. What was the extra clockwork for?'

'To measure where you were. If the alarm went off at the wrong moment you would have been in the blast when you stopped, not outside it. You didn't know to listen for it, so it had be variable. Makes it a bit heavy actually, I can take it out now if you like.'

'No … no.' He couldn't believe he hadn't seen that before. A man who knew he was listening for an alarm didn't need it to measure where he was. 'But I tried to get rid of it. If the pawnbroker had taken it …'

Mori smiled again. 'Have you read the warranty?'

'Of course I haven't read the warranty.'

'Paragraph three. All watches belong to their owners for life. If you break your watch, I'll repair it for no charge, and if you lose or sell it, it will be returned. Pawnbrokers won't buy them any more, they disappear too quickly. Obviously some people don't want their watches back if they've sold them, but it's good to have a bit of mystery around things.'

'You can be unsettling.'

'Sorry.' He looked at his knees. 'Anyway, I might go to bed. I'm getting drunk.'

He said his good nights and, once he had gone, Thaniel moved into the armchair. Sitting on the slate hearth had made the base of his back ache. From the chair, he could see through the half-closed door to the stairs, where Mori had stopped. He stood with his arms folded, his focus somewhere in the middle distance. It was a full minute before he went on again. The lock on his door turned, heavily. Thaniel listened for a while longer, because the silence was so deep and clear that he could hear ghosts of the thirty-six of thirty-seven possible worlds in which Grace had not won at the roulette, and not stepped backward into him. He wished then that he could go back and that the ball had landed on another number. He would be none the wiser and he would be staying at Filigree Street, probably for years, still happy, and he wouldn't have stolen those years from a lonely man who was too decent to mention that they were missing.

TWENTY

Iℕ ᴛʜᴇ ᴍɪᴅꜱᴛ of everything else, Thaniel had forgotten Sullivan's offer. He rediscovered the business card when he was emptying his pockets the next morning for laundry. The first rehearsal was on Sunday evening in two days' time.

When the day arrived, he went straight from Whitehall to the Savoy Theatre, arriving early so that there would be time to look at the music first. He'd been before, but only in crowds. Empty, it was cavernous. He walked backwards to see the galleries. There were two tiers, arranged in a horseshoe around the proscenium arch. A couple of violinists were already in the pit, which smelled of polish and dust. He sat down at the new grand piano and lifted the lid. The keys beneath were real ivory. He stared at them, watching his white reflection.

At last, he touched one key. He felt the thrum of the string behind it as the sound unfolded around the quiet pit. The music was already on the stand. He played the first line, very quietly. Little colours fizzed. Something in his mind that had been dislocated for years clicked back into place, and although it was a tiny shift, it made him blink. He sat back and flicked through the manuscript until he found a more complicated section and tried that, but it was too shallow to be a useful test, so he tried a few lines of a Mozart concerto instead, from an unremembered storage vault in an unused part of his mind. It was still fresh.

So was everything else. Tallis with no pedal, Handel with, even the horrible organ piece that had been written for someone with three hands. He had thought it had all gone, but all he had done was lock himself up in a few little rooms and assume the rest of the house had fallen down. It hadn't. There were doors and doors, and dust, but when the curtains opened and the drapes came off, it was all where he had left it and hardly faded. He took his hands from the keys and sat with them in his lap instead, because his thoughts were echoing in the new space.

Somebody plinked two of the upper keys purply. Mr Sullivan smiled.

'How's the score? Good God, are you all right?'

'I'm – it's just the dust, I think I'm allergic to something. The score's easy to follow. Thank you.'

'Excellent, excellent.' He leaned down close. 'I was hoping to get this all polished well before October, when we have a rather special guest coming. Around the twentieth. Do you think that'll be possible?'

Thaniel nodded. 'Who is it?'

'A minister from Japan, a Mr Ito. He'll be here for a formal something-or-other at Whitehall, but the Japanese ambassador here mentioned the operetta and he's asked to come and have a look, so, naturally we said yes. It's going to be a special performance at the show village.' He smiled sheepishly. 'I was rather flippant about a visit from an oriental minister, but it turns out that he's a bigger fish than I thought. Heard of him at all? You're at the Foreign Office, yes?'

'Ito is their Home Secretary.'

'I see? I see.' He looked worried. 'If you could manage not to trap your hand in a door the week before, I should be most grateful.'

Thaniel nodded and thought that it was all a big flaming coincidence, and made a note to himself to ask Mori if perhaps he hadn't arranged things so that his friend would have an interesting show to see, very close to home, where they might run into each other without his having to ask. It sounded typically shy.

A telephone rang out shrill and silver. It made Thaniel jump, which provoked a smile from Sullivan as he hurried to answer it. It was built into the wall of the pit.

'Mr Gilbert doesn't like to come in every day, so we installed a line between here and his flat so that he can listen in.' He picked up the receiver. 'Yes, yes, got you. Tune up, everyone!'

Thaniel's chest tightened. Playing with a room full of professionals was different to running through a few old things by himself, but there was no escape now. As Sullivan propped the receiver upright in its hook, facing into the pit, Thaniel leaned on a chord and the strings section produced a familiar tide of sharps and flats. They were all shades of seaspray around the Atlantic blue, almost exactly like Katsu's higher hummings. Thinking of a small octopus made everything homely. A young violinist just beside him had trouble and looked lost, so he hummed the difference for him. While they adjusted the strings between them, Osei Yamashita glided by, dressed in her blossom-coloured kimono. He was confused to see her at first, until he remembered why Gilbert had been at the show village in the first place.

She had come to speak to Sullivan about costumes, which, she said, needed a third layer if they were to seem authentic. He looked uncertain in the face of her accent, and she had to repeat herself twice before he understood. Embarrassed, he then agreed to everything, although there was a scritchy protest from the telephone, which seemed to think that the budget might not stretch. If Sullivan heard, he ignored it. Osei swept away again, but stopped when somebody in Japanese clothes went past her.

'Yuki-kun! What are you doing? Come back here!'

'The manager gave me a message for Mr Sullivan.' As always, Yuki sounded irritable.

He delivered the note to a startled Sullivan, and when he returned to Osei, he gave Thaniel a hostile look. Thaniel tried for a smile. Yuki ignored it. He looked like a prisoner of war. He still wore his sleeves tucked up, and there was a small dagger in his wide belt, with a ribbon-bound hilt. Osei must have forced him to come. Thaniel watched them disappear back into the gloom of the backstage passages, trying to think of a polite way to forbid him the knife.

'Oh!' Sullivan exclaimed. 'Excellent. Everybody listen up; the date of Mr Ito's visit has been confirmed by the Foreign Office. Our debut performance will be on the twenty-eighth of October, at the Japanese show village in Hyde Park. You will be performing outside in autumn, but there will be fireworks and wine afterwards to make it worth your while.' His cheer cracked and he looked wretched underneath. 'It seems to be turning into quite the diplomatic gathering. Anybody found to have double-booked himself therefore will be summarily beheaded.' Laughter rippled around the pit. 'Oh, isn't that delightful,' he muttered. 'You all think I'm joking.'

PART THREE

TWENTY-ONE

TOKYO, 1882

MORI HAD A habit of walking through traffic as though he couldn't see it. Ito usually attributed it to absent-mindedness, but at a place like Shinbashi station, it struck him as wilful. Shinbashi was the terminus of the trunk line from Yokohama, a great Western-style building with wide ticket halls that horseshoed the end of the tracks and stood twice as tall as anything around it. The road outside swarmed.

While everyone else gathered outside the station, waiting for a lull in the traffic, Mori came straight out and straight across. Ito wondered how many generations of knights it took to produce one who came with a guarantee that even a Tokyo rickshawman could spot good breeding and get out of its way. Bastardy, it seemed, was no obstacle. He looked just like his mother. The old noblemen of the court tended to say it with a certain reverence.

Of course, the good breeding was at double strength today, because he was walking with Kiyotaka Kuroda. Always vain of his name, the man was wearing all black. Even discounting his personality, Ito would have disliked him vigorously just for that. It was a special sort of bad taste for an admiral to go about advertising a name that translated into what sounded like a copy-cat pirate. Blackfield: between that and his triannual invasions of Korea, he might as well have sewn matches in his beard. But Mori had always liked him. Kuroda was walking close to him now, and as they approached, Ito caught snatches of their conversation, half whipped away by the passing traffic that never quite hit them.

'—should make a fuss. Damn embarrassing.'

'—no reason – you idiot.'

'A *baronetcy* for services to the throne when you should be Duke of Choushu. Might as well have slung mud at you. Why haven't you stabbed anyone yet?'

'I'm better off. The castle land was requisitioned but—'

Kuroda's voice dropped into an indistinct gutturalness that eventually resolved itself into, 'I'd better leave you to the bookseller.'

Ito waited for Mori to defend him, but he said nothing about it. 'Remember to come tonight.'

'What's happening tonight?'

'The opening of the Rokumeikan,' Mori said.

They were just on the pavement, a few feet away. Ito turned his back to them and watched the river to give, at least, the impression of not overhearing. It didn't work. He felt Kuroda notice him.

'The whatkan?'

'The new foreigners' residence. You burnt the invitation.'

'Oh, that. Is it mandatory?'

'The Emperor says so. Foreign relations.'

'I'll show him what foreign relations look like, when he can be bothered to stir himself and get on a battleship. Why has it got such a stupid name? What have foreigners got to do with deer? *Deer Cry Hall*,' he said, pronouncing the words very separately. He had pitched his voice for Ito to hear. 'Sounds like a pub.'

'It's a Chinese poem. A general sees deer grazing near his camp and thinks what good guests they make.'

'I've got deer in my garden. Used to have orchids.'

'The Americans don't read Chinese poetry,' Mori said, and the gem edges of his Imperial accent showed much more, suddenly, now that he had enough of the games. 'They won't know if we've accidentally called them vermin. The point is, put in an appearance. Hysterical as it would be to see the Emperor shout at you and demote you to midshipman, I really haven't the time to soothe your ensuing alcoholism. The ball finishes at one o'clock in the morning.'

'I'll be there at ten to, then.'

There was a bump that sounded like an elbow meeting ribs, and then Kuroda's sudden roar at a rickshaw boy. Ito didn't turn around. He had no doubt Kuroda was looking back to see if he would.

Mori came to stand next to him. 'Afternoon.' He had a leather case over one wrist, but it was not the right shape for documents.

'Yes, good afternoon.' He sounded stuffy after their roughness.

'What are we looking at?'

'Nothing in particular.'

'You know,' he said in his solemn way, 'I sometimes think this country could be quite a good place unabsorbed by the British or the Chinese if you and Kuroda could face each other without spitting.'

'And I think it would be quite good if he would see that these parties have a far greater impact on foreign policy than any of his battleships. I hope you've brought a change of clothes,' he added. Mori was in greys and old tweed and looking, as usual, chronically unofficial. 'It's white tie. I did tell you, ten or twelve times.'

'I would have if you hadn't had one of your aides bring one for me.'

Ito didn't ask him how he knew. Mori was paid to know things and in all fairness it would have been odd if he didn't know the whereabouts of his own dinner jacket. It was still irritating. He felt as though a trap had been laid for him.

Mori put his free hand to the rail of the bridge just before Ito felt the judder too. It began like an ordinary earthquake, but then the ground jumped and the road was full of falling rickshawmen and stumbling horses. The plant pots that decorated the upper windowsills of the station all fell and burst on to the pavement. On the river, the barges tipped. A haul of barrels splashed in and, roped together as they were, bobbed away in line.

It lasted a long time, about a minute, and when it died down, Ito straightened and tugged down his jacket, rattled. Other than the plant pots and one teetering carriage, there was no obvious damage, although of course there would be in the parts of the city where the buildings were old and wooden rather than new and stone. Wooden houses had a strangely complete way of collapsing; they fell flat, as if they were designed to be packed away. He imagined rows of little flat heaps along the canals and pushed his hand over his face.

'Right. Let's go and make sure our vermin hall hasn't fallen down,' he said, setting off at once so that Mori was left behind.

Mori caught up easily. He had lately proven himself to be one of those men designed much more for middle age than youth. Where Ito was starting to thin and grey, he had broadened from the unhappy frailty of his twenties, and brightened.

'I'm sorry about Kuroda,' he said.

'No, no. I'm teasing.'

Determined not to talk about Kuroda, Ito turned over a few other things in his mind, but couldn't find anything of substance to introduce. The point came where anything at all would have thunked in the quiet. Mori turned his head away to follow the path of a swarm of dragonflies.

They came to Hibiya Park from the small gate in the south wall. It brought them in by the lake, where the trees were turning now. The last of the cicadas had stopped singing a fortnight before, and so the place was quiet except for the hoots of the crows. Where the trees leaned together over the path, spiders hung in the lower branches, quite big enough to see easily. There was a ripping noise and Ito jumped, thinking it was the battle cry of something upset and arachnoid, but it was only Mori tearing a bouquet of seeds from a grass stem, like he always did when they came through. He smoothed his waistcoat down again and gave himself a talking to. He had grown used to the solid ground of London and Washington, and now earthquakes made him jittery.

As he turned his head, he saw a human figure among the trees. The man was standing still and watching them. He was not a groundsman; he was in a full evening suit. Ito lifted his hand, thinking that he must be an early guest come strolling, but the man did not wave back. Unsettled, Ito glanced forward again to check where he was going, and then looked back to find the man still watching them.

The ground shook again, not so badly this time, though the trees still rained down dead leaves and insects. The man had disappeared when Ito looked back a second time. He brushed bits of twig from his jacket sleeves and tried to brush off the memory of the unbroken stare. People did stare when they saw a man they knew from the newspapers, after all.

Beyond the lake, they came out into a tailored garden where small streams ran under red bridges and by new stone lanterns. Some of Ito's aides were set up under the pagoda, drinking tea from English china. They had not yet changed for the ball, and so they were still in kimono and bowler hats, and in one case a fez.

'Evening, sir!' one of them called. 'We're about to have a game of baseball – care to join in?'

'Oh, heavens, I can't play baseball,' Ito laughed. 'But don't let me stop the young and vigorous being young and vigorous.'

'Mr Mori?' he said hopefully. The aides were all frightened of Mori, but he was well known for his reflexes. 'Please? Baseball, the modern man's swordsmanship?'

'Not … this time, thank you,' said Mori. The young man winced. Ito nudged his arm. 'Be kind.'

'I didn't say anything.'

'Well then, come down off your high horse and take off your damn armour: you're clanking,' Ito said. He had meant it to be a joke, but it came out snappishly. 'And while you're at it, you might see Kuroda less often. I know I said liaise, but you're on the point of turning it into a liaison, if you haven't already.'

'All right. Our plans to overthrow everyone in cufflinks are almost complete anyway.'

Ito sighed. He yearned for a row, sometimes. 'Do warn me, when you act on them. Are there bombs in that briefcase?'

'No. He's going to be an octopus.'

'Octopus?'

'I want a pet,' Mori explained, insufficiently.

'Gone off your bees?' Mori kept bees. He lived in the middle of nowhere, in Shibuya, next door to a monastery. He let the monks come in to collect the honey. The hives had glass sides so that you could see when the combs were ready, and the peristalsis writhing of the drones. Ito had always hated them and asked why he bothered with them at the beginning of every visit, because Mori was hardly a keen entomologist, but he never had much in the way of a reply.

'They aren't pets.'

'Then ... I know a fellow who sells puppies?'

'Clockwork doesn't bark all the time and it's easier to take on a ship.'

'I've told you, you're not going to England until you explain why.'

'And I've told you, I've a friend in London.'

'No, you haven't got a friend in London. You've never been to London, and you don't write to anyone.'

'I'm not secret-selling to the British,' he said.

'But you can see why this worries me?'

'I've been telling you for years, you can't say you've had no notice.'

Ito was quiet, because it was true; after having initially said he would leave in ten years, Mori had brought it up every now and then to show he meant it. But he had never explained, and lately it had begun to make Ito nervous. That being so, he had given Mori's photograph to every harbourmaster between here and Nagasaki, and strict instructions. He had no doubt that Mori knew, because he could feel the heaviness in these moments when neither of them mentioned it. Or perhaps Mori would have mentioned it now, because he looked as if he wanted to say something, but then he put his hand in front of his face and caught the baseball that would otherwise have broken his nose. A flock of apologies came from the aides and whatever it was he had meant to say was forgotten.

There was, near the edge of the lawn, an enormous, ancient pear tree. Mori veered to it and dropped his handful of seeds among the long grass that had already grown around the trunk. He did the same thing whenever they came, and by now he had cultivated a lush patch of the stuff. He had a pathology of un-neatening overly neat things that matched his aversion to new houses and ironing his shirts. It was no accident he had chosen the one spot the gardeners absolutely could not mow without resorting to a pair of nail scissors. The roots were risen and twisting, and they wrapped all about the trunk making nooks and pools of withered pears, and little havens for weeds.

In the warm evening, the Rokumeikan was a rosy colour. A double bank of Roman arches ran the whole width of the building, one along the ground and one along the balcony above. Even in comparison to the train station, which was hardly elderly, it was magnificently new and clean. The earthquake had not unseated even a tile, which did not surprise him now he was here. It had a look of immense permanency, like a church. As they crunched on to the gravel drive, the great double doors of the balcony opened, and the Foreign Minister's young wife stepped out, already in her evening gown. The air was so still that Ito heard the silk hiss. The gown was Parisian, the bodice a sheaf of grey and pink pearls that sheened.

'Oh, hello, gentlemen,' she called down. She spoke English with a beautiful American accent. 'Baron Mori, it's been such a long time! What do you think, now the scaffolding is gone? Will all those fussy foreigners take us seriously now?'

He shook his head once. 'No. The moment they take Japan seriously will be the moment she defeats an existing Western power in a war of sufficient significance.'

She was a woman of grace, and so she laughed. 'But I guess it's better to try a dance hall before we order a thousand ironclads from Liverpool, right?'

'Exactly right,' Ito said, kicking Mori's ankle. 'I'm afraid I've been working him too hard, Countess Inoue, he's forgotten what few social graces he used to have.'

'Oh, it's okay. It's important to have blunt men around. Why don't you come in?'

Ito pushed Mori to the door before he could refuse, and the Countess turned inside again. Another little earthquake rattled the teacup she had left on the banister. Behind them, the pear tree creaked.

*

Few by few, the grand ballroom filled with glittering girls and tall foreigners in military tails or white ties. So many purple banners waved in the heat of the lamps that it felt to Ito like being inside an inflating hot-air balloon. Imperial chrysanthemums crowded everywhere, on the stairway, round the doors, in looping arches around the floor, a forest's worth. Over the past year, Ito and Count Inoue had poured more than fourfold more funds into this building than had gone into the new Foreign Ministry, and it showed. Mori of course had looked at it as if it were a casino and taken himself and his case of clockwork off to the balcony, which was empty except for six of the Empress's ladies, who had lost no time in making it clear they had been ordered to come.

Ito turned away from the buffet with a saucer full of chocolate strawberries to find the man from the woods looking at him across the room. Ito looked back at him, thinking that there must be something wrong with him. The man began to walk toward him, and as he passed under a chandelier, it traced the shape of his hands in his pockets, and the gun in his left. Ito stood still and realised that he was about to die holding a plate of chocolate strawberries. He couldn't move, only think how stupid it was.

Mori stepped between a pair of dancers as they spun and stood between Ito and the man. Ito lurched, because every inch of him expected a gunshot, but the man only froze and stared at him. Mori handed him a slip of folded paper. Without opening it, the man turned from him and almost ran.

Ito swallowed, and after what felt like a long time, set down the saucer and went to Mori.

'Who was that?' he said.

He saw Mori prepare a lie about the man having needed directions to the balcony, but then give up on it. 'Assassin.'

'What was that paper you gave him?'

'I didn't give him anything.'

'You did, I saw.'

'I didn't.'

Ito made an impatient noise that his wife would have called rude. He would have too, if he had been talking to someone less impervious. 'You are an astonishingly poor liar, for an intelligence officer. I'll go and ask him, shall I?'

'Ito—'

'What, something else you don't want me to know?' he snapped as he made for the stairs.

Mori lifted his hands but didn't bother to chase him. Ito was downstairs in time to see the man running through the front door.

The fine afternoon had turned into a cool night. The wind was up and even from the drive, he could hear the old pear tree shivering. The man was going that way now. Ito hesitated before he stepped off the drive and on to the grass, but then, feeling angry with himself, followed more quickly. Kuroda had once said that the difference between noblemen and commoners was the same as that between warhorses and donkeys. Mori was modern but not liberal. He thought the same, Ito knew he did. He had let him go because he thought the bookseller's boy would, as an inevitable consequence of his unimpressive breeding, prove a coward.

The man slowed as he reached the pear tree. Ito moved to the left so that he would not pass from view, and saw that there was a horse there too, grazing its way through Mori's patch of long grass. The man stopped and stood still. He had unfolded the piece of paper. As Ito watched, the man took out his watch and took more than usual care over the time, then looked around, all the way, so that Ito had to duck behind a hedge. Then he screwed up the paper and shoved it in his pocket, shaking his head as if he thought he had been conned somehow. His hand went to the gun again and he stood fingering it, but didn't move back toward the hall. He glanced around, as though waiting for something, but nobody else was coming.

'What did he give you, just now?'

The man jumped and held up the gun.

'If you're afraid of him now, I wouldn't like to imagine what he will be like if you kill me,' he said quickly. Hiding behind Mori's name became no less shameful when the man let his hand fall again.

Looking anguished, the man took out the piece of paper instead and came across to show him. As he did, the earth gave a little shrug, the last of the aftershocks, and the pear tree crashed down an inch from the horse. The horse shrieked and bolted. The man stared at the tree. Ito took the piece of paper from his hand.

It was a list of names, dates, and times. There were five. The final name was listed by today's date, beside which was the time, nine forty-seven. Ito pulled out his watch. The minute hand was just now easing to nine forty-eight.

'Is your name Ryosuke, then?' he asked into the echoing quiet. It was not silence; the broken tree trunk was still clicking, and the air was full of insects disturbed by the fall. A waltz reached them quite clearly from the open doors of the club. There was a shadow of earth in the grass. The tree had fallen so hard that it had ploughed a harrow.

'Yes.' The man pulled his gaze away from the tree again. 'I should find my horse,' he said in a faraway voice.

'Wait. Who are these others?'

The man looked at him strangely. 'Don't you know?'

'No?'

'They came after you too. He killed them all.'

Ito stopped following him. 'What?'

'I've got to find—'

'Wait!' Ito called after him, but he did not wait, and because the horse had run into the denser trees near the lake, he disappeared within twenty yards, into the dark.

The offices of the Choya Newspaper Company were closed by the time he arrived. Having made a good deal of money from being leery of the new government, they had acquired a grand brick building in Ginza, in sight of the clock tower, with high pillars and a fine arched doorway. The door was locked, but there was a lit window on the ground floor. When he tapped on it, a young man came out with a fountain pen stuck under the left strap of his braces. He stopped still when he recognised his visitor.

'All due respect, Mr Ito, sir, but you cannot come and shout at us for reporting the news, however unfavourable it happens to be for the government—'

'I'm not here to shout at you, I'm here to ask if I might look at your archives. Particularly obituaries, if you keep them. I'm terribly sorry for the late hour, but I'm afraid it's urgent and newspapers keep altogether better records than the ministry does.'

'Oh, of course,' the young man said, perplexed. 'We keep everything in the cellar. I'll just unlock ...'

Ito followed him inside, down a shallow flight of steps to a cold cellar. Leaving behind two lamps, the young man retreated, and Ito had to explore a little to get his bearings. Six or seven years' worth of papers had been stored in wide drawers – flat, first and uncorrected editions. They were in good order, and it did not take him long to find the broadsheets for the dates on the note.

The newsprint crackled as he sifted through it. Because the cabinets were wood and the drawers not sealed, the summer damp had got inside a few, and in some places sheets were stuck together, rendered so thin that they looked and felt like a single page that had been over-printed twice. It was on one of these that he found the first name. He had to bring the sheet right out and hold it over a light box to read it properly. He had expected a shooting or a mugging, but the man in question had been struck by lightning. He had been poaching birds in the grounds of the Palace, it said, and the lightning had struck him through his rifle.

The second man had been killed in a traffic accident in Kojimachi. By then, Ito's eyes were beginning to sting from the close focus and the difficult light, but he found the third too. Caught in the crossfire of a robbery, again very close to Kojimachi, perhaps two streets away from Ito's own house. He vaguely remembered hearing of it at the time, but not in detail. Of the fourth man, though, there was no mention, even in the days surrounding the one on the note. He sat back and pulled off his spectacles, and looked over at the enormous cabinets. It would take his entire staff weeks to sift through everything in search of one name, and even as he tried to think of ways to do it, he could see it was hopeless. But three was enough to be getting on with. Three men dead in accidents, a fourth unaccounted for and a fifth whose possible accident had been predicted to the minute. Ito sat gazing down at the crumpled note, translucent over the light box. He had always assumed that Mori's knack for pre-empting things was subconscious.

When he sat back, he thought that his watch was wrong. He had been there only for an hour and a half; it was not yet midnight. He stood up slowly, stiff, and put everything back before making his way up the stairs. The young journalist nodded as he saw him out, his fountain pen hooked over his pocket this time. Ito stepped outside into the cool air, knowing that he would have to walk back. The street was deserted now. The rickshawmen had long since got cold and gone home, and the trains had stopped an hour ago. It was less than a mile, but he was tired and felt disproportionately grateful when hooves clopped along beside him, and a black horse huffed at a firefly that had looped too close to its nose. The firefly veered off and, to Ito's tired eyes, left behind a trail of light.

'Mr Ito?' the driver said.

Ito looked up. 'Yes?'

'To the Rokumeikan?'

'Oh, thank God. You did well to recognise me in the dark.'

'Well, I was told to pick up the man on the steps of the newspaper office, and there was only you,' the man laughed.

Ito fell quiet. 'I don't suppose a Mr Mori made the reservation.'

'Didn't get a name, sorry. Do you still want the carriage?' he added anxiously.

'Yes – yes.' Ito climbed up and lapsed on to the leather seat.

As the cab stopped gently on the gravel drive, he saw Mori on the balcony. He was working at something by lamplight. Although he must have heard them, he did not look down. Threading his way through the foyer and the crowded stairway, where people had lined the rail to watch the dancing from above, Ito went up to him. Even the white men didn't have to duck to pass through the chrysanthemums.

Mori's lamp shone over the cogs spilled across the table top. Among them were sparks that cast rainbows. Ito sat down opposite. Under Mori's hands, the octopus was recognisable but split open, and there was a galaxy of clockwork inside. Parts of it glittered different colours to others, some bigger, some tiny and buried deep, all making winking networks of shapes that shifted and clicked softly, like something sleeping.

'You were planting grass seeds under that tree six months ago,' Ito said at last.

'Yes,' Mori said to the octopus. He was wearing glasses; Ito could see the clockwork reflected in the lenses. The rainbow-making sparks were diamonds. As he clicked another cog into place, a new section of the workings began to spin. The moving bearings threw more bright specks inside the casing.

'Those other men, the ones on the list. They were all near the Palace or in Kojimachi. They were going to kill me, weren't they?'

'Yes.' He was still speaking to the clockwork. Ito could not have said when it had begun, but he became aware then that the mechanisms were singing. It was a strange noise, one that made the hairs on his arms prickle. It was the after-tone of a struck tuning fork. 'The last one believed me and went to a monastery in Kyoto.'

He was speaking as he always did, dry and clear.

'Why would you let me find out about this?' Ito said at last. He felt like he had when he had broken his wrist. Altogether worse than pain was that maddeningly clear vision of having not tripped, not broken anything, when logic held up a lamp in the straight tunnel that time drove humans through, and showed that the walls were made of glass. His chest was stiff with the dismay of it. He could still see what would have happened if he hadn't chased the man to the pear tree. He need only have decided, as he often did that, like gravity and wives, Mori was one of those things best trusted and not over-scrutinised. He realised Mori was waiting for him to finish the question.

'You can kill a man by planting grass seeds in the right place. What can I possibly do now that I know that? Take your word for it that Kiyotaka Kuroda won't one day persuade you that world war is a good idea?' He could hear his voice rising but couldn't stop it. 'He's on the edge of it already. I should lock you up and throw away the key.'

'It was necessary to frighten you. Now you won't send anyone after me when I go to the ship,' he said. 'There's no point stabbing a man when you can arrange for him not to be in the way in the first place.'

'Oh, how philanthropic of you! Are you going to enlighten me about London now? What's there? What's so damn important?'

'A friend, like I said.'

'There isn't.'

'He hasn't met me yet.'

'I can't let you go anywhere.'

Mori let his breath out. The last of the clockwork across the table was gone now. He clicked the octopus's hatch closed and the thing shifted, waking, and wound its tentacles through his hands. He lifted it into his lap. 'I'm sorry about this. It's the only way to make you change your mind.'

'Oh, do your worst, I think you'll find—'

'Your wife is unknowingly but extremely allergic to bee stings,' Mori interrupted, quietly.

Ito fell still. 'No.'

Mori only watched him, as if he were very far away.

'Get *out*!' Ito exploded, and didn't care that it made the court ladies jump.

Mori did as he was told. The octopus sat with its beak on his arm. Ito half thought it would wave, but it didn't. Once they were gone, he leaned forward against his elbows and pushed his hands through his hair. He had always prided himself on his politics. Not left or right or old or new, but the mechanics of it: compromise, diplomacy, and the avoidance of war, which was what happened when statesmen failed. War was punching the clock instead of looking at the broken mechanisms. He had never failed like that in his life. He normally made fun of people who flew into rages. He closed his eyes and waited for his heart to subside, but it cantered on and on.

The balcony door opened and Kuroda came through, looking left and right. Ten to one already.

'You've just missed Mori,' Ito said. 'He's gone to England.'

'Mm,' he said, unbothered, and began to turn inside again.

'Kuroda,' he said suddenly.

'What?'

'About Korea.' He had to pause and feel his way around the idea. 'It frightens you. Why does it frighten you?'

The admiral looked as though a dog had sat up and talked. 'The Chinese, of course.'

'Why? We have the treaty—'

'Balls. Ask your British friends what they think about treaties.'

Ito took a deep breath. 'Just … come here a moment and tell me what would be best.'

'What d'you mean?'

'I mean I'm not a military man. I need someone to explain.'

Still frowning, Kuroda bent into Mori's seat and etched a map on the mahogany table top with his penknife. Ito winced, but stopped when Kuroda pointed it at him to ask if there was something he wanted to say. When the dawn came, the clouds were like smoke. He thought of trains and ships, and Mori probably already on the sea. Now that he was calmer, he was confused. Mori was rich enough to persuade anyone who followed him to stop, without giving himself away. He sighed. Kuroda gave him a salt cellar to hold in place of the Russian fleet and told him to pay attention.

TWENTY-TWO

LONDON, OCTOBER 1884

THE KENSINGTON HOUSE had a narrow garden and eight pear trees. They stood four on either side of a flatter patch of grass that had once been a gravel path, which still crunched in the most worn-down places. After weeks of the to-ing and fro-ing of painters and carpenters, the garden was the only aspect of the house that remained as her aunt had left it. The nettles were as thick as the grass and ivy stuck an octogenarian rake to the wall of the outhouse, which had a little stained glass window in the door. Grace had spent all summer catching her hems on things that stuck or stung, and trying not to look too closely into the branches of the trees, where alarmingly big crows had made their nests alarmingly close to head-height. Thaniel, who had been efficient in all other aspects, was oddly unwilling to put it all to rights. Even on chilly days, he sat outside with his Japanese dictionary pinned down with a rock rather than come indoors. Whenever she brought it up, he mumbled and found something else to do.

That was not to say he fabricated things. There was plenty to do, and it was made more difficult by the workmen, who were typical of their breed and imbued with a mortal fear of speaking directly to a lady. The house had been cluttered with the accumulated rubbish of her aunt's lifetime, and to clear it alone had taken weeks. Then the crumbling floorboards had been taken up and replaced, and then the laboratory kitted out, and the gas lines seen to, for her aunt had still run on oil. Piece by piece the house had become bright and new again, but still Thaniel kept to the garden, and still did nothing to it. Because they could only go on Saturday afternoons – with her father having flatly forbidden her to go alone and Thaniel at work in the week and rehearsals on Sundays – he managed to drag it out. Two Saturdays before the wedding, the cold came down fast and the garden whitened. Powdery snow hazed about the trees whenever the wind blew. She was working between two Bunsen burners lit on blue flames, but she knew better than to light a fire upstairs for when he arrived. She might as well have tried to settle a deer there.

When she heard the ice on the gate crack, she looked up. The laboratory was finished, and as a sort of christening, she had invited Mori to come and see it. She had not seen him since first meeting him, but when she had gone to the post office to send him a telegram, there was already one waiting for her saying that yes, quarter to two this Saturday was good. She sent hers anyway, because something about his wording suggested that he hadn't anticipated her exactly, but forgotten that he hadn't had the request yet.

Her watch said it was still an hour early, but she climbed up on the bench anyway when she heard the gate and pushed open the window to see. It was an unusual window; mostly it was grisaille glass, but just off-centre, the glazier had set a circle of bright colours mosaicked together from half an angel and some family crests, scavenged, probably, from a cathedral. The light was bright and cloudy at once, and the glass put coloured reflections over her arm. Thaniel was by himself.

'Is he still coming?' she called.

'He'll be by when he said,' Thaniel promised. He came toward the window and bent briefly to wave before he took the old ladder and propped it against the nearest pear tree.

'Does he seem put upon?'

'No. Why would he?'

'I had the powerful impression last time that he didn't like me.'

He laughed. 'Why invite him, then?'

'Because I might be wrong and I'd like to know what he has to say about this experiment. He could help. What … are you doing?'

'I thought I'd work out here for a bit.'

'Really?' she said curiously.

He held up the basket he had just set down by the ladder, angled down for her to see. It was full of golden pears, real gold, or at least a veneer. 'He had them kicking around the attic, so I stole them.'

'Won't he mind?' she said, thinking of all the stolen clothes of Matsumoto's she hadn't returned. She had meant to, but when the end of term had come, she hadn't found the time, and told herself she would see him in London anyway. But then after the Foreign Office ball, he had gone straight to Paris. He hadn't said good-bye. That was a frequent complaint of his friends. Friends were things that he liked to surround himself with for a while, like good curtains, before he moved on and forgot them and bought new curtains elsewhere.

Thaniel waved his hand as he went up the ladder. 'He would have said before I found them if he did.'

While he clipped the pears into the branches by their magnetic hooks, he chatted as usual, but not much, because he was working his way along the garden, away from her. He belonged with the trees. He didn't seem to mind touching the branches, though they were full of moss and old splinters where the wind had snapped off twigs. She wanted to go out too, but she could see that if she did, she would notice the splinters and the moss too much, and it wouldn't be the same for her. She closed the window and climbed back down to the laboratory floor to get on with the labelling of her chemical drawers.

'It isn't that cold,' she heard him say a while later, his voice carrying down from the gate on the small wind. Mori was here, then.

'You don't know anything; you burn in candlelight.' It had been odd to hear his voice when she could see him, but it was bizarre now that she couldn't. It was a foot taller and three shades whiter than the rest of him. She had thought before that he had a north-ern accent, and perhaps it was still there a little, but it was much more standard now. She wondered if it was conscious or not. 'Mind those. They'll drop if you don't clamp them on well.'

'Why?'

'It's autumn.'

'How do they know?'

'Interior thermometers,' he said.

'Not tiny elves, then.'

'That was my original plan, but they proved difficult to catch.'

'She's in the cellar,' Thaniel laughed.

She put her pen down and pushed her hands together. It was difficult to see where Thaniel found the confidence to joke with him. She wished she had it. She was reasonably sure that Mori would want to help with the experiments whether he liked her or not, for the sake of hurrying along a future he was no doubt bored of waiting for, but it would be better if she could persuade him that she was worth the effort.

Mori was too quiet for her to hear him on the cellar stairs, and so the first sign of his arrival was the turning handle.

He came in slowly, like somebody else's cat. She couldn't tell if that was wariness. He had a strange way of moving anyway, sometimes sudden and sometimes slow, one she had noticed when they first met at the house on Filigree Street. If she had been forced to offer up a theory, she would have said it was what happened when a man could recall being old, but every now and then remembered that he was young still and that there was no need to be careful of his bones. His black eyes caught on the grisaille window, which dotted points of colour into them. His hair was darker than it had been in June.

'Mr Mori, come in.'

'Miss Carrow,' he said.

'So, I've been working on an experiment to prove the existence of ether,' she said abruptly, because she didn't much like small talk even when she didn't know the exact wording ahead of time. 'It's there and there must be a way to see it – I don't mean see, I mean record the effects, of course – but nothing has worked so far. Thaniel told me about you a little while ago, and how you remember. I was wondering if you knew how do to it.'

'It's something about electricity and … I think it's icing sugar that works well.'

She laughed. 'I don't suppose you'd happen to know any numbers or suchlike that might be less vague.'

'I don't. Sorry. It's not my area.'

'Not your area? How?'

He shifted. 'Well, I know that light is fascinating and full of scientific mystery, but mostly I use it for not walking into objects, and mostly I use ether for not walking into events. It's there, it's useful, it's ... not something I can study for more than ten minutes at once without falling asleep. I like mechanics. I'm not the right person to ask for mathematics.'

'But you can understand anything now that you ever could understand.'

'I'll never understand. Advanced physics is about describing things you can't know intuitively, so you describe it in numbers, but I've got it in front of me.' He was looking around the room rather than at her. He seemed to like it, and since coming in, he had eased closer to the burners. 'It's like listening to blind people with no sense of touch prove atom by atom the existence and possible features of an elephant when I'm not even very interested in elephants. I'm sorry,' he said, and he really did look sorry. He opened his satchel and held out a book. 'I think this helps.'

It was a collection of fairy stories. She took it slowly, and felt completely left behind. In those stories, there was always someone who was too unmagic to hear the trees speaking or see the elves in the branches, or who the woods quietly closed out of their own accord. She had never thought it would be her. 'Thank you, I suppose.'

He nodded and turned to go.

'Wait, Mori. I thought you would want to do this. I think you could, if you wanted to.'

'I really am sorry,' he said again, without denying it. 'But you don't need me. You'll get there by yourself soon.'

'Actually I think you're perfectly interested, but I've stolen your favourite toy and now you're teaching me a lesson,' she murmured, careful to keep any impatience from her voice.

He lifted his head and looked straight at her for the first time, not so much with anger as a sort of half-surprise. She felt suddenly as though she had thrown a stone, badly aimed, but still a stone, at a navy sniper.

'Please come along and forget it; you of all people know there will be other toys. This work is important.'

'You've stolen my favourite toy,' he repeated slowly, landing hard on toy, 'and now you've invited me down here to play with a new toy whose mind is a reasoning engine running on rails. But I don't like train sets, they're dull, and there is a certain urge to arrange a wreck for the sake of variation.'

She swallowed. 'Yes, I deserved that for rather a patronising metaphor. I am sorry, I meant it to be a joke.'

'There's no piano upstairs,' he said, more like himself.

'The ... floors need to be laid first.'

'But this floor looks new.'

'It is,' she said, confused.

'I see. Anyway, I'd better go, the Christmas orders are coming in already.'

'Oh, no ...' she mumbled, and trailed off, because he had started up the stairs without waiting for her to say anything.

After a lag, she followed him up on an automatic urge not to let a guest see himself out. Because she rarely heard real hostility, it was only on the way, very gradually, that she understood he had not just been punishing her for speaking down to him. It had been a very straightforward threat.

'Do these grow their own pear trees?' Thaniel called to him from the ladder. Her ribs panged. She wanted to pull him indoors.

'No, I couldn't fit enough clockwork inside for a whole tree,' Mori said. He picked up the next pear and climbed up on to the tree's low fork to hand it over. The gold surface striped briefly as it reflected their fingers. 'I'm going home, I'll see you later.'

'That was quick.'

'I couldn't help.'

'Oh. Never mind. I'll be a while, I'm waiting for a man with some carpets.'

'Ten minutes.'

'Why don't you stay a bit and wait with us, then?'

'No, I ought to get on.'

'Mori ...' Thaniel began.

'I can't, I can't, I've left bread in the oven,' he said, already down on the ground again. He let himself out through the rusting gate and then disappeared among the traffic.

Grace reached the ladder as Thaniel was climbing down. Once he was back on the grass, he brushed splinters and moss from his hands. He smelled of the leaves.

'He doesn't like me,' she explained, and her voice came out tight. 'He was out of the laboratory within about forty seconds of coming in.'

Thaniel sighed. 'He's always strange, you shouldn't take it to heart.'

'I suppose it's no shock. He'll miss you terribly.'

He pushed his hands through his hair and found a leaf, which he dropped from shoulder height and watched as it sycamored down to the ground. 'He'll change his mind eventually.'

'How? There's nothing that could prompt it; he already knows what all the prompts are and if he's not convinced now, he never will be.'

He looked as if he might have disagreed, but the wind blew again then and a pear fell from the tree. He made a small sound in the back of his throat and started forward to find it in the long grass, then stopped suddenly. There was no time to ask him what was the matter before a thin gold stem crept up through the grass, along the tree trunk. It twisted around it, and grew its own small offshoots and creepers, which fastened themselves to the shape of the bark and the old, risen roots. Tiny leaves clicked as they opened, not as real ones did but unfolding like paper until they were ivy-shaped. They both stood back, and the ivy slowed and stopped at just about the height of a person, gleaming in the cold afternoon. Thaniel laughed. 'Not bad!'

She touched his arm. Other pears had fallen too, and the golden ivy had climbed up around the other trees. The vines creaked and sang as they stretched out their very last inches. It made her teeth ache. The gold was reflecting the leaves and the sky, and from any distance it looked like bright water that had become muddled and run up the tree trunks rather than down. By all accounts it was exquisite, but she wished that it was not right outside her front door.

'His name,' she said. 'Doesn't it mean woods? Forest, something?' She knew random snippets from Matsumoto.

'It … probably used to, before aristocratic spelling interfered. Why?'

She shook her head. It was unlikely he knew anything about oriental poetry. 'I don't know. He unsettles me. He threatened me just now, I think. Something about my being a reasoning engine and his not liking trains. It sounded like years of accumulated dislike. To the point of wanting to hit me with a steam engine.'

'If he was going to hit you with a steam engine, he'd have done it by now,' Thaniel pointed out. 'Actually, if he hated you that much, we would never have met.'

'Why did he say it, then?'

'Probably to make sure you didn't invite him again. Sorry. I'll shout at him later.'

'No, don't. I don't want him to be angrier with me than he already is.'

He glanced down at her with a smile in his eyes. 'So he can change his mind for the worse but not for the better?'

'I think he can give in to an extant temptation,' she said, more precisely than was good-humoured.

He seemed not to recognise it as snappishness. A cart had stopped outside their gate. 'The carpet people are here.'

'Make sure they sort out the dining room properly, won't you?' she said, naming a random room at the back of the house. 'I'd like to get that one right, what with my mother wanting to visit.'

He looked at her as if he didn't know at all, but it was his habit to take her exactly at her word and do as he was told.

Once he had gone towards the dining room with the man in charge, Grace stepped in front of a younger man and cornered him in the hall. He looked surprised, but not suspicious, and so she ploughed ahead.

'You do all sorts of flooring, don't you? Not just carpets?'

'That's right, ma'am. Hardwoods mainly, lots of oak. Had you got something in mind?' he said hopefully.

'Well, actually my husband was hoping you could do us a favour. You see those trees out there? We really don't want them any more, but it would be a shame to burn pear wood. If you cut them down, you can have them for nothing.'

'Are you sure, ma'am? With all the gold—'

'There's a gardener coming tomorrow morning, so I'd cheerfully pay you extra to get it done quickly. Unless pear wood isn't so in fashion these days. Is it?'

'Oh, it is,' he said quickly. 'Well, if you're sure, ma'am, I'd be bloody delighted. I mean—'

'It's all right, I've married a very nearly Yorkshire man, you're not going to out-swear him.' For the sake of speaking to workmen, she tended to say they were already married, and so did Thaniel: because my husband says so, and even better, because my wife says so, were rather more powerful phrases than 'Mr Steepleton' or 'Miss Carrow'. She wore her engagement ring backwards so that only the band showed.

He laughed at that and went straight back out to fetch some saws. She turned inside and made some tea, probably badly, and took it through to the dining room, where the master was rather ostentatiously re-measuring the complicated dimensions under Thaniel's grey eyes.

She had thought he would stray back into the garden at the first opportunity and she would have to make some excuse, but the carpet man was from Lincolnshire too, and they made friends. The dining room had its new floor fitted nicely by the time he came away, and by then the trees were all gone. The branches had been cut off and stacked neatly by the firewood shed, and all that was left were the stumps, very fresh and yellow, and a debris of leaves over the grass. Among them winked little rags of gold. The whole garden was bigger and brighter. Thaniel stopped as if he had walked into a wall.

'What?' was all he said at first.

'The carpenter asked if he could have some pear wood cuttings. So I said he could take the lot. That's all right, isn't it?'

'Where's the clockwork?'

'In the basket there.'

It was; the carpenter had unwound it carefully, and some of it had snapped like real vines would have, but it was largely intact.

'I'd better give it back to him,' he said. He looked down at it for a while. 'I'll just take it round, I'll be back in half an hour.'

He picked up the basket and set off down the newly bright garden, without looking to either side or back. She watched him turn left, toward Knightsbridge, and realised that she had upset him much more than she had meant to.

TWENTY-THREE

Unconsulted, LORD CARROW had arranged the wedding for the day before Gilbert and Sullivan's show, and so Thaniel was scheduled to miss beheading by twenty-four hours. He wasn't worried about the performance, but he had spent more time at the piano than he had at the Kensington house. He had added up the hours on his way home with Mori's broken clockwork. He was still absently multiplying when he pushed open the workshop door.

'Oh, never mind,' Mori said before he could get out an apology. 'They would only have gone to waste in the attic.'

He set the basket down by the door. In the cold snap, Mori had acquired a brazier that had stayed lit for the last few days. The embers in the middle of the grate waved the air. Thaniel unwound his scarf and hung it up by the lotus clock. Mori was still wearing his, and when he wasn't talking, he ducked his head so that he could breathe into it. The shop was closed today; he was doing his taxes. The book in front of him was all columns of Japanese numbers. Because he wrote with his left hand on the left page and his right on the right, the figures slanted in opposite directions and looked as though he had written only one page, then printed it against the other while it was still damp. In the basket, some of the gold ivy leaves flapped in the heat.

'Are you not coming to the wedding because you don't like her?' Thaniel asked.

Mori lifted his eyes. They reflected the snowy window panes. Because the dye in his hair had faded, he was more foreign. 'No. I'm a Buddhist. You might have a Christian obligation to catch pneumonia while you sit for two and a half hours listening to some twerp in a dress drone on about the virtue of wedded life but, dear as you are to me, I don't.'

'This is like brown tea, isn't it,' said Thaniel.

'It isn't unreasonable.'

'Of course it's unreasonable, you xenophobic gnome,' Thaniel said, laughing to cover the disappointment that had settled over his thoughts like sleet. It was stupid: he had anticipated hitting a pocket of Japaneseness over the church, and when Mori had first said no, weeks ago, he hadn't been surprised. 'So you're not … upset.'

'I would be. An oriental man in a church is a target for evangelism.'

'All right. You're excused, if it's so distressing.'

Mori nodded, but then put down his pen. 'Surely if an angel appears in the middle of a ravening mob, best practice is not to throw them your daughter by way of distraction but to suggest that the angel flies away? The defining characteristic of angels is their aerodynamic capacity.'

Thaniel frowned. Mori rarely spoke that much at once and it was only now that he had that it was obvious he had lost the north in his accent. It was a tiny, meaningless, sharp loss. He struggled to find the thread of what had been said.

'I've said you're excused; you can't continue to be annoyed about what the vicar would say to you if you did go.'

'I'll do my taxes,' Mori said, and bent his neck over the ledger again. Then, without looking up, 'Everything all right?'

'Mm.' He sat down in the other high chair to soak in some of the heat. Despite having put down his basket of gold, he still felt heavy and tired. He pulled Fanshaw's dictionary across the desk and stole a supernumerary pencil, and kept on with the small stories he made up in order to remember the pictograph characters. He let his elbow rest against Mori's and every now and then, when he couldn't find the characters' constituent radicals in the smaller dictionary he had bought from the show village, nudged him for an explanation. It was much sooner than usual that his eyes became tired and refused to recognise that they knew any of the writing at all. It turned into a meaningless jumble and he sat back.

'What in God's name is a needlemouse, anyway?'

Mori paused and wrote it out to see what he meant, and then inhaled at it and tipped his head forward.

'Something wrong?' said Thaniel.

'I've just written annual hedgehog income in the middle of my expenses column.'

Thaniel laughed without expecting to, until Mori jabbed him with the end of his pen and told him to take himself and his needlemice into the kitchen to make some more tea. He did as he was told, but stopped once he was standing. He could feel the laughter seeping away too quickly through otherwise arid thoughts.

'Mori,' he said. 'Why did you change your accent?'

Mori was cutting out the mistake with a scalpel. 'I didn't change it, it changed. I can speak English because I remember it from ahead, and most of it was from you, but we're not going to talk so often any more. I'm getting everything from open lectures and arguing with Mrs Haverly.'

'Kensington is twenty minutes' walk away.'

'You're going to be busy.'

'With what?'

'It's ... you know. Ordinary things pile up.' He knocked the drawer beside him shut with his elbow. Thaniel had not seen what was inside, but the little bump made whatever it was hum, very quietly. It was a distinctive noise; it was what you got when you closed the lid of a music box.

He didn't let his expression change. 'I'll never be that busy,' he said, because it was what he would have said if he hadn't heard the hum. 'You'll see. You've been wrong before, you're wrong all the time. Anyway: tea.'

Mori looked relieved. Thaniel closed the kitchen door after himself, and stood still while he waited for the kettle to boil. He liked children. The house in Kensington would be a good place for a child to grow up. But he wanted to lock himself upstairs and sleep until he could wake into something else.

The weather stayed cold all week. The mudbanks along the Thames froze, and then so did the shallows. Near Westminster, the ice was bumpy where the cockle-pickers knocked holes in it and the river water seeped up again. The newspapers became excitable about the possibility of a winter cold enough for frost fairs, although he had his doubts. A cold snap so early usually meant one of those zigzagging winters that saw everyone buried under snow one minute and going about without coats by Christmas, only to catch pneumonia at New Year. But the wind was sharper than ever when Thaniel went to King's Cross to meet Grace's friend Matsumoto. As the train from Dover applied its brakes, it slid on the tracks and slammed into the bumpers. The bang made everyone wince. A woman spilled some tea that froze into a sheet of amber. Not for the first time, he wondered irritably why trains ran on the same level that people walked. If they were to have been even two feet down from the platforms, they would be safer.

He was meeting Matsumoto in Grace's place; she had been cornered by her mother, something about the dress, and since the man was coming back from France for the wedding, it seemed ungrateful to leave him to do his own welcoming. Grace had told Thaniel to look for an overdressed socialite, so he did, and quickly found him. Matsumoto shook his hand and clapped his arm and called him Thaniel, which, after months of being Steepletoned by Mori, felt like being called ducky. Thaniel spent the cab ride studying him. He was much younger than Mori, and, like Grace had said, almost inappropriately well dressed. The iris in his buttonhole was more than enough to put Thaniel off trying to talk much.

Because he had assumed Matsumoto would stay at a hotel, he was puzzled when the cab pulled up by the red gate of the show village. In fact, Matsumoto's family had a London flat. It was on the top floor of the same pretty block of townhouses where Yuki's father had his workshop. Since Thaniel had last been that way, scaffolding had gone up the side of the building. Some workmen were sitting on the roof with their legs dangling, sharing something from a small flask. They had been working on the chimneys, where the half-constructed brickwork was new and bright. One of the men put the flask in a bucket and wheeled it down on a squeaking pulley to a boy on the ground, who giggled.

There was an elevator inside. At the flick of a lever, they glided five floors up to the carpeted hallway where the best suites were, passing flashes of flower-arrangements and differently coloured carpets on the way.

The flat was large enough for Matsumoto to show him around while they waited for the kettle to boil. It must have been recently done over, because the floors shone and smelled of beeswax. On the walls were ancient Chinese prints, except for one modern corner where there were four paintings in almost the same style as the one Mori had bought months ago from the depressed Dutchman. Embarrassingly, theirs was hanging in the parlour beside a sketch Thaniel had made of the Kyrie from Mozart's *Requiem*. Mori had rescued it from a wastepaper basket and then hovered with a packet of watercolours and a hopeful expression until Thaniel had painted the other movements too. He had tried to say you couldn't put up pictures of a requiem in a parlour, but Mori had proven selectively deaf. Whenever Thaniel intended to take them down, Katsu poked him with a pin. He was coming to the very gradual conclusion that Mori hadn't only been being polite, but really wanted it. Why was still a foggy point.

The tea was brown. Matsumoto was as English as Francis Fanshaw.

'It wasn't too much trouble to come, was it?' Thaniel said at last, when they had exhausted the weather and the paintings.

Matsumoto shook his head once. 'No, no. But I really must get straight home afterwards.' He sighed. 'Truth is, I'm rather anxious about Matsumoto Castle. My father's there by himself and the government have been bullying him about selling it for a while. I didn't think they were serious at first, but his letters are becoming more urgent, so I shall be hopping it straight after the party, I'm afraid. There's a thing called the Castle Abolition Law that—'

'I know, I know,' said Thaniel. 'What will happen if they do take it?'

'New house in Tokyo, I suppose. Gosh, no, the Emperor isn't in the habit of making beggars of his noblemen. He's not as bad an egg as all that,' Matsumoto said, but he looked bleak. 'God, it's cold in here. I didn't tell anyone I was coming, there's no wood.'

'Let's go and stand outside for a few minutes, then. It should feel tropical when we come back in.'

'I shouldn't have said anything, should I,' Matsumoto said, but he picked up his tea and came obediently outside.

The balcony had a wide view over the show village, then far across Hyde Park, although it would have been better had the scaffolding not blocked out everything on the left. The sky was indigo around the horizon, and lights sparkled in the village below. Not far away, the pagoda was being decked with paper lamps and streamers. Carpenters hammered up a wide stage before it. They had already erected a copy of the village's gaunt, curving gate on the stage to make a proscenium arch, and now some boys flicked their brushes at each other while they painted it red.

Grace let herself in behind them. She had a sparkler from Nakamura's shop downstairs. As she came across to them, she spun the light in spirals.

'Escaped at last,' she said. 'What's going on down there?'

'Gilbert and Sullivan's show,' Thaniel said. 'The debut will be here on Sunday.'

'Thaniel's playing the piano,' Grace explained to Matsumoto, who only murmured something generally polite in a way that made Thaniel think he hadn't heard.

The three of them watched the women with the lamps. They stood on ladders to reach the rafters of the pagoda, while the men passed up lit candles to test the integrity of each paper shade. The firelight made the folds of their kimono sharp, and rippled in black hair and silk belts. The lights were bringing late village visitors over to see what would be happening.

Directly below them, Yuki's familiar, ramrod figure emerged from the firework shop.

'Oh, I say!' Grace called down. 'I left some change on the counter, I took a sparkler!'

Yuki looked up and nodded, and then his eyes caught on Matsumoto. 'Western monkey,' he said in Japanese.

'Monkey yourself,' Thaniel called after him. 'You *live* in London, you little bastard.'

Matsumoto's shoulders twitched back. He was still young enough to be flustered by the disapproval.

'Look, when in Rome,' Thaniel said.

Matsumoto shook his head. 'I'm not so sure. I feel like such a popinjay in these clothes, sometimes, and I wonder if in wearing them I'm not helping chip away at what makes us ourselves.'

'What are you talking about?' said Grace.

'That boy was rude to him because he's wearing Western clothes,' Thaniel explained.

'Why?'

'Because he's a fledgling nationalist lunatic, so he wants everyone from Japan to dress like a samurai and go about snarling. That's his father's workshop, there. I've said it isn't clever to leave him with fifty tonnes of gunpowder and a grudge against anyone in a jacket, but apparently it would be wrong to boot him out for something he only might do,' he said, thinking that he ought to mention to Mori that Yuki showed no sign of changing his mind about his politics. Mori would already know, but there was value in making it clear that *he* knew as well.

'Better a jacket than those idiotic kimonos,' Grace said.

'I'm going to talk to him,' Matsumoto said.

'Matsumoto! You can't bear it, can you, not being completely adored by everybody who sets eyes on you ... no? Not listening? I was only talking to myself anyway,' she muttered as the elevator whirred.

Thaniel leaned his forearms on the balcony rail so that he wouldn't miss any explosions if there were any. He saw Grace's hands flatten slowly on to the stone too.

'I upset you before, didn't I?' she said. 'Because of the trees.'

'No. Leaving home jitters is all.'

She paused. 'Mori still won't come?'

'He won't come.'

'I know you'd like him to, but I'm glad.'

He looked side on at her. 'He's not a witch. He's a lonely man with no one to talk to except a machine in the shape of an octopus.'

Her eyebrows lifted. 'Thaniel. Wake up. He can remember anything but a random process. That's anything except coin tosses and dice throws. Spinning magnets, like Katsu's random gears. He's sensing ether disturbances. He knows the moment you *intend* to do anything, because the electricity moving through your brain is pushing ether as it goes. Is that not remotely worrying for you? It means he knows how to make you trust. He knows how to make you change your mind, because he can isolate the second in which you could change it.'

'I know he can. I wouldn't have touched a piano again if he hadn't put me in front of Arthur Sullivan when he did. A thing done on purpose isn't necessarily bad.'

'But you wouldn't know if he didn't want you to. I'm afraid of him because if he ever gets tired of me, he will be able to convince you that you are too.'

'It would be interesting if we could imagine for half a minute that I'm in possession of more common sense than a chicken,' he said quietly. 'I live with him, I can see when he's arranging things.'

'I don't mean that you're stupid. I mean that you're an ordinary man who works in an office and sometimes plays the piano, and Mori is a genius who could engineer worlds. I'm ... explaining why I'm worried, that's all.'

Thaniel absorbed that in silence. Down by the pagoda, Matsumoto had found Yuki. There was a photograph to be had there, he thought, with the one in a morning suit and an iris, the other in a faded robe, sleeves tied back, though the wind was spitting snow now. 'I know what you mean. But I think you've got him wrong.'

'I don't. I don't think you'll make any real choices until you're away from him.'

'Grace. We're getting married. He doesn't want us to. But we still are.'

'Yes. That makes me immeasurably anxious,' she murmured. 'I feel as though I'm waiting for the other shoe to drop.'

He shook his head.

She was quiet for a while. 'Has it occurred to you that clairvoyance and bombmaking aren't mutually exclusive? You know he could have made it to bring you to Filigree Street. In any case, he knew it was there and didn't disarm the thing.'

'You could always throw him off a roof somewhere just in case.'

She sighed. 'I wish Matsumoto would hurry up. I'm freezing to the tiles.'

'Let's go down, then. I should be getting back anyway.'

'Why? Plans?'

'Reservations,' he lied, because it would have been needling to say he wanted as long a last night at home as he could have.

He found Mori trying to tempt Katsu from one of the top cupboards, where there was a new nest of stolen foil wrappers and springs from the workshop. The octopus had developed a love of shiny things, which he had cunningly installed well out of Mori's reach. Thaniel stretched up and lifted him out with both hands. Katsu wrapped himself around his arm and refused to let go.

'It must be your cufflink,' Mori said helplessly. 'I'm sorry, I really didn't set him to do any of this, it's his random gears, it's like throwing tails twelve times in a row on a coin toss ...'

'Or he's alive,' Thaniel suggested.

'If he were really thinking, he would have intentions, so I would know what he'd do next, but – I – don't.' He tried to reach the panel that would expose Katsu's inner workings, but Katsu only cooed at him and skittered off over the floor. They both watched the lamp under the stairs go on, and a flustered spider hurry out. Then, 'Oh, I almost forgot: I've got an early wedding present for you. I would give it to you after the ceremony, but that would defeat the point.' He led the way into the workshop, where the lights hummed on as soon as he crossed the threshold.

Thaniel followed, curious. 'What do you mean, defeat the ...'

Mori stretched to lift down a fine cherry wood box from the shelf above his workbench. He set the box gently in front of Thaniel and put his hands behind his back to show who should open it. Thaniel lifted the lid. Inside, cushioned on a blue velvet lining, were three glass vials. They were all corked and sealed with glossy wax, and they all seemed empty, except for very faint differences of colour. Moulded around the vials were tiny bronze labels etched with ornate, miniature borders of the same pattern as Mori's watchpapers. They were marked in English and in Japanese. The first was 'sun', the second 'rain', and finally, 'snow'. Thaniel looked up.

'What are these for?'

'You can choose the weather tomorrow.' He lifted out the 'sun' vial and held it up to the light. The glass was tinted yellow and inside a faint powder floated weightlessly, winking like dust motes. It cast a golden shadow across his hand. 'If you release these particles into the air from a sufficient height – the church tower would do nicely – they will take effect within a few seconds. This one will disperse cloud. These two will gather it. The new conditions last a few hours.'

Thaniel touched the vials one by one, watching their coloured shadows on his fingertip.

'Whichever you want, half a vial should do the trick. And if you save some, you can decide what you want for the operetta too. That building where Nakamura lives is high enough. Obviously the sun mixture will only get you a clear sky at night. Personally I recommend that you rain the whole thing off and make them do it in the Savoy, like civilised people.' He dipped his eyelashes at the rain vial.

'What's wrong with outside?' Thaniel said absently. The vials weren't made of glass. They glinted differently, and they didn't feel fragile. He had thought, when the box first opened, that they were jewels, and he wondered suddenly if they might be made of diamond. He had dropped some of the stuff before, he realised, when he had been searching the workshop; God knew what would have happened if he had done that outside. Mori was good at his unbreakable inventions. He put his hands behind his back. The vials looked as though they belonged in a glass case in a museum, or locked in a vault.

'This is England. It will be horrible, whatever the weather.'

'But you'll come? Your friend Ito will be there, so ...'

'Of course I'll come; I've been looking forward to it. And forget Ito, you will be there.' He had lifted both hands impatiently when he spoke, and as he let them drop again suddenly in his broken-doll way, Thaniel caught his elbow to keep him from bumping his wrist on the corner of the desk. Mori took his arm back, and Thaniel thanked him too formally for the present.

Grace shivered by the pagoda while she waited. She had come down from the balcony by way of hinting that Matsumoto ought to hurry along, but he hadn't noticed. Yuki had scowled at first, but he was talking now, and Matsumoto showed no sign of stopping him. He was enjoying having tamed somebody. Behind her, the smell of hot wax from the lamps reminded her of Christmas. It was still two months away, and she hoped the weather would continue as it was. She liked frost fairs.

Matsumoto came back at last, looking irritatingly happy. 'How would you like to come with me to a nationalist meeting in town?'

'There are Japanese nationalist meetings in town?' said Grace.

'No, Irish, but a few of the men here go. The sentiment's the same.'

'It is the night before my wedding,' she said. 'I'd prefer not to spend it with the Irish Republican Brotherhood of Twaddling about the Oppressors.'

'Yes, of course, how silly of me. You'll be out with all your other friends.'

Grace slouched. 'All right. It won't be long, though, will it? I'm frozen already.' She dug her heel into the layer of packed-down ice on the ground.

'We can leave early. It's only in Piccadilly, we'll take the train.'

She lifted her head. 'No, we will not take the train, unless you'd like to die of bronchial failure—'

'Nonsense,' said Matsumoto. 'I'm in London; I must go on the underground.'

'You do understand that the trains run on steam, produced by coal, which, when burned, gives off sulphuric vapours?'

'Are those bad?'

'Do you know, let's go. The onus on the Japanese public school system will be much relieved if I can kill you off before you have a chance to breed.'

'Splendid,' he said, and beckoned to Yuki.

The station was not far, and as soon as they were below ground the cold lost its bite. Even before they reached the platform, she could taste the soot in the air, which was gloomy with it. The people were too. She was surprised by how many there were. Of course, it was cheaper than a cab and less horrible than the omni-buses, but still it was bleak. In his Japanese clothes, Yuki attracted curious looks, which he ignored. His expression was faraway, as though he could see something in the distance that nobody else had noticed.

As the train roared through, hot air plumed ahead of the engine and set the soot particles whirling. Matsumoto handed her up into a first-class carriage. It was otherwise unoccupied. Just beyond the window was the tunnel wall, pasted with a decrepit poster for throat lozenges. Matsumoto looked out as the train moved off again, delighted with the novelty. For a long time, there was only pitch darkness, but then there came a flit of dim light. It was the drillers' lamps in a half-finished tunnel, leading steeply downward. Although they passed it quickly, she saw the light gleam on the circle of a tunnel shield, and the men working in its square compartments. Since the beginning of the standard use of the shields, which edged forward foot by foot as the men inside dug out the space ahead, it had become impossible to track the progress of the underground. There was no more cutting up streets; the tunnels ran too deep for anyone above ground even to hear the digging. The carriage jerked suddenly and her hands closed of their own accord over the edge of her seat.

'I hate trains,' she murmured.

'I'm sure they rarely crash,' Matsumoto said, laughing.

'Anything that moves at forty miles an hour and crashes is fairly catastrophic, however rare. There's no such thing as a mild train crash, is there?'

'Oh, buck up, Carrow.'

The meeting was in a town hall that smelled of varnish and damp coats. They sat at the back, Grace on the end of a row and Yuki beside a group of men who greeted him warmly. Hoping that Matsumoto wouldn't notice, she took out a book from her coat pocket. She had bought it earlier that day. It was by Oliver Lodge, the Liverpool man working on weather control. He had, apparently, had some more successes in laboratory conditions, but as usual, a lack of funding was getting in the way of anything like commercial application. Between pages, Grace paused to listen, but always faded out of it again. She didn't much like Irish republicans for the same reason she didn't much like suffragists. There was a lot of talking, and little understanding that the problem would not go away if one only complained sufficiently.

'I want to leave,' Matsumoto said.

'Hm? What? But we've only just—' She stopped. 'I'm not complaining. Let's go.'

'Aren't you listening to him?'

'Of course I'm not listening to him.'

'He's praising the bombing of the Yard in May,' he said urgently. 'And Parliament, and – Carrow, we must leave. Yuki, I'm terribly sorry, I feel unwell.' And then they were out. Grace looked back in time to see one of Yuki's friends pat his arm, though he looked disappointed. Matsumoto shook his head.

'I'm sorry. He told me it was just a nationalist meeting. He didn't say it was the unofficial gathering of Clan na Gael. Christ.' He looked back toward the doors as they crossed the road again. 'That was a call to arms. I can't believe they have meetings like that. Anyone could have gone in.'

'It isn't illegal,' Grace pointed out. 'There were probably police-men there. Clan na Gael is only the extreme arm of the Irish nationalists. They have a representative in Parliament. Parnell. I've had tea with him. They're not just madmen in a little room somewhere.'

He laughed incredulously. 'I am continually surprised at the political leniency of a government that's already been bombed half out of Whitehall. That's the British for you. What's the time? Only seven. We can walk back, if your aversion to the trains is too much for you.'

'Hold on, should we not extract Yuki first? If he's listening to all that and living in a firework shop—'

'He says he's been going there for months and the firework shop's still there. Besides, it belongs to his father; he'd be destroy-ing his own living if he did anything silly.'

Grace nodded. They had only gone on a little way, and she had taken a breath to remark on the horses that were sliding on the ice as they tried to pull their cabs up the hill, when Matsumoto cut in first.

'I meant to say; are you all set for tomorrow? Your mother's had a talk with you?'

'I hope you don't mean what I think you do.'

As usual, he couldn't have been less embarrassed. 'Look, I've heard your views about biology. I seem to recall your claiming that it's the study of yeast and ooze. That doesn't bode well.'

'Kind of you to be concerned, but no need.'

'Are you certain? I don't trust your mother. I imagine she explained it in the terms of something like an appendectomy. That's wrong, you know. A man does not want to feel like a surgeon working without anaesthetic.'

'For the love of God, Matsumoto, shut up.'

'You can't say I didn't warn you.'

She looked up at him. 'We're marrying because I want a labora-tory and he has a widowed sister with too many sons. It's a business arrangement.'

'No, no, hiring one's tailor is a business arrangement. You're going to live with this fellow and he isn't bad-looking or unpleasant.'

'Matsumoto.'

He took a breath, but then let it out again, and his levity faded. 'I'm sorry. I didn't mean to … one says silly things, you know, when one is … ' He struggled, then shook his head. 'When one is in shock over the marriage of one's ugly friends.'

She thumped his arm and they walked on bickering, and slipping every now and then. Matsumoto complained bitterly about the Arctic weather, and Grace thought of the way Thaniel had walked on the ice, lightly, with both hands in his pockets. She didn't know how he did it, but he suited the winter. His eyes were the right colour for it. With any luck, the snow would come tomorrow to match him, and the old graveyard of the little Kensington church would be hidden and pristine, and her mother's flowers would seem all the brighter. And Mori, if his views of the weather were anything like Matsumoto's, would be less likely to change his mind at the last minute.

TWENTY-FOUR

ALTHOUGH ST MARY'S spire was not especially high, it was high enough to see that the tallest things in the city were other church spires. Thaniel cracked the seal of the snow vial, spraying little shards of red wax over his hands, and then held it up to let the wind take the winking dust. He was doubtful about it. London sprawled under a white sky, interrupted only by the patch of frosted green that was Hyde Park; half a vial of powder was not much beside such a wide space. Above him, the bells made a shimmering sound as the particles brushed them. While he waited, he looked down into the street for Mori, who was easy to find because his was a grey coat in among all the black. He was walking west, away from home. There was time to wonder why but not to reach any conclusions before the first snowflake stung his cheek. He leaned out through the open arch. The clouds were gathering and the air was turning grainy with ice. By the time he was at the altar, the snow spun and eddied, and the frozen mud of the churchyard was hidden under a fresh white.

When Grace arrived, she had a white parasol for the snow. He saw her spin it through her hands on the porch to shake off the damp before she let it down. Because her father still disapproved, it was Matsumoto who brought her down the nave.

The ceremony was over quickly, though it felt long in the cold, and then they moved on to the Westminster. It was much warmer there. In the dark afternoon, they had lit candles along all the tables. Thaniel's nephews soon set to playing with the wax. They sounded Scottish now – so did Annabel, who had aged since he had seen her last. He sat watching them and listening to Grace and Matsumoto on his other side. Having not seen him since they were tiny, the boys were nervous of him and, when forced to speak, kept looking uncertainly at their mother. They weren't precocious. He didn't push them, because he could remember, vividly, how much he had hated being forced to chat to obscure relatives he didn't know. He wished that he could have learned Mori's knack for speaking to children.

Across the dining room, a pair of bronze birds flitted in through the open doors. Some of the women diners squeaked, but the birds were clearly unaccidental, because they executed an elegant loop-the-loop in tandem, glimmering oddly as they flew. Thaniel recognised them a second before they both shed a cascade of colourful sparks along the length of the table. The guests ooed and laughed. Delighted, Annabel's boys ran after them as they sang off around the hall, making shapes with the fireworks. Before long, the birds looped back and hopped on to Grace's wine glass, one on either side. She lifted one of them down. Like a real swallow, it held her finger tightly, leaving six pale marks on her skin. It puffed up its bronze feathers and shivered, clinking.

'I'm sorry that Mori didn't come,' Grace said.

'Are you?' said Thaniel. Since everyone was distracted, he had slipped a tiny packet of Lipton's out of his pocket and into one of the white coffee cups. When she spoke, his mind was still taken up with the question of how to call for some hot water without alerting Lord Carrow. The champagne must have cost a fortune, but he hated champagne.

'No,' she said. 'But he should have come. It's your wedding.'

'He should,' he agreed quietly. He had thought that if he didn't say anything, Mori would come and sit at the back of the church. He had known there was a chance he wouldn't, but he hadn't realised how bleak it would be without him.

On Grace's other side, Matsumoto leaned forward. 'I don't suppose I might see one of those birds?' he said.

Grateful for the interruption, Thaniel cupped his hands around the nearest and handed it over.

'I didn't mean to eavesdrop, but just now, you were talking about...' Matsumoto hesitated. 'It's Keita Mori, isn't it?'

They both turned to him. 'How do you know that?' said Thaniel.

'This is his clockwork.' Matsumoto looked between them. For once, he didn't smile. 'How well do you know him?'

'Well,' said Thaniel.

'Then you know the circumstances in which he left his home town?'

'No, it's never—'

Matsumoto tucked his chin down in the most fractional nod. 'No. Well, let me tell you. Keita Mori is the bastard son of old Lord Mori's wife. His legitimate brothers were killed in the civil wars and so the familial castle went to his cousin, Takahiro. Takahiro was not an easy man, but not a bad one either. He was honourable: he believed in blood and nobility, so he never much liked Mori. Of course, Mori didn't like him, either.' His brown eyes caught briefly on Grace. 'Then one day, they argued, and an hour later Takahiro was killed under an unstable section of the castle wall. I saw it happen. Coincidence indeed, but coincidences follow Keita Mori. I should think you've noticed.'

'Yes,' said Thaniel. 'But you don't land a wall on someone's head because you vaguely dislike him.'

'That's not the point,' said Grace. 'Matsumoto, you said coincidences, not coincidence. Are you saying that there are others who have died?'

Thaniel's nephews crept up and tried to steal the other bird, which soared a little way along the table, then again when they chased it. When it flew, its metal wings beat so quickly that they hummed a clear, sunny yellow. It gave Thaniel the odd feeling of sitting in broad daylight, despite the candles and the dark winter afternoon. He shook his head, aware that Matsumoto had been talking.

'—don't know. I was only eight when Takahiro was killed. I think one would have to know Mori very well indeed before one could tell between a train derailing by chance and a train derailing because he distracted the engineer at the right moment.'

'He doesn't derail—' Thaniel began.

'Thaniel lives with him,' Grace interrupted. 'He doesn't like me.'

'Then I suggest you try for an embassy posting in Morocco,' Matsumoto said to Thaniel. 'Before she's hit by an omnibus.'

'For God's sake, he won't do that. He's spent three months not hitting you with an omnibus, I really doubt he intends to begin now, don't you?' To ensure that neither of them could reply, Thaniel called to a waiter. Grace's eyebrows rose slowly when he asked for hot water.

'You've smuggled in your own tea.'

'Yes. I'm sorry. I don't like champagne.'

She kissed his temple. He caught a snatch of her summery perfume and its Italian spices, too strong today. Matsumoto stood suddenly and said that he would have to go if he was to catch his train, so they both saw him out into the snow and laughed when he put up his umbrella with an operatic flourish. Thaniel began to turn away, but Grace went with Matsumoto right to the door, her dress hissing as the hem spun. He had caught her arm.

'You know,' he said, pitching his voice softly, 'Mori spent twenty years not landing a wall on Takahiro. If you're going to stay here ... well. You must know what you will do, if you think he's on the edge of something unfortunate.'

She nodded once. 'I've a vague idea.'

'Not vague would be better.'

'It wouldn't. If I think, I'll decide something, and he will know it the second I do. I'm trying to hold it in stasis.'

Thaniel watched their voices change to the colour of the snow.

Matsumoto looked worried. 'Can you?'

'You know when you've two big numbers to multiply, and you could do it in your own head if you made the effort, but you feel lazy and you hold them still until you can reach an abacus?'

He glanced out into the snow. 'Yes,' he said after a small pause. 'I see what you mean. You're quite clever enough to puzzle it out if the time comes. Well. Best of luck. I had better go.'

She put her hand out to shake his, but he stepped back from her and bowed at her instead, leaving her to clench her hand uncertainly in his wake.

'Come back in,' Thaniel said quietly. 'He'll be all right.'

She rubbed her arms as she came back. 'Of course he will. There's an opera ballet in Paris.'

With an air of great reluctance, Lord Carrow announced that he was needed at Horse Guards in half an hour. After that, the rest of Grace's family left in slow twos and threes. Grace shepherded out the last of them while Thaniel waited for her at the foot of the hotel stairs. They had a suite for the night. When she came back, she caught up the hem of her skirt so that she could climb the stairs, awkwardly, because none of her usual dresses were so long. Thaniel went slowly to keep pace with her, close to the wall so that they wouldn't knock elbows.

'Thaniel!' Annabel said.

'I thought you'd gone? I'll follow you,' he added to Grace, and went back down.

Annabel smiled and put her arms around him once she could reach. 'Dear me,' she murmured. 'That was all a bit strange. Are you sure about her? She looks like a boy.'

'I like her. Were you all right tonight?'

'We had a lovely time, yes.' She looked behind her, where her sons were waiting by the door, well away from them. 'I'm sorry about the boys. I thought they remembered you more.'

'They're better than I was with uncles.'

'All our uncles were fat anglers who smelled of fish,' she pointed out. She sighed and pushed her hair from her eyes. It was a duller colour than it had been. The rest of her was dull too. He hadn't recognised her when she had arrived on the sleeper from Edinburgh, and when he had, he had cried and pretended it was because he was happy. 'There wasn't another girl, was there? Poorer but better?'

'No. Where do you think I'm meeting women? There aren't the hours in the day. I go home from work, argue with my mad landlord about cats or suffragists and then I go to work again.'

'Well. It's a very smart match, then. Are you sure about sending the boys to school?'

'For God's sake, what am I for?'

She looked relieved. 'I'll see you in the week, then.'

'Is it Thursday, you're going?'

'Early, yes.'

He saw them out to the cab and stood in the snow for a while, half to watch them go, half because a little dying hope at the back of his mind was waiting for Mori. The street was nearly empty. He turned back inside with snow on his sleeves.

When he found it, the room, or rather rooms – there was a parlour – had the immensely clean hotel smell that comes of everything being boiled and ironed, and repainted, much more often than usual. There were deep carpets and chairs in different shades of blue and white, and on the low table by the fire was the remains of the wedding cake. The porters had brought it up ahead of them.

'I'm changing,' Grace called from behind a pair of closed doors. 'Don't come in here for a moment. How is your sister? I didn't speak to her.'

'She's well. She says you look like a boy.'

She snorted. 'The two of you are from the same mould, then.'

'I get it from her,' he said, taking off his tie and collar. The big windows looked out over the Thames and Waterloo Bridge, where the cabs crawled along with lit lamps. The river had frozen completely now, and there were lamps moving there too as pedestrians cut across to save climbing the bridge. The light sparkled where it caught on the frosted bulkheads of ships stranded in the ice. Snow was criss-crossing again. He thought that he could see the steeple of their church in Kensington. He counted sideways until he found a point of electric light that might have been Harrods. Filigree Street was somewhere behind it.

The fire snapped and sent a flight of sparks up the chimney, although for all its determination it was not giving out much heat. He clasped his hands, feeling the cold. He never would have before, but Mori's expectations of temperature had spoiled him. He had looked up Japan on the map a while ago. The south shared a latitude with Morocco. He went to the hearth to put in another log and then edged the chairs closer. Grace came back in a dressing gown too white for her colouring.

'I think I might turn in,' she said. 'Or, cake first, then bed. I'm exhausted. That was an awful lot of standing up and putting up with my parents.'

'I'll just steal a pillow and a few blankets to bring out here, then.'

'Oh, you can ... I don't mean for you to sleep out here,' she said.

'It's all right.' He went through and opened cupboards until he found extra bedding. Grace's wedding dress was draped over the end of the four-poster bed. He rescued it gently and put it on a hanger, then turned to find her by his elbow.

'I mean to say I should rather you stay,' she said. She winced as if it had come out badly and curled her fingers around her sleeves. 'It is our wedding night, after all. You mustn't spend it on a couch.'

'I'd never be able to sleep on a feather bed, I'd only keep you awake.'

'I don't mind.' She took his hand and squeezed it. Hers were colder than his, and so was her silk sleeve. He caught her perfume again, strong because it was in her hair, which had been set into as much of a curl as it would hold. 'You deserve a proper bed after all that.'

'I know it sounds as though I was brought up down a mine, but I'd really prefer the couch,' he said, easing his hand away so that he could go back to the fire. While he moved the cushions from the long couch, which creaked quietly with horsehair, she cut some cake and held out a plate. He took it, though he was starting to feel tight, as if he were getting a cold and the muscles across his chest were stiffening. It hurt when he pressed his fingertips under his collarbone. She was right; there had been too much standing up.

'Well, good night,' she said.

He smiled. 'Night.'

She kissed him too lightly, so that it was only a cold brush of damp and the chalk smell of her powder. He flinched and pushed his hand over his mouth before he could stop himself.

'Sorry – I'm getting a cold. I don't want to give you—'

'Oh. Yes; you don't look very sparkling. Sleep well, anyway.'

He nodded and turned out the lights once the space under the bedroom door turned dark, but didn't lie down or undress. He waited until he stopped hearing her turn the pages of her book, then stood up, quietly. It was too dark to find his coat, so he left without it.

The lights were on at home. When he let himself into the workshop, heat furled out to meet him. The brazier was on as always, but Mori was using a soldering iron too, the pen-fine tip of it glowing red as he traced steaming lines along something inside a watch. It was how he etched the cogs. The thing was so hot that he did it standing, so that he could step back in time to save his hands if he dropped it. He had pushed his chair off to the left. Katsu was draped over it, basking.

'Is it warm enough for you yet?' Thaniel said, trying to sound offhand.

'Nearly.' He had taken off his tie, which was looped under the left strap on his braces so that it hung against his hip like a jockey sash. He set the iron down on its own flint bowl of hot coals carefully. There was a dew of sweat between his collarbones. 'Did everything go off well, then?' he said.

'Yes – it was lovely.'

Mori poured his teacup over the coals, then leaned back when they hissed and steamed. 'Good. I thought you were staying at the hotel?'

'I am, I am. I'll go back later. Grace is … her family are still there. You should have come,' he said suddenly.

'I know. I'm sorry.' He gave Thaniel a pensive look and began to turn away. 'It's late for tea, but there's some wine, or—'

'Mori, wait.'

When he stopped, Thaniel went round the desk to catch him and pressed his cheek against Mori's darkening hair. His clothes smelled of steam and lemon soap. Through them, he was solid. He held Thaniel tightly for a while before tilting him back. He had an ego-saving trick of not looking over-concerned, only curious.

'It was—' Thaniel began.

'Don't tell me, just intend to. And then I'll forget, if you change your mind.'

Thaniel nodded once and saw him listen to what he could have said while the filaments of the light bulbs made fireflies of themselves in his eyes. Annabel, Matsumoto, Grace. When he ran out of thoughts, he looked down and brushed the loop of the silk tie where it hung over Mori's hip while he let other things rise to the edge of speaking. Mori held his elbows, watching him straighten the knot. He drew him closer by them and then held his arm out to the door. The lights switched off and hid them from the dark street. The fading orange in the filaments showed clear in his eyes, then disappeared when Thaniel kissed him. His shoulders came forward and Thaniel breathed him in, the lemon soap on his skin, and the water vapour and the charcoal. Though he had shaved that morning, his cheek was rough.

'Where did you go this morning?' Thaniel said quietly, against his temple. 'You didn't walk back this way. I saw you from the church tower.'

'I went to see Six.'

'The little girl from the workhouse?'

'Mm. We went to see the vivarium in Hyde Park. I've been going on Saturdays, when you go to Kensington.'

'Good...that's good,' Thaniel said. Whenever he went to see Grace, he imagined that Mori's clockwork stopped and that he only sat in the workshop, waiting for someone to wind him up again. It was odd to think he kept himself wound up and went off to visit orphans while nobody was watching. He felt left behind, hypocritically.

Mori stepped back and let his arm drop again, and the light bulbs hummed bright. 'Mrs Steepleton is on her way to fetch you back now.'

'Would you mind if I stayed here until the first morning train?'

'No,' Mori said, frowning. 'But that's a waste of a night in a hotel. This place has been here since the thirteen hundreds, it will still be here tomorrow.'

'But I'm not going to come back much. Am I?'

'Well, it isn't—'

'That music box in your desk. Is it for Six?'

Mori was still. 'No.'

'No, I didn't think so.'

'I'd better light the fires upstairs, then.' He paused, looking at the street lamps outside. 'The wood's damp, so it will take me a while.'

'No, that's all right,' Thaniel said. He sat down to wait, absently teasing Katsu while he watched the snow fall past the reflection of the workshop.

TWENTY-FIVE

Grace pushed open the workshop door. Thaniel was waiting inside, by himself, close to the charcoal embers in the small lock of a soldering iron on the desk. She had heard him leave the hotel, but it had taken her a while to dress, and she had not managed to catch the same train. When she had reached the curve of Filigree Street, she had thought nobody was awake, but then the workshop lights had come on, and they had already been inside. She had stopped still for a second, because they hadn't looked as if they had just walked in. They had been there together in the dark. Her stomach twisted nastily. Everybody had their bad habits but she had wanted not to know Thaniel's, not until they were used to each other and they could laugh instead of flinch. Thankfully Mori had taken himself off elsewhere now. It was hot inside.

'Hello,' she said. 'What's the matter? I heard you go.'

He didn't look surprised to see her. He was sitting very still, and although he usually smiled when he saw her, he only glowed dully.

'Nothing. I just came for a cup of tea. I thought you were asleep or I would have said.'

'Well, come back with me, or you'll miss the last train.'

'I can come on the early train, it's all right.'

'Rather a long cup of tea.'

'I was going to do some sleeping as well,' he said, not quite laughing. 'Why does it matter where I am?'

'Because you've been skittish about the Kensington house for months, and you plainly don't want to leave Filigree Street, and I think that wherever you are tonight will be where you stay. This is ... if you were going to regret things and go back on it all, it was always going to be today.'

He frowned. 'Grace. I'll come back in the morning. I'm not going back on anything.'

'I know I sound strange. But will you humour me?'

'I'd rather not. This once. Please.'

'What kind of tea do you drink in the dark, anyway?' she said quietly. She hoped it would scare him, but it didn't.

'Come again?' was all he said.

She pressed her fingernails into her palms. 'Do you remember when I said that one day he would get tired of me, and on that day, you would agree with him? It's today.'

He inclined his head, very slightly, so that the light in his hair only shifted rather than disappeared. 'Do you remember when I said I'm not stupid?'

'Of course you're not stupid—'

'No, I'm an ordinary man who works in an office and sometimes plays the piano.'

She didn't recognise the words at first, and when she did, it was with a prick of irritation at being quoted, and then a creeping dismay. She had not thought he listened so closely. 'I never meant—'

'I'll come back tomorrow,' he said again.

'No, come back now. I know you only want the night, but tomorrow you'll want another and another, and you'll never leave. Do you not understand what would happen then? Thaniel, if we're seen to separate – for Christ's sake, my father is best friends with Lord Leveson. You know, the Foreign Minister? He'll see to it that you lose your job no matter what I say to him, and neither of us will see anything of the rest of the dowry. What will happen to your sister then?'

He closed his hand on the desk at the mention of his sister. 'I want to stay because I'll hardly ever come back after this. Grace, there's going to be a child before long. And I'll love you, and her, and he'll be left behind, like he always is, but I won't care, because we will have drifted by then and I'll have my own family to think about. I want to think of him while I still can.'

'What rubbish has he been telling you?' she demanded, aware that her voice had risen. It was one thing to know the man was clever, but another to see how he could apply it. If it hadn't affected her, she would have admired the strategy of it. 'Thaniel, it's only to make you—'

'I don't think so.'

'Good God, I feel like Cassandra! I've been making true prophecies and still you don't believe me. Just for a moment, push past the fact that you aren't so clever as he is, and see what he's done.'

'I'm not clockwork.'

She wanted to shake him. 'You are. But you are such good clockwork that you don't know. Please, see it. It's my life you're holding, as well as yours. I can't keep the laboratory going without the dowry money.'

'I know that. Which is why I will come back, in the morning,' he said, with a dead calm she realised that she had often heard before. Like an idiot she had thought it was because he was never angry.

She let her breath out. 'In the morning then. I'm sorry about all that. I'm sure we'll see, soon enough.'

His expression opened. 'Yes. Tomorrow.'

'All right. Well, I shall go and enjoy a cavernous hotel room to myself.'

He smiled.

'My best to Mori,' she added.

She let herself out into the powdery snow. The door clicked behind her. With grains of snow tapping against the hem of her skirt as the wind blew it in rivulets from Knightsbridge, she looked back in time to see him go into the kitchen through the heavy, old door at the back of the workshop. Once he had gone, the lights faded by themselves, and there was only the dim glow of the dying brazier.

In the cab on the way back to the hotel, she closed her eyes, wanting to rest, but saw things behind her eyelids. She had never seen a stone wall fall, but Matsumoto had showed her a photograph of Crow Castle. It was, he said, much smaller than some of the great old castles in the south that had come down over the past decade, but it was still a colossal thing, standing on inward curving walls above a black lake. The process of multiplication ticked as she tried to think what one of the stones would weigh, and then how many stones went into a wall that size, or bigger, and then what that weight would do to human bones. There would hardly have been bones to speak of.

'The Westminster, miss,' said the cabby, waspishly.

She straightened, and realised that the cab had been still for more than a minute. The yellow light of a street lamp cast a shadow of the window glass across her knees, where it seemed to run liquid. She got out and paid the man. Her joints were moving badly, all unoiled hydraulics.

Upstairs, she pushed open the unlocked door of the suite. The lamps she had lit before leaving were still burning. The carriage clock on the mantelpiece chimed half past eleven and the floor shook, just perceptibly, as a train left Westminster station underground. She pressed the heels of her hands against her temples and blew her breath out. Her engagement ring caught on a strand of her hair.

As she sat down, a sovereign fell from her pocket and rolled off under the chair. Heads. She picked it up and imagined the disturbed ether billowing as it closed over the dead chance of tails. The trails in it would be everywhere, stacked in layers; there would be Grace-ghosts making tea, locking the door, standing in the window, doing all the things she faintly meant to soon. There would be shapes made by the cleaning woman who would come at ten o'clock tomorrow, and faint ones from guests who still hadn't decided whether or not to take this particular room. The particles were so fine that they were knocked about by the pressure of flashing nerves in minds ten miles away. A hundred.

She turned the coin over in her hands and tossed it again. Heads. Heads. Heads; it was funny, that. With every throw that turned up heads, it was tempting to think heads was less likely for the next, but it was still even chances. A memoryless process. The coin did not know it had thrown heads four times in a row. Before every throw, the ether would split two ways, in equal anticipation, always. It didn't matter who did the throwing or why. The chances would be the same, just as unpredictable, even if by some extraordinary fluke, heads appeared twenty times. Which was how Katsu worked, of course.

She held the coin and, at last, let her mind work. She had been holding the ideas still for so long that they had developed by themselves, with little intervention from the rest of her. She glanced at the clock. Twenty-five to midnight. The last train would go on the hour. There was time, if she hurried.

Outside, the wind hummed around the gutters and clattered frozen leaves against the window pane. Some caught in spiders' webs and threw uneven shadows across the floor. With his back to the wall and his arm across Mori, Thaniel could feel the heat of the fire along the back of his hand and his forearm, and the cooler air behind his shoulder. He hid from the light against the nape of Mori's neck. He could feel sleep coming; his grip was gone and his thoughts had turned mirrorish. Under his arm, Mori curled forward. If he had been standing, he would have let his head drop.

'I've got to go. Mrs Steepleton is about to go missing from the hotel room.'

'What?'

Mori's silhouette sat up and pulled on his shirt, leaving Thaniel cold for a second before the dense heat of the fire had time to fill the gap. 'Everything's wrecked, or it will be, by the time I get there.'

He understood what he was hearing then. He sat up too. 'Someone's – taken her?'

'I don't know. You're not coming,' he said, before Thaniel could say it. 'Stop intending to say things and listen to me.'

Thaniel bit his tongue.

'I can't remember where to find her,' Mori said, 'which means that it hasn't been decided yet. If I go now, I could still see her. I can remember seeing her all around London after that, so I'm going to try and catch up, and then I'll be close by when the decisions are made and I'll have a chance of overtaking her. You would slow me down.' He hesitated, as if he had meant to add something else, but then got up suddenly and went to the door, wrapping on his scarf. Thaniel lurched after him.

'You know something else,' he said from the top of the stairs. Mori was already by the door, halfway into his coat.

'I don't,' he said.

'You can't lie for your life. What is it? What happens if you can't catch up?'

'No time,' Mori said. The front door snapped shut. By the time Thaniel had dressed and followed, the snow was falling again in flurries and he could see no sign of him. He stared down Filigree Street through the lamplight stripes. The wind blew snow between the buttons of his shirt.

There was nothing to do but sit at the piano and wait. He practised for the operetta to distract himself, a candle on the piano top, although he no longer needed to see the music. The snow came down and silently down. There was snow in his thoughts too. Matsumoto had been afraid. So had Grace. Through the snow, he couldn't see whether it was because they both understood things he hadn't, or because they had failed to understand something. And so he couldn't tell whether he had just watched Mori go to do just what he had said, or just what Grace had said he would.

Over the bright colours of Sullivan's score came a sudden, sharp creak. He lifted his hands off the keys and leaned to see past the doorway. It was too heavy to be Mori. He followed the sound upstairs, passing the susurration of the clocks in the workshop, then the downy silence of the snow on the landing window. Tiny green echoes danced in the penumbra of his candle. He eased open the door of Mori's bedroom, letting the candle trickle light inside. It was empty.

'Mori?' he said uncertainly.

The candle only shone over Katsu. The little octopus was lying on the pillow, tentacles arched around an invisible shoulder. There was even a kink where Mori's collarbone would have been. Thaniel felt weight settle on to his diaphragm. Mori had expected to be here, then.

A knock at the front door made him jump. Thinking it was Mori without keys, he went too quickly downstairs and didn't feel it when candle wax spilt on to the back of his hand.

Dolly Williamson was outside.

Thaniel looked past him for uniformed men, but there were none.

'Pax,' said Williamson. He held up his hands. 'Sorry for the time. Thought I'd better come myself.'

'What's going on?'

'May I come in?'

Thaniel stepped back. Williamson led the way into the parlour and watched him light the lamps.

'Your wife has gone missing from her hotel,' he said, sitting down on the piano stool. 'The stewards reported it about half an hour ago. Someone found the door open. They thought you had too, at first, but then one of them said you had left earlier.'

'Missing.'

Williamson nodded. 'So, we've looked at the hotel. There does seem to have been a struggle. There was blood on the door, but it was nothing like enough to have been a lethal injury. I assume your wife is alive.'

Thaniel realised that his hand hurt and peeled off a still-soft disc of fallen candlewax.

Williamson leaned down a little to force him to meet his eyes. 'Why did you leave?'

'I wanted a book. I stayed for a while to get warm and then missed the last train.'

'A book. On your wedding night.'

'Horsehair couches are hard to sleep on.'

Williamson took a breath, then let it out again. 'I see. And where is Mr Mori tonight, then?'

'York. There's a clockwork fair.'

'He didn't come to the wedding?'

'No, it was only family.'

'How do they get on, he and your wife?'

'I think they've spoken twice.'

'I hear she's a clever woman. Scientist. I wouldn't put it past a girl like that to work out there was something not right about him. Or to ask him about it.'

Wrong, but not in the wrong field, he realised. She must have seen them. If she were angry enough with him, or even just scared enough of Mori to report it – those cases never went through, but he saw suddenly that Williamson would latch on to it and damn well make it go. There wasn't the evidence to convict Mori for the bombings but second best was to get him into a prison for something else. The sentences were long. He would have known the second Grace decided to go to the police station. She knew that too. Thaniel had to close both hands over the candleholder to keep himself from pushing the left across his face.

'It wasn't him, Dolly. He doesn't make bombs.' His voice might have come from a very far-off phonograph.

'All this is nothing but a screaming coincidence? If you think that, then . . .' He stopped. In the garden, small lights flared and cast coloured shadows on the far window's frames. 'What's that?'

'I don't know.' Thaniel led the way to the back door and opened it. Nobody was there, but the floating lights he had seen on his very first night had returned. They hovered over the snow, their glow more than enough to show the single set of footprints leading away from the door.

'So he was here,' Williamson said. He looked Thaniel over. 'Were you lying or didn't you know?'

'He wasn't—'

'Stay where you are,' he said, and set out to follow them around the house.

Thaniel crouched down to see the prints. Mori still had only that one pair of brown boots with the Japanese manufacturer's mark imprinted in the sole, and there was no mark in the impressed snow. Williamson came back a few minutes later and shook his head.

'They go out to the road, but I couldn't follow after that.' He looked hard at Thaniel. 'I'm going to arrest you, and then you might tell me something worthwhile.'

'These aren't his! His shoes have Japanese in the soles—'

'Thaniel. How many other small men live here?'

'None, but he won't buy English-made clothes.'

'Is it really beyond the realms of possibility that he might have bought new shoes without your noticing?' Williamson demanded.

'Arrest me, then, but I won't have anything different to say.'

'You're under house arrest. Constable Bloom will stay with you,' he said as the front door opened. An austere constable stopped just inside to shake the snow from his boots. Williamson must have seen his lantern coming through the workshop window.

'Find my wife, in the meantime. Please.'

Williamson shook his head, his hand on the door. 'What the hell has he said to you to blinker you so much? He made the bomb and your wife found out, and now he's taken her. What did he do, when you first came here? Really, it would be magnificent to know. I can put it in a training manual.'

'I'll tell you after you find her.'

Lifting his hand helplessly, Williamson let himself out. Constable Bloom stopped Thaniel before he could close the door and did it for him. Thaniel went back to the piano, where he sat down for a while without touching anything before he turned to the back of Sullivan's score, where there were two spare pages, and started to reconstruct Griszt's piece from memory.

The next morning Lord Carrow came to the house. He said nothing, hit Thaniel in the face with his riding crop, then left again. Another officer came to relieve Constable Bloom. Nothing yet, he said. Thaniel left him in the kitchen with a good supply of tea and sat in the workshop to read.

When five o'clock came around, he said he was going upstairs to sleep, found his old coat in the cupboard – the new one was still

271

at the hotel – and climbed through Mori's window and on to the small porch of the back door. He reached the snowy ground with nothing but a few scrapes. Skirting behind the birches in order not to leave obvious tracks through the middle of the lawn, he found the stream along the back of the Filigree Street gardens and followed it north. It came out on the very edge of Hyde Park, so near the show village that he could hear voices and a singing violin as someone practised a strain from the operetta.

He went slowly, willing Mori to be waiting for him. The crowds and the twilight were safer than home, stocked as home was with policemen. Outside Osei's teahouse was a tight knot of people using it as a meeting spot. He wove through them, looking for a grey coat. Although he could cope with arrest and Lord Carrow's riding crop, and whatever had happened to Grace, he could feel himself going ragged at the edges. His ribs hurt with wanting Mori to come and be his ordinary self and explain it was not what he thought, but still there was no grey coat. He stilled and stilled as the hope seeped away, his hands loosening in his pockets in the same way Katsu did when his springs ran down.

Someone brushed his arm. It was only Osei. She bowed tinily and lifted her hand in the direction of the pagoda to show he ought, perhaps, to hurry up now.

He pulled himself together, although the ragged patches didn't line up as well as they should have. Osei's dark eyes had caught on the mark on his face. He went on ahead of her so that he wouldn't have to speak. He should have gone back to Filigree Street before the police noticed his absence but part of him clamoured to say that Mori was only late, and something might have happened, and he might still come during the performance. He had said he would. Only two days ago, he had said it. And that Katsu was going wrong proved it. He had meant to be here.

The pagoda was hung about with hundreds of paper lanterns. He had thought that the outdoor performance would be miserably cold, but in fact it was plenty warm enough. An open marquee protected the audience's seats, though there was no more snow yet tonight, and at the end of each row was a coal brazier. The heat waved out above the cushions, distorting the lamplight. Even so, the women were wrapped in fur stoles, and some people had brought blankets. The glow and the white ground made it all seem like something put together on the whim of a musical czar, somewhere in the grounds of the Winter Palace. It was very far away from the silence at Filigree Street.

He found the orchestra to one side of the stage and only felt when he sat down and the glass plinked on the under-edge of the piano that the weather vials were still in his pocket. He moved them carefully, not sure what would happen if all of them broke at once. He slid them into his waistcoat pockets instead. There was no rush. The audience were still finding their seats. Musicians waxed strings and adjusted keys while stagehands fussed over the paper lamps. Outside, men hurried in and out of Nakamura's shop with rockets and lists, preparing for the firework spectacular after the show. It took a little while for Thaniel to notice a group of oriental men in immaculate clothes near the front. Most of them were young, but they surrounded an older man, benignly ugly. He sat in the same way Mori did in the cold, hands pushed under his coat sleeves. Thaniel glanced back at the orchestra, but it was still in relative disarray. He ghosted away and across to the front row, as yet unoccupied.

'Mr Ito?' he asked the ugly man.

He looked up with robin-bright eyes. 'Yes?'

'My name is Nathaniel Steepleton, I live with Keita Mori. I don't suppose he's spoken to you today?'

Ito's expression closed. 'What's going to happen?'

'Pardon?'

'Why are you here?' He had a delicate American accent.

'I'm playing in the orchestra. But Mori is missing. Have you heard anything from—'

'Is he supposed to be here?'

'Yes?'

Ito slipped through the space between the front row seats and steered Thaniel to the side. He was a tiny man, much smaller than Mori. 'Then he sent you to do whatever he meant to here. Something must be going to happen tonight.'

'No, nobody sent me. I'm playing the piano, that's all.'

'Who arranged for you to do that?'

Thaniel opened his hands between them and had to clench them together tight to stifle the need to hit something. 'Yes. He did.'

'Indeed,' said Ito. 'Can you think of nothing ... ?'

'Oh, I don't bloody know, he makes a toy and then I'm working for the Foreign Office, it's not generally an obvious train of thought. Sorry,' he added, more quietly.

'No, it's quite all right. My feelings toward Mr Mori exactly.' Ito shook his head and cast a long look around the audience and the stage. 'Well. You had best get back to your piano. Watch for anything ... odd.' He flicked a look up at Thaniel. 'It is a pleasure to meet another trustee of the Mori Futures Preparation Society, of course,' he said, with no pleasure whatever. 'Although I had hoped I was an alumnus rather than an active member now.'

'I thought you two were friends?'

'Friends? I threw him out of Japan,' Ito said. He drew his lower lip under his teeth to moisten it. Then, 'He could have killed my wife, you see.' There was a little silence. Thaniel couldn't fill it. 'Please excuse me,' Ito added, and returned to his aides.

When Thaniel sat down at the piano again, the oboe-player tapped him and said it was time to tune up. As the seaspray whine of tuning instruments sounded around the marquee, the audience stopped their rustling and settled. Sheet music clattered, and in the strings section, one of the rickety metal music stands collapsed and had to be repositioned. Thaniel watched the starry squeaks as somebody tightened the screw. The oboe-player touched his temple, looking faint. One of the violinists passed him a flask and smiled. It smelled of coffee. *Could have killed my wife*. No one asked him if he wanted anything or if he was all right. It was Mori who asked those things.

Mr Sullivan sailed in and bowed to the audience, who clapped. Having rearranged his music, he waved at the orchestra and counted with his baton. Thaniel pushed his knee against the leg of the piano stool, trying distantly to think if anything seemed out of place, but nothing did. He didn't look too hard. If Mori had left him here to see to whatever it was, it would make itself obvious before long.

The operetta began and the actors swept on to the stage in glorious, floor-length kimono that made them seem to glide. He played watching the stage. Everything was just as it should be.

Nothing happened throughout the first half, except when Yuki kicked at the line of costumes just at a solemn moment. He thought that there might be something when the audience dispersed to stretch and buy tea from Osei's shop, but there was only the usual chatter, and an overlay of excitement, because the performance was going beautifully. He started to think that Ito was wrong and that there was no plan, and nothing would happen, but he was wary of the thought. The last time he had been convinced that nothing would happen was May, when he had nearly exploded.

Ito was staying near the second row's brazier instead of venturing out into the cold. One of the aides had been dispatched for tea. There was no sign of Mori.

Already aching, his neck started to hurt, and he stood up to stretch. He paused when he saw what he thought was a police uniform near the stage, but it was only one of the actors in costume. Even so, it made him nervous. He wanted to hope that if he was missed and if they found him here, then having escaped in order to play for an operetta would be a benign enough thing for them to waive a real arrest, but he doubted it. He tried to feel around the idea of prison. The edges of it were too sharp to touch.

Somebody bumped into him. When he looked around, Mr Nakamura, the firework maker, ducked into one of his cringing bows.

'I'm sorry ...'

'Everything all right?' said Thaniel, thinking he looked even more worried than usual, but that was perhaps only because the lines on his face were clearer in light than in the dimness in his workshop. He carried the strong smell of gunpowder with him, and he shuffled away from the nearest brazier.

'Have you seen Yuki?' he said in a small voice. He sounded like an old man. It wasn't kind, but Thaniel felt a flash of impatience with him. He would have been going to nationalist meetings and picking fights with samurai too if he had had more of a dormouse than a father.

'He's around somewhere. Breaking things, I'd imagine.'

'There are some packets missing from the workshop, I need them for the display later. He must have moved them ... silly boy ...'

Thaniel caught his shoulder. 'What kind of packets?'

'I only know the Japanese names. Chemicals,' he said hopelessly. 'For fireworks. For the fire. Oh, there he is. Yuki! Yuki, what have you done with the—'

Yuki was at the edge of the stage, watching the audience. He usually stood with his arms folded, but they were by his sides now. He was holding a heavy revolver. Thaniel pulled Nakamura back by the belt of his kimono to a feebly surprised protest. It was time wasted, because Yuki had clicked back the safety catch. Nobody else heard. From within the circle of braziers, the boy was invisible.

Thaniel tackled him and the gun went off. He had never been so close to a gunshot. The noise was like a lightning flash and for a moment he couldn't hear anything except a high, familiar whine.

As things came back into focus, silence filled the room. Nothing moved. Thaniel had his hand under the gun's hammer, the sharp point sinking into his skin because Yuki was still holding the trigger down in an effort to hurt him enough to make him let go. It was all he could do; he wasn't tall, and there was hardly any muscle across his shoulders.

'Put it down,' Thaniel said, beside the boy's ear. Usually his Japanese escaped him the moment he was faced with a Japanese person who was not Mori, but it came as easily as English did now. 'I don't want to hurt you.'

'I'll kill you,' Yuki said with a strange calm. 'That man will destroy Japan.'

'We can talk about that later, but this is not honourable. These people are musicians, they've done nothing. Look, Mr Ito has gone.'

The boy looked to the side. Ito and his aides had melted away. Yuki went limp and Thaniel felt the sudden jerk of his ribs as he began to cry. The pressure on the hammer released. He skimmed the gun away from them. It skittered under the seats and came to rest when it bumped into a cello, where the small impact made the strings sing.

Then there were other men, hauling Yuki up and pulling him outside. Someone was calling to the audience to leave as quickly as possible, although most of them didn't need telling; the marquee was almost empty already. Thaniel stepped back, away from them all, and retrieved his coat from the piano stool. His hands were steady, though there was a red graze from the gun hammer. The Yard bomb, he realised, had spoiled him for fright. Having lived through that, an unhappy boy with a revolver was not frightening, though he should have been. As he shrugged into his coat, stiffly because his neck hurt again, he couldn't help thinking that if there had been no chance he might have to save Ito today, he wouldn't have lived through the fire at the Rising Sun.

He turned to go, trying to construct a quiet way of getting back inside at home unseen, and walked straight into Mori.

TWENTY-SIX

OFF TO THE WEST, the Kensington churches chimed half past six and tinged things briefly blue. Mori was standing awkwardly. His clothes looked as though somebody had dragged him through a coal mine. With a backward glance to where the violinists had found a beat constable, Thaniel hauled him round to the other side of the stage out of sight, more roughly than he meant to. It made Mori stumble. Something had happened to his ankle.

'Where in God's name have you been? Where's Grace? Dolly Williamson is on the warpath, I was arrested—'

'There is going to be an explosion,' Mori said.

'Good, then. Delighted to be involved. Am I going to be in this one, or is there some chance of watching it from further away?' He checked himself when he saw Mori struggle with the sarcasm like the ambassador sometimes did. On the tail of the thought came a little spark of dismay. He had never known Mori have any trouble with English before. He looked exhausted. 'Where is it?' he corrected himself.

'Over there. Nakamura's shop.'

'Better tell the police. They've already got Yuki, he'll tell them where it is. Nakamura said he was missing chemicals.'

'No,' he said. 'Mrs Steepleton is in Matsumoto's flat, on the balcony, she's waiting for the ... the ... fire, the *hanabi*—'

'What?' He looked up at the building and counted along to find Matsumoto's balcony. It was the only flat with lights inside, but the doors were closed and nobody inside would have heard a shout. He dug his fingernails into Mori's sleeve, wanting to shake him. 'Never mind. Come on,' he said. He pulled him toward the lamplit archway that led into Matsumoto's section of the tall townhouse. 'You did this, you can damn well see it through. What happened to Grace?'

'I don't know,' Mori said, and there was something halting in the way he spoke. 'She was on the underground. I saw her this morning, but someone ... but I fell on the tracks and I think I did know who was there, but I can't remember now. I should never have – but ... I don't think I knew she would come here.'

'Just go and take apart the bomb before it explodes.'

'I can't. I can't find it. It keeps ...' He shook his head with frustration and swung his hand to and fro. 'Moving,' he said in Japanese.

'What do you mean, moving?'

He only shook his head, and then winced when his neck cracked.

Thaniel frowned. 'Did you say that you fell?'

'In the tunnel.' He looked lost. 'I don't know why I was there now. It took a long time to get out. And by then she was back on the ... the ... *kisha*.'

Trains. 'Mori, you're forgetting words. Did you hit your head?'

'No. I'm forgetting things I won't hear again.' He said it to the ground, and gave up on the English halfway. Because he was favouring his ankle, he was moving unevenly. 'I can't remember anything after five minutes from now.'

Thaniel stopped. They were at the door in the rounded trapezium of light from the expensive lamps. The need to frighten him snuffed out under a cold, creeping frost of an understanding that something had gone wrong. He saw him properly for the first time. There were grazes on his hands, and two parallel dark marks on the inside forearms of his coat. They would have lined up if he put his hands out in front of himself. He had fallen across a railway track and landed almost flat.

'Then you're going to leave here now and let me fetch her,' Thaniel said, and willed his English to come back.

It didn't. 'I can't. There has to be rain, otherwise the fire will ... you will never make it away before the other buildings catch. Everything here is wooden. You've got it,' he said, then took the rain vial from him when he didn't understand.

'How long is there?' Thaniel asked.

'Th—ree minutes.'

'That's enough,' he said. Three minutes was enough to play a reasonable sonata. It was more than enough to go up to the top floor of the building and down again.

Thaniel pushed open the elevator grille and was about to press the fifth lever when he saw that Mori wasn't with him. He was looking at the top of the elevator. The ceiling was nothing but copper mesh, and through it, the darkness of the high shaft stretched up and up, striped with light from the upper floors. He came after that tiny lag, but he had clenched his hands so hard that he had cut his palms. As the lift hummed upward, he stood very still, looking at the floor so that he wouldn't see the flashes of the other hallways they passed, or the gaping darkness above them. Thaniel pushed a handkerchief between his hands to soak up the blood. Mori watched him do it as though his hands belonged to someone else.

'So, Grace and I will go down the stairs,' Thaniel said. 'You'll need the elevator to get down again from the roof. We'll meet you by the gates. Is it ... going to be as big as the Yard?'

Mori lifted his eyes. 'I don't know. I won't see all of it.'

'Don't be stupid. You can get down in time, you'll just have be quick. Look at me. You haven't forgotten completely, it's only hard to remember because it's unlikely.'

'Yes. Probably true. But I still can't remember.'

'Christ, your hands ...'

'What happened to your face?' he said quietly.

'Just Lord Carrow.'

He closed his fingers over Thaniel's to stop him chasing the blood that had pooled again along the lines of his palms. 'Be careful with yourself. Please. She will make you much less than you should be, if you aren't careful. I don't mean you won't be happy. But you will be small.'

'Don't ...'

The elevator stopped. Thaniel swallowed hard and opened the grille again, and flicked the last lever for the roof, so that Mori wouldn't have to. 'I'll see you soon,' he promised.

The elevator disappeared upward. Mori had closed his eyes.

Thaniel shoved open Matsumoto's door. It banged against the wall, and in the doorway that led out to the balcony, Grace spun around. She was waiting, he realised, to see if the fireworks would start. The balcony was at the wrong angle for her to have seen what had happened by the pagoda, only the general commotion. She was wearing Thaniel's clothes, holding his coat closed across her chest against the cold that had seeped into the unheated room. The grate was dark.

'Thaniel, what—'

'There's a bomb somewhere in here. Yuki tried to kill a Japanese minister, he just shot at him and this must be his failsafe. Stairs, quickly, Mori's got the elevator. Come on!'

'What do you mean—'

'Now!' he shouted at her. He couldn't speak and keep count internally at the same time, but the elevator had taken at least a minute. He pulled her out and down the corridor. Five floors: thirteen, fifteen steps between each, probably. The staircase was wooden when he found it, creaking and old, and the heels of their boots thumped hollowly in the empty space that must have been beneath the steep risers.

He slowed, because he could hear something peculiar. It was coming from inside the elevator shaft, a skitter of something smooth and steel against the wall, moving irregularly. It wasn't anything much larger than a rat, because its colour was pale and thin, a watery blue that deepened as it moved further and further down the shaft. There came a greenish slither as it slid down the counterweight's steel cord, as if the thing had managed to hold on. The shade of it was familiar. It made him think of the tide, and the way the salt water thinned at the edges of incoming waves and grasped the pebbles.

'Thaniel?'

He lost the sound over the noise of their own steps. 'Did you see anyone else in here on the way up? There weren't any lights, but—'

'No, everyone was at the operetta.'

When they reached the ground floor, he ran back from the building to see up to the roof, and realised with a sick feeling that Mori was still there. The lamps on Kensington High Street cast an orange glow behind the chimneys, just enough to silhouette him.

'Mori!' he shouted. 'Now is not the time to be afraid of heights! Come down!'

His heart was loud in his ears from running on the stairs. Grace was already nearer the pagoda than to them. A small wind ruffled the paper lanterns around the empty stage, and the sheet music still clamped into place on the stands. Everyone else had gone. It had been more than three minutes, he was sure of it; still no explosion and still no sign. 'Climb down to the balcony, you can come down the scaffolding, it looks—'

Something plinked. It was a neat little noise, the same watery shade as whatever had been falling down the elevator shaft. A strange sigh billowed from the firework shop, and then flames that burst outward. Thaniel was thrown backwards, but as he fell, he saw the blast race up the shaft – he could see the flashes through the windows as it moved upward – and Mori turned around on the roof, looking toward where the explosion would emerge first. It tossed him backwards too, off the edge of the roof. Then he was lost in the smoke. So was Thaniel. It was deep and dense, and strobe flashes of different colours flared somewhere deep in the heart of it, not sound, he realised, but fireworks. The back of his head cracked against the ground. Embers helixed red above him. He didn't think that he was hurt, but part of him remained sceptical, and was unsurprised when everything faded to an endless grey. From a long way off he heard thunder.

TWENTY-SEVEN

THANIEL OPENED HIS eyes. There was a ceiling above him, and part of a window. Creaking footsteps walked by. He sat up. It was a hospital ward. He had never been inside a hospital before. It smelled of fearsome disinfectant. Across the far end, two nurses scrubbed the floor on their hands and knees. Stiff, he twisted his head from one side to the other. It must have been a quiet day. The beds around his were empty. Beside him, Grace was slouched in a stiff wooden chair, watching him over a science journal.

'Morning,' she smiled.

'Where are we?'

'St George's.'

He shook his head, confused. The ward was airy and well proportioned. It was not the kind of place that treated people for nothing. He didn't have any hospital subscriptions; they cost something absurd, two or three guineas a year. 'But I haven't—'

'I paid. How are you feeling?'

He felt as though somebody had stuffed his head with wool and left its more usual contents in a jar. The idea of a whole sentence was daunting. 'Hazy,' he said instead.

'The nurse says you've a concussion. Lots of scrapes and bruises.'

'What happened to you?'

'Nothing, I was much further back. Bumped my arm.'

'No, I mean before.' He swallowed, and tasted smoke. 'Everyone thought you had been kidnapped.'

She blinked. 'Kidnapped? No. I might have knocked a few things around. I just left. I was angry.'

'But where did you go?'

'I walked round town. Then I got on the underground when it opened.'

His head hurt. 'I'm sorry.'

'Never mind that now. We're both all right. So is almost everyone else. The police are saying it was a miracle that it rained. There were sixty people in the teahouse when the roof caught fire, but the storm put it out before the smoke could trap them.'

He looked down the empty ward. 'But he's dead, isn't he?'

'Who, Mori? No. He's in surgery.'

'Surgery for what?'

'No idea. Thaniel – stay where you are,' she said, pushing her fingertips to his chest.

'Yes,' he lied. He leaned back a little. 'I can't believe he didn't see it coming,' he said, to distract her. 'Modernist Mr Ito visits the home of Yuki the mad nationalist, whose father makes fireworks? I told him from the start to get Yuki away, but he wouldn't listen.'

'It could have been anyone,' Grace said quietly. 'That firework shop was so busy when I went up that a man dressed in a gorilla suit might have strolled in unremarked.'

'No. You don't know Yuki, he attacks people. He tried to kill Mori once. Tried to shoot Ito at the show.' He coughed. The back of his throat was raw and dry, and the water she gave him only made it itch. 'Mori sounded like it had taken him by surprise. Nothing ever surprises him. And none of this surprises me, so I don't see how—'

'Think about it later,' she said gently. 'Listen, I must sort out fees and so forth, and then see my parents, if they think I've been kidnapped. Good God, I go for a walk and the world goes mad. You get some rest.'

Thaniel promised that he would, waited until she had gone, then called over a nurse and told her that he wanted to be discharged. Once they had both signed the papers and she had given him back his clothes, he pulled the curtain around his bed closed. He dressed behind it. There were small cuts across his chest, splinters from the blast. The middle of his back felt stiff from the graze there. Nothing terrible.

He lost count of the number of loops in his tie and had to start again.

When the surgery was over, the nurse told him, Mori would be taken to the Jewish ward. It was upstairs. The staircase was hung with huge oil paintings, which gave way to long windows on the wards, all slightly open in order to let the air circulate. Beneath one of them was a warning poster about the dangers of mephitic odours. He knew vaguely that they had to do with the spread of disease, but he had no clear idea of the subject. He could smell only the cleaning salts and over those, the chemical sweetness of carbolic acid. When he opened the double doors of the ward, he found it mostly empty. Some Yiddish men were playing cards. Another was suffering an epileptic fit while two nurses struggled to hold him down. A third nurse saw Thaniel and shooed him out.

'Visiting hours do not begin until three o'clock!'

'Could you tell me—?'

'No! Wait outside the hospital, or in the galleries.'

He tried to argue and was shown out by one of the taller doctors, who left him halfway down the stairs. He stared after him. His eyes still stung from the smoke and he rubbed them, then stopped when he saw that his fingertips had come away wet.

Below him in the entrance hall, a pair of nurses hurried in through the front door, letting in a gust of cold air. Best not to wait outside in the cold in this state. His logical capacity was divorced from the rest of him, observing from a few inches to the left of his head. It directed him along the long corridor that led away from the door. After some drifting about, he found the gallery. It was tucked away to the left of the back door, which opened out into a conservatory overlooking a wide garden. The windows were all shut, the air warm.

As he stepped into the gallery, the floorboards creaked. They were old. In glass cabinets stood wired skeletons of all sizes, adults and children, and in one, a pair of strangely conjoined twins, whose two spines curved from one pelvis. Each had two ordinary arms and a head. He studied the wiring, certain that it was a fake, but then he saw that the tailbones were fused together. Whoever the skeleton had belonged to, he – they – had been nearly six feet tall. It was difficult to see how they could have walked. It must have been a matter of one leg each and a good deal of trust. They had clearly managed. The bones weren't warped or uneven. Everything was symmetrical and strong, cleaned to a pearlescent shine. He moved on to look at the other cabinets, avoiding his own reflection.

Further on were pictures, mainly paintings of dissections or operations. The people didn't look real. Half-formed things hung suspended in bell jars. Around them were more cabinets filled with waxworks. One showed a face, stripped of skin on one side to expose the complicated muscles underneath, another a flayed hand. A family of skeletons leaned over an anatomy book that had proven so interesting that being dead hadn't distracted them. He wandered for a while, bending to see into cabinets but never touching them, not wanting to cover them in fingerprints. Someone had cleaned most of the soot off him, but it was still in the lines of his fingertips.

He was glad that the gallery was so strange. It was keeping his mind off surgery. He wished he knew what kind. If it was serious, they would use chloroform. Chloroform was better than a large whisky, but he knew a little about it, Annabel's husband having died under it. It killed some people. It triggered a form of allergic reaction. Nobody knew why.

He sat down on the floor beside the twins' cabinet and tried to think of nothing. It worked best when he counted. After every nine hundred or so, the city bells rang to mark the quarter hour. Towards half past one, a doctor came by and pulled him up by his elbow, assuming he had escaped from somewhere. Thaniel assured him he hadn't, but the doctor sent him outside anyway.

At first it was numbingly cold, but that was only because he had been sitting still for so long. After he had walked around for a while he didn't feel so bad. Yesterday's thunderstorm had washed away the snow, but the puddles had frozen and the street crackled with the sound of ice splintering under boots and cartwheels. While he waited, a small crowd gathered outside the double doors; other visitors, with seedcake or fruit or small bottles of gin hidden in their pockets. At three, a fat janitor opened the doors and stood between them as people passed through. Whenever the man saw a suspicious bump in a coat, he snatched it out and laid his prize on the table to the side of the corridor. He seemed disappointed when he patted Thaniel's pocket and found only his watch which was, despite everything, not broken. Thaniel watched him confiscate an apple from an old woman. He couldn't see what was wrong with bringing food on to the wards, but he was too tired to ask.

When he found the Jewish ward again, he saw Mori almost straightaway. He was still asleep. Beside him, a doctor made notes on a chart.

'Are you a relative?' he said to Thaniel, sceptically.

'I'm a cousin, he's half English. Is he going to be all right?'

'He is,' the doctor said. 'Damn miracle. Fell from the roof, apparently. Rope burns on his hands; he must have caught hold of something. He was found in a doorway at the base of the building. Astonishing luck. We're keeping him here tonight to sleep off the chloroform. If he doesn't wake in an hour, tell the duty nurse.'

Thaniel nodded again and sat down in the chair by the bed. He cast around for a newspaper. There were none. Visitors were not encouraged to linger. He leaned forward against the mattress, his head cushioned in his arms, and faded to nothing but listening. Gas shushed as the lamps flared on. The bells, sometimes. Half past three, four, half past four. Twice, footsteps paused near him, but no one asked him to leave.

A cold hand pushed itself through his hair. 'Are you asleep?'

He jolted upright. 'You're awake. My God, the surgeon more or less told me you'd die from the anaesthetic—'

Mori smiled a little. 'Don't exaggerate.'

'I'm not!'

'I'm not allergic to chloroform. I'm not allergic to anything but yellow liquorice allsorts and those haven't been invented yet.'

Thaniel took his hand back before he could touch the bandages that just showed through the hospital night shirt. 'What did they do?'

'They took out some shrapnel, that's all.'

Thaniel watched him for a long time. 'Well,' he said at last, 'now we know why you're afraid of heights.'

Mori smiled properly. The lines around his eyes were deeper than usual now. They made him look like an old photograph of a young man, often crushed, but ironed carefully so that only the ghosts of the marks remained. Thaniel moved the edge of the blanket over his arm. With the windows open, the ward was frozen.

'What in God's name were you doing?' Thaniel said. 'Grace was only on the underground trains, and then she went up to Matsumoto's flat to see the fireworks after the operetta. Why couldn't you just have tied Yuki up somewhere until Ito was gone? He shot at him before the explosion; it isn't as though any of us were surprised when the bomb went off, and – for Christ's sake – how could you have even allowed for there to *be* a bomb? How could you not have known?'

'It was so unlikely that I couldn't even remember why I was afraid of heights.'

'How? How was it unlikely? I saw this coming and I don't remember any futures at all. Yuki was always going to do it!'

Mori sat up, slowly. 'I don't think it can have been Yuki.'

'Why not?'

'Because I would have done something more useful than fall off a building if he had meant to do that.'

'Mori, you ... you fell, before, on the underground tracks, you said. You hurt your ankle. That would have made you late for everything else. He must have decided and done it and before you could have even reached the village, never mind ...'

He trailed off because Mori was already talking over him. 'I don't need to stop things in person. If it was Yuki, there would have been something in place that would stop him as soon as he decided. I wouldn't have let it all hinge on my not falling in pitch dark, I'm not that stupid, or I hope not.'

'No, you're not. I was there to keep him from killing Ito.'

'Even that has a last-resort look about it to me. I don't think ...' He shook his head. 'I'm so sorry. I don't know what I can have been thinking.'

'I don't care. You're alive.'

'You should care, if I'm putting you in the way of idiots with guns or—'

Thaniel closed his hand over his arm. 'No, no. He couldn't have hurt me, I'm twice his size, and after the Yard I don't think my heart even beat faster. I was well qualified.'

Mori only shook his head again. He was looking at the folds in the blanket. His eyes were clouded. Watching him try to find the pieces of himself he had forgotten was worse than imagining him on an operating table. Thaniel moved on to the edge of the bed and hoped Mori could feel the future in which he did dare, despite the frowning nurses, to put his arm around him, but he didn't think he could.

'Just leave it now,' he said quietly. 'It's done.'

'I don't understand why the bomb was moving,' Mori said. 'That makes no sense. I should have been able to find it.'

'He must have strapped it to a dog, or something.'

'What for? That was risky. Anyone could have seen it. Why didn't he hide it in Nakamura's workshop? Anyway, it wasn't a dog, I would have seen a dog, it was ...' He let his breath out. 'In the walls. Something small.'

'I think it might have been a rat, I heard something in the elevator shaft.' He stopped. He remembered the seawater colours.

'What?' Mori said.

Thaniel let him go and stood up. 'Listen, I ought to find Grace. She went to see her parents; she should be back by now.'

Mori's focus strayed to the middle distance. 'She's in the foyer.'

'You get some rest. Real rest. No inventing things ahead of time, or frightening the nurses. When will you be discharged?'

'Half past ten tomorrow morning,' he said, and then stopped and set his teeth together, and looked up at Thaniel with eyes full of questions. The vowels had been short.

'I'll come back for you then.'

TWENTY-EIGHT

GRACE UNBUTTONED HER coat as she came into the hospital's wide foyer again, chased by a spray of sleet and grateful for the clinical quiet. Her father had almost stopped shouting at home when the police superintendent had hissed that she was a stupid little girl, which had set him off afresh. She had left them to it, not certain why he was so angry about it when in fact his opinion agreed exactly. Rather than sit down, she paced slowly, studying the oil paintings and probing the weave of the last two days for loose threads. Since they had argued at Filigree Street, she had started to sink under the feeling that the simple way Thaniel spoke had never been a reflection of the way he thought, but a spectrogram. She had always seen the odd pauses and dark lines in the colours of his words and assumed they were accidental hitches. They were emission lines. She had done everything she could to ensure Mori couldn't know what had happened, but Thaniel was different, and she couldn't tell what he would have noticed. God knew there had been near misses. She pushed her hands through her hair and tried to see it from the beginning again.

It had been half past – no. Twenty-five to twelve on the wedding night. The carriage clock on the mantelpiece had not looked symmetrical as she watched the second hand go round. She had watched it for a little while, like a metronome, holding the coin.

Then, everything had been quick. She pulled open the small suitcase that Thaniel had left under the bed. As she had hoped, there was a change of clothes inside. She pulled off her own clothes and left them scattered over the floor, then shrugged into his, tying a knot in the back of the shirt to make it fit her shoulders. She wrapped on his tie while she went round the room knocking things on to the floor with one elbow. Fully dressed, she scraped the icing from the long cake-knife and cut her arm twice before smearing the blood over the mirror and the door handle. Nobody would come if it didn't look like violence. Thaniel had left a handful of change on the mantelpiece, so she swept it into her palm, along with her own stray sovereign. At the last moment, she remembered to pull off her earrings and her wedding ring.

Leaving the door bumping open on its latch, she took the empty suitcase and went quickly down the back stairs. They were nicely decorated, despite being the province of the staff. She looped around again to the warm entrance hall and stood just shy of the corner by the desk, out of sight of the door. She could feel her watch ticking in her pocket, almost exactly in time with the hotel clock. It was ten to midnight already. Mori was late.

'No, no,' called the night watchman, just as the front door opened. His loud voice made her jump. In the doorway, Mori ignored him and came in. 'We don't want your sort in here.'

Grace squeezed her eyes shut. Mori started toward her before she called his name, but she was already running for the kitchen and the back doors. She heard him ask one of the cooks if he had seen a woman go by, and the cook said, truthfully, that he had not.

The snow was fresh and brittle, and she was able to run unslippingly to the station. The midnight train pulled in just as she arrived. She ducked past an antique ticket inspector, provoking a shout, and opened one of the carriage doors before the train had wholly stopped. Inside, she sat down by the window and cupped her hand to her eye to see out into the station, an iron taste in the back of her throat. If the train left before Mori could catch it, he would have no way home except a cab, which would take at least ten minutes longer. Ten minutes would be enough to find Katsu, if she was lucky.

She was breathing hard after running, and she had to clear the condensation from the glass twice while she waited. It felt like hours, and she began to feel coldly certain that there was some delay. Mori appeared on the station steps, distinctive in his grey coat among all the black, but then the train sighed and ground forward. Grace slumped over her knees.

'Er – I say?' said a voice just beside her. She jumped. It belonged to a little clerk. 'I say, my dear, what are you doing out late at night dressed as man? Is everything all right?'

'I'm in disguise and running away from my husband's best friend, who can remember the future,' she said, because her mind was too full to conjure lies. 'I'm trying to beat him back to his house now, so that I might steal his clockwork octopus, which runs on random gears.' He stared at her. 'You look confused. Random gears are clockwork gears governed by spinning magnets, and the switch that each one controls will flick depending on whether the magnet is facing its north or south pole. Why do I want an octopus with random gears? That section of things is still on the drawing board I'm afraid.'

'Young ladies ought not to drink,' he said coldly.

'You ought not to wear that colour tie.'

He made a point of changing carriages at the next station. Grace checked her watch again. Five past midnight. Gently, she opened the back panel and watched the clockwork bird peck at its imaginary scraps. She wondered if Mori had known it was for her when he made it. If he had, she couldn't see why he had chosen a bird. It was Matsumoto who loved swallows. She set the watch down open on the carriage table and crumpled back in the wooden seat. She was tired. The softly illuminated carriage seemed, as it moved through the black tunnels, like a cabin built away in the countryside, folded up tight in a night unpunctuated by street lamps or stars. It made her sleepy, despite everything.

She had expected to find that somehow he had reached Knightsbridge ahead of her, but the little station at South Kensington was empty. She still ran from there to Filigree Street, borrowed clothes slowly soaking in the snow. There was a light on at number twenty-seven. Thaniel was still up, playing the piano. He was gaunt in the light of the single candle, but the tune was jaunty; he was practising for the show tomorrow night. She wanted to knock on the window.

Instead, she eased round to the back door, snow creaking under her shoes. It was unlocked. In the clean, warm kitchen, the stove still held a glitter of dying embers. Katsu was nowhere in sight, but she knew where to look. Thaniel had often complained about the octopus living in his dresser. She crept up the stairs. The landing was dark. She had never been up before, but the first door she chose was the right one, judging from the sheet music over the floor. She went through the drawers one by one, but no Katsu. Aware that Mori would be back in a few minutes, she cast about hopelessly, then tried Mori's room. It was spartan. She saw the little octopus straightaway. He was curled on the pillow, one tentacle curled up over an invisible shape in the air. A step creaked on the stairs, and she froze for a second before sliding under the bed.

It was only Thaniel. He leaned in through the door and said Mori's name, and then stood still for a long time. She squeezed her eyes shut and tried not to breathe. Someone banged on the front door and he turned away. She lay still for a moment longer. Mori was a fastidious housekeeper – there was no dust beneath the bed, no cobwebs. The floor was so well polished that her breath clouded it.

Katsu remained stiff even when she picked him up, so she folded his tentacles down one by one and closed him into the small suitcase. She had to wait in the gloom at the top of the stairs while Thaniel led a big man she didn't know into the parlour. Then she darted to the back door again. Her incoming footprints had already been obscured by new snow, which sank down further than before when she stepped out. Almost as soon as the door was closed, a swarm of little lights rose from the back of the garden. They drifted toward her like living things, but they came with a hum of clockwork. Something of Mori's. She stole into the passage between terraced houses, not wanting to find out what they might be.

*

The electric lights of Harrods illuminated the whole width of the road. Although she felt exposed standing by them, she waited for a cab there; it was the only place in the dense night where a cabby could spot her. Still, not many cabbies had chosen to brave the weather, and she was on the verge of leaving on foot when one finally guided his plodding horse across. He was puzzled when she said she didn't mind where they went, and more puzzled when she chose their turnings by flicking a sovereign coin. But since she said he could have the sovereign at seven o'clock the next morning, he didn't ask many questions and seemed only to put it down to some Belgravia fad he hadn't heard of. In the suitcase beside her, Katsu rattled every now and then as it tried to shift and move. It was reassuring: it meant Mori had not expected the octopus to be in a suitcase at all. The cabby stared at the case once or twice and then fixedly at the road.

Seven o'clock found them just beside the Clock Tower, where the bells sang out the hour over London. A pale line glowed around the edges of the sky, just enough to show through the vapour rising from the frozen Thames. The ice was so solid now that some adventurous tinkers had set up little stalls beyond the quays, where they were hanging up small lamps along the awnings.

'Seven o'clock, miss, you'll be wanting to be on your way, I expect, thank you very much for your custom,' the cabby said in a dislocated rush. Katsu's clatterings had become more frequent and more noticeable during the past hour.

Grace did as she was told. Her throat was sore and, faintly, she could still taste the sweetness of the icing from the wedding cake.

Then, 'You shouldn't be out by yourself all night, miss,' he said as she shut the door.

'I know,' she said tiredly. 'Can you tell me where the nearest underground station is? And – will it be open at this time?' She had meant to hail another cab, but the trains were warmer, and the more she relied on whim, the harder it would be for Mori to follow her.

'Westminster station, up there,' the cabby said. She had come a full circle. 'The underground's always open early. It will be packed, mind.'

She gave him his sovereign coin and set off for the station, limping because her legs had stiffened from yesterday's running. She hadn't run so much since she was ten years old.

The cabby was right; Westminster station was crowded, and it was easy to slide unnoticed past the guards, who she couldn't have paid now even if they had caught her. The cold snapped at her ears and her hands. Condensed steam had frozen in drops along the ceiling above the tracks. Sometimes one of the bigger drops fell off and plinked on the rails. While she paced to keep warm, she passed a dead beggar in an archway. She saw others notice him too, but everyone was too cold to risk missing the train in favour of telling a conductor.

When the train steamed in, it didn't stay long. The carriage door had hardly closed behind the last man when a whistle keened through the smoke and the wheels jerked. The clerks – they all looked like clerks – read newspapers by the lamps. Some coughed. Nobody looked at her, but there was a little shuffling to make room for her in a seat at the edge of one of the small tables. She was the only woman. Not trusting herself to catch her last penny if the train were to hit a bumpy patch of track, she spun it on the table. At first, it spun so quickly that its edges blurred and became the surface of a copper ball. As it slowed, it drew circles on the table top, then fell. Heads. She would get off at the next stop, wherever that was.

Two minutes went by, then five, and then the train paused in the tunnel to wait for another. The next station, she realised too late, was Victoria, where there were a dozen lines criss-crossing each other, bound over and underground. They waited for another five minutes. She pinched her own wrist hard, unable to believe she had been so stupid as to spin the coin as she boarded. She should have waited until the train was stopping. She had just handed Mori ten minutes, at least, to reach the station before her, and if she decided not to get off there now, he would still know which line she was on if he was within ten minutes of Victoria and able to remember the chance of seeing her there.

She was coming to the conclusion that all she could do was make it fifty-fifty and throw the coin again at the station when she realised that it would be better to get off as she had meant to.

Mori must have known what was happening by now; he must have known that someone was throwing a coin or a dice. It was camouflage. She had thrown the coin and the fact that she was deciding to get off at Victoria did not, therefore, look like a real decision, only a decision to follow the coin. If he was anywhere close, he would be there soon, and then he would follow her if he saw her. At a station honeycombed with underground tunnels, that was not, in fact, a bad thing. She shifted the suitcase on her lap and thought about sheep in order not to think about Katsu, because she could feel gears turning in her mind.

Victoria. The cold had blown in from the overground tracks. She hunched in Thaniel's coat, scanning the crowd. The platform was lit by the big globes that hung on chains in all the underground stations she had seen, glowing eerily because the glass was frosted. She couldn't see a grey coat. She walked the length of the platform, watching the cloakroom at the top of the steps beyond the ticket office. In order to come down to the lines, everyone had to go past it. Through the open doors, she could see inside it too. It was a big room, and everything about it – the doors, the luggage rails, the round lamps and the paintwork – looked new. A Clan na Gael bomb had gone off here in February and the railway company must have finished the repairs only recently. Around her streamed half the civil service on its way to Whitehall.

Gazing out at the swarm of black coats and black hats, the endless, identical men, she thought of disappearing altogether. It would be easy. She could go to Paris and find Matsumoto again. She would only have to follow the line of swooning ballerinas.

She crushed her knuckles against her eye. There was no laboratory waiting in Paris. There wouldn't be one here unless she did what she had set out to. And Thaniel: there would be no Thaniel either. Not very long from now, he wouldn't be a man any more, only a clockwork copy of one with a clever veneer of character. That he couldn't see it made her feel still and hollow. It was listening to tuberculosis rattle in the lungs of a man who thought he only had a cold. He had been good, and kind, and he was going to vanish, along with everything else.

There was a flash of grey in the black. Mori was standing on the platform between the two underground tracks, turning slowly as he looked for her. The back of her throat tasting of copper, she waited until he saw her, then waved urgently at him before she jerked backwards into a crowd of clerks, all taller than her. She looked down the tracks, where two rats were playing. There was no rush of hot air to announce the arrival of a train. Without giving herself time to think, she stepped over the small kerb, between the rails, and ran into the tunnel.

There were no lights inside, but further ahead, around a curve, a glow came down in narrow lines. It was lamplight, filtering through one of the steam grilles in the pavement up above. She picked her way slowly along the tracks, the back of her neck prickling as she listened for the thunder of an engine, on steps behind her.

A train crashed past as she rounded the next bend. The headlamp was bright in the dark. Though she pressed herself to the opposite wall, the blast of hot air from the engine was searing. Steam flooded everything long after the train had gone. She coughed, tasting soot. A burst of laughter reached her from up above, through another grille. She stared upward and tried to think at what point it had become inevitable that she would be here today, running through underground tunnels from a man who nobody in their right mind would have challenged. She was becoming more and more sure that it was the second she had bumped into Thaniel at the roulette table. More pressing was the question of what she meant to do now. Walk back to Westminster along the line God willing. If Mori caught up with her – she banged her fist to the wall to stop herself thinking or planning. A weird laugh echoed around her. She jumped before she realised it was her. Any moron could tell you that running blind without thinking was stupid, but thinking was far more dangerous now. She tried to embrace the panic and the illogicality that came with it, because that would be what saved her if Mori caught up.

Once she had passed under the grille, she was in solid darkness again. She walked with her hand to the wall. It was gritty with old soot. In the brief light from the train, she had seen that everything was opaque black from the smoke. She tripped on something, but she didn't know what, and when she stopped, she heard it shuffle away. She took a deep breath and started again, feeling her lungs stiffen. The corner of the suitcase bumped against her leg. Katsu was heavy.

The tunnel wall disappeared.

She stepped backwards and found it again, but it took a sharp turn that led back the way she had come. She stood still for a long time before crossing the tracks as quickly as she dared. The other wall carried on smoothly. She had come to a junction, a Y shape, of which she had just walked the upper left line. Suddenly she wasn't sure of where she was. She couldn't see a clear map in her mind's eye; she couldn't remember if another line joined this one between Victoria and Westminster. With a slow unfurling of new, real, unmanufactured panic, it occurred to her that the track had already split without her knowing, from the other side, and that instead of walking to Westminster, she was heading down a new tunnel, a dead-end half constructed, or one of the older, abandoned lines, where there would be no trains and no workers to find her.

'Mrs Steepleton?'

She flattened herself against the wall and her hand to her mouth.

'Are you here?' he said.

He was less than a foot away. She could hear his clothes moving, but the dark was so complete that it was impossible to make out even his outline. She didn't speak. If she didn't speak, he would not remember later that it had been her.

She waited until she heard him a fraction of an inch away from her, then punched him as hard as she could, straight forward into his chest rather than risk missing his face. They were the same height, but she had more weight. It knocked him flat. She heard a thud as he fell against one of the rails and waited, but he didn't get up again. She knelt down and found his shoulder, then his temple. His hair was soft, and the structure of his bones felt sharp and fragile. It sent a tingle up her arm. At first it made her shudder, then sad.

She hit him again, with much less force and more nerves. She had no idea how much a human skull could withstand. With her knuckles hurting and her hand shaking, she held her palm over his nose and mouth to be sure he was still breathing. He was. She lifted him to the side of the tracks, close to the wall, in case it wasn't a dead line after all.

Slowly, she felt for the other wall, the one that led down from the fork in the track. It bent her fingernail backward. She winced and clenched her hand, then she ran in the dark. When her lungs hurt from running and smoke, the tunnel gave way to the lights of Westminster station. A train waited on the other side of the tracks. She cried when she saw it. Even if he had come round a few minutes after she knocked him down, he would be hard pressed to follow her now, but she still got on with everyone else, and flicked her coin only as station lights approached.

Mr Nakamura's workshop was full of people. They were going in and out with fireworks and lists, making ready for the display after the operetta. Nobody paid her any attention, though she was the only one who did not have black hair. On the last train, she had lined up her possibilities. The firework shop; her own laboratory at the Kensington house; the armoury at Horse Guards, behind her father's office. They were all full of explosives. The penny decided, in the end. She tried again, hoping for Horse Guards, but it fell on tails.

She went quickly. It had been hours since she had run from Mori on the tracks and she was gambling that he hadn't yet managed to get out of the underground in the state she had left him in, but he was strong. He might have. Like she had at the Bodleian, she walked as if she knew where she was going. The labels of the chemicals were all in Japanese, but she knew what she wanted by smell. She only had to open a few bottles and packages on the main worktop before she found it. She took the whole packet, parcel-sized, and knelt down behind the desk. All of the fireworks in the bundles around her had snap fuses of the kind that pulled open and ground a few grains of gunpowder between two rough slips of card to make a spark. She took one out and looped one end through the top hoop of her watch, then guided it all the way around the case and trapped the other in the back panel with the clockwork swallow. She pressed the catch experimentally. The lid opened and pulled the paper, and it snapped and sparked. Good. With the dial at the side, she set the lid to lock and to open in half an hour, and put on a new fuse.

The octopus waved when she took it out. It seemed no worse for having been in the suitcase for so long, and it had not wound down. She held it still between her knees as she tied on the makeshift bomb. She had almost finished when someone stopped just beside her. She froze uselessly, afraid to look up, but nothing happened. She lifted her head half an inch. It was Yuki, Matsumoto's nationalist friend. He hadn't seen her; he was only going through some papers. Someone, an old man's voice, called at him. His expression changed into indignation and he shook his head, making his hair sway in its long tail. She eased to the left, around to the next side of the desk. The old man came to talk to him and went through the chemicals on the worktop. He was looking for what she had just taken. His voice rose and the boy shouted back at him, holding up his hands. She had no idea what they were saying, but the sign language was universal. I didn't take it.

The old man slapped him and the boy pushed past him, aiming for the door. Almost immediately, the man bleated at him and hurried after him, but he was ignored, and the boy soon had a good start over him. They disappeared outside.

'Why don't you speak English!' Yuki shouted. 'You should! You are just like them!'

She sat holding Katsu for ten long ticks of her watch, working up some nerve again. An explosion in a firework shop wouldn't be viewed with suspicion by anyone but Thaniel. She had to hold the certainty tightly, because the idea that Yuki might be arrested for it made her want to untie the bomb and take Katsu back to Filigree Street. He was an unhappy child with an idiot for a father. She could remember being that. If she kept him with her on the way out, nobody could say anything against him.

Very carefully, she set Katsu free on the fifth floor, from the door of Matsumoto's flat. She had been afraid that it wouldn't go anywhere, the settings all wrong, but it shuffled off happily enough, exploring the walls and then the elevator, where it disappeared into the small gap between the floor and the lift. She felt wretched. It was a beautiful piece of machinery. Nobody would see anything like it again for a hundred years if Mori decided not to make another.

She folded her arms tightly across her ribs to keep her hands from shaking and went to the window to watch St Mary's clock tower. It was itchy to have nothing to do but wait. She had to be here right before the explosion so someone could see her come out, but she did wish she could have arrived closer to the operetta's interval, so that she wouldn't have to wait for so long. Another five minutes should do it. She pushed her hands over her eyes. They were still sore from the smoke in the underground. There had been a sharp fear at the back of her mind all day, since the tunnel. It was that although Mori was prescient and strong, he had been knocked out by a scientist who had never hit anyone in her life. In all probability, that was because it had been very dark, and she hadn't known when or where she would hit him, so he hadn't either. But there was a chance that he had let her do it.

She saw people streaming away from the pagoda and decided that it was as good a time as any for her to go too. There was no need to be here for the last minute. Thirty seconds to go down the stairs, there was time for that.

She was just beginning to turn around when the door banged open and Thaniel was there, telling her to get out. Confusion took over on the run down the stairs as she tried to understand why he was there, but her brain had run out of fuel and she couldn't think of anything but not tripping. When they reached the ground floor, she went to the firework shop and dragged out Mr Nakamura and his wife, who were both crying. There was no sign of Yuki. They said he had been taken away, but couldn't put together the English to explain why or how.

She jumped when someone touched her arm. Thaniel had come down the stairs quietly. She couldn't read his expression.

TWENTY-NINE

THE OUTSIDE AIR was hazy with vapour, and frost crunched beneath their shoes. Crows sat in the trees and watched the smaller birds in Hyde Park, which was on the other side. Thaniel aimed to walk under the big oaks rather than over the open grass. It was very fractionally warmer in their shade. Beside him, Grace was in her own clothes again, the hem of her dress scratching as it brushed over twigs and old acorns. The garden was at the back of the hospital so that the ward windows opened on to fresh air rather than train steam.

At last, he said, 'The only way to make a bomb he can't follow is to put it on something that moves randomly. It was on Katsu. I heard him in the elevator shaft.'

Her brown eyes flared. 'Are you certain? What does a clockwork octopus in an elevator shaft sound like?'

'Seawater. You broke in and stole him, didn't you? I heard someone. It was your footprints outside. And then, with a watch and a shop full of fireworks I don't think it would have taken you long to put something together. No one would have noticed. It was too busy. Mr Nakamura thought it was Yuki who took the chemicals.'

There was a long silence, long enough for him to notice the crows calling. Grace sighed, and her breath curled white.

'I never meant to hurt him,' she said. 'I intended for there to be an explosion, that's all – just something dangerous. I went up to Matsumoto's room and I was about to go back down when you arrived. I thought that if you believed I'd almost been killed in a way he could have prevented, then ... you would tell him to leave us alone. All I want is for him to leave us alone.' She glanced up at him. 'I had no idea he'd send you. There was no need.'

'He sent me because he needed the rain. I had it, he had made some weather vials so I could choose the weather for our wedding. So he took it to the roof and I fetched you. He didn't know you would have come down of your own accord later. He couldn't remember living long enough to see you.'

He saw her take a breath to ask how, and then accept that Mori could arrange the weather. 'I see.'

'I don't,' he said. 'What I don't see is, how you knew that you would have time to come to the village and make a bomb, and wait, without his stopping you.'

'I don't know that either. I knocked him out underground, I punched him. But ... I shouldn't have been able to.'

'It's his fault you knocked him out?'

She pushed her hand over her mouth. 'You're going to tell him.'

'No, of course I'm not, because I wouldn't have a leg to stand on then if he did hit you with a steam engine.'

'I suppose.' Grace folded her arms more tightly in the cold. She was very white above the upturned collar of her coat. 'But you must know that this was all a magnificent trick. He knew about all of this, right from the start. You are clever enough to wonder if he chooses things for you, so he let you stray away with me for a while to give you an illusion of freedom before reining you back. Yes, argue away. I'm sure he's said that it was all so unlikely that he didn't recall, but it's so beautifully organised. Cogs don't make themselves into a watch in the wind.'

'This isn't a watch, it's a mess.'

'And you're never going to doubt him again, are you?' she snapped. 'You blind fool.'

Thaniel was quiet, and she looked away. They had reached the conservatory door. He opened it for her.

'Why didn't you just report him to the police? You saw us. You said so. What kind of tea do you drink in the dark? That would have been enough, from a Belgravia lady. I thought that's what you meant to do.'

'Those never stand up in court, it's impossible.'

'It would have. Scotland Yard had him pegged for the bombings but on no evidence. The Superintendent was boiling to get him for something.'

'Oh, well, lucky for you I didn't know that, did I. I thought they'd left him alone. But you won't mind terribly if I divorce you,' she said. She shook her head. 'I'm at your mercy and I know I should be saying I wish you all the best. But ... I don't.'

'Let me sign your house over to you first.'

'Why are you being kind?'

'I'm not. If I keep it, he'll know something's going on.'

She looked as though she preferred that to kindness. She nodded, a quick, broken nod, and went on alone to the front door. He stopped to let her go on ahead. He turned back up the stairs. A nurse tried to stop him, but he brushed past her. In the attic ward, Mori was reading a newspaper, or pretending to; the nurse looked as though she had just forced it on him. He put it down when Thaniel came in.

'It's not tomorrow,' he said. Thaniel could hear the clockwork in his mind grinding. He hated not knowing what was going on, and the edge of it was brushing against his voice. Just for a moment, Thaniel enjoyed being the more informed. 'What's happened?'

'Settle down,' the nurse told him.

'You settle down,' he growled.

'I won't be long,' Thaniel promised her. She sighed but waved toward the bed as though she would wash her hands of Mori if he died of over-strain. Thaniel sat down on the edge of the bed. 'You really don't know what happened, do you?'

He frowned. 'I did, in the underground. I don't know now. Do you?'

'No. No, I don't know,' Thaniel lied again. He bit the inside of his lip. He wanted to tell him everything, but to say anything now would be to tempt fate, or worse, tempt Mori. He sighed. 'Listen, I've a question. I don't very much want to ask it. Will you forget what you're saying halfway through your answer if I don't?'

Mori nodded apologetically.

'All right. Yuki tried to kill Ito yesterday. And I was there, in the orchestra, three feet away from him and conveniently able to speak Japanese.' He hesitated. 'I spoke to Ito. He didn't seem to have much time for you these days, but he's going to be the prime minister soon. Did you save me from the Yard bomb so that I would be there to stop Yuki? You got me into the Foreign Office where I learned Japanese, you arranged for me to work with Sullivan on the operetta. You always said that you would stop Yuki if he tried anything, and you said just now that that was why I was there.'

'I came to England for you.'

'What?'

Mori breathed in so deeply that Thaniel saw his chest move under his shirt. 'Look, there are only so many people in the world who can put up with me, and of those, not many who I like too. You are my best friend, you have always been that. I worked for Ito while I waited for you to grow up. I didn't arrange for you to play the piano for Sullivan because I wanted you to save Ito, I did it because you're a pianist. You saved him because you could. If you couldn't have, there would have been something else. It was just ... efficient. And slapdash. I didn't think you would have to do it.'

'Oh,' Thaniel said softly. He looked away. 'I wish you'd turned up five years earlier. You needn't have been so long working for Ito.'

'You weren't my Thaniel yet. You weren't finished. You wouldn't have liked me.'

Thaniel smiled slightly. It was true. Before the bomb, he had been a smaller version of himself.

'I'm sorry,' Mori said.

'Don't apologise for having made me better. I was ...' He shook his head. 'If I hadn't seen the Yard go, I'd have died a clerk instead of a pianist.'

Mori smiled, then turned away and coughed.

Thaniel frowned. 'Have you caught something here?'

'No, it's the cold. They won't shut the windows.'

'You should be more careful,' Thaniel said, aware that he sounded hennish, but also aware, suddenly and sharply, that Mori was much older than him. In a flash, he saw that by the time he was in his fifties, it would all be over: he would be one of the lonely men who walked in Hyde Park in the early mornings, feeding the starlings and not thinking. He cleared his throat. 'Anyway, I ought to go before they frog-march me out. I'll come back in the morning.' He stopped halfway to rising. 'Don't go without me.'

'I won't,' Mori said, looking puzzled.

Thaniel glanced at the nurse, who stared hard at him. He stood up and shook Mori's hand. 'Sleep well, Keita.'

Mori smiled slowly, and nodded.

THIRTY

HE HAD HEARD, either from an article in the *Illustrated London News* or something else that used the same typeface, that total immersion would cure a fear. It was untrue. When they returned to Filigree Street, Mori refused even to go upstairs. Instead he hid under a quilt in the parlour with Thaniel's never-read copy of *Anna Karenina*. The Russians, he said, knew how to write genuinely boring novels, and he would only stop being afraid when he was bored enough. They were all the more boring because he could remember reading the end in the recent future.

Outside, the snow kept on. London ground to a halt. Usually Thaniel would have complained, but Fanshaw had given him the week off, so the furthest he was forced to venture was the grocer's. Since the surface snow never had time to freeze solid before more snow arrived, it remained more like powder than ice for days; the Haverly children's snowballs disintegrated into miniature blizzards of their own, and the wind blew streams of it along Knightsbridge.

The workshop came steadily back to life. A clockwork forest grew in the front window, its branches warped and host to a flock of tiny birds, its floor carpeted in the white, coralline moss that grew in Scandinavia. In a lull between chapters of Tolstoy, Mori walked around the workshop with a basket of tiny glass balls, each magnetised and charged with phosphorescent dust, lobbing them gently in the air, where they hovered and formed constellations around the orrery. One afternoon, a swarm of clockwork fireflies soared in through the kitchen door and arranged themselves into a bell jar, where they pulsed different shades of yellow and orange.

'I didn't want to say I'd made them,' he said when he saw Thaniel watching. 'I hadn't got one to show you. I think if you go about claiming at strangers that you make clockwork flying things they start to feel doubtful about any sort of elongated tenancy. But I showed you Katsu, didn't I? Maybe I didn't think at all. Anyway, I made them,' he said, lifting the jar a little, then sighed. 'I've forgotten something, haven't I?'

'No.'

'Tell me if I have. Please? I don't like being a future goldfish, it makes me perpetually mistrustful of my past self.'

'I don't think you have,' Thaniel said dishonestly. Anything else would have sounded accusatory, and he didn't want it to. He was nearly sure that Mori had known the fireflies would be important, but hazily, like other people saved money in a special account for some unforecast rainy day, or absently made more than the necessary number of friends because of a bad feeling about a business venture. Lately he was starting to think that they were surrounded by things that had been made for the same reason, but had missed their purpose as time overtook them. The gold locust clock was striking, and strange, but it had no reason to be a locust. Grace's watch had had its irrelevant swallow, and now, there was the half-finished music box in the desk drawer. He had seen Mori looking at it yesterday as if it were a fossil whose original shape he couldn't make out.

Mori looked tiredly at the window. 'When I forget something, I forget what I've said about it. Or written. It's like having learned some French at school and then forgotten it later, but being able to recall that you used to understand.'

Thaniel felt a pang, as if he'd seen him catch himself on the tip of the soldering iron. 'Is something wrong?'

'Not wrong. But the police are coming now. They found another bomb at the new Yard. I can stay and we can talk to them together. Or I can go out for an hour and ... leave you to it, and by the time I come back it will be over and I'll have forgotten they could have come. That's cowardly, but I'm still held together with thread. I don't normally mind a few pushes, but it will hurt more than usual. Do you mind if I ...'

'Christ, go. Why are you staying to ask me, you idiot?'

'I'll just write it down so I know what you've done. You ought to have some credit for this,' he said ruefully.

Thaniel took the pen from him. 'I'd rather have some more of that good coffee from the pretentious shop on Knightsbridge, actually.'

'Pretentious-shop coffee. All right.'

'I'll start out with you, I think I'll wait for them at the top of Filigree Street. Is Dolly Williamson with them?'

'Yes. How do you know him?' Mori said curiously. He handed over Thaniel's coat, being nearest the hooks.

'Just over the telegraph wires. I used to take his messages at the Home Office. Do you know who made the bomb? Might help to convince him it wasn't you.'

He had not meant it to come out so suddenly, and realised what he had done halfway through the question when Mori stopped winding on his scarf and only held the ends of it wrapped over his hands, close to his breastbone. 'Yes. I should have told the police before, I know that,' he said carefully. He seemed to see that he had frozen and, very slowly, in a way that looked as though his gears were being pulled in the wrong direction, finished the knot of his scarf. 'But there was . . . well, you wouldn't have stayed if I had. I don't know why. I have a note of it, it's underlined.'

Thaniel stared at him and Mori mistook his expression and looked down.

'No . . . no.' He closed one hand over his elbow and tried to think what to say. He wanted never to say that he had worked for Williamson. It was bad enough that Mori had let six policemen tear his workshop apart for the sake of not being abandoned, without knowing that they had come because Thaniel had told them to. 'Thank you,' was all he could find in the end.

Mori gave him the kind smile of a reprieved man. 'Frederick Spindle,' he said.

They went slowly in the snow, but since it was all powder, it wasn't slippery. It blew from the ends of gutters like the thin waterfalls on mountainsides, pattering as it hit windows crosswise and drifted against the bicycles propped up outside the shops, most of them frozen into place and unused for days. Mori left him to go on along Knightsbridge. Thaniel waited against a lamp-post. It was still broad daylight, but the snow made the roads difficult, and the lamplighters were already out.

He didn't wait long before the black police four-wheeler turned on to Filigree Street, inching along as the horses struggled against the wind, even with their blinkers. He stepped out in front of it to stop them, then went round to the door. He tapped on it.

'Dolly.'

Williamson opened the door. 'You', he said, 'should thank your lucky stars I haven't done anything about your little escape from house arrest. If it weren't for the Foreign Office telling everyone you're a bloody hero, you would be in a cell by now. Step back and let us get on.' He paused. 'How did you know to come out?'

'What are you here for?'

Williamson sighed irritably and climbed down. He looked ill. 'I'll meet you there,' he said to the others, and then, to the driver, 'On you go.'

Thaniel stepped back to avoid the spray of snow from the wheels. Williamson hunched forward in his coat.

'We found another bomb. It was hidden in the ceiling above my office. Full of his clockwork of course. Fred Spindle has just confirmed that it's the same workmanship as the first. Perhaps your wife might tell us what really happened to her now we have proof coming out of our ears.'

'What happened is what she told you. She went walking round London for a while.'

'And then happened to miss being blown up in a firework shop explosion by about ten seconds the following evening—'

'Come with me,' said Thaniel, suddenly too angry to bother with a logical pretext.

'What? No, the others are waiting—'

'No, you're going to come with me and I'm going to show you who did it before your officers arrest the wrong bloody man. You'll just have to make the effort.' He pulled Williamson by his elbow toward Belgravia. They had to take a cab, because although it was only a short distance, Williamson began to cough.

The bell rang demurely in Mr Spindle's shop when they came in. Behind the desk, Spindle himself straightened and smiled.

'Superintendent Williamson—'

Thaniel dragged him out from the desk by his shirt front. Williamson swore and Spindle gasped as the back of his head knocked against his meticulously organised counter. Thaniel ignored both of them. 'It was you. I came in here with that watch, and you thought Mori knew all about the bomb, so you made up that rubbish about the diamonds knowing full well he had the money to buy them himself. You'd already used his clockwork to be sure of the accuracy, so it was only a matter of spooking me and stressing it to the police. All you needed to do then was show them the comparable parts.'

Spindle tried to prise away his hands. 'No! No, I didn't—'

'Give the bomb to another watchmaker to look at, Dolly, and I'll bet you my life that they'll tell you it's not Mori's workmanship, even if they are his parts.'

'They forced me to!' Spindle exclaimed. He looked between them desperately. 'You can't say no to these people. I was – I had boasted too much about being a consultant for the police, and they heard, and a man came to the shop. I thought he would kill me. He would have, if I hadn't made—'

'You were calm enough to make a bomb.'

'Williamson! They would have—'

Williamson had closed his eyes. He looked more tired than ever. There were new lines on his face since Thaniel had seen him last. 'You'll have to come with me now.'

Mr Spindle stared at him. 'It's treason.'

'Is this your coat? Put it on.'

They waited while Spindle put on his coat. Williamson steered him outside, then blew his whistle. A constable came running, and then another not long after him. Belgravia was well patrolled. Thaniel resisted the urge to shove Spindle in front of an approaching cab. Williamson stood by him in the snow and silence for a few moments. Although the road was busy with cabs and carriages, the snow muffled the sound, and the only thing he could hear clearly was the clucking of water under the drain beside him.

'How do you explain how Mori knew about the Yard bomb early enough to leave you that watch?' Williamson asked at last.

'Same reason I knew to come and meet you today. You wanted to know what he said to me, before. He's a clairvoyant, Dolly, a real one. My wife proved it. In chalk, on a blackboard.'

Williamson faltered. 'What are you talking about?'

'I know it sounds ridiculous, but come and meet him.'

Williamson smiled uneasily. 'I don't go in for clairvoyants.'

'You will for him. Please. It's warm at home, and you're ill. So is he, you can complain together.'

With an expression caught between scepticism and anxiety, Williamson consented.

Mori was still out when they arrived back at number twenty-seven. Williamson murmured to the men in the waiting police carriage to go to the Kensington station, and waited awkwardly at the kitchen table while Thaniel made some tea. The kettle sang just before the front door opened.

'Can you make four cups?' Mori called from the hallway.

'Four?' He turned around, and so did Williamson. Mori came through the door with a small child in front of him. It was Six, wrapped in his scarf. She looked up at Thaniel with doubtful eyes.

'I see?' said Thaniel.

Mori looked set upon. 'It's freezing at the workhouse. Six, don't steal anything, this is a policeman.'

She studied Dolly. 'A real one?'

'A real one.' He put his hand out to Williamson, who shook it slowly. As always, Mori seemed smaller beside an ordinarily sized person, but the warm colour of his skin made Williamson look haggard. 'You think you're dying, but you aren't,' he said gently. 'You need to eat some proper fruit and go to the sea. This is the address of a house of mine in Cornwall, it's lovely there. They're expecting you there on Saturday. It's cold there, but no snow, and there's going to be an interesting storm on Thursday. If you catch the ten fourteen train down, first class, you'll be sharing a carriage with the woman in the blue coat who you sometimes see along Whitehall Street. She's visiting her aunt.'

Williamson stared at him. 'If you really know the future then you know who made the bombs.'

'Spindle.'

'Why the hell didn't you report him?'

'No one would have believed me,' he said. 'I'm a little Chinaman and a business rival, and he's a government consultant.'

'I ... well. Interesting,' Williamson said, sounding shaken. Thaniel gave him the tea and they sat down together while Six looked at Williamson's whistle. He seemed grateful to have a child there; she made a good distraction, and she had several solemn questions about police work that sounded to Thaniel as though she had been talking to Mori about it beforehand.

'Don't try to take the train,' Mori told him when he said he would leave. 'There's a man about to commit suicide on the line. You won't get there in time.'

'There's ...?'

'A cab for you outside instead.'

After Williamson had gone, Thaniel gave Six some more tea. He wouldn't have thought such a small child would go in for tea, but she had finished hers faster than any of them.

'Is your funny octopus here?' she said.

'No. I don't know where he's got to,' Mori said. He looked sad, not for the first time.

Thaniel's heart turned. He had been hoping that Katsu was as bomb-proof as his watch, but it had been days, and no one had found him in the wreckage.

One of the Haverly boys threw a snowball at the window. Through the glass, he looked a little shocked that he had been accurate. He had climbed over the fence between the two gardens.

'I'll give you a cake if you get him in the stream by the end of the afternoon,' Mori said to Six.

'Hold on,' Thaniel said. 'No making criminals of the orphans, Fagin.'

'But I want some cake,' Six frowned. 'And his name isn't Fagin.'

'I mean you needn't throw anyone in a stream.'

'Nobody gets anything for nothing. What do you want?'

He straightened, alarmed.

'You've got until...' Mori looked at his watch. 'Five o'clock. Extra for his brothers. But not the baby, it hasn't done anything objectionable yet.'

She nodded and let herself out through the back door, having to reach upward to turn the handle.

'So that was dreadful,' Thaniel said flatly. 'We're keeping her. Not just while it's cold.'

'I don't want any extra people in my house,' Mori protested, fadedly.

'It's your fault for bringing her back; you must have known what I'd say.'

Mori sighed. 'I hardly ever know what you're going to say. You change your mind too often.'

THIRTY-ONE

IT WAS A small gathering, but some effort had gone into it none-theless. Grace sat in the second row. The occasion was in honour of Thaniel, who had saved the life of an important Japanese minis-ter during the Gilbert and Sullivan operetta. Now he was being given some sort of medal, although since the ceremony was in Japanese she couldn't understand anything. She had known noth-ing about any of it until he sent a telegram inviting her yesterday, and since the annulment was not yet legally final – there was no larger bureaucracy than the British civil service – she had felt that she ought to attend. Wearing black, she was invisible among the men in their lovely suits. There was a certain security in it.

Thaniel had said a well-rehearsed hello when she arrived, because Mori was with him, and introduced a tiny girl called Six, but after that she had pretended to find the punch bowl of sudden and great interest so that he wouldn't ask why she was in black. In fact, the little girl was distraction enough, although not in a havoc-causing way. She had been introducing herself to people in Japanese. Twice, she reported back to Thaniel, who drew lines in the air to show the length of syllables as he corrected her pronun-ciation. The gathered Japanese men seem to find them both a fabulous novelty, which she supposed they were, like Mori and his Lincoln accent, which had returned.

For the hundredth time, she doubted herself. It was possible, maybe, that everything would have been all right had she simply not done anything, if she had taken a slice of wedding cake in a paper box to Mori, and said nothing but good things of him.

Thaniel had said there would have been a child. She couldn't decide if that was true prophecy or only something Mori had told him to rattle him.

The ceremony finished. Nearly as one man, everyone in the room got up and gravitated toward the buffet. She saw some men bow at Thaniel and then shake his hand, Western-fashion, with white-gloved hands. The small crowd was dominated by Mr Ito's aides and by the few Japanese noblemen who happened to be travelling in Europe and had heard of the occasion in time to attend. She had never felt so tall in her life.

Someone sat down beside her. She glanced to the side, feeling hostile. It was a distinctly human thing to walk on to a large, empty beach, and set up one's deckchair two feet in front of the only other soul there. Matsumoto smiled briefly.

'They sell *The Times* in the Gare du Nord. Your husband was on page six. Curiosity got the better of me. I'm sorry to be late. I was on the train from Paris to Berlin. Damn thing blew a piston twelve feet away from the border. Quite harmless, but they wouldn't let us across because they thought it was a gunshot, so the train came all the way back.'

Grace nodded once and folded her arms. 'He's not my husband any more.'

'What?'

'Oh, you know. He decided he would prefer to live with his watchmaker.'

Matsumoto followed her eyeline. 'Then I'm glad you're away from it all. I'm not sure it's healthy even to be in the same room as Keita Mori. Is ... that why you're in black?'

'No, my mother died,' she said shortly. 'Don't fuss; I'm not upset. I didn't like her much, but I seem to have done for her at last.'

'All right,' Matsumoto murmured.

'I'm glad you came,' she said. She hadn't meant to say it and swallowed hard, waiting for the barrage of inevitable teasing, but he only nodded. He was still watching the crowd, twisting one of his swallow-shaped cufflinks. Having gone to school in England and been raised on an English diet, he was taller than his countrymen and made the scale look mistaken, as though they were further away than they really were.

'I've missed you,' he said at last. 'The world is not quite the same when nobody is stealing my good jacket.'

'I don't know what you're complaining about. All your jackets are good jackets.'

He touched his lapel and then clasped his hands to stop himself. 'So ... what's your situation now? You've gone back to live with your father, I presume?'

'Yes.' She forced herself to say, 'I rather feel that I ought to hurry along and find some work. I'm not welcome in the house. A girls' school has offered me an interview. Chemistry mistress.'

'Oh, don't be absurd. I was telling my father about you, via telegram. He said he would be delighted if you'd like to come and stay for a while – he says the castle could do with an interesting woman in it, particularly since the government seem not to be tearing it down after all.' He aimed a pensive look toward Mori, who was speaking to Ito with his arms folded. Ito looked like an accomplished doctoral student who had settled into believing he was good enough to get on by himself, only to be faced with an old tutor who asked casually about something he hadn't read.

'I thought you had sisters?'

'They like flower-arranging.'

'Christ.'

'His view exactly. He's rather eccentric. He wears a bow tie.'

Grace couldn't stop herself laughing. 'Really?'

'Oh, yes. Complete loon.' He inclined his head. 'So, would you like to stay? It will get you out of London for a while, at least.'

'I ... I don't think Alice would want ...'

'Never mind Alice,' he said gently. 'We can hire a chaperone on the way. If you feel that you need one.'

'I don't know what to ...'

'Splendid,' he said. 'That's settled, then.'

Grace hesitated. 'Listen, I've done very stupid things lately, horrible things really—'

'Aimed at Mori?'

She nodded.

'That man ought to be shot for the general good of humanity, before he loses his temper.'

Grace wanted not to cry in full public view, but she could feel that she was about to. Matsumoto put his jacket around her shoulders and raised the collar so that her face was hidden. It smelled of his expensive cologne. She tried to shrug out of it. 'There's no need to coddle me, Matsumoto—'

'My name is Akira. Please.'

She lifted her head. 'Grace, then.'

He smiled a little and held out his hand. When she took it, hers looked small by comparison. Aware that her skin was rough from overexposure to chemicals, she started to slide it back, but he closed his other hand gently over her knuckles to stop her, and inclined his head at her with an amused sort of tolerance. She squeezed his fingers and did not let go.

'I should have asked you before,' he said quietly.

She pushed her free hand against her eyes again. 'Twelve feet from the border, did you say?'

'Yes. It was missing some nonsense, a bolt from the pivot or something. God knows how it came off, they're big things. Lucky, mind.'

'I'd like to go with you,' she said.

Not far away, she saw Mori detach himself from Ito's chattering group and collapse into one of the chairs in the front row. He held himself awkwardly, although since he had bad posture anyway, she wasn't sure if it was habit or surgical scars. He pulled something out of his pocket. At first Grace thought it was a watch, but it was too small. He flicked it into the air to let the light catch it. It was a heavy-duty bolt.

ACKNOWLEDGEMENTS

I'd like to thank everyone at the University of East Anglia who looked at the early chapters of this book and crossed out all the rubbish; especially Tala White, who insisted on the value of both fantasy and octopuses, and Professor Rebecca Stott and her excellent historical fiction seminar.

Also Jenny Savill, my agent, and Alexa von Hirschberg, who between them turned this from a long ramble into a story.

The Daiwa Anglo–Japanese Foundation, meanwhile, made it possible for me to write about Japan from the standpoint of a person who has lived there. I'm pretty sure that if they could have arranged for me to live in Victorian London too, they would have. So thank you to Jason James and everyone at Daiwa House, and thank you Katsuya and Mitsuru Shishikura, and the Uemoto family, who looked after me in Hokkaido and made sure that a) I didn't annoy any bears and b) I had access to fish and chips.

With regard to historical accuracy – there is some, mainly courtesy of Lee Jackson's *Dictionary of Victorian London*, which includes brilliant resources on the early days of the London Underground, the Knightsbridge show village, the bombing of Scotland Yard and a thousand thousand other interesting things. Natsume Soseki's sad and hilarious *Tower of London* provides a very good idea of what a Japanese man thought of England in the early 1900s. Many of the policies of the Meiji government can be found in old editions of the *Japan Times*. The Edo-Tokyo Museum has a model of the Rokumeikan, along with accounts of one of the parties held there.

Finally, thanks to my mum and dad, who taught me how to imagine. And thanks to Jake for making sure I sometimes talk to people who are not imaginary. Surprisingly important.

A NOTE ON THE TYPE

The text of this book is set in Bell. Originally cut for John Bell in 1788, this typeface was used in Bell's newspaper, *The Oracle*. It was regarded as the first English Modern typeface. This version was designed by Monotype in 1932.